Praise for *The Midnight Plan of the Repo Man*

"A joy to read! At once original, absorbing, hilarious, gripping, and emotionally satisfying. A deftly written, small-town family chronicle wrapped in a laugh-out-loud premise, wrapped even tighter in a page-turning thriller. I marveled at every page!"

—Andrew Gross,
New York Times bestselling author
of *No Way Back* and *Everything to Lose*

"Cameron has delivered a highly engaging and funny novel that is reminiscent of the early works of Carl Hiaasen and Christopher Moore. It's so easy to get wrapped up in Ruddy's misadventures that readers may well finish the novel and only then realize that they've read it in one sitting." —*Library Journal*

"Hook up this book, put yourself in gear, and pull away."
—*St. Louis Post-Dispatch*

"Ruddy's first person narration is light and breezy, verging on comedy, and the story is very clever. . . . This repo man has legs." —*Booklist*

"As witty a narrator as I've encountered in a long time. He's about the most fun voice to have in your head as a reader can imagine. High entertainment."
—*Bookreporter*

"Offbeat and engaging . . . very funny . . . Readers will look forward to more of Ruddy's good-hearted efforts to protect those he loves in the promised sequel."
—*Publishers Weekly*

T0191229

BY W. BRUCE CAMERON

The Midnight Plan of the Repo Man

The Dogs of Christmas

A Dog's Purpose

A Dog's Journey

Emory's Gift

8 Simple Rules for Dating My Teenage Daughter

How to Remodel a Man

8 Simple Rules for Marrying My Daughter

The Dog Master

For Younger Readers

Ellie's Story

Bailey's Story

THE
MIDNIGHT PLAN
OF THE
REPO MAN

W. BRUCE CAMERON

A TOM DOHERTY ASSOCIATES BOOK
NEW YORK

This is a work of fiction. All of the characters, organizations, and events portrayed in this novel are either products of the author's imagination or are used fictitiously.

THE MIDNIGHT PLAN OF THE REPO MAN

Copyright © 2014 by W. Bruce Cameron

All rights reserved.

A Tor Book
Published by Tom Doherty Associates, LLC
175 Fifth Avenue
New York, NY 10010

www.tor-forge.com

Tor® is a registered trademark of Tom Doherty Associates, LLC.

ISBN 978-1-2509-0723-3

Our books may be purchased in bulk for promotional, educational, or business use. Please contact your local bookseller or the Macmillan Corporate and Premium Sales Department at 1-800-221-7945, extension 5442, or by e-mail at MacmillanSpecialMarkets@macmillan.com.

First Edition: October 2014
First Mass Market Edition: June 2016

P1

To W. Chase Cameron

My son, my best man

THE
MIDNIGHT
PLAN
OF THE
REPO MAN

Prologue

I'm afraid.

I'm afraid, and I don't know why.

I glance around out my windshield. If I'm in any danger at all it's from this road I'm bouncing along on, a rutted indentation in the leafy forest floor that looks like it was last traveled by covered wagons. At any moment the two-track might fade away like an old rumor and then I'll just be driving cross-country through the Michigan woods in an Oldsmobile station wagon, plowing into trees and rocks. I'm alone and if I break an axle it will be a long hike back to the highway.

But that's not what's bothering me. The vehicle I'm driving was built by General Motors during what must have been a national steel surplus—the front end sticks out like the prow of a battleship. It looks as if it were designed to run into things. I'm not afraid of crashing.

No, this is more basic, more primitive, a chilling call from somewhere in my deep subconscious that startles my pulse rate and causes my eyes to widen involuntarily.

Just as I crest a small rise I ease my foot onto the brake, coming to a groaning halt.

There is absolutely nothing to see but acres of stunning oak and maple trees, lit up by a blazing autumn sun and waving their branches in the gentle breeze as they drop their leaves to the forest floor in an audible rain of color. I am deeply committed to a road to nowhere and can't reverse course save by driving backward for at least four miles—I doubt my car would forgive me, and I know my neck wouldn't. But that's what my instincts are urging me to do: back up. Get out. Escape, an inner voice whispers.

Escape from what?

After a time I overrule my instincts and push ahead, rolling my eyes as if I have a passenger to whom I am apologizing for such squeamishness. It's a beautiful day, and the property I'm heading out to show is a pretty piece of land on the river—the leaves will be dancing by on the clear water in a colorful flotilla. I was looking forward to it until I came down with a case of the jitters.

At a sharp bend I see something that gives me a start: two men standing beside a pickup truck. They both raise their heads and stare at me as I bounce past, not reacting at all to my attempt at a jaunty wave. I know one of them, it occurs to me, but for some reason I can't think of the name. From their surprised expressions, I can tell that neither of them is the person I'm meeting—besides, my prospect said he'd bring his wife.

After less than ninety more yards the road ends and I've arrived at my destination: the remains of a cabin that burned down nearly ten years ago. Rusted bedsprings and flattened tin cans among the broken glass tell the story of a place that nobody bothered to rebuild after some campers apparently got the bright idea of starting a fire in a chimney full of debris. Now the chimney is all that's left, crumbling with age but still standing defiant. I wheel my car through the yellow weeds and stop where the front door used to be. When I shut off the engine the resulting quiet makes me want to turn it back on. I'm still that uneasy. Still don't know why.

I slide out of the car, hesitate, and then walk a few paces to peer at the rusted handle of an old-fashioned icebox lying by itself in the grass. There's not much else to look at except the river, just ten yards across at this point, so I stroll down to its banks and stare into the dark-green water.

A flash of gold catches my eye. Curious, I reach for it, the current numbingly cold against my wrist.

I'm holding a class ring: Kalkaska High School. It's probably valuable to someone—I decide to put it in my pocket and drop it off at the principal's office the next time I am in that small town. The ring has initials stamped into the inside. Someone would probably like to have it back. My resolve to turn it in makes me feel good about myself, a mission with unselfish aim.

I climb back to the flattened, burned-out footprint of the cabin. The couple I'm meeting isn't here yet: I hope they aren't intimidated by the sad shape of the road and are back at the turnoff, trying to decide whether to risk their car's suspension. I don't want to spend any more time here alone than I have to.

I whirl and gasp, then laugh weakly. The two men by the truck have followed me on foot, and are marching toward me now with oddly serious expressions. Perhaps they believe I am trespassing; I will have to explain my business.

"Hi there," I call, clearing my throat. "Incredible day, isn't it?"

They are less than twenty yards away. The one I know—now what is his name?—is average height, midthirties. It strikes me that the reason I can't remember what to call him is because he looks different; he has a full head of jet-black hair now, whereas the last time I saw him his scalp was covered with only a few wisps. A toupee. I must remember not to stare when I am talking to him, even though it looks as if he's covered his head with a dead house cat.

The toupee guy's companion is short and muscular, with green eyes and skin still dark from a summer working out of doors. He looks like a laborer, one of the men I've seen engaged in an interminable road project in town, and as if to dress the part he carries a short shovel in his hands.

The one I know exchanges a look with the other as they close the gap between us. Neither of them answers.

And that's when it hits me: It's these men I'm afraid of. I fling an arm up just as the laborer swings his spade at me.

I catch the blade of the shovel with my forearm and crash against the side of my car, gasping. The other one is reaching for me but I keep spinning, trying to ignore the pain. I fall to the ground and roll and the shovel misses me, biting dirt instead.

They are both right there but the one with the toupee slips a bit in the mud and that is all I need to leap to my feet and run, my numb arm flailing uselessly at my side. They are right behind me, making their first sounds as they grunt and gasp in pursuit, but then after twenty, thirty yards, they fade away.

I'm in shock, but out of the fog of my confusion it occurs to me that I can run. I'm good at it. I look down and I am wearing runner's shoes, and even with the fear coursing through me my legs are almost joyously strong, pumping up and down in an even rhythm. I can run faster than they can, faster and longer, and I am going to get away.

As I pound down the road I think about the one with the shovel. No expression, his green eyes watching me, looking at the place on my head where the blade of his weapon would hit. He was trying to kill me. Why did this happen? How could something like this be happening?

I hear their truck and look over my shoulder. Like a fool I have been running on the road, I am still on the road! They are less than thirty yards away, coming very fast. I turn and leap into the woods to my right. A low branch slaps my shins and I stumble and fall, sliding on the wet leaves. It's okay, I'm okay, and I'm back up. They won't catch me now. I duck and weave, stumbling over the stumps and fallen trees littering the forest floor.

Then I'm down again, falling hard. My right leg is completely numb, and when I roll and try to leap back up, it won't cooperate, sliding uselessly beneath me. What? *I stare in disbelief at the crimson stain of blood soaking through my pants at the calf. I touch the muscle and it feels shredded; my finger finds a small hole in the cloth.*

I've been shot.

No fair, no fair, I want to sob. Now that I understand what's going on I can compensate, and I am hopping forward on my left leg, gritting my teeth. I am moving much more slowly now.

No fair that they have a gun.

Then a mighty blow knocks me forward and I don't even feel it when my head bounces against the dirt. When I come to a stop I am on my back, looking up at the clear blue sky, orange and red leaves cascading in lazy circles down onto me.

This is the last thing I am ever going to see, *I tell myself. Towering over me is a massive oak tree, more than four feet in diameter. A wet, black hole big enough for a man to sit in lies just below the split of the oak's two mighty limbs. I stare at the tree, memorizing it, wanting to take something with me when I die.*

I hear the two men approach, moving slowly. They stand above me, just out of my vision. I am unable to turn my head to look at them, to ask them why they have killed me. The question asked by everyone ever betrayed: How could you do this to me?

"Thought you said no one ever comes out here," one of them accused. "You know who he is?"

"Never seen him before."

Liar.

"I didn't want to shoot him. Now what?" *I get the distinct impression he spits as he poses his question.*

"Well, we can't just leave him. There would be forensics on the bullet. And a murder right now . . ."

There is a sigh. "I suppose we'll have to bury him right here, then."

"I think so, yes."

A gust of wind and the oak creaks, then there is a rattle as hundreds more leaves release their hold and cascade to the ground.

"He breathing?"

There's a crunch and a shadow falls over me as one of them leans over for a look.

"*Nope. He's dead.*"

No, I'm not, *I want to say, though I'm not altogether sure it's true anymore.*

"*Guess I'd better get another shovel, then.*"

After that I hear only silence, though the light takes a long time to fade away.

1

A Conversation with Albert Einstein

Computers and insurance companies call me Ruddick McCann—to everyone else I'm just Ruddy. I work for a collateral recovery agency run by a guy named Milton Kramer. When people can't make their car payments, I help them get back on their feet.

I'm a repo man. Get it? "Back on their feet." That was repo humor, there.

Milton does some financing—mostly people from our small town of Kalkaska, Michigan, who can't get credit anywhere else—but usually our business comes from banks and finance companies. We'll get assignments to repossess folks who can't pay, won't give up their vehicles voluntarily, and who usually hang up on collectors who are calling to try to work something out. It makes collectors mad when you hang up on them, so they pay me to go out and express their displeasure in person.

I've been relieving people of the burdens of automobile ownership for more than six years and I still don't understand why it is necessary. If you can't afford to make your car payments, why not just drive it back to the dealership and hand over the keys, instead of making Ruddy McCann come after you?

Of course, a better question might be, "If you aren't making any money, why don't you move someplace where you can find a job?" Most of the time my customers give the impression that having their vehicles repossessed is far from the worst thing to happen that week. When they invite me into their homes to hear their complaints about life, I have to shed my coat—they always keep it hot, their wood stoves pumping out heat and carbon monoxide in equal measure. Their TVs are always on. The local economy has been stuck in a recession since the term was invented. Nine months of the year it's cold and wet, and then it turns hot and humid. No rational person would stay here longer than the time it takes to pack up his belongings and leave.

I should know. I've lived here all my life.

Today I was looking for a twenty-five-year-old man named, of all things, Albert Einstein. Albert Einstein Croft was his full name, though I suspected everyone called him Einstein—how could you resist? He worked on the assembly line at a place called PlasMerc Manufacturing—something told me he wasn't exactly living up to his parents' expectations regarding his intelligence. Einstein didn't feel morally or ethically bound to pay for his used pickup truck anymore and had crudely suggested to the woman from the bank that she go somewhere to have anal sex with herself.

When I met up with Albert Einstein Croft I'd ask him to explain the physics of how that was supposed to work.

The PlasMerc factory had only been open a few years

and I'd never been there before. I was surprised, when I located the place, that the employee parking lot was fenced and paved, with a guard in a booth, no less. Most companies in northern Michigan were more considerate, leaving their workers' cars out in the open where the repo man could easily get to them. I pulled up in Milt's tow truck and nodded at the guard, hoping he'd figure I was from AAA and punch the button for the gate to swing open. Instead, he gave me a stony stare, so I sighed and rolled down my window.

"Hey, how's it going?" I asked in what sounded to my ears like a falsely cheerful voice. I'm not really known for doing "cheerful."

"Help you?"

I had to make a quick decision on how to play it. I decided to shrug and look dumb. "Got a call, guy named Croft, an employee here? I'm supposed to pick up his truck, haul it in."

He didn't move to open the gate. "Yeah?"

We looked at one another. The guard was my age, around thirty, and had my build—solid and big. It was obvious we didn't care much for each other's attitudes.

"I know who you are," he said finally.

It was my turn to say "Yeah?" So I did.

"You're Ruddy McCann. Everybody used to look up to you, and then you let us down."

"Well, sometimes that's how these things go."

"Now you steal cars for a living."

I had to admit, it sounded less glamorous when he said it.

"You had everything anybody could ever want, and you pissed it away," he continued. His eyes were cold and pitiless.

I sighed. "So could you let me in?"

"Get out of here. This is private property. You show up here again, I'll have you arrested."

We looked at each other for a little bit more. I thought about getting out of the truck and reaching into that booth and pulling him out by his shirt, and he could see me thinking about it and his gaze never faltered—that's how much he hated me. So I threw the truck in reverse and backed away, my face burning.

There was nothing to do for the next couple of hours except fantasize about punching the guard in the nose. I was sort of driving aimlessly and after a few minutes I was in what passes for a downtown in East Jordan—a tiny, clean little main street with a few shops and no people, as if they were filming a zombie movie.

My idle thoughts eventually drifted around to the nightmare I'd had a couple of nights ago, my sleep disturbed by the violent windstorm that wound up knocking out power all across the county. The memory of it was more like something real, as if it had really happened. I clearly remembered the two men, the guy swinging the shovel, and running down the road, thinking I was going to get away.

He's dead.

No, I'm not.

The dream seemed like it happened in the fall, but right now it was April in northern Michigan, a balmy forty degrees with a light drizzle starting to film my window. I flipped on the wipers and with the first sweep my vision cleared and there she was.

Attractive, midtwenties, curly red-brown hair falling to her shoulders, wearing a bulky all-weather parka and slacks, smiling. And waving. At me.

This was not the sort of thing I expected to happen to me, either in East Jordan or in my lifetime, but despite my disbelief, I stopped. She trotted over to my window, which I hastily rolled down.

"My car won't start," she told me. "Could you help me?"

"Why won't it start?" I asked, as if reading from a book of Stupid Responses for Men.

She shook her head, wiping her wet bangs out of her blue eyes. "I don't know."

I swallowed down my disappointment over how I'd been conducting my end of the conversation and finally came up with the right thing to say. "I'll see if I can jump it."

I swung the tow truck into the parking space next to her little Ford and in short order determined her battery was dead. She stood in a doorway and blew on her hands while I pulled out my jumper cables. "Your battery looks pretty old and the posts are corroded," I advised, wanting to talk about anything else but her car. "I can probably get you started, but you'll want to get a new battery."

"Oh, great. How much does something like that cost?"

"Maybe fifty, sixty bucks. I don't know."

She nodded in resignation. Her car roared to life with one crank, and I disconnected the cables. "I'm so glad you came along," she told me.

There had to be something witty I could say to that. I stood there, staring at her, trying to think what that might be.

"How much do I owe you?"

"What?"

She reached into her purse, digging out a wallet. "Oh no, no," I protested. "No, I'm not a tow-truck driver."

I could see the skepticism in her eyes: I was, after all, driving a tow truck.

"I mean yes, this is a tow truck, but I'm not from a towing company. It's . . . it's hard to explain." Particularly if you want to impress someone and thus don't want to use the term *repo man*. Her skin was blemish free, perfect, and her teeth were white and perfect. Probably I would think her elbows were perfect, too.

"So you just drive around looking for what, women in distress?" Her clear eyes sparkled in merriment.

"Wet women," I affirmed. Then I realized how that might sound and wanted to throw myself on the tow hook. "I mean, from the rain. Not, uh, you know." Oh, God.

We stood and looked at each other for a minute. "Well, thanks very much, then."

"Ruddy. My name is Ruddy McCann."

"Ruddy. You mean, like the complexion?" Her smile lit up her face.

"It's short for Ruddick; it was my mother's maiden name." I bit my lip, remembering the reaction from the guard. Everybody used to look up to you, and then you let us down. I desperately didn't want this woman to already know anything about me.

My name didn't seem to register. "I'm Katie." Her hand was cold and wet from the weather, but it warmed me when I took it.

She hesitated, perhaps sensing that I wanted to say more, and then gave me another smile. She opened her car door and slid inside. "Well thanks again, Ruddy."

"Sure. Uh, wait!" My heart was pounding. Katie beamed her beautiful blue eyes up at me and did as I asked: she waited. My brain flailed around, groping for words.

"Uh, I was wondering if maybe I could buy you a cup of coffee?" There.

"That's sweet, but I need to get back." Her expression seemed to indicate she really did think it was sweet, so I plunged ahead.

"Maybe some other time? Tomorrow?" Could I sound more desperate?

"Well, I'm dating somebody right now, Ruddy. So, you know . . ."

Yes, I knew. Pretty, intelligent women with humor in their blue eyes didn't wander around in the gray drizzle of East Jordan, Michigan, without a man lurking somewhere in their lives. "Okay," I told her.

She cocked her head as if to look at me from a different angle. Then she turned and dug into her purse, possibly to hand me a gun so I could put myself out of my misery. "Look." She wrote her phone number on a piece of paper—I even found her handwriting attractive. "Coffee would be fun. Yes, I'd love to. Here." She handed me the paper and our fingers brushed against each other. "Call me, okay?"

I spent the rest of the afternoon rewriting my conversation with Katie, talking to myself and being almost excruciatingly witty. I gave Albert Einstein Croft enough time to get home from work, then swung the tow truck up his steep driveway, hoping to find his Chevy pickup out in the open at the top.

It was there, but a severe bend at the top of the drive made it virtually impossible for me to back my tow truck up to his bumper. He'd parked his vehicle with a brick wall at one end and some cement stairs at the other, a tight parallel parking job that must have taken him some time. I couldn't haul the thing out of there with anything less than a crane. I'd have to appeal to Mr. Croft's sense of fairness.

I stepped out of my truck and a large white goose peeked at me from a small shed. We looked at each other with baleful expressions.

Einstein came to the door wearing an open plaid shirt and a scowl, holding a beer in his hand. He was lean, but with a soft belly spilling out over his belt. Another five years he'd be thirty and people would describe him as having a "gut." His hair was black, long, and stringy; eyes dark and cold. He regarded me through his storm door, a "who the hell are you?" expression on his face.

"Mr. Croft? I'm McCann, from Kramer Recovery."

"So?"

"So you want to talk through the glass, or do you want to open the door?" I asked, considerably less friendly.

He cracked open the door and a sour odor drifted out on a blast of warm air. Over his shoulder I saw pizza boxes and dirty clothes sharing the same space on the couch. "It's about the Chevy, Mr. Croft. You're three payments behind again and the bank sent me out to pick it up. I need you to collect your personal property out of the vehicle."

Croft looked contemptuous. "I told them I'd pay next Thursday."

"It's not up to me. They said you've broken promises before. So unless you have those three payments, I need you to surrender the keys."

"Get off my land."

I put a fatherly expression on my face: time to roll out my best material. "Look, I know times are probably tough right now. But sometimes all a man's got in life is his signature on a piece of paper, and I've got your sig-

nature on a contract saying if you can't pay, you'll surrender the vehicle. You have to stand up for your good
name, Mr. Croft."

This little speech had succeeded for me a lot of times
in the backwoods of Michigan, where people often really
don't have anything left in life but their honor. Einstein's
expression was derisive.

"Kinda crap is that? You guys knew I paid late when
you financed it."

"It was financed because your dad cosigned for it. You
really want us to contact your old man, tell him his son
isn't living up to his word?"

"Hell if I care."

Milt had told me the cosigner had lost his job and
couldn't pay. I blew out a breath, exasperated. "Come-
on, Croft, make it easy on yourself. You really want to
go around through life parking your car between brick
walls so I can't get at it? Never knowing when you're
going to come out of the bar, finally talked some babe
into going home with you, and it's gone from the parking lot? Let's get this over with now."

"You come on my property again, I can shoot you
legal," he responded.

"Actually, that's not true, it has to be hunting season,"
I advised.

He blinked, then twisted his expression into sour disgust and slammed the door in my face. I stood in the rain
for a minute, then turned and trudged back to the tow
truck. The goose observed me with an unblinking eye.

The truck was sold used, so I didn't have the original
invoice in the file. No invoice, no key numbers to access
to cut myself a set of keys to his truck. Normally with
used cars I just tow them away, but that wasn't an op-

tion with the way his driveway turned and how he liked
to park it. But this truck was built with one of the old-
style, steering wheel-column ignitions. What I could do
was slim jim the lock on his door and use a dent puller
on the key collar, disabling the security lock on his steering wheel and ripping out the starter contacts before
Einstein could recite the theory of relativity. Once I
started the truck, though, I'd have to rock back and forth
a few times before I got a good enough angle to back the
thing down the driveway. He'd obviously gone through
the same rocking process to park it there. If he really did
have a gun in his house, I'd be a pretty easy target.

I'd have to come back later.

Midnight. I did my best work at midnight.

2

Money for Nothing

The drizzle became more ambitious on the one-hour drive back to Kalkaska, making a ticking sound that meant it was changing from rain to sleet. I thought for a while about Einstein Croft's truck, then about beautiful curly-and-brown-haired Katie, her phone number safe in my pocket, and then finally about the nightmare again.

By the time I dropped Milt's tow truck off at the lot, the ice was coming out of the sky like bird shot, stinging my face as I hustled down to the Black Bear Bar. I pushed the door open and wiped the wet off my coat.

The bar was just starting to gather its Friday night together, some guys from the insurance agency turning their liquid lunch into an early evening and a couple of construction workers messing around at the pool table. I could tell from the pristine set of the booths that we hadn't sold any food all day.

My sister Becky and I disagree about the kitchen she tries to run out of what had been nothing more than a place for booze back when my parents owned it, but in

the end the business belonged to her and she tacked up a
BAR AND GRILLE sign over the door a few months ago,
as if the extra *e* was going to convince anyone to actually
eat there.

Becky was hunched over her ledger book, chewing on
the end of her pencil. "Becky, hey," I called, sliding around
the bar and pulling down a glass of beer. The spigot
sputtered and spat foam. "Great," I muttered.

"Be sure to clean the hose this time," Becky reminded
me absently.

"This time," I shot back. More than two years had
passed since I'd neglected to clean the rubber hoses that
ran the beer from the keg to the tap, with the result that
we served a bunch of college students a few brews with
some moldy-looking crap floating on the surface. Apparently I was never to be forgiven.

Grunting loudly, I wrestled a new keg out of the back,
then pointedly set about running soap and water down
the hoses. "You won't believe this dream I had."

"Uh-huh," she replied, so fascinated she couldn't bring
herself to look at me.

"The night of the big storm, knocked out the power?"

"That was some storm. Windy," she answered absently.

"It was incredibly real. I've never had a dream like
this. I was driving in the woods and these two guys hit
me with a shovel."

She glanced up. "Who?"

Becky is two years younger than I, but I can't help but
think of her as my older sister. While I was raising hell
with my football buddies in high school she was always
serious, like right now with her glasses smudged and her
brown hair lifeless and stringy after working the bar all
afternoon. It was as if she had a tapeworm or something

that was always draining the fun out of her, turning her dour and sad.

It started with her teeth. Some sort of medication my mother took when she was pregnant caused Becky's baby teeth to come in a dark gray, almost black. I'll never forget waiting for those teeth to fall out, and the slump in my parents' shoulders when the adult teeth finally sprouted and they were as dingy as the first set. She was the girl with the gray smile. Becky spent her whole childhood trying not to grin, and it seemed to make her mouth small, somehow, pulling her face down into a point. Bleaching at the dentist's office eventually became affordable and effective enough that she now had a real smile, but she doesn't deploy it very often.

"I don't know who. Two guys. They hit me with a shovel, then they shot me."

"Shot you," she echoed listlessly.

I found myself somehow hurt she didn't care more. Wasn't she listening? I was *shot*. "Yes, shot! And then I died in the dream. That's never happened to me. I mean, I could just feel myself die. Last thing I remember was lying there looking at this big old tree, and then I just slipped away."

"And came here." She gestured around the Black Bear Bar and *Grille*. "Heaven."

"It's bad luck to die in a dream," I persisted. "It supposedly means you're going to die in real life."

"Supposedly, you *are* going to die in real life."

"What's eating you, anyway?"

She tapped her glasses with her eraser, regarding me with her sad eyes. "We're pretty far behind on our food bill. When I called in the order this morning they wanted to know when we'll be sending them some money."

"Oh, that again."

"Yes, that again."

"Okay. I'll talk to Milt tomorrow, see if he has something for me." I shrugged.

"We need a thousand dollars by the end of the month." I figured I knew why the accusatory tone: Against her wishes I'd extended some credit to a few people who'd been oddly absent from the bar since the night of my generosity. "If we don't have it, we'll be cut off again, have to pay cash for everything. We could go out of business."

"Okay, I'll talk to Milt," I reiterated. "Man, that was a weird dream."

"Ruddy, you're not listening to me. A thousand dollars or we could lose the bar."

I weighed the chances of pulling in four repos in a week. It made stealing Albert Einstein's truck a higher priority. "I'll think of something, okay?"

I turned away from the distress in her eyes. What could I say? This time of year was always bad for the Black Bear, all of the cash reserves sapped by the winter's lack of business. Becky bent her head back down, tapping her pencil. I wanted to comfort her, but Becky doesn't really do *comfort*. The Black Bear had been in existence our whole lives; I really couldn't imagine it closing, despite her dire pronouncement.

I went back to cleaning up, thinking there was something else about the nightmare I needed to tell Becky. Something important, but now I couldn't remember.

Slow night. An hour later the insurance salesmen were gone, dropping a pile of crumpled bills on the center of the table that covered the tab but left virtually nothing extra to acknowledge that Becky had been running back and forth to the bar on their behalf for four hours. I slipped the money into the till without telling her. The construction workers had added a third person to their party, which I supposed made it a crowd, but they made one pitcher of Coors last for two hours, as if having clean hoses made it taste funny. To please Becky I tried suggesting they might like some nachos and they acted as if I were joking.

I couldn't blame them; our nachos tasted like roofing material.

Claude and Wilma Wolfinger made a boisterous appearance at around eight o'clock, looking as if they had already invested a considerable amount at one of Becky's competitors. They were both sixty years old and it seemed like they had been married for at least that long.

Claude waved at me expansively. "Ruddy, come here a minute," he greeted.

Claude was a thin man with white hair growing from his wiry, spotted arms. His cheekbones were nearly always red from the harsh weather and the strong drink he used to ward off the cold. His shirt proudly stated that he was a mechanic at a used car dealership, and his hands were never quite clean. When I was a little boy he and Wilma would sit in the Black Bear and regale me with stories of the world travels they were about to undertake. Twenty years later and he was still here in Kalkaska, overhauling truck engines.

Wilma worked for the county, patiently telling people they were in the wrong line or that they had filled out the wrong form. She was an inch taller than Claude's five foot eight and outweighed him by fifty pounds. She wore violently bright colors and huge sparkly earrings that resembled miniature chandeliers. Some of Wilma's ancestors were here when the white man came and apparently liked the new arrivals enough to marry them— all that remained of her Native American heritage was her black hair and dark eyes, but it was enough to give her a bit of an exotic look, particularly when she was angry at Claude, which frequently happened at the Black Bear. They always paid for whatever dishes they threw at each other.

"Ruddy, Ruddy, come sit down," Claude urged, clamping a hand on my wrist. Wilma was smiling at me joyfully, positively beaming. That they were this happy together was so unnatural it made me instantly suspicious.

"Ruddy, I've got a plan that is going to make us all rich."

"I haven't got any investment capital, Claude."

"No! Listen." He winked at Wilma and she nodded encouragingly. "You can say good-bye to your finances with this one, Ruddy."

"That's exactly what I'm afraid of."

"What?" Claude asked, puzzled.

"He means your finance *problems,* Ruddy," Wilma corrected. "This is going to fix everything."

Claude was looking over my shoulder, his face drawing tight. "This deal's just for us," he said hurriedly, "so don't say anything to Jimmy about it. Act natural!"

I turned. Jimmy Growe was making his way across the floor to my table, his face scrunched in concern. "Hey, Claude. Hi, Wilma. Ruddy," he greeted us.

"Hi, Jimmy," Wilma responded softy, while Claude and I acted natural. Wilma was reacting to Jimmy because she couldn't help herself; he has a clean, innocent face that seems to make women want to mother and love him from the moment they see him. He was what I think they call "black Irish": green eyes, smooth skin, jet-black hair—he looked like a movie star and had even been in a TV commercial once, though his career as an actor was somewhat hampered by his inability to act.

"Ruddy, you got a minute?"

Claude's hand grabbed my wrist again in a firm message I ignored. "Sure, Jimmy, everything okay?"

He eyed Claude and Wilma. "Uh, I need to talk to you. It's kinda important."

I struggled to my feet, Claude clinging to me like a wrestler. "Okay, sure, let's go over by the bear." I gave Claude a look and he reluctantly released me.

"See you in a minute, then, Ruddy," he told me, with so much emphasis I half expected him to pull out a stopwatch.

Jimmy and I wandered across the bar to the bear. When I was nine years old my father and my uncle shot one of the last black bears seen in Kalkaska County, a fact that gave him no end of pride back then and which now occasionally came up as a barbed reference by the environmentally minded editors of the local paper. The carcass was taken to a taxidermist, who stuffed it full of, well, stuffing, and posed the animal in a position of fierce anger, its teeth bared and its arms lifted for a totally unbearlike attack. My dad nicknamed the bear Bob. Not too many people wanted to sit under it and get drunk, so Jimmy and I were alone. We pulled our chairs up to a small table and sat, Jimmy hunched over in a position of such distress that I was sure he'd gotten a girl pregnant. I crossed my arms and waited for him to find his way to the right words.

"*Where the hell am I?*" the bear asked.

I whipped my head around. I'd heard it in my right ear

as clear as if the bear had leaned over and spoken, but there was no one there. "What?"

Jimmy frowned. "Huh?"

"I . . ." I pointed to the bear. "Did you hear that? It sounded like the bear talked."

Jimmy was clearly baffled. "The bear?"

I cranked my head around all the way, surveying the whole bar. We were completely alone, ignored except for the frantic looks from Claude. Yet the voice had been right there, closer to me than even the bear, really. "It said, 'Where the hell am I?' Did you hear it?"

Jimmy gazed at the bear with a perplexed expression.

"Okay, never mind." It didn't make sense so it must not have happened. "Tell me what's up."

"Oh, yeah. Okay. Yeah." Jimmy hunched over again, poking at a cigarette burn in the wooden surface of the table.

"Jimmy . . ." I prompted after a minute.

"It's like this. You know Milton Kramer, right?"

This was going to take awhile. I sighed. "Yes, I know my boss. Are you behind on some payments, Jimmy?"

"Oh no, nothing like that, Ruddy. It's these checks."

"Checks? From the hotel?" Jimmy might look like a fashion model but he lacked a certain focus and thus far had managed only to secure full-time employment as a low-level maintenance man at the local hotel.

"Well no, huh-uh. These are checks I got in the mail."

"In the mail?"

The door opened and two young women came inside, blinking at the bear in a way that let me know they'd never been here before. Then they fastened their gaze on Jimmy. I nodded at them encouragingly, but apparently I was invisible.

Jimmy glanced at me with hooded eyes. "Uh-huh, yeah. In the mail. For a thousand dollars."

"Who sent you a check for a thousand dollars?"

Jimmy shrugged. "I dunno."

"You don't know."

"Yeah."

"So someone sent you a check for a thousand dollars and you don't know who."

"Yeah. Five of them."

"Five of them? Five thousand dollars?" I stared incredulously.

"Yeah."

I sat and regarded him with the same lack of comprehension he was showing me. "So you have five checks for a thousand dollars. Made out to you?"

"Yeah."

"Made out to you," I proclaimed. "Jimmy, I wish I had a problem like this. Are you sure you don't know who sent them?"

"Don't know," he muttered.

"So what's bothering you, Jimmy?" I prompted. At the bar the two young women were talking to Becky, who chatted with them and then glanced at me in a way that instantly communicated what was happening: The girls were buying Jimmy, but not me, a beer. I shrugged at my sister, indicating I thought they were too young for me anyway. Her eyebrows lifted in skepticism.

"Well . . . you know Milton Kramer?" Jimmy asked.

For heaven's sake. "Jimmy, would you please get to the point? Claude and Wilma want to make me an instant millionaire and there are two girls at the bar who want you to sleep between them tonight."

"Huh?"

Becky came over with Jimmy's drink and a sympathy beer for me. "Maybe the one who doesn't get Jimmy will settle," she teased. I scowled at her and she almost smiled for what would have been the first time in weeks. Jimmy and I raised our beers in thanks to the two girls, who appeared delighted with Jimmy and alarmed that I had somehow become part of the process. When Becky returned they enjoined her in emergency consultation.

"Milton Kramer," I suggested, making it sound like a toast.

Jimmy nodded unhappily. "Well, it's like this. I cashed the checks with Milton."

"All five thousand?"

"Yeah. Ten points."

"He charged you five hundred dollars."

"Right. I don't got a checking account anymore because of the mix-up with the bank," Jimmy explained.

"That mix-up where you wrote checks with no money in the account to cover them."

"Yeah. Goddamn banks," Jimmy stated without heat. Jimmy doesn't really get mad at people, but in his mind there was something unfair about a system that required you to keep track of your checking account when the bank had all the money anyway. It had been up to me to arrange a way for Jimmy to pay off his debts a little at a time.

Jimmy is three years younger than I and had always been something of a little brother. I'd been protecting him from the world for as long as I could remember. He and Becky were the two people I cared most about in this life.

I sighed again. "Let me guess what happened with the checks."

"They bounced."

"That was going to be my guess."

"So now . . ." Jimmy spread his hands.

"So now Milton wants his money back. Which you probably don't have anymore."

Jimmy stared at his beer.

"Somebody sent you checks and you had no idea why, so you cashed them, Jimmy? Didn't you wonder what the hell was going on?"

Jimmy shrugged. "Well, there was no name on the checks. They were the starter kind," he said, as if that explained it.

"Ahh."

"So I was wondering, could you like, talk to Milton and get him to see reason here?"

"See reason? Jimmy, he's out five thousand dollars."

"Well yeah, but I didn't know they were going to bounce. I mean, it's not my fault or anything."

I let that statement lie there for a while.

"See, I was thinking you could maybe talk to Milton, and then you could, like, find out who was sending the checks and get the money back."

"Get the money back."

"Yeah, and like, I'd let you have this. Endorse it over, you know." Jimmy reached into his shirt pocket and pulled out a crumpled piece of paper, which of course turned out to be a check made out to James Growe in the amount of one thousand dollars. I stared at Jimmy's clear green eyes and saw no indication of anything approaching irony. I turned to the bear. "Never mind you, where the hell am I?" I demanded.

"What?" Jimmy asked, baffled at my behavior.

"Look, Jimmy. I'll check into this. And I'll talk to

Milton. But you're going to have to pay him back the five thousand, you know that, don't you? What did you buy?"

"Uh, a bike. And I gave some money to some friends."

"Can they pay you back?"

"Well, you know."

I sighed. Yes, I did know. "Okay, well first, you'll have to sell the bike." Jimmy looked unhappy. "Sell it and give the money to Milt. I'll work out a payment plan for the rest. And Jimmy, if you get any more checks, don't cash them, all right? Understand?"

Jimmy nodded with relief that I was going to help him, but I could see he was lying. He didn't understand, not really.

I suddenly became aware of something in my pocket and pulled it out. "Katie," it said, along with a phone number. For a moment I thought of asking Jimmy what it meant when a woman told you she had a boyfriend and then handed you her phone number. Jimmy's had more experience with ladies than anybody I know. But then I thought better of it—what if Jimmy said it didn't mean anything special? I wasn't ready for that kind of news.

When I stood the two girls at the bar went on high alert, preparing to swoop as soon as I stopped polluting the situation.

Claude looked ready to have a heart attack. "Where the hell have you been?" he grated, despite the fact that I had not been out of his sight for a single second. "I told you this was important!"

"I went backpacking across Europe," I told him, sitting back down. "What's up, Claude?"

Wilma leaned forward. "Claude and I are going to be set for life," she announced triumphantly.

"Wilma!" Claude barked, irritated with her.

"Tell him, honey," she urged.

"It's my idea, and then you go and spoil it," he pouted.

"I didn't spoil it!" she snapped, her voice rising. Becky raised her head up in alarm, worried the Wolfingers were getting ready to start throwing things. I waved a hand at her.

"Claude," I said sternly. "Wilma didn't say anything. You want to tell me your plan? Because I could really use some money right about now."

"Yeah, okay. Well, like I was saying," he started, giving Wilma a fierce look, "you ever heard of a little thing called the Witness Protection Program? Where they set you up in business, give you a new name and a house and everything?"

"I'm going to have a pet shop," Wilma proclaimed.

"Wilma! Would you let me tell it?"

"We're moving to Florida!" she added happily.

"We're not going anywhere if you don't learn to keep your trap shut!" Claude thundered.

"Hey!" I shouted. They turned to me, blinking as if just noticing I was there. "You mind telling me what this is all about?"

"Well, remember when I saw that guy smashing the headlights on the front row of cars at the dealership?" Claude asked.

I nodded.

"They caught the guy," Claude announced delightedly.

I looked at the two of them beaming at me. "And?" I prompted.

"I'm a witness!" They clinked glasses in congratulations.

"What a couple of idiots," I heard the bear say. I froze, then turned my head slowly, looking for what had sounded

like someone bent over and speaking directly into my ear. Jimmy had joined the two girls at the bar, and the bear was still immobile in attack, lips not moving, all the way across the room. There was no one else within ten feet of me.

"Witness Protection Program," I repeated, just to hear my own voice. I sounded like myself—the bear's voice, while male, was pitched higher.

"I'm going to tell them to make me a pharmacist," Claude avowed.

I pulled myself back into the conversation and gazed at the glowing couple. "Sounds like a great plan," I told them with as much sincerity as I could muster. "Tell me again why this is such good news for me?"

"We're going to ask that you be our personal body-guard, Ruddy," Wilma informed me. "Just until we leave Kalkaska, but still."

"You know how much money those guys make?" Claude wanted to know.

I opened my mouth to answer when a motion caught my eye. I turned and watched in amazement as Jimmy Growe, his arms waving, flew backward across the room, falling to the floor with a crash.

3

Something Feels Wrong

In the shocked silence following Jimmy's fall I tracked his trajectory back to its source: a nasty-looking guy I hadn't noticed coming in, with long, black hair and a goatee clinging to a threadlike existence on his chin. He was one of those guys for whom black jeans and a black T-shirt can only be accessorized with black boots and a black belt, both sporting pointed silver studs that had mostly fallen out like rotten teeth.

Sitting on one side of the two girls was a beefier version of the same guy, also in black but his T-shirt had words printed on it, so he was probably the brains of the outfit. It didn't take much imagination to picture the scene that must have ensued just prior to Jimmy's backward tumble. Two greasy guys try to move in on the girls, ignoring Jimmy because he was about as intimidating as a Calvin Klein underwear model. Jimmy attempts to make the bad boys back off, and one of them changes the nature of the exchange with a quick punch.

"Hey," I observed, using my best bouncer voice. I stepped over Jimmy's prostrate form and he stared up at me blankly, not yet capable of processing thought. "That's enough of that."

The guy with the goatee sized me up. I was considerably larger than he, but he looked anything but intimidated: Delighted, would be the best description. "Who're you?" he challenged, his voice quavering with something I swear sounded like joy.

"I'm the guy who's telling you to leave," I answered quietly, stepping into his space. I was aware of Jimmy's playmates standing just behind him, their eyes wide as they regarded this exchange, and sucked in my stomach a little.

The guy with the goatee didn't back away, even though he had to tilt his head to look at me. He still had an odd smile playing across his lips, as if he had a secret he was dying to share with me.

A change settled over the both of us, a realization. With twin motions we glanced over our respective shoulders— my opponent at his buddy still sitting with the girls, and me at Becky, a slight head shake telling her to take her hand off the telephone.

"So you think—" I started to say, but with a fast motion he struck me in the ribs hard enough to erase the rest of my sentence. The sparse crowd, most of them my friends, gasped a little.

I rubbed my side and stopped talking, watching my opponent dance back on his feet. I stepped forward, following, bringing my arms up. I jabbed hard and hit the air where his head had been an instant before, which put me in a bad mood. He slid sideways, feinted with his open hands, and then slugged me with something. No, I realized as I staggered away from the blow, he kicked me. In the head, the guy actually kicked me in the head!

I fell as hard as big guys are supposed to, the whole room echoing with the impact. Little points of light danced in a conga line across my vision, and the back of my skull joined the chorus of pain as I struck the floor. For a moment, the room seemed to grow dark, and as I lay there I imagined I was looking up at a hole in a large oak tree.

He's dead.

No, I'm not.

When I thought about it, I rolled away from his feet, but he wasn't a stomper; it was too much fun to knock me down. So that was the secret he'd been so eager to share with me; he was some sort of martial arts guy.

I reconstructed my stance a segment at a time, unhinging legs, then waist, then chest. Finally erect, I raised my hands.

"Come at me, fat boy," he snarled.

"Fat boy!" I halted and stared at him. "I weigh less than I did in college, for God's sake."

"Come on, college boy," he suggested.

"Better," I muttered. I followed him around the room, accepting a couple of light hits to the face in order to set myself up for a gigantic, fight-ending punch, which arrived long after he'd jumped out of the way.

"You're fighting his fight. You can't do that," the bear's voice whispered in my ear.

I whipped around. "Who said that?" I demanded.

The crowd of watchers glanced at each other nervously. One of the women raised a tentative hand, looking apologetic. "Not you," I snapped in irritation. She yanked her arm back down. No one else looked like a ventriloquist.

I swiveled back and faced my opponent, who was beaming with enjoyment. I took aim at the smile and went after it with viciousness in my heart, expending a lot of energy in what would have been a skillful attack if I'd hit him. I managed to connect with his shoulder a single time while he peppered me with blows—not a very good trade-off. My lip started to swell and my eyes stung. I was panting so hard that my throat felt like it was on fire. "Give up?" I gasped at him.

"He's faster than you. You weigh more. Get him pinned in the corner," my voice advised.

"Someone tell the bear to shut the hell up!" I shouted.

My opponent was waiting for me to recover enough to put up a pitiful resistance. *"The corner!"* the voice urged.

I pressed forward. This time, when my opponent jinked left I moved only to block, backing him up toward the corner. I hunched my shoulders and accepted punishment to my ribs again. Okay. He was running out of room to retreat. At the last moment he seemed to sense my plan and tried to dart to the right but I lunged and had him against the wall. My arms came around him and I squeezed.

He grunted and tried to pull my arms away. I held on and we toppled to the floor like drunken dancers at a wedding. He no longer looked happy.

Once he had squirmed around a little it seemed like the easiest thing in the world to catch his wrist and bend his arm back up behind him. He knew that was the end and went limp, surrendering. I lay on top of him and tried to suck in enough air to ensure continued consciousness.

"You wanna get off of me?" he finally suggested.

"Where you from?" I responded pleasantly, content to press down on his arm and watch his face turn gray.

"Cadillac," he finally spat.

Cadillac is just down Highway 131 from Kalkaska. They don't make Cadillacs there. They actually don't make much of anything there, which leads to a high rate of frustration that often makes its way north on a motorcycle and winds up in my sister's bar.

"Tell you what." I stood up, careful to take his wrist with me, and he struggled to follow, wincing. "Next time you're coming through from Cadillac, you get to my bar, you just keep going. Understand me?"

He nodded and I let him go, but carefully, like releasing a snake. He shot me a look but didn't try to get back into it. Some of these guys, when I throw them out I spend the next week wondering if they are going to come back and set fire to the place, but I could see that for this one, the fun was using his karate moves on dumb, unsuspecting bouncers. I'd spoiled the game a bit by listening to the bear and falling on him like a dead tree.

Naturally everyone wanted to come up and tell me what a hell of a job I'd done, though if they'd had their eyes open they'd plainly seen the guy taking all the points up until the final round. I caught Becky staring at me darkly, and when I met her gaze her eyes shifted to the two girls who were cooing over a finally upright Jimmy. She turned away in disapproval.

Would I have handled it differently if the possibility of winning one of Jimmy's hand-me-downs wasn't in the air? No! Well, okay, yes. Was that so wrong? They both had that quality I found irresistible in women—they appeared to lack better options. If I hadn't felt their eyes on me, I probably would have shouted at Becky to call the cops, which usually lets the air out of things pretty fast because then the bouncer wins no matter how many flying kicks you land on his cranium.

Not that my victory did me any good: The girls were so unimpressed with the champion fighter of the Black Bear Bar that they seemed to have forgotten I existed. After half an hour I waved at Becky. "Can you handle it from here? I need to go home and bleed internally."

She peered around the bar. Other than Jimmy and his new girlfriends, we had Claude and Wilma in the corner, and the remaining two construction guys were back at the pool table, staring sightlessly at the cue ball even though it had stopped rolling. "Yeah, it's quite a crowd, but I think I'll be okay."

"Good night, sis."

"See ya, hero."

Milt's fifteen-year-old tow truck wanted to keep sleeping, but the dual batteries methodically cranked the engine until it finally rumbled like a grouchy lion. I scraped away the ice from the windshield and eased out into the night.

It was just past twelve. Time for a physics lesson.

Out of habit I hit the repo switch as soon as I was close—dousing lights, instruments, and anything else that glowed—with one click. Milt had invented it and called it "stealth mode," but I was pretty sure I was still visible to Russian radar. It was simply a kill switch for everything emitting light so that I could sneak up on people in the tow truck, which meant there were no brake lights as I parked about fifteen yards from Einstein's house, sliding into a dark place under the trees where my truck would be impossible to spot on such a black night. The precipitation had let up but a light patter of melt-water falling from the branches smothered my footfalls as I approached his place.

I paused at the bottom of the driveway and reviewed my plan: (a) go up to his truck; (b) take it. A thin blade of flexible steel, notched on one end—the slim jim—would gain me access to the cab. The dent puller was a claw with a thickly threaded screw on one end. Turn the screw and the claw would pull the ignition switch right out of the steering column. Once the switch was dangling there like a loose eyeball, I'd stick a screwdriver into the contact points, twist, and the truck would hopefully start faster than mine had.

New vehicles no longer used the steering column switch, but Einstein's Chevy was one of the last trucks built during an era when manufacturers were more considerate of car thieves and repo men.

When the engine was running I'd have to do some back and forth before I could clear the cement steps, and backing around the abrupt elbow in the driveway would be more than a little difficult, but I was betting Einstein's Friday night had ended with him drinking all of the brothers and sisters of the beer he'd been holding in his hand when we had our productive little chat, and that he would snooze through the whole thing.

So why was I hesitating?

Being a repo man requires what Milt calls "nerves of stupidity": I usually handled danger by not thinking about it. And I wasn't thinking about it now. Einstein didn't scare me, his threat to "shoot me legal" didn't scare me, and his goose didn't scare me. I wasn't picturing him with a gun. I wasn't picturing anything, but my heart was pounding and my hands shook when I tried to read my watch in the black night.

What if the dream was some sort of foreshadowing? You dream about your death and then you die trying to steal a Chevy truck out of some Einstein's driveway.

I didn't like this. Something was wrong—I could feel it, even if I couldn't see anything. Then I thought about Becky needing a thousand dollars to keep the Black Bear open. I'd get $250 for this repo. I had to have it.

So okay. Still shaking a little with anxiety, I crept up the driveway, slipping a little in the wet slush. There was the truck, jammed in right where it had been earlier. A half-inch of snow covered the windshield; hopefully it wouldn't leave a film when I wiped it off.

I took another two steps forward and nearly shouted when three large outdoor spotlights flashed on, bathing me in harsh white light. Cursing, blinded, I scrambled away and rolled into the bushes by the goose shed, hugging the mud, trying to stay low. Motion detector.

The door banged open. Einstein Croft stood on the threshold, even uglier in his boxer shorts than he had been in a lumberjack shirt, though I'm sure part of my assessment came from the objectionable presence of the deer rifle in his hands.

He swung the rifle around in a slow circle, sighting over the top of it. I pressed down into the dirt, scarcely breathing for fear the fog of my breath would give me away. My heart hammered at my chest wall and I stared at him, willing him to see me as nothing more than a shadow under his sparse shrubbery.

A full minute passed and then the lights abruptly shut off the show. Now he was illuminated from within the house, and I saw the eagerness go out of him, the barrel of his gun drooping in disappointment. He'd been hoping to bag himself a repo man.

I lay there for a full five minutes after he went back inside, willing my body to calm down. In this part of the country a lot of people own guns and I'd had a few of them pointed in my general direction, but most of the time it was just to scare me. This had been to shoot me. I thought of the nightmare, of the sensation of a rifle bullet hitting me in the back of the head, dropping me onto the forest floor. I desperately did not want that to happen in real life.

After a moment my fear bled out and left me with anger. What did that idiot think he was doing? You don't kill someone for repossessing your pickup truck! Forget the $250; this was personal now.

I pondered my options. Home motion detectors were usually not very sensitive. If I moved slowly, chances were the lights wouldn't pop on until I put the truck in gear. I mentally ticked off the seconds it had taken Einstein to come to full alert once the spotlights flared. What had seemed like mere moments now, on reflection, felt like maybe two minutes. If I couldn't start a pickup and back it down the driveway in less time than that, I didn't deserve to be a repo man.

Once I decided to try it again, the same uneasiness settled over me—a dread-filled foreboding that I couldn't shake off. What the heck was my problem?

I was just snaking forward through the muddy snow when I felt a stabbing pain in my Achilles, like something biting me. I rolled over and there was the goose, its neck uncoiling as it delivered another attack on my leg. "Hey!" I whispered sharply. I was trying to avoid setting off the motion detectors and here was this dumb bird, well, goosing me.

It hissed, parting its ridiculous lips and sticking its tongue out at me in what I was sure was some sort of insult. I pulled my legs away. "Stop it! That really hurts!" I commanded with all the authority of being from a superior species. I slithered another few feet and the goose launched itself into the air, flapping its wings.

The night was flooded with the searing white glare from the spotlights. I flung up an arm and the goose wings pummeled me as hard as the biker from Cadillac. Where were its survival instincts? It should have been terrified of me; I eat geese!

All right, the heck with this. I sprinted down the driveway, my shoes sliding and sending me down onto my butt. I heard the back door fly open again as I tripped and fell and rolled in the slush.

"Doris!" Einstein yelled.

I made it to the bottom of the driveway and paused. Of all the insults I'd suffered that night, having Albert Einstein call me Doris was the most surprising.

"Get back in the shed, Doris, you stupid duck!" he raged.

I felt my energy drain out of me as I trudged back to my truck. I'd been outsmarted by a man who named his goose Doris and thought it was a duck. I could not have been more depressed.

By the time I got home the woodstove in my small living room was down to a few coals; I stirred them and threw in some pine. My dog Jake thumped his tail at me and I bent down to scratch his head. Jake was maybe eight years old, a dog of unidentifiable and suspect DNA. His soulful eyes and floppy ears made it appear there was a basset hound on one of the lower limbs of his family tree, but from there he was fifty pounds of anyone's guess. I'd found him in the back of a repo—not the backseat, but the trunk. We're supposed to return all personal property from a repossession but I'd decided on the spot that Jake's people had lost their right of ownership.

"Hey, Jake, you got any goose hunter in you?" I asked.

Jake used to ride with me on repos, but he was middle-aged when I found him and lately had decided he'd rather nap. I didn't blame him—the second I found someone to feed me and give me treats I was going to retire, too.

"Jake, busy day today?"

Jake gave me a "you have no idea" look, rolling his big brown eyes at me.

"You need to go out?"

Jake has a dog door but more and more often was too lazy to use it unless I firmly suggested he do so. I gently tugged on his collar and he groaned to his feet, slipping outside in front of me and then giving me disgusted looks over how wet it was. He lifted his leg quickly and then briskly went back to the door, pointedly sniffing at it so I'd take the hint. We went back in and he hustled to his blanket and collapsed as if he'd spent the day mining coal.

I sang him the "good boy" song—basically me just singing "good boy" over and over, "good boy good boy g-oooo-d b-ooo-y." Big finish. Jake didn't applaud.

A bottle of Patrón tequila slapped into my hand with easy familiarity from its perch on the counter, and I sat down in a chair, watching the woodstove flames licking at the wood. The increasing light soon was illuminating the beer bottles on the coffee table. I stared at the reflection, taking very tiny sips from the Patrón every few minutes. The college boys who somehow found the Black Bear in the summer always poured the stuff in shot glasses and messed around with salt and lime, but my dad had taught me the way to drink tequila was from a snifter, neat, doing little more than wetting your tongue and allowing the fumes to fill your nasal cavities before you swallowed.

Over time, I'd sort of given up on the snifter.

Taking stock of my life: I was broke; I lived alone; I'd had two fights in the past couple of hours; won one, lost one (to a bird)—though both of them left me much worse off than my opponents—and I had a phone number in my pocket I somehow doubted I had the courage to ever call.

"*What a dump,*" the bear's voice pronounced.

I sat stock still, turning my head to the right only after I mentally followed myself into the house, recalling locking the door before I threw on the piece of wood. No one had slipped in behind me; Jake and I were by ourselves in my home. Bob the Black Bear was, as far as I knew, still down at the bar.

Who said that? I asked within my head.

Nobody answered.

4

Repo Madness

When I opened my eyes the next morning it took me about ten minutes to do an inventory of my injuries. My ear hurt from the kick in the head, my ribs throbbed, my arms were bruised, and my shins ached from where Doris had pecked them. I staggered into the living room like a hundred-year-old man. "What a dump," I muttered to myself. Jake sighed in agreement.

After being so severely beaten by man and fowl I would have expected to sleep easily, but I'd spent most of the night brooding over what it meant that I could hear a voice in my head. I wasn't sure *schizophrenia* was the right term for it, didn't know if there was a pill you could take or if it required surgery—I was just pretty sure that whatever was going on, it wasn't covered by my health insurance because I didn't have health insurance. And was it Bob the Bear? No, I'd heard it speaking here, last night. (I was careful to mentally regard the voice as an "it," believing that calling it a "he" would somehow make it worse.)

Whatever was happening, though, I knew I had to

play it cool. If I screamed in surprise every time I heard it, I'd wind up in the loony bin.

I fished around in the refrigerator for something edible and came up with the meat loaf Becky had given me a few nights before, still wrapped in foil. I cut a piece, squirted on some ketchup, poured myself a cup of instant coffee, and sat down for breakfast.

"You've got to be kidding," my voice said.

Sticking with my game plan, I didn't gasp and jerk around to see who'd spoken. "You hear that, Jake?" I asked calmly. Jake didn't even seem to hear *me*. He lay motionless, not even coming over to check out the meat loaf.

"You can't eat like that for breakfast, you'll clog your arteries," the voice admonished.

"So I've developed a split personality and it's become a nutritionist," I announced out loud.

"No, I'm not," it answered defensively.

"So you're what, a boxing manager?"

"No, I mean I'm not a split anything, I am my own person."

"Yeah? Where are you, then?"

There was a pause. *"I'm not sure."*

"Well, you sure as heck aren't here. Unless . . . you're not an eight-foot rabbit, are you?"

"I'm not Harvey. My name is Alan Lottner."

"Alan Lottner." I cut another slice of cold meat loaf. Play it cool, play it cool. "Uh-huh. Well, what can I do for you, Alan?"

"I'm . . . I'm not sure what is going on."

"Well, I think I have a pretty good idea. I've been living alone for a long time now so my brain has furnished me with a friend to play with. An invisible friend who will soon start telling me it's okay to set fires."

There was a silence. I stopped eating and cocked my head. Maybe all I had to do was identify the problem and the neurosis would simply go away. Self-administered psychotherapy.

"I admit this is weird," the voice stated slowly, *"but somehow I am inside of you. When you look around, I can see what you see."*

"Great, I am a man trapped in a man's body."

Alan Lottner chuckled: I actually heard him laughing in my ear. The sound unnerved me—whatever was going on inside my head, it couldn't be good that I could hear *laughter.*

"I don't know how I got here," he confided after a moment.

"Well, as soon as you figure it out you can leave the same way." I was pretty pleased with how cool I was playing this—maybe he would leave.

"At first I thought it was a dream. It's like that, because even though I can see and hear and even feel everything, I don't have any control over my body."

"Whose body?"

"Okay, your body . . . but where's my body? What's happening to me?"

"Sorry to have to tell you this, but I think the real concern is what's happening to *me,"* I corrected. "I'm having a conversation with a voice inside my head. Clearly, the stress of living life in the fast lane in Kalkaska is getting to me." I finished my meat loaf and tossed the aluminum foil at the trash can. It bounced off the rim and joined the pile of missed shots cluttering the floor.

"Are you going to pick that up?"

"No, it's how I keep score," I answered. The silence I received in reply had a huffy quality to it. Great, my voice had no sense of humor. "So Alan, why don't you go out and do some work while I stay home and watch a little basketball?"

"I . . . look, is your name Ruddy?"

"Ruddy McCann."

"I thought so, though at first I thought they were saying 'Buddy.' Like Buddy Hackett."

"No, it's Ruddy, for Ruddick. Mother's maiden name."

"Ah."

I pulled on some clothes and went into the bathroom to comb my hair and brush my teeth. *"Stop!"* Alan commanded.

I froze, raising an eyebrow.

"This is just really strange, looking at my reflection, only having it be somebody else," he told me.

"Didn't we already have this conversation? Whose reflection is it?"

"You know what I mean. I guess I sort of halfway thought that it would be me in the mirror, and that I would find out that I had amnesia and suddenly woke up six four and three hundred pounds."

"Six two and two-twenty. Watch it."

"What happened to your nose?"

"Broke it. Car accident. What happened to your body?"

"I guess I lost it."

"Tough break. Hate it when that happens." I pulled on a jacket. "Well, I guess you might as well come along," I told him. "Let's go, Jake."

Jake considered it briefly, then lowered his head back down. *"Now*, boy, let's go," I commanded sternly. He didn't move. "Hey!" I snapped my fingers. Sometimes you have to show them who the alpha male is.

Jake closed his eyes.

"Please?"

I finally got him to move by pulling a box of dog biscuits out of the cupboard. Once up, he grudgingly allowed me to walk him around the block, lifting his leg on a few leafless shrubs out of moral obligation, but when we got back he fell on his blanket with a "thank God we got that out of our system" expression.

I drove over to Milton's office. Milton Kramer is a short, stocky guy who wears white short-sleeved shirts every day of the year and has a head that looks like it has been waxed and buffed. His skin appeared to have never been exposed to even a moment of sunshine. Milt's life revolves around his work—I've almost never seen him out with his wife, whose name isn't Ruby but that's always what I want to call her when they have me over to their house for dinner.

"Hey, Milt."

"Hello there and good morning, Ruddy. Say hello to my nephew, here. Ruddy McCann, this is Kermit Kramer."

Kermit didn't get out of his chair, but he extended his hand with a smile. He had Milton's pushed-in-looking nose and thick features, though his hair was dark and curly and his complexion a Mediterranean shade. "Kermit" was a good name for him; he was shaped a little like a frog, with narrow sloping shoulders and big wide hips.

"Kermit's going to help me out a little this summer."

"Summer," I agreed dubiously. I looked down at the wet snow I'd tracked in.

"Yep. Maybe you'd take him around, show him the ropes?"

I nodded carefully. Milton didn't need two men; was I being asked to train my replacement? Milton was the sort of person who always looked out for his family, even his brother's sons. I was painfully aware that if I weren't a repo man I'd be nothing.

I sat in the metal chair facing Milton's desk. "Got anything for me?"

"Yeah, believe so." Milton put on a pair of reading glasses and looked over the tops of them at a file. "Ford Credit. A guy somewhere in Traverse City, said he'd make up the two payments he's behind and then disappeared instead. Ford Mustang."

"Okay." I reached for the file.

"Mind if I matriculate a little?" Kermit asked, intersecting my reach with his own.

"If you what?" I asked politely.

"I just would like to see. You know, if I have any ideas."

"Sure, sure, that's a good idea," Milton beamed. "Let's let him metic-whatever, see if he can find the guy."

"Okay." I paused. "Milt, I heard you got some bad paper from Jimmy Growe."

Milton glanced up sharply. "Who told you about that?"

"Jimmy."

"Ah." Milton took off his glasses and rubbed his eyes, as if looking at me over the top of the lenses was tiring him out. "Yeah, that's right. I guess he spent the money already."

"He bought a motorcycle with some of it. I told him to sell it."

"Good, good. I don't want the damn thing."

"What's the deal with the checks, though? Jimmy said he didn't know where they came from."

"That's right. Bank is up in Traverse. They won't tell me the name on the account, and they're those starter checks."

"Why'd you cash them?"

"I know, I should have thought it through better. I knew Jimmy wouldn't be up to anything, is all. And I figured, why would someone send him the money, if it wasn't legitimate?"

"Want me to look into it for you?"

Milt shrugged. "I don't know what good it would do. No law broken, Jimmy never did anything to earn the money. I just should never have cashed them."

"I'll be up near Traverse anyway, tracing this Mustang. Something's not right, Milt. I mean, you know Jimmy. Sending him those checks was a deliberate way to get him into trouble. Maybe I can recover something from that end for you."

Milt grunted. "Sure, look into it. I took ten points; you can have all of it if you can recover my five grand. Last time he owed me money it took something like eight years for him to pay me back."

I nodded, understanding. Milt was fine with paying me, but if I couldn't track down somebody to make good on the debt in Traverse City, I would be collecting from Jimmy.

I exhaled. I hated this next subject. "So, Milt. I'm wondering if I could have an advance on some of the work I'm doing? We're a little short with our suppliers down at the Bear."

Milt loans money for a living, so the look he gave me was all business. "How's it looking with Albert Einstein?" he asked.

"I touched the collateral yesterday." I told him about the goose named Doris, and both Kermit and Milton howled at the picture of me being run off by poultry, leading me to conclude that neither one of them had been clubbed with goose wings before.

"Ya know, if the goose really attacked you, they should euphemize it," Kermit advised.

"Euphemize? You mean, call it 'Christmas Dinner' or something?" I smiled.

Kermit frowned. "No, I meant put it to sleep."

I decided it wasn't worth trying to explain. I was watching Milt pull out his big checkbook and scrawl in it. He handed me more than I was expecting: $750. "There's advance on Einstein—I know you'll get him if you've seen the truck—plus the fee on Jimmy. I figure with you babysitting him I'll get paid one way or another." Milt wagged his finger. "One percent of the balance per month on Jimmy, my interest rate on that."

I nodded. Twelve percent per year, better than the credit cards. Milt lends money but he's not the Mafia.

"And hey, would you mind taking Kermit along with you now? You're headed up to Traverse, right?"

"Only if he brings a dictionary."

Milton laughed. "He does have a hell of a vocabulary, doesn't he?"

Kermit and I stood. On his feet, he appeared to be no more than five foot six; next to him I felt like a giant. In high school he would have played center—all of his weight down low like that. In college he would have sat in the stands along with everyone else his size.

I turned at the door. "Hey, catch up with you in a minute, Kermit." Once he had passed outside I came back into the room. "Milton, can I ask you something?"

He nodded carefully.

I jammed my hands in my pockets and glanced around the room. "Have you ever had voices in your head? Talking to you?"

Milton stared. "You got voices in your head?"

"No, forget it. I mean yes, I do, but it is only one voice. He says his name is Alan."

"You got a voice in your head named Alan?" Milton's eyes were looking sort of milky. I wondered if he was calculating how long it would take the cops to arrive if he lunged for the phone.

"Forget it, it's nothing."

"I'm afraid you've got the madness, son," he whispered.

"The what?"

"Repo Madness. It happens. The stress of snatching units off the streets, one day, you just crack up. I once saw a guy bigger than you sit right down on the curb and start to cry like a baby. Madness got him bad. He was never able to take another car after that day." Milt beckoned and I reluctantly leaned forward. "Why do you think I never steal any of my own cars anymore, Ruddy?"

I thought about it. "Because Ruby would kill you?"

He blinked. "Ruby? The hell is Ruby?"

"Your wife?"

"My wife is Trisha."

"That's her name! Trisha!"

"Jesus, you got voices in your head and you think I married some bimbo named Ruby?"

"For God's sake, Milt, it's just one voice and I have always thought your wife's name was Ruby. I mean, I knew it wasn't, but I couldn't think of her any other way." Already, the name Trisha was fading from my brain, replaced by a giant neon sign blinking RUBY, RUBY, RUBY.

Milt eyed me for a minute. "It's the madness, Ruddy," he pronounced finally. "I just got the madness. One day everything is fine, and the next, no matter how easy the snatch, I start getting so damned scared I can barely move. Then I'm pulling a voluntary, guy voluntarily hands me the keys, and the same thing happens—my heart starts to pound and my hands shake. That's when I knew I had to give it up, before I lost it completely." He looked at me shrewdly. "Before I started hearing voices."

I remembered the dream, and how my heart had been pounding the "Night of the Attack of Doris the Goose." Could this really be what was going on? Repo Madness.

I shook it off. "Look, just forget about it, okay? I'm fine. Thanks. No problem. I'll find this skip and look into Jimmy's checks, okay?"

Milton nodded sadly. As I backed up, my heel caught the lip of the rug and I tripped a bit, stumbling. He just watched with wise eyes, probably thinking this was another symptom.

"So you're a repo man? That's what the whole thing was about last night? I thought you were a cop or something," Alan complained as I left Milt's office.

"You don't like it, go inhabit someone else's psychosis," I growled silently, keeping the dialogue in my head where it belonged. I expected a flip response, but instead I got back silence, with a bit of an impatient flavor to it. I stopped in the hallway. "So, no lippy comment? I just called you a psychosis," I challenged him mentally.

"Well?" he finally demanded. *"What are we doing? Why don't you say something?"*

"You mean you can only hear me if I talk?" I asked out loud.

"Well, of course," Alan replied a bit indignantly. *"You think I can read minds?"*

There were just too many things wrong with that question to respond to it. "Listen, Alan, we have to discuss something. I think I am handling this pretty well. I mean, I have a voice inside my head, but I'm not over-reacting. But this isn't normal. I'm obviously losing my grip. You have to go away now, Alan."

"I can't go away, Ruddy. What do you think, I can just float out and up to the stars or something?"

"I don't know what I think. I'm not sure it matters what I think. All I know is, I can't go around talking out loud to this voice in my head because people just don't do that. Not mentally healthy people."

"You're saying I am just some sort of figment of your imagination. I resent the implication," he said loftily.

"You resent? You? Let me ask you, do you hear a voice in your head? Huh? No, you don't. You can't even hear me in my head! So don't tell me about implications. The implication is, I am going crazy and am going to wind up in a room with soft walls, that's the implication."

"Well, obviously there's no talking to you when you're in this sort of mood."

"What I am saying is there's no talking to me, period."

I paused, glaring at the wall, because what else was I supposed to look at?

When Alan spoke his voice was suddenly plaintive and small-sounding. *"But Ruddy, I need your help. I think I know why I'm not . . . not in myself anymore. My body, I mean. I think I know what happened."*

"Okay, let's hear it."

"I'm dead."

I blinked. "Dead?" I repeated incredulously.

"Murdered. I think I was murdered, Ruddy."

I stood frozen, still staring at the wall.

My Repo Madness seemed to be getting worse by the minute.

5

Exactly Fifteen Miles an Hour

On the way to Traverse City Kermit checked his mobile phone every ten minutes, announcing over and over "no signal here," and "weak signal here" as he frowned at it. "That's why I leave mine in my kitchen. Signal's good there," I responded, but mostly I wasn't paying attention. I was brooding over what it could possibly mean that the voice inside my head now claimed to be a murder victim. It sounds, well, crazy, but I realized that somehow I had started to buy into it all—I was actually beginning to think of the voice as a separate person, as Alan Lottner, and could see myself eventually growing comfortable with my conversations with him. There was just something so normal about it—another man's voice, seeming to be coming from my ears and not from within my brain. That's really what all human interactions are like, right? Kermit at that moment was yammering away about some way he could make money; it was a separate voice, a separate person, and I wasn't looking at him. And when you talk on the phone, you can't see that particular person, either. So none of this *felt* any different than how life usually goes, even if I knew it wasn't.

But murder? What was next, would he want me to avenge his killer? And who would that turn out to be, the president of the United States or somebody? How long before I complacently went along with this idea, too?

Traverse City is right on Lake Michigan and has fifteen thousand people in the winter and what seems like two million in the summer, as opposed to land-locked Kalkaska, where I think I know just about everybody by their first name. Kalkaska only really has a crowd control problem during deer hunting season, when the boys from the city arm themselves and wander around wearing camouflage pants, drinking beer.

Kermit was happy for me to drop him off at a drugstore to mess around while I checked into Jimmy Growe's mystery checks. The silence he left behind when he jumped out made me realize just how much talking he'd been doing—I had a voice both in my head and in my truck.

All of the checks to Jimmy Growe had come from one bank. I walked into the lobby, looking around for the Department of Checks from Nowhere That Bounce.

The person who agreed to help me was a large woman, her bone structure as solid as mine, and I could picture her being a Campfire Girl leader for the three daughters whose framed photographs owned most of the real estate of her desk. She was about my age and wore her auburn hair so that it curled a little off her shoulders. Her dark eyes softened in concern as I spread Jimmy's six checks—five NSF, one uncashed—across her desk. She told me to call her Maureen.

"Oh my," Maureen murmured.

I explained my connection to Jimmy and Milton, showing her my business card and Milton's corporate endorsement of the checks on the back. "What I need to know is who wrote these checks. You can see that the signature is not really legible. It could be Whitmore, or Southmore, or Sophomore. Or Whilnose, or Whilmore." Those had been my best guesses. None of the names I'd suggested were in the Traverse City phone book, and I doubted anyone on the planet was named Whilnose.

Maureen agreed that the names were hard to read, and even pointed out something I'd missed—the signatures didn't really appear to be the same from one check to the next. "This one is definitely Wilmore," she pronounced.

"Wilmore," I agreed, making a note. She watched me write down the name, frowning.

"Please understand, I am not confirming that as the name on the account," she warned me, somehow sounding less like Maureen the human and more like Maureen the bank.

"Oh, I understand, it just helps. Most people, when they want to assume a name, pick a variation of their own name." She looked at me dubiously. "Well, that's what I read in a mystery novel," I explained defensively.

"So you think these are all pseudonyms?" she asked.

"I don't know, really. I thought you could give me the name of the owner of the account. Maybe it will turn out to be this Wilmore."

She bit her lip. "We've never had a case of a returned check where the payee didn't know the remitter."

"It certainly is interesting," I agreed brightly, watching the doubt etch shadows into her expression. She wasn't going to tell me.

"You see, Mr. McCann, it would be against bank policy to give out a name on an account."

"But these are bounced checks!"

"I'm sorry, even under these circumstances."

"But you said it has never happened before. Come on, Maureen, you mean you have a policy for something that never happened before?"

"Great idea, get her pissed off," Alan admired.

A slight flush crept onto her cheeks, but she maintained her composure. "I'm sorry. But the owner of this account . . ." She paused, frowning. Her head came forward sharply. "These are all different accounts!" she exclaimed.

"They are?"

"Look!" She pointed to the hieroglyphics across the bottom of each check. "You have six checks drawn on six separate accounts."

I wanted to encourage her curiosity. "How in the world could that possibly happen, I wonder?"

Our eyes met. "Someone must have opened six separate accounts with our bank, receiving a packet of starter checks each time."

"And not using them at all," I agreed, finally doing some noticing myself. "See? These are all check number one hundred. That would be the first in the series, right?"

She nodded. "Right."

I held my breath, watching her mull it over. Then the part of her brain that stood guard over bank policy slammed the door on this line of thinking. "Well," she murmured, searching for the words to tell me I still wouldn't be getting any information out of her.

Glancing around the office in my frustration, I noticed

her degrees and certificates. "Hey, you went to Michigan State!" I exclaimed.

She blinked at the abrupt change in subject.

"Me too!"

We beamed at each other, and then her expression changed. "You're Ruddy McCann. *The* Ruddy Mc-Cann?" she gasped.

"That's me."

"Oh my!" She half rose in her chair as if to shake my hand again, then sat back down. "I didn't know you lived here."

"Right down the road in Kalkaska. Went to high school there and everything."

"What a small world," Maureen breathed. "I had no idea."

We spent a moment looking inward at our college memories. "What happened to you, didn't you play professional football? I remember everyone saying you were going to win the Heisman Trophy, and then . . ." Her face turned gray as she remembered what did happen to me. "Oh my."

I waited. People have various reactions to my past, and I didn't know what direction Maureen would take.

"I'm so sorry," she murmured. I could see that she was; her deep brown eyes were sagging under the weight of tragedy.

"It was a mistake I will regret for a lifetime," I told her sincerely.

"*What was?*" Alan demanded.

The silence was awkward but I let it build for a moment, then I leaned forward. "Maureen, Jimmy Growe is a very simple guy. I kind of take care of him, like the big brother he never had. He pushes a broom for a living.

When these checks arrived, he felt like he had won the Lotto. Now, you and I would probably wonder what the heck was going on, but Jimmy just ran out and cashed these with my employer. And, Jimmy being Jimmy, the only tangible item left from all that money is a motorcycle. Which, knowing Jimmy, he bought from someone who probably took him to the cleaners, so when he sells it he will be thousands of dollars in debt. If I don't get to the bottom of this, it is going to take Jimmy years to get out of trouble. He still doesn't really understand what is going on—he offered to pay me by giving me this last, unendorsed check here."

Maureen made a noise in sympathy. I could see her mothering her image of Jimmy, so I decided to leave out the part about him being the hottest stud in Kalkaska.

"Couldn't you please look into this? If it is a joke, it has gone way, way too far. These checks are doing Jimmy a lot of harm."

Her maternal instincts pushed her over to the dark side of banking. "Yes, all right. I'll be right back." She swept the checks off her desk and left the room.

"You were a Heisman Trophy winner?" Alan demanded.

"No," I told him.

"What was she talking about, then?"

"Alan, is it lonely in there? No one to talk to?"

"You don't know the half of it. When you're moving it is all I can do to hang on, like when you were driving and that Kermit was talking about how he was going to make all that money by processing credit card charges. But when you're sitting still and I feel more in control, I want to scream, because—"

"Alan, shut up."

He bit off his rant in what I swear sounded like hurt silence.

"You are not in control. I am in control. And when I am conducting a conversation with someone, I want you to be quiet. If you are, then when we're alone, I'll talk to you. If you're not, then I'll never answer you again, and you'll never have anything approaching a dialogue with anyone unless you leave me and go into somebody else's head. Okay?"

He didn't answer.

"Alan?"

"Oh, am I allowed to speak now?"

Maureen was back in the room, carrying a ledger book. "This is very disturbing." She sat down heavily and stared at me, wrestling with what she had just learned.

"Maureen?" I prompted.

"Well, we still maintain this log in addition to the computer. Whenever we issue starter checks we write down the name and date, here." She pointed to the list and I looked at it from an upside-down angle. Customer information flowed across the register in neat rows. I sensed there was a lot more, and waited for her to tell me.

"The thing is, Mr. McCann, none of these packets were ever issued to a customer. See? The account numbers are printed right here. Someone has drawn a line through them."

"Why would anyone do something like that?"

"Well, sometimes an error is made, and we just void out the account. Under those circumstances, we would mark through the number here and destroy the starter packet."

"Does that happen a lot?"

"Well, not a lot, but it does happen. Someone should have noticed this, though. Oh."

"Oh?"

Her eyes were now unreadable as they met mine. "Oh my."

"What is it, Maureen?"

Wordlessly, she spun the book around for me to see. I glanced down the list of names, noting that the starter packets with the lines through them were grouped together, all issued in December, all within a day or two of each other.

"The handwriting," Alan murmured.

"The handwriting," I repeated stupidly.

"Yes. The word *void* looks like it could be the same as on the checks," Maureen agreed helplessly.

I looked at her in amazement. "So the *bank* has been sending Jimmy these checks?"

"No! Oh no, Mr. McCann. Not the bank. An . . . employee."

"Why would they do that?"

Maureen shook her head, her look as blank as Jimmy's had been.

"I need to talk to the employees," I declared grimly.

Maureen appeared shocked. "Oh no, we couldn't allow that."

"But . . ."

"No, I'm sorry, that won't be possible."

I don't like it when people tell me something I want to do isn't possible. When I spoke again, it was slowly and deliberately. "Maureen, you need to understand, Milt isn't trying to go after the bank. We just need to get to the bottom of this. Can you look into it, figure out what happened, who did this? You know. Just compare the log here to people's handwriting. We'll keep this quiet. There is no need for Milt to report this to the authorities."

Maureen's eyes searched mine. Alan was silent but I swear I could feel his distaste for my subtle threat. Finally she pressed her lips together, nodding unhappily.

"Good, I'll call you in a day or two to see if you found anything out for me, okay?"

Maureen nodded again, and I shook hands with her and left the office. I was the first to speak in the parking lot. "What, what is it?" I challenged.

"She was helping you and you made it sound like if she didn't cooperate you'd haul her down to gestapo headquarters," Alan sniffed.

"Alan, I'm a repo man. I collect money, and if people don't have any I take away their cars. How do you think I do that, send a Hallmark card with a puppy on it?"

"It was mean."

I stopped walking and faced a small snowman some children had built so that anyone watching would assume I was arguing with it and not with a voice in my head like some crazy person. "Yeah, well, what do you do for a living?"

"I sell real estate," he answered loftily.

"You what? Would you listen to yourself? You do nothing. You live off of the welfare state of Ruddy McCann. You don't even have a body."

"Well, I'm sure if circumstances were reversed I would be a little more understanding."

"I'm sure you would, Alan, because you know what? I'm not understanding any of this!"

"I told you I was dead, murdered, and your lack of concern could not have been more apparent," he ac-

cused. *"You're selfish, mean to people, and you don't floss."*

"I . . . what?"

"Your dietary habits are inexcusable. Your house is a wreck, and you never exercise."

"What are you talking about?" I sputtered. "I don't have to exercise, I'm an athlete, I get it from sports! And I do too floss, sometimes, and how is it your business anyway, and shut up! I mean it, stop talking now, Alan. Not another word."

I kicked ice chunks out of my way as I strode down the sidewalk to the pharmacy. I had a split personality and we didn't like each other. I peered up at the overcast sky, thinking I was the butt of some cosmic joke. It was not the first time in my life I'd entertained that particular notion.

I entered the drugstore and started hunting for Kermit. He was reading a *Playboy* magazine, hunched down by the display so the pharmacist wouldn't notice him. "You're not supposed to read them if you're not going to buy them," I called out loudly. He fumbled the magazine back into the rack and followed me outside. Soon we were in the truck, headed out to try to find the Ford Credit account.

"This guy we're looking for bought himself a brand-new Ford Mustang and stopped paying for it a couple of months ago," I told Kermit, mostly to prevent him from talking. "A lot of the vehicles I drag in are sports cars. Hardly the most practical vehicles for around here—we're buried in ice half the year. Young guys fall in love with an image of themselves roaring around in their hot cars and sign papers for payments that are hopelessly out of their reach."

"I used to own a Trans-Am," Kermit piped in irrelevantly.

"That's nice, Kermit. Anyway, by the time they find out what the insurance is going to cost on their new toys, they start to get a little buyer's remorse. But they can't sell the things—the most expensive option on a new car is the depreciation, meaning they'd have to come up with thousands of dollars to undo their mistakes. Most guys wind up turning them back in. The ones who refuse to drop them off at the dealership find themselves dealing with me. Unless they're like this guy—he went to ground. His car hasn't been seen around all winter, and he doesn't seem to have a home, he just sort of drifts from friend to friend's place. No permanent address."

"First thing we should do is run a background check," Kermit speculated.

"Yeah?" I glanced over at him. He looked completely serious. "What does that mean?"

"You know, on the computer."

"You know how to do something like that?"

"Um, no, not especially."

"Okay. So I thought the first thing we'd do is check out his place of business."

For employment, the customer had listed "logger" on his application. There's no such thing anymore in northern Michigan; what he did for a living was run a chain saw, cutting down second-growth forest for small-time firewood operations. One of the regulars at the Black Bear did the same kind of thing and told me where our Mustang customer had been working this past winter.

Kermit had the file open in his lap as we bounced down the rutted two-track deep into the woods, my tires biting at the mud in four-wheel drive. "What are these?" he asked, holding up a set of what were clearly car keys.

"When you buy a new car, the dealer retains the key numbers, so you can cut a new set if you lose them. Or if the repo guy needs some," I explained.

We came to a halt in a clearing with jumbled stacks of hardwood. It was Saturday, so the place was abandoned. Two hydraulic splitters, a couple of mauls, and an old flatbed truck with dual rear wheels all appeared to be rusting at about the same rate. "No signal," Kermit pronounced, holding his phone up for me to see. I ignored him.

"Hello?" I called out as a formality. There clearly wasn't anyone around.

"Hello! Yo! Anyone here? Hello!" Kermit shouted. "Hey!"

"That's enough, Kermit."

"Hello there, hello! Anybody?"

"Kermit!" He looked at me, startled. "It's okay, I don't think anyone's here."

"Oh."

"Why don't you look around, see if you can spot the car anywhere. A lot of these guys think I'll never look for it out here in the forest."

He agreed, the black mud sucking at his boots as he wandered off down one of the trails. His thighs were so big he had a natural waddle to his gait, which the tricky footing only accentuated. I couldn't recall ever meeting someone who carried all his weight in his legs and butt like that. Unconsciously I pinched a fold of flab over my hips, then patted my stomach. When I realized what I was doing I sighed and shook my head. So what? I always gained a little weight in the winter. It was perfectly normal. Sometimes I even lost some of it in the summer.

I looked around. Everything in the clearing was a boggy mess. The earth was deeply rutted where their truck had backed up to the six-foot-high piles of split firewood. To the left, trunks of fallen trees lay ready for the saw to cut them up, and sawdust was nearly a foot thick in some places.

"Well, hell. I half expected to find the car here," I muttered. Alan didn't reply, apparently deciding to punish me with silence. I wondered how I could induce him to keep it up.

I strolled around, looking hopefully behind the woodpiles. In the shadows the ground was still buried in deep snow, and I tried to imagine what it was like to stand here all day and cut up logs while the Michigan winter poured wet blizzards on my head. What a life the poor guy led.

"Well, that's that," I announced in disgust. Kermit had come wandering back twice like a lost dog, and was running out of trails to explore. I could hear him blundering around about thirty yards away.

"*Wait,*" Alan blurted.

"Oh, are we speaking now?"

"*Look at the ground. Not there. No . . .*" He grunted in frustration. "*Please, look at the woodpile. To the left. Farther. Now down. Look at the ground. There! Look at the tracks.*"

Along the forest floor where Alan was directing my eyes, muddy ruts went right into the woodpile, as if someone had driven under the logs. I glanced at the other places and noted they all looked the same: When the loggers unloaded their truck, some of the logs obliterated some of the tire tracks. I didn't see anything special about the area in which Alan was interested.

"Walk over there," Alan urged. I obliged, curious. *"Do you see?"* he demanded.

"See what?"

"The grooves from the tires. Look at them."

"Uh-huh."

"Not only is there a double set like everywhere else, there's also a more narrow, single set. Like someone pulled a Ford Mustang up to the woodpile."

"Right." I thought about it. "Or maybe the woodpile wasn't here when the Mustang made these tracks."

"Yes, exactly!" Alan agreed excitedly.

With effort, I climbed up the precarious stack of wood until I was on top. I kicked aside a few logs. "If there's a sports car under here, it is dented all to hell," I commented. I started tossing logs off the top of the pile. Just a few layers down I hit heavy chipboard, three-quarters of an inch thick. "I'll be damned. Hey, Kermit!"

An hour later we had exposed a large wooden box, fortified within by two-by-fours and which, once I'd broken out the crowbar, proved to be home to a cherry-red Ford Mustang. I used the winch on the back of the truck, unspooling the thick black cable, attaching the hook to the Mustang, and pulling the car slowly out into the open. Milt's truck was old but the winch was state-of-the-art, well oiled and repo-silent.

"Whoa, nice car, can I drive it?" Kermit wanted to know.

Something about the lustful look in Kermit's eyes made me think that would be a bad idea. "Better let me," I advised. "I'll let you do the next one."

My keys worked but the battery was lifeless. I peered

up at the darkening sky. "Tell you what, Kermit, I'd like to get the hell out of here. Instead of jumping it, why don't you just push me down the road. Once we get going I'll pop the clutch and we'll start it that way."

Kermit shrugged. "Whatever."

"The road's pretty slippery, so I imagine you'll need to get me moving about ten, fifteen miles an hour or so for the tires to get enough bite to start it. Okay?"

He sullenly shrugged again, apparently hurt that I didn't trust him with the car. I slid in behind the wheel, put in the clutch, and moved the shifter into first gear.

The car rocked. I glanced in the rearview mirror and saw Kermit hunched over the trunk, gritting his teeth. *"What an idiot,"* Alan muttered.

"Kermit." I stood up out of the car. "I meant push it with the truck. The truck, Kermit."

"Oh." He stood up, scratching his head.

"Did you really think you'd get going fifteen miles an hour pushing it yourself?"

He shrugged.

"Okay, try the truck. And Kermit, no faster than fifteen miles an hour, all right?" I slid behind the wheel again. "Guy would probably try to hit eighty if I didn't say anything," I remarked.

"So how did a Heisman Trophy finalist wind up a repo man in northern Michigan?" Alan wanted to know. *"What was she talking about back at the bank?"*

"Later, Alan," I responded, knowing I would never tell him. It wasn't something I talked about. I frowned as I watched Kermit in the cab of the truck. He had turned it around so that the big rubber front bumper was facing the rear of the Mustang I was sitting in, but now, for some reason, he was backing up. Where did he think he was going?

Kermit turned on the headlights. He was a good fifty feet away. Suddenly the truck lurched forward.

"What is he doing?" I sputtered, watching the tow truck bear down on me.

"I imagine he is approaching the rear of this vehicle at a speed of exactly fifteen miles an hour," Alan observed calmly.

There wasn't time to say anything else before the crash.

6

The Slander Clause

It was dark and starting to snow with real hostility when I hit the door of the Black Bear, pushing it open like I was hoping it would smack into someone on the other side. I pulled a beer off of the tap and stood behind the bar and drank it while the regulars sat in their chairs and gaped at me with expressions verging on fear.

"Bad day?" Becky asked innocently, moving close to wipe down the keg machine with a rag.

"Don't ask. I've got your thousand dollars, though."

Her eyes flared with life briefly, then went dark again. "Okay."

"I've got seven-fifty now, and I'll give the rest of it to you tomorrow, after Milt pays me for today's repo."

"Okay."

"Come on, Becky! Isn't that what you wanted?" I bit off the impulse to shout at her.

"Sure." She passed a hand over her brow, leaving a smudge on her glasses. "Sorry. Thanks, Ruddy."

She tried out a pursed smile, but it was so rickety and

weak I had to look away. When I turned back, she'd given up on it. "Listen, a couple more months and the summer crowds will be here. Things always go better in the summer. We just have to hang on," I encouraged.

"I'm not sure we can make it until summer, Ruddy," she said in a voice so quiet I wasn't sure I heard correctly.

Janelle Lewis sat down at the bar, and I turned to serve her, glad for an interruption. "Hey, Janelle."

"Hello, Ruddy." She was, as always, carefully made up, though the flip in her professionally dyed blond hair looked like it had spent a little too long out in the wet weather.

Janelle's husband divorced her hard when she turned forty, applying every insult to the injury by marrying a woman who was herself forty. Janelle had brown eyes and freckles and had lost so much weight after her husband left she could probably still wear her Kalkaska High School "Blue Blazers" cheerleader outfit, but she'd abandoned her innocent look in favor of tight jeans and loads of fake jewelry that made her look sharp-edged somehow.

Janelle's bar tab tracked bourbon to the exclusion of everything else. She was lonely, and the way her eyes often lingered on me told me that she saw me as a possible cure for the emptiness in her life. The thirteen-year age difference between us didn't seem as relevant as the wide gap between herself and her happiness, and I'd never been tempted. I poured some bourbon in a glass and waved the soda nozzle at her—sometimes she wanted it, most of the time, like tonight, she shook her head and took her first gulp like it was medicine, her eyes tightly closed.

"I heard about the fight here the other night. I'm sorry I missed it," Janelle observed.

Kermit slunk in then, not sure I was going to allow him inside. He sort of slithered across the floor, finally winding up at the end of the bar. "Stick around," I told Janelle, "you may get to see another one."

I wandered off to check on the other customers, conscious of Kermit watching me like an elk eyeing a wolf. I got the sense that if I suddenly whirled and glared at him he'd flinch and fall to the floor.

Eventually Becky came up to my side. "I replaced the evaporator fan in the back fridge," she greeted.

I glanced up to where the television was playing the Home Repair Network or Fix Your House Network or whatever it was my sister kept it tuned to twenty-four hours a day. Even with the sound off, it annoyed me—a bar should have the game on. We'd talked about it, though, and it was her bar, so unless a customer requested something different we got a steady stream of unreasonably handsome guys ripping down walls and laying carpet. I used to play football—believe me, nobody is that attractive and that muscular; it's an impossible combination. "I would have helped you with that evaporator fan," I told her.

"I know that." She gave me a neutral look while we both didn't mention that after I helped her put in new shelves she had to basically tear out my work and do it again. "Wish we had the money for me to replace the lighting in the kitchen."

I grunted noncommittally. If we didn't try to cook food, we wouldn't even need a kitchen.

Becky was lingering at my elbow as if wanting to talk about something. I gave her a questioning look. "Who's your friend?" she asked, nodding at Kermit.

I was glad we were off the topic of problems at the

Black Bear. "He's not a friend. More like an unsightly growth that I need to have removed."

"Introduce me?" she queried after a pause. I peered at her but got nothing back but pure Becky-style blandness.

I shrugged and she followed me down to where Kermit was clinging to the end of the bar. He looked exquisitely alarmed at my approach. "Kermit, this is my sister Becky, she owns the place. Becky, this is Kermit, the reason why your brother needs a chiropractor today."

They shyly shook hands. "You're bleeding!" Becky exclaimed to him, giving me an accusatory look. Kermit had a bruised lip, but it wasn't a gift from me. Next time he used his uncle's truck to ram a Ford Mustang he should keep his mouth off the steering wheel. I turned away, not caring what she thought. I refilled my glass and sat heavily in a chair.

Claude and Wilma soon joined me. Claude's stained sweater bore the name of the place he'd worked about three car dealerships ago, and Wilma was tented in a blue dress that flashed like aluminum foil. "If it isn't the Wolfingers," I greeted. "Oh wait, you probably have new identities now. Let me guess: you're Mandrake the magician, and your wife here is the ambassador to Spain."

They were still at the stage of their drinking where they found everything hilarious instead of an excuse to scream at each other. They laughed for what seemed like three full minutes—a stand-up comic would kill to have an audience like them. Finally, wiping their eyes, they calmed down. "The government. They don't care about anything. Worst people on earth," Claude lamented.

"Wilma works for the government," I pointed out.

"Not the county. I'm talking about the feds. They acted like I was an idiot when I told them I wanted to join the Witness Protection Club," Claude spat indignantly. Then he leaned forward. "Doesn't matter, though. We've got something else going, you won't believe it."

"Please no," I replied honestly.

Claude told me his plan, laying it out like it was a bank heist. I was keeping my eye on things, mainly on Kermit talking to Becky, and didn't really listen. I gathered, though, that it had to do with Claude and Wilma's homeowner's insurance policy. "That's a quarter of a million dollars, Ruddy," Claude announced dramatically. Wilma nodded happily in agreement.

"Now what, again?"

Claude shook his head in exasperation. "Weren't you listening?"

"It's the slander clause," Alan advised. Apparently he could pay attention even when I didn't, which I had to admit might occasionally come in handy.

"The slander clause," I repeated.

"Exactly," Claude beamed. "It says we're covered for slander for up to two hundred fifty thousand dollars."

Wilma leaned forward. "That's a lot of money, Ruddy."

"I can't argue with that."

Claude glanced at Wilma triumphantly, as if my endorsement settled the matter. "Right. So what we do is, Wilma and I get a divorce. And she gets the house, I let her have it."

I blinked. "You and Wilma are getting a divorce?"

Claude shook his head in exasperation. "Dammit, Ruddy, pay attention to me now, this is complicated and we can't afford any screw-ups. We get a divorce, and Wilma gets the house. That means she gets the homeowners' policy, which covers her, see? And then she slanders me, so I sue her for the full extent of the policy. The insurance company says, 'Holy cow! It's slander all right, let's pay this before it becomes another . . .' What was the name of it, that company lost all that money?"

He snapped his fingers at his wife in a way I could see instantly irritated her, but she suppressed her reaction because they were going to be rich. "Golden Sachs," Wilma prompted.

"No, that's not it."

Wilma's eyes flared, but Claude ignored her. "Whatever it was. They can't afford that, bad for business. So they write me a check, and then we remarry, have the wedding right here at the Bear."

Wilma frowned, not sure about that part.

"But they can't make me give the money back, so we're rich!" Claude exulted. "The little guy wins!"

I gazed back at the two beaming con artists. "What could Wilma possibly say about you that would be considered slander?" I asked at last.

They laughed gaily, propelled by their foolproof plans and probably a quart of vodka between them. "Oh, I'll come up with something, I promise you." She winked.

"And Ruddy"—Claude's hand was back on my wrist like a manacle—"I want you to know, you'll get your share. I promise."

"Thanks, Claude," I said sincerely. "And why do I deserve a cut in this completely foolproof, completely felonious plan to rip off your insurance company?"

"Because I'll be living with you!" Claude announced happily.

There was a long silence. "With me," I repeated.

"Sure, on the top floor. Nobody's using it, right?"

When my mother died half a year or so after Dad, Becky got the bar and I got the house. I turned an outside staircase into a separate entrance and tried to rent the place as a duplex, but Kalkaska didn't have much of a market for that sort of thing and I'd gradually lost my momentum. Claude knew the place had been empty for nearly a year, after I kicked the last fellow out for failing to understand the relationship between occupancy and rent.

I sighed. "I'll have to charge you something," I warned, feeling helpless. I was reminded of the time we all watched Claude and Wilma attempt to sell ten-foot teepees to tourists from their front yard, probably sinking their whole savings into the idea. Were they really going to try this mad scheme?

"Yeah, and more important, you need to keep quiet about when Wilma comes to visit for, you know." They both giggled like kids, and I had to suppress a smile.

"Okay."

Claude became serious. "We'll have to stage a fight or something, so that people will think we have a reason to be splitting up," he speculated.

"Claude, anyone who was here when Wilma tried to break that chair over your head will believe you've got a reason to be splitting up."

The two of them stared at me blankly. Incredibly, I could see that neither one of them remembered the incident.

I served Janelle another bourbon and gave two ice fishermen the pitcher they wanted, offering menus which they refused without looking. I wondered if Becky was as trapped by Kermit's nonstop yapping as I had been earlier, and decided not to go rescue her. Good life lesson. Tough love.

Jimmy came in. I nodded and he headed right over.

"Hey there, Ruddy, did you get a chance to look into my whole . . . the thing with the checks?"

"Yeah, but I don't have anything for you yet."

"Because I got another one."

I sat forward. "You did? Let me see it."

"Well . . ." He stared down at the floor.

"Wait a minute. Jimmy. Jimmy, look at me." His eyes were as evasive as a dog caught sleeping on the couch. "Don't tell me you cashed it."

"Well . . ."

"Where? Milt wouldn't take it."

"At work."

"At the hotel? They cashed it for you?"

"Yeah."

"Jimmy, why would you cash it? I told you not to do that!"

He shrugged, looking miserable. I sighed. "Jimmy."

He glanced up.

"It is going to bounce. And when it does, they will take it out of your paycheck." I watched him process this, a clever look stealing into his eyes. I held up a hand. "Do not try to tell me that it's somehow okay because a thousand bucks is more than your paycheck. You weren't really going to say that, were you?"

He drew himself up. "No, course not."

I explained to him that until the hotel got their money, he wouldn't be receiving any paychecks at all, so he'd better not spend the cash that was probably burning a hole in his pocket at that very second. He sorrowfully agreed. "And if you get any more checks, you give them to me, okay? You cash another one, I'm going to wring your neck."

"Sure, yeah. Sorry, Ruddy. Hey, Ruddy . . ." Jimmy

looked left and right, then lowered his voice. "Is it true what they say?"

"What do they say, Jimmy?"

"That you got Repo Madness and everything?"

"Great."

At midnight we were treated to the Claude and Wilma Show, a loud production featuring such incredibly faked anger I found myself laughing a little. How could two people who battled each other every single night be unable to repeat the performance when it was theater? "That's it, I'm throwing you out of the house!" Wilma shouted at the climax of the play. Claude pressed a hand to his heart as if he'd just taken a bullet and staggered around the room.

"She's throwing me out of the house!" he yelled in the faces of several people he probably pictured would make good witnesses at the slander trial. As he came up to me he was grinning hugely. "Ruddy, what am I going to do? Where will I live?"

"Don't worry about it, Claude. She'll get over it. She always does," I encouraged.

His face fell. "Uh, no, no, Ruddy! That's not the . . . She really means it this time!"

To punctuate his declaration, Wilma slammed the door of the Black Bear behind her as she stormed out into the night.

"I'm a broken man," Claude declared, sitting down in a chair. He shook his head. "A broken, broken man." He looked up brightly. "Well. Can I buy you a beer?"

"Didn't she throw you out of the house like last week?" Jimmy wanted to know.

"That was different," Claude corrected fiercely.

"I have to make a phone call," I announced, shocking

myself. I went to the back room and shut the door and regarded the telephone as if it were a poisonous snake. Katie's phone number was starting to get a little smudged from riding around in my pocket. I took a deep, steadying breath, my fear stronger than anything Repo Madness had ever served up. It used to be easy for me to call up girls—hell, there was a time when they called *me*. Now, though, I was a completely different person, not sure I even deserved to have a conversation with a pretty woman.

"Is this Katie?" I blurted when she answered on the third ring.

"May I ask who this is, please?" she responded, not unfriendly but not gushing with warmth, either.

"This is Ruddy McCann. Like the complexion? I gave you a jump." I winced. "I mean, in the rain the other day, you were in East Jordan—"

"I remember, Ruddy," she interrupted, laughing a little. "That sort of thing doesn't actually happen all that often."

"Okay, good! Well . . ." My brain was having what mechanics term *vapor lock*. I simply could not get anything out of my head except for the various ways "I gave you a jump" could be interpreted as something sexual.

"Ruddy? This isn't a good time for me to talk," Katie said, smoothly but a bit hurriedly.

Relief flooded through me as if I'd just been pardoned by the governor. "Okay then," I told her. "Bye."

"Bye-bye."

As she disconnected I heard a male voice in the background. The boyfriend, I presumed, probably wondering who the hell was on the phone.

About half an hour later the Black Bear emptied as if

it had been punctured. Becky was still pinned down by Kermit: I grinned at her as I walked out into the night. "She's going to be pretty pissed off at me next time I see her," I chuckled. There was no answer. I cocked my head. "Alan?"

And then it struck me: I couldn't feel him there anymore. I hadn't realized it, but from the moment he'd given me boxing lessons, Alan had had a presence inside me, an almost physical sensation of another human being. But now there was nothing. "Alan?" I asked again. I listened carefully, probing my consciousness, but there was no response.

Alan was gone.

7

There Never Was an Alan Lottner

Alan had been like a loose tooth—irritating and constantly demanding attention—but when it is finally gone the hole it leaves behind is, in some ways, worse. I sat in my living room, watching the firelight reflect off my empty beer bottles in a festive fashion, and wondered what the psychiatrists would say if I told them how much I missed my psychosis.

Sensing something, Jake wandered over and nosed my hand, staring up at me with soulful eyes. "You're right, Jakey. I'm not alone at all." I scratched his ears and he groaned, his eyes half-lidded, until he collapsed at my feet.

I reached for my book, my schizophrenia behind me. My mother had been a nonstop reader and when I inherited the house I found boxes and boxes of novels stacked in the basement. I sorted out a couple that I vaguely remembered her carrying around and set them out as if she had just been there reading and had put down her book to start dinner. Maybe that was the start of my Repo Madness, because I knew it was irrational, but the sight of those books gave me comfort.

Eventually I became curious and idly picked one up and started to leaf through it. It was *The Charm School* by Nelson DeMille, and I honestly thought it would be about women learning manners from some uptight lady with her hair pulled back in a bun. But it was a thriller—my mother was addicted to suspense novels and mysteries, and before long I was hooked on them myself.

When I could afford to I added to the collection—Carl Hiaasen, Andrew Gross, Dave Barry, Lee Child—and when money was tight I went to Mom's boxes and revisited old classics. Right now I was on an Alistair MacLean jag: I'd picked up *Ice Station Zebra* because it sounded like it was a novel about Kalkaska, and now I was rereading *The Guns of Navarone*. I had my book, my dog, and my chair. What else did a man need?

I forgot to grab the Patrón bottle, and once I was sitting down it was too much of an effort to heave myself back up to get it. I turned the pages until my eyes sagged shut of their own accord.

About an hour later I jerked awake to the sound of a great crash, the noise so startling that even Jake got to his feet. I went to my door and yanked it open.

Claude and Janelle were on the porch, laughing at each other while Claude tried to extract his hand from her blouse.

"Oh, Claude," I said in dismay.

"Ruddy! Ruddy, I'm getting a divorce, you know," he blurted when he saw my expression.

"Claude," I repeated sadly.

Janelle gave him a long and disgustingly wet kiss on the mouth, which Claude accepted hungrily. "Welcome to the single scene in Kalkaska, darling," I think she said. Her eyes were deliberately evading mine, and the way she clung to Claude, less from lust than for structural support, told me a lot more bourbon was flowing through her veins than was typical. Janelle had always straddled the line between being a drinker and a drunk—apparently tonight she felt she required some extra juice to help her go through with her decisions.

Jake decided he'd had enough of this nonsense and brushed against my legs as he turned and went back to his blanket on the floor.

"I need . . . I need the key for upstairs, Ruddy," Claude gasped as he pulled away from Janelle's lips. He gestured up the outside stairs to the door of the second-floor "apartment."

I opened my door. "Come on in, Claude."

They both stopped groping and stared at me, blinking in noncomprehension.

"You can sleep on my couch." I reached for my jacket. "I'll drive Janelle home."

"But . . ." Claude crashed in through the doorway, blasting me with vodka breath as his whisper found my ear. I winced as he leaned against the bruises in my ribs. "But Ruddy, remember the slander plan. . . ."

"Claude." I grabbed him by the shoulders and peered into his bloodshot eyes. "Are you out of your mind? Wilma would have your balls for breakfast. Get in here." I yanked and the force of my pull propelled him across the room, where he twisted and fell onto the couch as if it were a special gymnastic trick we'd been practicing together.

"Come on, Janelle," I told her, gripping her elbow so she wouldn't slip on the ice. She accompanied me without protest, but in my truck she huddled against her door like an animal caught in a cage. I fished for something to say to her but didn't catch anything. I looked at her light blond hair and for some reason it made me sad that it was so stylishly cut; she'd probably spent an hour on it before going to the Black Bear and hooking up with Claude Wolfinger.

I pulled into her driveway and stopped. She didn't get out; she just sat there, and I sighed, thinking I should apologize somehow, but not knowing what she needed to hear from me.

When she turned and met my eyes it was as if we were having a conversation about loneliness, and had gotten to the point in the discussion where we were asking ourselves why we didn't just go ahead and cure two cases of it with one shot.

The "single scene in Kalkaska." Who was she kidding? We were it.

I stared back at her. Since coming back home I'd been sleeping exclusively with myself—would it be so wrong to reach out for a little human warmth, maybe give some in return?

I might have turned off the truck and followed Janelle into her house if it weren't for the piece of paper with the name "Katie" written on it. Janelle and I could collapse gratefully, or at least desperately, into each other's arms, but what if Katie turned out to be real? Or, if not Katie, someone like her, and then I would be just one of a series of men dropping Janelle for another woman. The thought of participating in that process made me recoil.

Janelle read the answer in my eyes and her lips formed a bitter smile. She pushed open the door and walked away from me with her head at a stiff angle. I waited until she had turned on the lights in her house before backing into the street, and my last view of her was of her shadow watching me from her front window.

It was just past two in the morning. I was wide awake and in the kind of bad mood that could only be fixed by stealing someone else's car.

At Milt's lot I swapped my vehicle for the tow truck, then drove down and let myself into the Black Bear without turning on the lights. The only illumination came from Becky's TV show, where some guy who probably doubled as an underwear model was ripping insulation out of an attic. Bob the Bear stood sentry in the corner, silently watching my approach as I stood on a chair and unscrewed the bolts on the back of his neck.

Something about Bob I don't think Becky even knew: his head came off.

I unbolted the bear head and stuffed it and a big rain poncho in the front seat of the tow truck. From the storeroom in the back, I felt rather than saw the couple of rifles in my dad's old gun closet, pulling out the pellet gun I'd received for Christmas when I was fifteen. I stood in the ambient light drifting in through the front windows and turned it over in my hands, examining it.

"What is that?" Alan demanded loudly.

"Agrhh!" I shouted, staggering back. "Geez, you scared the hell out of me, Alan! Don't do that!"

"Why are you so jumpy?"

"Where have you been? I thought you were dead. I mean, not dead the way you say you are, but dead as in not in my head anymore."

"Oh. I was asleep."

"You sleep?" I responded incredulously.

"Sure. Mostly it's just been little naps, but today I think I was out for a couple of hours. I needed it, too."

"Wait a minute, what else are you doing in there?" I demanded.

"I'm not going to the bathroom, if that's what you're implying," he huffed.

"I have no idea what I'm implying. I can't believe you sleep, that makes no sense to me." I closed up the bar and returned to my truck. "As opposed to the part of this that does make sense," I added after a moment. I looked down at the rifle in my hands and actually heard him draw in a breath, proving my point—none of this made sense. He couldn't draw in a breath, he had no lungs.

"What are you planning to do with that gun?"

"I'm going on a little wild-goose chase," I explained, starting the truck and heading north to East Jordan.

"You're going to shoot Doris? You can't do that!" he protested indignantly.

"What do you want me to do, euphemize her?"

"Huh?"

"The goose bit me and nearly broke my arm."

"I know, I felt it."

"Well okay, then. Alan, I need that repo. I've already been advanced the money on it. Milt will carry me a bit but soon he's going to want interest payments at the least—and meanwhile, I have my own expenses. You need to go along with me on this; I know what I'm doing."

I parked the tow truck a hundred yards down from Einstein's place and wandered into the trees, circling so that when I approached his home it was from the rear, where I had a perfect view of his truck—and the open doorway of the shed, where I could barely make out the white form of Doris, sleeping peacefully. I looked at her over the gun sight.

"Ruddy! Please," Alan begged.

I swung the gun barrel over and sighted down on the three floodlights, squeezing the trigger and taking each bulb out with a satisfying plink. Doris stuck her neck out curiously, but didn't leave the shed.

"Why did you do that? Make me think you were going to kill the goose," Alan demanded as I made my way back to the tow truck.

"Just having fun."

"Well, I think you're a horrible person."

"You're welcome to leave anytime, Alan." I lifted the snarling bear head and set it on me like an ill-fitting hat, holding it up there with one hand and draping the poncho over the whole assembly with the slit in front so I'd be able to see. I grabbed a gallon jug of water and headed back to Einstein's house.

I'm not sure what Doris thought she saw coming up the driveway, but it was huge and had the face of a bear in a bad mood and that was enough to keep her quiet. I slipped over to the pickup under cover of uninterrupted darkness, making motion without detection, and poured the contents of the water jug directly into the gas tank. Doris eyed me uneasily the entire time from within the safety of her shed, and didn't respond when I waved at her as I departed.

I didn't know what time my customer left for work in the morning and didn't want to take a chance of missing him, so I settled in the driver's seat of the cab and tried to make myself comfortable. From where I sat I could easily see Einstein when he left for his job at PlasMerc, where he probably worked on the line, assembling sub-atomic particles.

"Hey Alan, you awake?"

"Yes. Where did you get the bear head? That was a pretty good idea."

I told him about my father, how I grew up playing at the feet of Bob the Bear, and how he showed me something no one else in the world knew, that a couple of bolts in the back were all that held Bob's head on.

"How about you, Alan, you grow up around here?" I asked carefully.

"Why do you ask it like it's a trick question?" he responded.

I blew out some air in exasperation. "Just answer me, okay?"

Alan told me he'd moved to East Jordan because that was where his wife Marget lived. He met her on an airplane, sat next to her on a flight to Denver, where he was living at the time, asked her to dinner that night and every night for the next six, and when she left Denver to return home to Michigan he made up his mind to follow. Her father owned a real estate company in East Jordan, and that's where he found himself working. In Denver he'd managed a movie theater complex in the Cherry Creek area but the work wasn't portable—not too many theater complexes in a town of twenty-five hundred people. Working out of East Jordan, though, Alan was able to do pretty well for himself selling lakefront property and hunting cabins.

As he spoke I ticked off the things he was telling me. I'd never even been to Colorado and had never heard of Cherry Creek, but I could look it up and see if such a place existed. He seemed pretty knowledgeable about both movie theaters and real estate sales, competently fielding my questions as I put them to him. If he wasn't real, how could he know all of this stuff? If I were schizophrenic, wouldn't my split personality be confined to my own knowledge base?

I started the tow truck to pump a little heat into the cab. "So, Alan . . . I'm sorry about when you told me you were dead. I've just . . . I mean, what do you say when someone tells you that? It's not exactly something that ever gets covered all the time in Dear Abby."

"I felt completely ignored."

"Well, okay, but I said I was sorry."

"You think this is easy for me?"

"What is your problem?" I snapped. "I said I was sorry. What more do you want, a box of candy?"

He was silent for a bit. *"I want you to find the people who did this to me and bring them to justice,"* he finally said.

"Oh ho, now we're down to it! You want me to kill somebody, don't you?"

"No, of course not!" he sputtered.

"No? No? Are you sure? Because a second ago it sure sounded like you wanted me to find some people—not just one person, now, but a whole group of people—and do to them what they supposedly did to you."

"Not a whole group, just two people, two men."

"And then I suppose they'll be in my head, too," I raged. "And they'll want me to kill somebody else, and pretty soon the TV networks will be in my neighborhood, interviewing my friends who'll be saying, 'Gee, he seemed like such a nice guy, who knew that he had all those bodies buried in his basement?'"

"You don't believe me," Alan replied, hurt.

"Which is weird, because this is all so plausible."

"Look, couldn't we just . . . we're in East Jordan. Won't you just let me prove it to you? We can go to my house, talk to my wife, see my little girl. Then you'll know."

"Your little girl? How old?"

"She's sixteen. Her name is Kathy, Kathy Lottner. My wife's name is Marget Lottner."

I mulled it over. "I can't believe I'm going to do this," I finally muttered.

"Great!"

"But not right now." I shut the truck off, and it rattled into silence. "Right now, I'm on what we professional repo men call a stakeout."

"That's what cops call it."

"Right, they stole it from us."

It was cold when I lurched awake at dawn. Shivering, I started the tow truck and let the wipers and defroster work on the layer of ice on the windshield. Alan was quiet and I could feel that he was asleep, now that I understood what it meant when I experienced the peculiar sensation of him not being there.

About half an hour later, just as I was talking myself into abandoning my post for the time it took to get a cup of coffee, Einstein Croft wheeled down his driveway and gunned his truck, his back end sliding as he headed off for work. I gave him a half mile and then unhurriedly crawled off after him; I knew where he was going—PlasMerc, home of the surly gate guard.

I was close enough behind him on the highway to see him speed up and slow down twice, his tailpipe blowing clouds of black smoke as he tried to clear his engine by stomping on his accelerator. Satisfied that his erratic progress was a sign that the water in his fuel line was doing its job, I pulled a U-turn and sped off in the opposite direction.

Half an hour later I cruised back down the road and there was his pickup, all by itself, emergency flashers blinking away. Einstein must have thumbed a ride to work. I eased up to his truck and hooked it with the hoist, drawing nothing but a curious glance from the few vehicles that drove by. Car breaks down, car gets towed, God bless America.

You might think you're a genius, Einstein, but you cannot outsmart the repo man.

I called Milton from the junkyard we used as a storage lot in East Jordan, and he grunted in satisfaction. "The cosigner's a real nice guy, too. Makes you wonder, since his kid is such a jerk."

"His kid's a walking jerk," I corrected, somewhat gleefully. Repo humor never gets old for me.

I hung up, feeling like the greasy phone had probably left a black mark on my cheek. Everything in the junkyard was coated with motor oil, even the people.

"This place is disgusting," Alan muttered. One of the mechanics was standing at the other end of the counter, so I didn't reply. I fished out the card I'd gotten from the woman at the bank in Traverse City, and dialed her number to see how things were progressing in the mystery of Jimmy's checks, leaving a thumbprint on the paper in the process.

"Yes, Mr. McCann, I remember," Maureen the banker told me when I introduced myself.

"I'm wondering if you were able to—"

"I'm sorry, but I won't be able to help you in this matter," she interrupted.

I blinked. This did not sound like the motherly person

I remembered. "But I thought you said . . ." I started slowly.

"I have no information for you."

"Maureen, are you saying you can't help me, or won't help me?" I persisted. "I'm confused."

There was a noise, as if her kind nature was being strangled, but she replied firmly. "I can't help you, Mr. McCann. Please don't call here anymore."

I listened to the *click* in disbelief. What could have happened to make her so uncooperative?

The good feeling from reintroducing Einstein to the concept of nonvehicular travel had evaporated. I felt tired and old as I fired up the tow truck.

"There's something strange going on," Alan observed.

"Right . . . this coming from a man who claims to be a ghost stuck in my brain."

"No, I mean, the change in her demeanor was striking."

"Yeah, all of a sudden she's mean."

"No, not mean. More like scared," Alan observed after a moment.

I cocked my head, considering. "You're right. She was frightened."

Since I had nothing else to do and we were already in East Jordan, I agreed to drive Alan around to check out his past. He directed me with barely restrained excitement up North Street, past homes that would probably cost a million dollars if they weren't located in what the locals awkwardly called "northern lower Michigan." Here, a nice four-bedroom house could be had for what would be a down payment anywhere else. Made you wonder why the people living in Phoenix didn't move here en masse. I flipped on my heater to dry up the puddle of melted snow at my feet.

East Jordan sits at the south end of Lake Charlevoix, which is a beautiful, deep blue body of water that joins Lake Michigan via a river. Tourists mostly ignore East Jordan—to its benefit, I believe. In the winter a few small factories plus a big one, the East Jordan Iron Works, keep the economic blood flowing, and a small flock of summer people come in for July and August to hang out in little cottages mostly built in the twenties. It's a poor cousin to Charlevoix, the town on the north end of the lake, where all the yachts bob up and down in the summer. I like the people in East Jordan the way I like the citizens of Kalkaska and the way I probably would dislike the yacht people in Charlevoix if they ever invited me aboard their boats.

Alan urged me to slow down as we approached his house, as if to savor the anticipation, and then went quiet. I eased over to the curb and looked at a vacant lot at the address he'd given me, the snow smoothly untracked and an old Plymouth up on blocks, both engine and hood missing. "Where's the house, Alan?" I asked softly. I moved my eyes slowly, carefully, like a searchlight probing for escaping convicts. I wanted him to take it all in. "Is that your car, maybe?"

"This is impossible. It has to be here!"

"Let's go check out the office," I suggested.

According to Alan, his real estate office was right on Second Street, a block from Main. We pulled up in front of what was obviously an ice-cream shop and nothing else.

"This wasn't here! It was an old two-story building with a bay window on top. Next to it was a shoe store; they're both gone."

"These stores have been here as long as I can remember,

Alan," I said gently. I couldn't really recall what had been here when I was in high school, but since I started working for Milt a couple of years ago, the shops had been open for business.

"It's like . . . it's like someone is following around after me, erasing my past," he whispered.

I didn't advise him that it sounded like my split personality was developing paranoia. Instead I sat there, letting his mind work on it. (Or was it *my* mind?) He recovered pretty quickly. *"Okay let's . . . let's go to the school, see if Kathy is there. I know she'll be there! And Marget wouldn't leave town, her parents are dead but all of her friends are here. I know! Let's go talk to the guy who runs the iron works, Mr. Malpass. I sold him a house on Highway 66, I'll show it to you."*

"Alan." I sighed. "Listen to me."

"I know what you're going to say, but dammit, Ruddy I can prove to you I exist!"

"Don't you think it's likely that the reason your house wasn't there, and your office wasn't there, is because I made them up, and I made you up, too?"

"For God's sake, Ruddy!" Alan replied, anguished.

I pulled the tow truck away from the curb. "I have to face the fact that I've been talking to myself, which isn't exactly a sign of good mental health."

"No, you're not! I'm a real person!"

"You need to face the fact, too," I told him, as if that made any sense.

I spent the afternoon picking up a voluntary repo way north in a tiny spit of a place called Cross Village. The man who owned the Ford Explorer had left his keys in it when he took his family and moved back to Detroit and, as a further assistance to the repo man, had taken an ax and whacked the living crap out of the thing. I knew it was an ax because the head of it was buried in the windshield, the handle snapped off and pointing skyward like the business end of a sundial.

The whole time I was occupied with hauling in the Ford, my voice was blabbering away, reciting from the *Book of Alan*. I learned his Social Security number and that his father's nickname was "Boots." He told me his first real girlfriend wouldn't kiss him unless he gave her chocolate. He recited the names of at least fifty people he claimed could verify that he'd once lived.

I snorted in derision. "I can see me calling them up. 'Hello, have you heard of Alan Lottner? Did you kiss him for chocolate? Because I've got him in my head.'"

It was dark and cold by the time I got back to Kalkaska, and my body ached from camping out in the tow truck, which I exchanged for my pickup at Milt's lot. Tonight, I decided, the Black Bear could do without a bouncer. I eyed the bear head on the seat next to me, wondering what people thought of Bob the Headless Bear.

Jake's groan of a greeting as I limped in the door matched my sentiment exactly: time for bed. But everything changed when I saw the note posted to my refrigerator. Becky's handwriting. *Ruddy, need you to get down to the Black Bear now. Hurry!*

8

The Soul of Lisa Marie

My heart lurching around in my chest, I sprinted down the street, my legs acting like they had never been asked to run before. A couple of blocks and I was drained of oxygen—how had I gotten so out of shape?

The bar was completely dark, which was all wrong. I fumbled with the keys, finally managing to fling the door open. When my hand found the light switch the room roared with noise. "Surprise!"

I staggered back. More than a dozen people stood there in party hats, grinning at me wildly. "Happy birthday, Ruddy!" Becky called.

"Holy smokes," I panted. I stumbled in and accepted a beer. "What are you doing? My birthday's not for a week."

"Yes, that's the nature of a surprise; it is unexpected," Becky explained calmly, putting a cone-shaped hat on my head and kissing my cheek. "Happy three-oh, old man."

My friends crowded around, including my boss and

his wife. I felt strangely awkward at the center of atten-tion, hoping they weren't expecting a speech. "Hey there, Milt. Hi, Ruby."

"Trisha!" Alan hissed.

"I mean Trisha!"

"Happy birthday to you," Kermit enthused.

"Kermit," I greeted a bit darkly. ·

"Be nice," Alan warned.

My cake was decorated with a tow truck hauling away what looked like a Ferrari, something that had never happened in real life. I blew out the candles and the smoke misted my gaze a little. There'd been a time when all of my cakes were decorated with footballs and goal-posts.

"Hey, you okay, Ruddy?" Alan asked. I felt myself re-senting his concern, a little.

I sat down at the table with a groan. "You do sound old," Becky teased.

"I am old," I told her with feeling. "My body's aching from spending the night in Milt's truck. My back mus-cles are all tense."

"You need a misogynist," Kermit advised me.

I looked at him. "A misogynist," I repeated woodenly.

"He's right, a massage would do you good, Ruddy," Claude told me, while Alan snickered in my ear.

"That's not what a misogynist does," I responded a bit too crisply. Everyone frowned.

"Well, what do you think they do?" Milt asked.

"A misogynist is someone who hates women," I ex-plained.

They glanced at each other. Claude cleared his throat. "Uh, but Ruddy, how could you make a living doing that?"

"Forget it."

There was a small pile of gifts. Becky gave me a sweater. Claude presented me with a beer cooler. Milt gave me what looked like an alarm clock without the clock part. "It makes noise to help you sleep," he explained.

I looked at him blankly.

"See, it has a river flowing, and wind and rain, and birds. I figured for at night when the voices start talking."

"Thanks, Milt," I responded, trying to sound sincere.

Jimmy Growe gave me a book. "*Son of Sam,*" I pronounced, reading the title.

"Yeah, I told the lady at the bookstore that you liked to read and that, like, I wanted a true story about a guy with madness, hears voices."

"Jimmy, this is about David Berkowitz." Becky was suffocating a giggle.

"Who?" Jimmy was leaning toward me, staring into my eyes as if trying to spot a piece of soot lodged there.

"Jimmy, please tell me you are not trying to see the person inside my head," I said pleasantly.

Kermit coughed. "Hey, Jimmy, maybe I could go in with you on that. I mean, I didn't know about the party in time to appropriate a gift."

Becky beamed at Kermit over his munificence. Oh, this was not good—what was going on between the two of them?

"*You haven't even thanked Jimmy,*" Alan chided. I put a crooked smile on my face and told Jimmy the book was a perfect gift. Becky left me to tend bar, Kermit following her like a duck that's been imprinted on its mother.

Claude nodded after them. "Who's the guy?"

"Absolutely nobody," I growled. For some reason I

twisted to look at Bob the Bear, reacting in shock to his decapitation. How could no one else have noticed?

"Listen, I . . . I won't be needing your room, after all," Claude told me, bursting to tell a secret.

"Oh? You and Wilma afflicted with a sudden rush of sanity?"

"No." His mouth curled into a sly grin. "I've got somewhere else to stay tonight."

I raised my head and saw Janelle watching us from across the room, her expression dark. "No," I said flatly.

Claude blinked. "Huh?"

"Claude, Janelle is . . . confused. She's had a rough time of it lately."

He snorted. "Haven't we all."

"Claude, Wilma will kill you."

That one made him think.

"What are you guys talking about?" Jimmy wanted to know.

A burst of laughter, strange yet familiar, caught my attention. I spun in amazement and caught sight of my sister standing at the end of the bar with her hand to her mouth. Becky laughing?

After a few minutes Wilma came in, stomping mud off her boots and sitting down at our table with a sigh. "Happy birthday, Ruddy. Hi, Jimmy. Honey, would you get me a vodka and soda? My feet are killing me."

"Wilma!" Claude hissed. "What the hell are you doing? You'll blow the whole deal!"

"Oh Claude, these are our friends," Wilma declared dismissively. She brushed back her thick black hair and her gigantic earrings flashed like disco balls.

I got up to fetch her a drink. When I came back, the

topic had shifted. "Ruddy, you have voices in your head?" Wilma asked, her eyes welling up with concern.

"It will all be in tomorrow's paper," I agreed heavily.

"What do the voices say?" Jimmy wanted to know.

"It's not voices; it is just a single voice."

"What does it say?" Jimmy asked insistently.

"It wants me to go to East Jordan and find a Realtor."

"Oh Jesus, no," Wilma breathed, making the sign of the cross.

"I don't get it," Jimmy confessed.

"Wilma, we can't be seen together. I'm gonna go sit over . . . over there. I'll sit with Janelle," Claude declared. Wilma's dark eyes flashed dangerously, but Claude was already standing up and turning away.

"A Realtor?" Jimmy repeated dubiously.

"Wilma, do not throw any furniture," I warned her. Her eyes turned and settled on me.

"He wouldn't, would he, Ruddy?" she asked plaintively. "I mean, we're not really separated, it's just for the slander clause." I couldn't meet her gaze.

"Hey, can I talk to the voice?" Jimmy wanted to know.

"That son of a bitch." Wilma stood up with a crash, silencing the bar. Over across the room Claude was sitting at the table with Janelle, attempting to look perfectly innocent while her hand stroked the inside of his thigh in plain view of everyone in the room. "Son of a bitch!" Wilma cried.

She stomped from the bar, slamming the door behind her with such force that the headless bear rocked a little in his stand.

Janelle didn't even blink; she was regarding me with an arched expression. Was that what this was about? Me?

"There's something not right about Claude and Janelle," Alan, a voice in my head—a goddamn *voice in my head*— murmured.

"Ruddy?" Jimmy persisted. "Can I talk to the guy in your head?"

I felt the world start to sink on me then, a heavy blanket of unhappiness. At the end of the bar Becky was paying Kermit rapt attention. Was she really so desperate? Claude and Janelle were building heat like two sticks rubbing together, and Jimmy wanted to have a personal consultation with Alan Lottner, The Man Who Was Never There.

I stood up and stalked over to the jukebox. I felt Becky's eyes on me and knew how well she was reading my mood as I hunched over the dusty glass and tried to find something recorded before everything had gone sour in my life. I fed in some coins and punched some buttons, then turned and surveyed the sparse crowd. "Jimmy!".

He was at my side like an obedient dog. There might not be a lot of light behind his movie star–quality eyes, but he was a good friend, loyal as they come. He helped me shove some empty tables away from the jukebox, then grunted with me as we wrestled Bob the Bear deeper into his corner of the room.

"Hey, his head is gone. How long has he been like that?" Jimmy asked.

"It doesn't matter. I want you to go ask Janelle to dance," I commanded him.

He blinked. "Janelle?"

"Go get her. Becky! Come here and dance."

"Oh no," she said, flipping her rag like a horse's tail. "No way, Ruddy."

But she didn't run as I came after her, and once I had

snagged her wrist she gave no pretense of struggling. Claude's mouth sagged open a little as Jimmy easily lifted Janelle out of their conversation about foreplay or whatever, bringing her out onto the small dance area exactly as I'd instructed.

At the next song Kermit came out and took Becky away from me, so I stood under Bob the Decapitated Bear and watched approvingly as Jimmy did another turn with Janelle. Wilma walked in at that moment—I knew she'd come back, we'd played out similar scenes before—and it saved Claude's miserable little life that he was sulking by himself at Janelle's table. The tension left her when I grabbed Janelle and Jimmy, caught up in it, dragged Wilma out for a turn.

I bought a round of drinks for everyone who was dancing, which motivated the entire room to get out there for the next song. The noise brought in people from the street and somehow we achieved critical mass then, the point where the place becomes one big, uncontainable party. I had to go behind the bar to help Becky, and she no longer had any time for Kermit.

It was the first time in a long time that I had to force people out the door at closing. I left Becky counting money and headed home, my boots crunching the ice. "Hey, Alan," I said tentatively.

"Yeah?"

"You were awfully quiet tonight."

"I know. Asleep for most of it."

I stopped. "Really? With all that racket?"

"It's strange, but when I go to sleep I can't hear or feel anything. It's the deepest kind of sleep you can imagine, like I've gone somewhere else."

"Heaven?" I suggested.

"I don't know."

Or maybe, I reflected, he didn't sleep at all. Maybe when he went away it was whatever had spun loose in my mind gaining a little traction and realizing there was no Alan Lottner.

Jake gave me a wounded expression when I whistled for him to come out for a quick walk—he thought we'd agreed I had no right to interrupt his sleep. "Jake, you're supposed to like walks. It's what dogs live for," I advised him. His look indicated I had no idea what I was talking about. He did his business with quick dispatch and then pointedly turned and headed right back home. By the time I got to the front door he was sitting there watching me with an impatient expression.

"All you did is nap all day, right? And now you want to sleep all night," I accused. I said it gently, though, and stroked his velvety ears once we were indoors and comfortable. "Okay, sleepy dog," I said. "You store your energy."

Becky, God love her, must have snuck over and given me an extra little birthday present by picking up my house, because when I awoke the next morning all the beer bottles were out in the trash and the dishes had been done. "Place looks great," I grunted, stretching out my muscles.

"Much better," Alan agreed from within.

I left alone the implication that Alan would prefer I wasn't such a slob. "Man, I'm getting old. Just a couple of hours dancing last night and I ache all over." I showered and went to the closet, pulling on a pair of jeans. I loaded a rake into my Ford pickup, cajoled Jake into getting into the front seat with me, and then stopped at the florist. The spring bouquet was already on the counter.

"Thanks, Ruddy. See you first Sunday in June," the woman told me.

"Who are the flowers for?" Alan wanted to know. I didn't reply because I wasn't sure how to answer.

The sun was hiding behind some dark-gray clouds, but it didn't look like rain. I headed north, fiddling with the radio. Jake sat in the passenger seat, blandly watching the scenery, clearly feeling the view was better from his blanket in the living room.

"When was the last time you gave your dog a bath?" Alan sniffed at me.

"You smell wonderful, Jake. Don't listen to him."

Jake seemed unoffended.

"Where are we going?"

"Suttons Bay."

"Where?"

"It's a little community out on Leelanau Peninsula. Kinda empty this time of year. Real pretty, though."

"I know what it is. I mean, why? Are we after another car?"

"No."

"What's with the flowers? Got a woman up there?"

"Why don't you go back to sleep," I suggested. Jake thought I was talking to him and circled three times in his seat and closed his eyes.

I steered along the bay. The ice had moved out but the water looked black with cold, and the lone boat I saw chugging along with lines hanging off the stern was manned by two guys looking huddled and unhappy. In the summer, Suttons Bay is a bright, active place with people from boats milling around buying artwork. This time of year, the second day of May, with six inches of slush melting everywhere, the place looked gray and deserted.

The dirt road was muddy. I stopped and opened an iron gate. *"We're in a graveyard,"* Alan pronounced.

The place was deserted. I winced as Jake lifted his leg on a gravestone.

Underneath the melting snow the ground looked dead. The yellow stems from last summer's grass stood up as I scrubbed at the gravesite with my rake, but I saw no green yet. The flowers I placed in front of the headstone made a bright splash of color.

"Who is Lisa Marie Walker?" Alan asked, reading the grave marker. *"Would you hold your eyes still for a second?"*

I did, but I was gazing at a stand of trees, remembering the first time I had been here. I heard Alan grunt in frustration; he wanted to read the headstone.

"So who is she? An old girlfriend or something?"

"Be quiet for a minute, Alan," I murmured. I took a deep breath, lowered my head, and prayed for the soul of Lisa Marie Walker.

"You!"

I turned, startled. A young woman in a wool coat stood just inside the iron gate, her face twisted in anger. "You!" she barked again, advancing on me with her finger pointed like a pistol. "I know who you are."

My shoulders slumped. "Uh . . . ," I started to say.

"Lisa was my cousin. How dare you come here?"

I spread my hands. "I heard that the rest of her family moved to California. So I thought, with no one here to take care . . ."

She was in front of me now, a woman in her thirties. Her face was white pale except for two burning spots on her cheeks. "We don't want you to do anything! We don't want you here. Haven't you done enough? Do you

know what it would do to her parents if they knew it
was *you* who's been leaving the flowers? This is a small
town—didn't you think someone would notice that the
first Sunday of the month somebody was always out
here tending the grave?"

"I guess I didn't, no," I admitted quietly. Jake's eyes
were on me, sadly taking in my discomfort.

"When I heard about it, I knew it had to be you. I
drove up Friday from Flint." Some of the anger seemed
to be fading from her, now that she was face-to-face with
me. "What in God's name could you be thinking?"

My throat was tight and I found myself unable to answer. I looked away from her glare, shrugging lamely. "I
just thought someone should . . ." I trailed off.

"Maybe someone should. But not you. *Never* you."

"Okay."

"Don't come back here again, understand? Please,
you've caused us enough pain."

"Yes, I understand. I won't come back."

I let her stare at me, let her examine my face. "You're
not what I expected," she finally said.

"Shall I . . . shall I leave the flowers I brought today?"
I asked faintly.

"No. Yes, yes, what does it matter—okay." She started
to turn away, then faced me again. "Look, I know you're
trying to be . . . decent. But you can't be. Not you, do
you understand me?"

After she drove away I pressed a hand to my face and
sighed. Alan, mercifully, was silent, and he remained that
way even as I began walking numbly among the tomb-
stones, reading the names of people long dead. The cemetery had been here since the 1880s, and some of the
graves were worn down by the wind and the rain, fad-

ing away like the memories of the people for whom they stood in silent monument.

Lisa Marie Walker. Cheerleader, a pretty blonde with a white smile. Her high school announced her name at commencement even though she died the day after Thanksgiving of her senior year.

"Looks like a fresh grave, over there," Alan noted, searching for a safe subject. I wandered over to where muddy tracks and wilted flowers surrounded a gray headstone, Jake following at my heels. This woman, unlike Lisa Marie, had lived a long, full life until she died three weeks before.

"Oh, my God!" Alan cried.

"What?" I answered, startled. "Do you know her?"

"My God, my God!" Alan shrieked.

"Alan, what is it? What's going on?"

"Look at the date, the date."

I looked at the dates. *"What's the date today?"* Alan demanded.

"The date? May second."

"The year. What year is it?"

When I told him he literally howled, so loud I gritted my teeth. "Hey!" I shouted.

"Ruddy, my God, my God. I thought I just died, but I didn't. It's been eight years!"

I stood blinking in the cemetery, trying to make sense of what he was telling me.

"Eight years," Alan repeated quietly. *"Oh, my God."*

9

To Swipe or Not to Swipe

Alan and I spent the half-hour drive from Suttons Bay to Traverse City with me trying to bring Alan up to speed on all the events of the past eight years—not easy to do when you're from Kalkaska, where nothing ever really changes, pretty much cut off from the rest of the world, where everything does.

As I pulled up in front of Maureen's bank, he was saying, *"This explains why my house wasn't there, and my office. Don't you see, Ruddy? I'm not crazy!"*

"Oh, don't worry, Alan. Of all the possible explanations for what is going on, it never once occurred to me that *you* might be crazy," I assured him. I gazed at the bank. Jake sat up and looked around, then eased back down with a "You handle this one, I'm going to nap" expression.

I stroked Jake's back and he gave me an encouraging moan. I stayed silent until Alan calmed down, my eyes on the bank so he'd know I was in the mood for a change of subject.

"So what's your plan here, more veiled threats?" Alan finally inquired.

"Thanks for your support, Alan."

"Did you see how she reacted when you talked about Jimmy? Why don't you try appealing to her maternal nature again; that seemed to work better than anything."

"Excuse me, did I ask for your help, here? Do I poke my nose into your business? Do I tell you how to be a ghost?" I opened windows for Jake.

Alan was still muttering as I entered the bank and asked for Maureen. I was escorted back to her office. Her face darkened a little when she saw me standing in her doorway. She finished her telephone conversation and hung up, motioning me in. "Hello, Mr. McCann."

"Call me Ruddy," I beamed, oozing charm.

She was shaking her head, opening drawers to indicate how busy she was. "I told you on the phone I can't help you further. There's nothing more I can tell you."

"Poor Jimmy, this is going to ruin him," I said mournfully.

She wouldn't meet my eyes. "Well, I'm sorry," she stated in clipped tones. She half rose in her chair, as if to indicate the meeting was over. So much for her maternal instincts.

I was opening my mouth to say something about going to the newspapers, because that's what always seems to work for people on television shows, when Alan interrupted me. *"Ask her why she is afraid."*

I bit back my irritation. "Maureen."

She finally looked at me.

"Why are you afraid?"

Her gaze turned inward for a moment, and then she sat back down in her chair, heavily, as if the burden of it all was just too much. Very slowly, watching her hand as if it belonged to another person, Maureen opened a drawer and pulled out a card. "This is an invitation to a party next month. It is at Mr. Blanchard's house. He's the president of the bank." She handed it to me. I opened it and saw what Maureen had seen.

"It's the same handwriting," Alan observed excitedly.

The signature was much more legible but obviously from the same hand as what I'd seen deliberately smudged on the starter checks. *"Please be our guest,"* the invitation began. It was signed, *"Alice Blanchard."*

"She worked here over Christmas when one of the gals was having a baby. She signed up new accounts. She issued the starter checks."

"And took some for her own use, voiding them out."

"It appears so."

"And sent them to Jimmy Growe."

Maureen was silent.

"Why?" I asked aloud, but I could see she had no idea. Alan was quiet, probably pondering the same question.

"Sooner or later you would have found out," Maureen finally suggested. She leaned forward. "I mean, you would have gone to court and demanded we turn over our records anyway, right? I just saved us the trouble of going through that."

"Of course."

"Ruddy, you won't tell Mr. Blanchard how you found out, will you?"

"Never, Maureen. You have my word. Absolutely not," I told her, meaning it. "May I keep this card?"

She nodded wordlessly. I assured her again that I would never betray her confidence and left.

"This is really bizarre. The bank president's wife? What's going on?"

"I don't know, why don't we go ask her?" I suggested, sliding into my truck and starting the engine.

The Blanchards' house was exactly what I would have expected for a bank president in a small town: very nice, not too flashy, and well kept, with a large front porch that creaked when I walked across it to the thick oak door. I liked the place, but Jake seemed unimpressed, though he did consent to follow me to ring the bell, which chimed but summoned no one.

"Try it again," Alan suggested, so instead I lifted the brass door knocker, heavy as the clapper on the Liberty Bell, and let it fall several times, loud booms echoing throughout the empty house. When I turned to leave Jake gave me a "you woke me up for *this*?" expression. "Sorry, buddy," I told him.

"You've got the wife of the bank president stealing starter packets of checks and sending them payable to Jimmy for a thousand dollars each," Alan reflected as we got back into the truck.

"She didn't exactly steal them. She lined them out in the log." I pulled away from the curb.

"Right, okay, but the point I'm making is that she took them and now she's sending them to Jimmy."

"I get that, Alan."

"I'm just reviewing the facts of the case," he huffed, sounding offended.

I didn't bother to tell him that repo men don't have "cases." "Don't get your shorts in a wad, I'm just saying I know this. I just don't have any idea why someone would do something like that."

"In a 'wad'? What a vile expression."

"Okay, fine. Right."

We drove in silence for a bit, and then I felt him leave, like shutting off a lamp. "You asleep, Alan?" I asked softly. He didn't respond. I decided I was thankful he didn't snore.

I dropped Jake off at home and then, putting my health at risk in order to demonstrate my loyalty to sister Becky, I had lunch at the Black Bear. She put a tuna sandwich down in front of me and then cocked her head at me. "What?" she asked. "Why are you looking at me like that?"

"You just seem different. Are those new glasses or something?"

"No," she responded scornfully.

I stared at her until she blushed. "Like a haircut or something? Tattoo? Boob job?"

"Ruddy." She slapped her dish towel in the air as if to whip me with it.

"Well, anyway. Thanks for the maid service; you didn't have to do that. Place looks great."

She turned and surveyed the bar, her face puzzled.

"Not here, you goof. My living room," I teased.

"What do you mean?" she asked innocently.

I smiled at her. It's against Becky's nature to take credit for anything—she could win the Nobel Peace Prize and she'd decline to accept it because she'd insist there were other people more deserving.

"I've never seen your sister with makeup; she looks nice," Alan observed, coming awake.

"Makeup!" I shouted triumphantly.

Becky's expression turned cold for some reason.

"I mean, you look great, Becky. I like your makeup."

"I wear makeup all the time," she declared frostily. She spun on her heel.

"Wonderful. Thanks a lot, Alan," I muttered.

"What did I do?"

I didn't respond because I wasn't actually sure. "How come you keep falling asleep?" I inquired, switching subjects. "You're like a loose lightbulb, always flickering on and off."

"I don't know, it just happens. It's not like falling asleep in a bed, where you make a conscious decision to lie down. It just overtakes me whether I want it to or not."

"Maybe you're depressed," I speculated.

"I am not depressed."

"You sure? I know I'd be depressed if I didn't have a body or any proof that I'd ever existed except as the paranoid inner voice of a repo man."

Alan made an exasperated noise. I noticed Becky watching me from across the room and realized that though she couldn't hear me, she could see my lips moving, so I stood up and nodded at her before leaving the Black Bear. Outside it was *cold;* my breath a frosty cloud. I shoved my hands in my coat pockets. "Are we going to do spring this year? Like, ever?"

With no repo business on hand, I let Alan talk me into driving back to East Jordan to revisit the issue of his past, now that he was claiming he'd been dead eight years. I agreed with him that yes, houses and office buildings can be torn down in that amount of time, though it seemed pretty coincidental for it to have happened.

"So where have you been all this time, Alan? Eight years."

"I don't know."

"I mean, what happened? You died, you were murdered, and then what?"

"I don't know."

"How could you forget something like that?" I fretted.

"I didn't forget, I mean I don't know. It's like there's a big blank. I have no sense of the passage of time."

"But you must have gone *somewhere*," I argued. "Did you see God? Other ghosts? Other Realtors? I'm serious—if this is true, you hold the answer to the most important question in the history of our species!"

"If what is true?" he demanded suspiciously. *"You mean, me? You still have doubts?"*

"Come on, Alan, you want me to believe you've been asleep for eight years? Nobody's *that* depressed."

"I'm not saying that. I'm saying I don't know."

"If you really are Alan Lottner, if you really have come back from the dead, it proves once and for all what millions of people have believed—that there's life after real estate."

"I do not understand your persistent refusal to acknowledge my existence," Alan said coldly, speaking over my laughter.

I shook my head in dismay. How do you convince your split personality that he's not real?

"Well, there's something I didn't expect to see." I slowed down a little. Kermit Kramer was walking along the opposite side of the county highway, kicking at the piles of snow. His thumb was raised in a pathetic bid to hitch a ride, too lazy to turn around and face traffic the way you were supposed to. He lifted his eyes and stared at me as I drove past. I stared back. "Now what the heck is he doing fifteen miles north of Kalkaska, hitchhiking?"

I flipped the truck around and drove back. Kermit had

resumed his trudge, but turned at the sound of my approach. I stopped and he seemed to hesitate, as if afraid to get in the truck.

I rolled down the window. "I know you're not supposed to accept rides from strangers, but you'll be safe, I promise."

He slouched onto the seat, his hand resting on the door's handle after he pulled it closed. I steered back onto the highway and headed toward Kalkaska.

"We're still going to East Jordan though, right?" Alan demanded. I ignored him.

"So what are you doing out here, Kermit?" I asked curiously.

Kermit looked really unhappy with my question. "I had to hitch back from outside Mancelona. I couldn't get any cell phone signal."

Mancelona is a tiny town midway between Kalkaska and East Jordan. "You're kidding! You walked what, two miles in this cold? What were you doing in Mancelona?"

Kermit sighed. "My uncle Milt dropped me off up in East Jordan to drive a repo back to Kalkaska."

"Yeah? It break down or something?"

"No. The guy took it."

"What guy? What are you talking about?"

Kermit looked sightlessly out the window. "The customer. He was following me with some guys. When I stopped at the light, he came up and opened the door and pulled me out."

"He stole it? Wait a minute, the customer . . . it wasn't Einstein Croft, was it?" I shouted.

Kermit looked miserable. "He said not to bother calling the cops because it was legal for him to take his own truck back."

"Is that true?" Alan asked.

I slapped the dashboard in frustration. "Kermit, how could you let this happen?"

He didn't have a response to that one.

"He must have spotted the unit at the shop having the gas tank dried out, and then just followed you when you drove off," I seethed. "Didn't you bother to even look behind you to see if you were being followed?"

"Well, who would do that?" Alan snorted.

"It's basic repo man procedure!" I stormed. "It's in the manual." Or at least it would be if there *were* a manual.

"How do we know it was Einstein?" Alan wanted to know.

"He told me his name," Kermit said, as if he'd heard the question.

"Wait, what? Did you hear a voice ask you how you knew who it was?" I demanded, agitated.

"Huh?" Kermit looked worried. "A voice?"

"Never mind," I stormed. I glared over at Kermit, who appeared ready to fling himself from the truck to get away from me. "Okay, look, this happens sometimes." Actually, it had never happened, but I didn't think that would cheer him up. "We'll just take it again. We know where he works, where he lives. We'll do it. Okay? We'll put him back on his feet, Kermit. There's no better feeling than outsmarting a guy like this and repoing his vehicle."

"No better feeling," Alan repeated. *"Not winning a million dollars. Not making love to a woman."* I slapped the dashboard again, signaling him to shut up.

Kermit perked up a little, straightening in his seat and nodding, seeing himself driving off in Einstein's truck, probably giving the guy the finger on the way past.

Apparently he felt that we had bonded somehow, because a few minutes later he lightly punched me on the arm like we were old pals. "Listen, I was talking to Becky last night."

"Becky," I repeated. The friendly smile dropped from my face.

"Right." He swallowed, but it was too late to back out now. "Becky. I was talking to her last night about this deal I have. See, you can run nonswipe transactions for your charge cards. So what I told her—"

"What you told Becky," I interrupted.

A full thirty seconds passed by while Kermit contemplated the fact that he was hurtling down the highway with a man at the wheel known to have voices in his head. "Right. Becky."

"My sister."

"Your sister," Kermit responded as if hypnotized.

"Who, if anybody ever hurt her, I would break his face into fragments."

"Why don't you let up on the guy, Ruddy?" Alan demanded.

"Yeah. Right," Kermit said after a moment.

"Okay. So you were telling Becky . . ."

"Right." He took a breath. "See, the Black Bear has what you call a merchant account, which I used to sell before I ran into some unfortunates and had to rehabilitate up here to the north with my uncle. That means that when someone hands you a credit card you can accept it and run it through your machine and the bank will credit your account."

"Sounds good."

"Right. So, if you run the actual card through itself, you get what is called a *swipe* account. But, if you don't have the card, you can still punch the numbers into the machine and you'll get credit for the transaction anyway. That's called a *nonswipe*. And you can do both!"

"Hot dog!" I said enthusiastically.

"So I got this client who can't get a merchant account. So you could, like, run his business through your machine, pay him his money, but you keep thirteen percent. Pay your three percent to your bank, and you're keeping ten percent of everything he sends you."

"Ten percent," I repeated dutifully, vacillating between not understanding and not caring.

"Right. He does credit card business, sends you the account numbers. You run them through your nonswipe account, and keep ten percent. Ten percent of a thousand dollars is one hundred. He can send you three thousand a day. You'll make twenty-one hundred dollars a week," Kermit advised, as if reciting a catechism.

"Kermit."

He looked at me.

"Is there something printed on the sign at the Black Bear that tells every person in the world with a get-rich scheme to stop in?"

"No, see, Becky thought it sounded like a great idea."

"She did."

"Yeah, honest."

"Becky."

"Uh-huh."

"My sister."

Kermit looked out his window in disgust. "She said you guys have had problems paying the bills. I thought this would help."

"Becky said that?" I asked incredulously.

"Yeah, Becky. *Your sister.*"

I hid my smile behind my hand. So maybe the guy wasn't a total idiot.

I expected him to ask me to drop him at his uncle's lot, but he said the Black Bear would be fine. He said it nervously, the way a boy acts when a girl's father wants to know where they're going on prom night.

I liked that.

The snow was falling steadily as I headed back to East Jordan. Twenty-seven degrees: a fifteen-degree drop in a couple of hours. "I'm joining the Witness Protection Club and moving to Florida," I announced.

Alan wanted to visit the East Jordan cemetery first, which surprised me. *"I want to see if I'm buried there. I purchased a family plot when Kathy was born."*

"Then why wouldn't you be buried there, if you paid for it?" I asked curiously.

"Let's just see," Alan responded evasively.

"What aren't you telling me, Alan?"

"Oh, my God! Kathy! She's not a little girl anymore, she's . . . she's twenty-four. She's a grown woman."

Alan began making an odd noise. I frowned, concentrating, then realized he was *crying.* "Hey, Alan, hey, you okay? Talk to me."

"I'll never see my little girl again. She's all grown up. She grew up without me. I wasn't there, Ruddy. I'm her daddy and I wasn't there for her."

I tried to imagine what he was going through. I thought about how I felt when I got the call from Becky telling me Dad was dead, how frustrated I'd felt that I had seen so little of him those three years. Mom was even worse, coming just six months later. "I'm sorry, Alan. Jesus, I'm really sorry."

Alan directed me to the cemetery, going quiet as I

pulled up to a heavy-gauge chain-link fence. There was not a headstone in sight. *"I don't understand,"* he said finally. *"This was the graveyard."*

I got out of the truck, the snowflakes landing on my face and melting. I walked up to the fence and grabbed it—it felt pretty new, coated with some sort of rubberized layer to prevent rust. From here I could gaze right down into the parking lot of the factory where Einstein worked. I scanned the area, looking for his truck.

"This makes no sense. This was the cemetery, I swear. The funeral home was about fifty feet from where we are standing, and the headstones went all the way down the hill."

"Well, it's not here now, Alan. There's a factory, instead," I sighed. Another indication that Alan was a figment of my imagination.

"What's happening?" Alan shouted in frustration. *"My house, my office, even the town cemetery, they're all gone, just like the past eight years!"*

I didn't say anything.

"You're thinking that this is just more proof that I never existed," Alan accused.

"Well yeah, Alan, I am."

The noise he made in response was full of defeat.

"What do you want to do now, Alan? Got any more ideas?"

"Let's just go."

I detoured down Main Street in case Katie was standing there with a dead battery. No such luck, though everything else about the day was pretty much the same. I swung the truck into the exact same parking slot and let a pleasant feeling akin to nostalgia wash over me. "I think I'll have a cup of java," I remarked. "That okay with you, Mr. Lottner?"

"*Sure,*" Alan responded listlessly.

I indulged myself by sitting at a small table and picturing what it would have been like if Katie had accepted my offer of coffee that day. Again, I was almost impossibly witty, and she laughed and laughed.

Alan winked out on me, off on one of his catnaps, and I took this as a sign that I should be impossibly witty on the telephone while I had some privacy. The woman who ran the coffee shop told me to help myself to her phone. I was pretty calm as I dialed, fully aware that Katie was most likely still at work. *I'm in East Jordan; before I leave, I want to make sure your battery is still . . .*

I heard five rings, and then a click. "Hello, this is Katie Lottner. I can't take your phone call right now . . ."

What? *What?* I hung up, my heart pounding.

Katie *Lottner?*

10

I'm Not Dead

Could this really be happening? How could she have the same last name as Alan? Was she Kathy, his *daughter*?

What was my mind doing to me? Or was it God, trying to teach me some lesson I hadn't any hope of comprehending?

I'd met Katie before I heard any voices in my head. Had she mentioned her last name then? I tried to recall. Maybe she told me, and I forgot, but it was trapped there in my subconscious. Mix in a little location—East Jordan, where I met her and where Alan claimed to have lived and died—and the whole story was revealed to be nothing more than a rather mundane creation by an imagination too lazy to go very far for the ingredients of its hallucinations.

Shaken, I drove down to the little park located where the Jordan River empties into Lake Charlevoix. For most of its length, the Jordan isn't so much a river as a clear, cold brook. As it approaches the lake, though, it widens, slows, and forms what in other waters might be termed a bayou. The water here looks still, deep, and dark.

I felt Alan come awake, but I didn't say anything. The very fact of first name Katie, last name Lottner, was rendering me mute.

I turned my back on the river and gazed out at the lake. The water was the same shade of gray as the sky. We were both silent, contemplating. A long way out a boat broke from shore and headed north—I could see its wake flashing white in the frigid water, but the wind carried off the noise from the motor before it could reach my ears. *"It's best for me like this, when you are looking long distance and not moving your eyes so much. When you're focused on something close it makes me nauseated,"* Alan finally said.

"Well, do me a favor and don't throw up in there."

"I remember coming down the Jordan River in a canoe with my daughter. We'd fish for trout. When you get down here to the end where the river flattens out, the current sort of dies, and you have to paddle pretty hard. She'd get tired. We'd pull up right about here. Then we'd sit and fish some more from the shore."

"Your daughter, what was her name, again?"

"Kathy."

"Kathy, what is that, a nickname for Katherine or something?"

"Actually it's 'Katrine.' Marget insisted we name her something Swedish. I called her Kathy, Marget called her Katrine."

"Katrine. Katie," I said. Alan didn't comment. I sighed. "I've done that. Canoed down the Jordan River before," I told him, returning to the original subject. Which was probably why Alan had the same recollection—we were both drawing from the same memory bank.

"Yeah?" He pondered this for a few moments. *"It was near the Jordan where I was killed."*

I sat down, careful to keep my eyes on the horizon so he wouldn't get sick. Time to see what my imagination could come up with. I had a feeling Alan's murder would exactly match the circumstances from a T. Jefferson Parker novel I'd just finished. "Tell me about that."

"I got a phone call from this guy who'd seen an ad for a listing in our office. There was this cabin out in the Jordan Valley, ten acres of land. Man who owned it used to hunt out of it. Then he died and his wife let it fall apart. Kids broke into it, and then somebody got care-less and it burned down. When she died it went to her niece, I think it was. She put it up for sale, but she was from California and wouldn't believe me when I told her how little it was worth. It was a pretty little piece, about five hundred feet of riverfront, lots of hardwood. We went through the motions but nobody was interested at the price she wanted. So then this guy calls me, says he might make an offer, wants to take a look at it. I arrange to meet him and his wife, but driving out, I think I saw something I wasn't supposed to."

"What do you mean?"

"Two guys. I think it must have been a drug deal, the way they reacted. I drove on past them to up where I had my listing, and a couple of minutes later I heard them coming up from behind. I turned and one of them had a shovel . . ."

"A *what*?" I demanded sharply.

"A shovel. He had this look on his face I'll never forget."

I stood abruptly. "Can you show me? Show me where this happened?"

"*Sure.*"

Alan directed me back down Highway 66 toward Mancelona. Even with the forest still looking dead from winter and snow puddled in the shadows, the Jordan Valley is a spectacular remnant of glacial action, heavily wooded and hilly. We turned once, then again, bumping down a mucky dirt road that was doing its best to turn back into untracked forest. I dropped my truck into four-wheel drive and powered over some small trees that had been felled during recent storms. My heart was pounding now, and I felt a little sick. We topped a rise and I eased to a stop.

"*What? What is it?*" Alan demanded anxiously.

"Here." I stared without blinking at a small clearing off to the right. "This is where you saw the two guys, standing next to a truck. One of them you knew from somewhere before, but the one with the shovel was a stranger."

"*The one I knew had a toupee,*" Alan whispered.

"Exactly." I pressed on the accelerator and shot forward. Without the autumn leaves it really didn't look much like the same place until the road ended at the remains of a burned cabin strewn across the forest floor. I slid out of the cab and walked up to where the front door had been, kicking at some loose bricks. "You were standing right about here."

"*How do you know this, Ruddy?*"

"The other one, the stranger, husky with a tan. Green eyes. He walked right up and swung the shovel without even slowing down." I rubbed my arm.

"*Hit me between the elbow and the wrist. Broke the bone, I think,*" Alan murmured.

I pictured the guy with the shovel, the expression on his face. "Yes." I turned and looked down the road. "So you ran back this way."

"I was running forty miles a week at that point. Once I got twenty yards ahead, I knew they would never catch me. I could hear them panting, even after that short distance. And then the sound faded away."

I found myself trotting back down the road, acting it out. "Didn't even notice their truck when you passed it," I said as I huffed past the clearing where it had been parked. I slid and almost fell in the snow-covered mud but didn't stop.

"I was too busy thinking, trying to figure out why they had done it. Maybe if I had seen the truck it would have occurred to me to get off the road."

"Because you didn't." I stopped, peering around. "If you'd made it into the woods, they never would have caught up with you."

"It was up here farther, I heard the truck."

I began moving. "I'm not sure we'll be able to tell exactly where; the woods look so different this time of year."

"Tell me how you know all this, Ruddy."

"I had a dream several days ago. Except it felt more like a memory, more like waking up and remembering something that had really happened."

"A dream."

"Don't start getting skeptical on me, Alan. Not you, of all people." I slowed down, panting with the exertion. "Here's where you heard the truck, right?" I began watching the side of the road. "So right along here somewhere . . ."

We saw it together, the place where he'd jumped the

ditch and fled into the woods. "There," we said in unison. Without hesitating, I stepped into the trees.

"Right along here. I'd just started running, I fell, and then just up here . . ."

"Yes. He must have had a rifle. Even then, a pretty good shot, caught you right in the leg."

"I don't know that he was aiming for the leg," Alan argued, as if it made a difference. *"And he might have shot five times; I never heard the rifle."*

I turned around in a full circle. "I'm looking for a big old tree. An oak," I stated.

The tree was there, but was no longer upright. Same large cavity in the huge trunk, but the massive oak had been toppled by nature, lying indignantly on its side.

It didn't go down without a fight, though—it clung to an enormous ball of earth with its gnarled roots, exposing a huge crater that had filled with brown meltwater. "Right here."

"Yes."

"This is where you died."

"Yes."

I stood there for what must have been five minutes, staring at the tree, thinking of the life ebbing out of me, of wanting to live and knowing I wasn't going to. Fixing my eyes on the sky and a tree and wishing I could have more time.

"You okay, Alan?"

"Yeah. I guess . . . I guess I'm probably buried right here somewhere. That's why I wanted to see the cemetery, see if I had a grave. I knew I wouldn't."

I turned and looked, kicking away the thin layer of melting snow. There was no mound, and whatever signs of digging that might have once marred the earth had been erased by eight years of active forest cycle.

"What do we do now, Ruddy?"

I jammed my hands in my pockets. The day was ending. The sun, which had been hidden behind a thick skin of gray all day, was fading rapidly away. "So one thing that could be happening is that I've been here before, forgot about it, and now, after my dream, I have created a split personality that 'remembers' a murder."

"Back to the 'I must be crazy because I have voices in my head' theory," Alan observed.

"Right. Repo Madness."

"You don't believe that, though," he said evenly.

"No," I admitted. "I don't. Because I know I've never been here before. I had a dream about it, but I would not have been able to find this place if you hadn't shown me."

"So now what?"

"So now I have to follow this thing through," I said grimly. "Because if you are a figment of my imagination, the fact that I believe your story means I really am crazy."

We drove back to East Jordan with the light nearly gone from the sky. Some locals were already in the Rainbow Bar, not giving me much notice as I slid up and asked for a beer. I sat there looking friendly for a while, finally breaking into a conversation between two guys about what great times they had three years ago ice fishing. "I'm looking for a guy named Alan Lottner," I told them.

They passed a doubtful look between them. I sipped my beer.

"Guy that ran off few years ago," someone speculated from another table.

"I didn't 'run off,'" Alan objected.

There it was: confirmation that àn Alan Lottner had really existed in East Jordan. Of course, I could have picked this up somehow, read his name off of a real estate sign, even met him at some point and just forgot.

Everyone was watching me curiously. I cleared my throat. "He ran off?"

"Oh, yeah," one of the ice fishermen said, brightening. "What happened to him? He wasn't from around here."

"Found him dead somewhere. I remember reading about it," said the guy at the other table. "Funeral notice in the paper."

"I still don't know who you're talking about," the other ice fisherman groused.

"Dressed funny," the guy at the other table recalled.

"Dressed funny?" Alan squawked.

"So . . . he's buried here in East Jordan?"

The man with all the information squinted his weathered eyes, trying to remember. "Yeah, think so."

"I tried to find the cemetery, but it's not where I remember it."

The ice fishermen both snorted. "That's because they moved the darn thing. Just dug everybody up and moved 'em all, so they could build the PlasMerc factory."

"New cemetery is up north toward Boyne City way. About four miles."

Alan was still upset as we drove north. *"Where do they get that from? I didn't run off."*

"It was a long time ago, Alan. That's probably all they can remember."

"And do you think they found my body in the woods, is that why I'm buried in the cemetery?"

"Let's just take it one step at a time, Alan."

"Dressed funny. This from a man in a Detroit Pistons

jacket, a John Deere baseball cap, and a T-shirt with a picture of a duck on it."

Grinning, I swung my truck into the parking lot of the cemetery, my lights sweeping past a funeral home that looked no more than a few years old. A shadow appeared briefly at the window, probably someone checking to see who had just pulled in. "I see somebody in there; let's go ask him where we can find Alan Lottner's grave."

Rock salt crunched under my feet as I mounted the cement steps. I pushed open a polished wooden door and stepped cautiously into the entryway of the funeral parlor. Tasteful carpet and dark paneling gave the place a solemn feel. I poked my head around the corner, looking into a large room with shiny wooden pews.

"Can I help you?" inquired a voice from behind me.

I turned and started in surprise.

He was heavier than I remembered, and his scalp was so bald it gleamed. But take a few years off his face and put a toupee on him and I would recognize him anywhere. In my dream he was standing next to a pickup truck in the woods, talking to a green-eyed guy with a shovel, gazing at me with an unreadable expression as I drove past.

We'd found one of Alan's killers.

11

Where the Bodies Are Buried

"My name is Nathan Burby," he told me, holding out what turned out to be a professionally soft, dry, funeral-director hand. I stared at him, astounded.

He was several inches shorter than I, with a rounded chin and dark, warm eyes. His suit was charcoal gray wool, his facial features bland. His smile was cautious—welcoming, but careful not to come off as too jovial in case I was here to discuss putting Aunt Mildred in the ground. Absurdly, it struck me that he looked like a really nice guy.

"Oh my God," Alan breathed, barely recovering from his own shock. *"Do you know who this is?"*

"I'm Ruddy McCann," I finally answered Burby, releasing his hand.

He gestured as if he had a staff of workers gathered around him. "How can I help you tonight, Mr. McCann?"

"I was looking for the cemetery," I replied faintly.

"Well, you've come to the right place, then." He smiled pleasantly.

"It's him! The one with the toupee! That day in the woods! He's one of the killers," Alan was babbling shrilly. I closed my eyes once, hard, trying to get him to shut up. Burby was watching me curiously.

"I meant the other one, wasn't the cemetery, I mean, didn't it used to be somewhere else?"

"That's right. We moved here about seven years ago."

"He must own the place," Alan speculated, calming down a little.

"Was that so they could build that new factory I noticed? PlasMerc?"

Something like discomfort flitted across Burby's face, but, smoothly practiced in suppressing his own feelings in order to allow his clients to indulge in theirs, he kept whatever it was under tight control. "Yes, that's correct."

"How could you do that, though? I mean, weren't the bodies buried and everything?"

"We moved everyone," he explained simply. "Everyone with a family member interred at the old cemetery was compensated, or at least those we could contact. For those with untraceable roots, we've established a trust fund, and we have hopes that eventually they'll come forward."

"What about you, though? Did you get compensated?"

Burby's eyes lost some of their softness. "What's this about, Mr. McCann?"

"I had a family member buried in the old cemetery," I lied.

"Oh? Who?"

"How much were the families compensated?" I parried.

He regarded me for several long seconds. "In the thousand-dollar range," he finally stated quietly. "May I inquire who it was you were related to?"

"Alan Lottner."

No amount of practice could have prevented the wild look from passing through his eyes then. "That's . . . impossible," he whispered.

I took a step forward and was rewarded when Burby took a fearful step back, tilting his head up to stare at me. "Why do you say that, Nathan? Why's that impossible?"

"I know the family," he stuttered. "No one has ever mentioned . . ." He gestured toward me.

"I had a whole group of cousins in Wisconsin," Alan advised me.

"I'm from Wisconsin," I explained. "Alan had a whole group of us cousins up there. All good runners."

"Runners?" Burby repeated helplessly.

"So is Alan Lottner buried here? Did you move his body from the old cemetery?"

That one took a while for him to process, but when Burby spoke next he had rediscovered his gift for imperturbability. "Actually, no. I don't know what you've been told, but your cousin left town without a word. After several years, he was declared dead, and his ex-wife and daughter had a service for him here. We placed a memorial headstone on the grounds in a very nice area, if you would like to see it."

"What does he mean, ex-wife?" Alan demanded indignantly. *"We weren't divorced!"*

"I'm confused about something. You said 'ex-wife.' I don't remember Alan being divorced."

"Ah, well, after he disappeared, his wife . . ." Burby spread his hands, hating to deliver unpleasant news. "It was a simple case of abandonment."

"What about Kathy? Does she still live here?" Alan asked.

"Does the family still live here?" I pressed.

"Yes," Burby answered reluctantly. "They are both living in East Jordan."

"Where? Ask him where!" Alan implored.

I was more interested in a different subject. "So you sold the cemetery to the factory. That must have made you a lot of money."

"Actually, no, that's not right. Burby's operated under a nonexclusive lease to the city of East Jordan. The city sold the land. Burby's surrendered lease rights in exchange for the deed to the property here."

There was something about that last statement that rang false for me, but I wasn't sure what it was. I pushed in a slightly different direction. "Well that must have saved you a bundle, not having to make those lease payments to the city."

Burby chuckled, but there was no humor in his eyes. "Hardly. Our lease formerly cost us a dollar a year. This new arrangement subjects us to property taxes."

"What does this have to do with anything?" Alan asked churlishly.

"May I ask why you are so interested in these matters?" Burby inquired, essentially asking the same thing. Maybe I should just shut up and let the two of them talk to each other.

"I'm just trying to understand. So the factory is on land formerly owned by the city?"

"Yes. Well no, not entirely," Burby admitted reluctantly. "Most of the parcel was a ranch belonging to a local family. The city land was less than a quarter of the total."

Far more interesting than his answer was his uneasy expression. In better lighting, I might have seen sweat on his shiny, toupeeless head. "What was the name of that family?"

"I really don't recall," he replied uncomfortably. "Mr. McCann, does any of this matter? Shall I show you where Alan Lottner's memorial is placed?"

"So you got paid to move every body? That must have amounted to a lot of money," I speculated.

Burby had had it with me. "I don't see how that's any of your business."

"Oh, just wondering if it wouldn't be a good idea to open a cemetery in Minneapolis," I joked.

"*Wisconsin!*" Alan corrected.

"Wisconsin. The funeral business pay pretty well?"

"I'd like you to leave, Mr. McCann." He made as if to nudge me forward, but someone Burby's size can't budge a bar bouncer without help, and I didn't move. We were now standing almost intimately close, like dancers, and I leaned down to murmur in his ear, the way Alan's voice sounded to me. "Man doing well like you, must own a second place, maybe on the lake?"

"Please. I've answered all your questions."

"What about on the Jordan River?"

Burby looked truly puzzled.

"*Ruddy . . . ,*" Alan warned faintly.

"Be nice to own a piece of property on the Jordan River someday, wouldn't it? Beautiful in the autumn. You ever go up there, take a look at a piece of land on the Jordan, some autumn afternoon?"

Burby's expression was slack and empty, trying to cope with the implications of what I was asking him. I slapped him on the shoulder and he flinched. I liked that. "Hey, just making conversation. Listen, I'll come back some other time to check out where Alan's buried." I turned to leave.

"Well, no, actually, he's not buried here. As I explained, it is a memorial."

"Oh?" I turned back. "Where is he buried, then, Nathan?"

We looked at each other for an open and honest moment before Burby decided he must be reading too much into this whole thing and relaxed. "From what I understand, no trace of him was ever found."

"Is that so." I nodded pleasantly and walked out the door.

"I can't believe you did that!" Alan fretted as I drove away. *"Why did you ask him about the Jordan River property, and where I was buried?"*

I waited to answer until I had driven out of eyeshot of Burby. "Why not? What did you want me to do?"

"But now he knows we're suspicious!"

"No, now he knows *I'm* suspicious. And so what?"

"I don't know, I just . . . you're just so different than me, I would never confront someone directly like that."

"You think that was direct? That wasn't direct. If I had confronted him directly he'd be in the hospital right about now."

Alan ruminated for a few moments. *"There was something strange there, at the end, when you asked him about the land."*

"He was lying. Something about the ranch, I don't know what it is, but it made him nervous. I've seen the same expression on people's faces when they tell me they don't know where their car is."

I realized I was grinning. Whatever doubts had remained were gone now: Alan Lottner had been a *real* person, he *was* a real person, and I'd just shaken hands with his killer. I wasn't crazy.

My smile faded when I thought about Katie. I might not be crazy but I wasn't exactly without problems. The first woman in a decade to make my pulse race, and I had her father trapped inside my *head*.

I tried to picture telling Alan that I knew his daughter, and how I knew her, and found myself almost shivering with dread. I could not think of a single reason to talk to him about it. Ever.

The East Jordan Library was still open. I started flipping through back issues of the *Charlevoix Courier* on the microfiche, irritated that Alan couldn't remember the date of his appointment to show the property on the Jordan River. "It was the date you died, how could you forget something like that?" I challenged peevishly. A woman at a table within earshot gave me an alarmed look, and I smiled weakly.

"I don't know, it's not like me to forget. But it's erased, I really can't . . . the past few months, I mean, the months before I went out there, are all blurred, like I was drugged. I can't remember anything."

"Well, you can bet that when I die, I'll pay attention," I grumbled.

Screaming headlines from the winter after Alan vanished caught my eye. 32 DIE IN EXPLOSION. "Oh yeah, I remember this," I muttered.

"I hate this. You read at a different speed than I do. I can't . . . it makes me a little sick," Alan grunted.

I bristled. "Are you saying I read more slowly than you?"

He didn't reply.

"Come on," I pressed, "that's what you're implying,

right? I'm a big dumb jock who moves his lips while he reads." The woman at the other table glanced at me again—I *was* moving my lips while I read.

"I don't think it matters which one of us reads more slowly," Alan proclaimed haughtily.

"Ha! So I am faster!"

"You're so competitive."

"And you're such a snob! It really burns you to admit a football player reads faster than you do, doesn't it?"

When he didn't answer I turned triumphantly back to the microfiche. "It was a firebomb that killed all those people," I recalled after a moment, glancing through the story. "An explosion in the basement of a nursing home, and all the residents there died. It was deliberate, and I don't think they ever found a motive for whoever did it. Just somebody out to kill off a bunch of local old people, plus I think a couple of nurses."

"Do you think it had something to do with me?" Alan asked.

"Is that some sort of gentle reminder that we're not here to catch up on old news?"

"I am just trying to understand where the investigation is taking us."

"Is that what this is, an investigation? Hey, here we are." I pointed to the story: LOCAL MAN MISSING.

Alan Lottner, 41, of East Jordan, failed to return home from work on Oct. 11th, according to his wife, Marget. A Realtor, Lottner often works long hours, so she was not alarmed when she went to bed on the 11th and Alan still wasn't home. "But when I woke up the next morning and he was still gone, he's never done that before," she stated. Authorities are asking local residents to be on the lookout for Lottner's automobile, a green late model Olds 98 Station Wagon, license BA 113 08.

Two photographs accompanied the story, and for the first time I got a look at Alan Lottner. The top photo was obviously from his real estate brochure—coat and tie, a fatuous grin, professionally lit background. Alan's hair was short and curly, his eyes dark, his teeth even and, I assumed, well flossed.

In the second picture he was standing on some steps, one hand reaching out of frame, probably holding onto his daughter, who had been cropped out of the shot. His pants were creased, his polo shirt pressed, probably underneath it all his boxers were ironed as well. I could see why a couple of ice fishermen might think he dressed funny.

"October eleventh," I noted for the record.

A week later another story surfaced.

STILL NO SIGN OF LOCAL MAN, MISSING SINCE 11-OCT.

This one was pretty brief, with little to say other than the fact that the local authorities were investigating the possibility of foul play but had no leads.

That was it. Flipping forward through the days on the microfiche eventually brought me to the stories about the nursing home bombing, the worst crime in the history of the area. *"I lived here for eighteen years, and when I was killed I got less coverage than a story about some kids spray-painting a trash Dumpster behind Glen's Market,"* Alan groused.

We left the library and headed back to Kalkaska. "But they didn't know you were killed, Alan," I pointed out. "They just thought you took off. Lots of guys do stuff like that."

"*I wonder . . . I wonder what Marget told them.*"

"Told who?"

"*The police.*"

"What do you mean?"

"*Well look, we weren't getting along very well. Marget was sleeping in the spare bedroom. She'd gotten so cold toward me. We really didn't have much to say to each other. We'd talked about divorce, you know, like maybe that would be the best thing. If she told the police that, maybe they wouldn't look very hard for me.*"

"That makes sense," I admitted.

"*But I would never leave Kathy. It's crazy to think I would just get in the Oldsmobile and drive off and leave everything: my business, my clothes, and especially my daughter, just because Marget and I were not getting along. It's stupid,*" he complained bitterly.

I watched the road. It was a dark, moonless night, my headlights carving out a bright tunnel between the ridges of snow that lined both sides of the highway. Down there at the bottom was the snow that first fell in November—it would be the last to melt away.

"*You believe me now, don't you, Ruddy? I'm not a figment of your imagination. Maybe it made sense that you had a bad dream and then got a voice in your head, but not after what we heard tonight. You know something's not right, here. Burby, you recognized him, and you know he's lying. And the newspaper. You didn't imagine that.*" Alan sounded plaintive and insecure.

"No. You're right. I didn't create you out of my imagination. You lived, you sold real estate, you ironed your pants."

"*What's that supposed to mean?*"

"I've just never seen so many creases on a living

person. You looked like you could give someone a paper cut."

Alan lapsed into a moody silence, and a few minutes later went to sleep.

The inside of the Black Bear was even quieter than the East Jordan Library had been. I slid up to the bar, massaging my thighs. You know you're getting old when you're sore from just driving your truck. "Hey, Becky," I called.

I took over for my sister at the bar, and heard her chatting on the telephone in the back room. Alan woke up and, after I swept my eyes around the nearly empty room so he'd get his bearings, asked to know where everybody was. I told him we were in Kalkaska—this was everybody.

Becky came back and slid up on the stool in front of me in a way I could tell meant she wanted to talk. "So Kermit told me he told you about this business deal he has," she began.

"He did?"

"Yeah, you know, the one about the credit card thing."

"Oh, yeah. Swipe or nonswipe."

"Right." She looked at me seriously. "We could make a lot of money, Ruddy."

I reached behind her for a beer, changed my mind and made it a glass of diet soda. "Becky, he wants us to run credit card numbers through our machine, here. Doesn't that strike you as being illegal somehow?"

She shook her head forcefully, her eyes sparking. I was a little taken aback: Becky never argued with me, never argued with anything, just accepted her fate with weary resignation. Something was happening to her. Could it be that Kermit Kramer, the worst repo man on the planet, with a criminally misaligned vocabulary, was responsible? "Kermit explained it all," she said, confirming my suspicions. "His customer is an audiotext business."

"A what?"

"Audiotext. You know, information and entertainment over the telephone. They take credit card numbers and give readings."

"Readings. They read to people?"

"No." She stroked a hand through her listless brown hair, and the eyes behind her glasses looked unhappy to have to explain it to me. "Readings. From cards."

I processed this without comprehension. *"Tarot cards,"* Alan suggested helpfully.

"Tarot cards? You mean, like psychic readings? Those people that advertise during the Tarzan movies in the middle of the night?"

She frowned. "There are Tarzan movies in the middle of the night?"

"Becky, what are we talking about here?"

She took a deep breath, preparing to be patient. "To get a nonswipe account, which is what you need so you can take credit cards over the phone, you have to be in business for a few years. But you can't be in business for a few years doing readings over the phone if you can't take credit cards! So Kermit knows this guy who has this business, and he is willing to pay thirteen percent off the top to anyone who will cash the card numbers his customers give him."

"If this guy is psychic, why does he need Kermit? He should be here himself right now, because he knows we're talking about him."

"Ruddy, please. Listen to me." Becky leaned forward. "We owe everybody in town. The money you make isn't enough to keep the doors open. We can't go on this way. We've been cut off from two suppliers, and the bank says no more."

"But . . . I just gave you a thousand," I protested, reminding myself that $750 of it was an advance from Milt. Losing Einstein's truck meant I was back in the hole on that one, since we couldn't very well collect our fee from the bank twice.

"That just kept us open for this month! What are we going to do when we need another thousand in three weeks?"

I shook my head stubbornly. "This always happens this time of year. Another month or so and repos will pick up, business in the Bear will pick up, we'll be fine."

"No, Ruddy, we will not be fine. We lose money every year."

I stared at her. "Milton would loan—"

"That's not a solution! You hear me? Are you even listening? You can't borrow your way out of a losing business. Something has to change." Her lips pressed together, trembling. "We're going to lose the Black Bear, Ruddy."

Even though any idiot could have seen them coming, her words still hit me so hard they knocked me back two decades, when our folks were alive and the Black Bear was a second home to us. Becky and I would play in the boxes in the storeroom and help Mom scrub the floors every morning. Dad had his buddies from the cannery swarming at one end of the bar, and at Christmas we put a Santa suit on Bob the Bear and piled presents at his feet. We couldn't lose the bar. I'd lost everything else in my life, but I would never let the Black Bear pass out of the McCann family.

"I'll sell the house," I decided abruptly.

"Oh, Ruddy."

"It's worth fifty, maybe more. Depends on what is going on with the zoning. Free and clear. I'll put the money into the Bear."

"That's not what I want. Don't you see? Things have to change. We need to attract somebody besides bikers and unemployed factory workers."

"What about the petty criminals and con artists?"

"Why do you always joke? Ruddy, the other night when everyone was dancing, we grossed more than four hundred dollars. If we could attract that sort of crowd every time . . . I want to sell something besides popcorn—you know how often people come in and ask for a menu? Because we don't serve anything but thawed-out chicken wings and nachos with that disgusting cheese sauce, after they come here for a drink they go somewhere else to eat. I want to put in a grill that actually works, paint the walls, get some new tables."

"People don't like our cheese sauce?" I responded, truly offended.

"*It's made out of plastic,*" Alan sniffed contemptuously.

"Please," Becky said impatiently.

"Okay, okay. I'll give you the money. I can sleep in the back for a while, until your business plan kicks in and we become as big as Burger King."

She shook her head. "No, Ruddy. Dad and Mom left the Bear to me. I don't want your money; I want to do this myself."

"By running credit card numbers through our machine."

"Right."

"Have you consulted a psychic about this?"

"I would think you of all people wouldn't make fun!" she snapped.

I looked at her. "What do you mean, me of all people?"

She shook her head. "Never mind."

"No, what is that supposed to mean? That I got a voice in my head, so I should start hanging out with psychics and people who have been kidnapped by UFOs?"

"I'm doing it," Becky said fiercely. Her eyes were blurred. "It isn't something I need your permission for."

"Dad would never allow it."

"Oh right, Ruddy. I'm the one who disappointed Dad."

That one hurt. I felt the heat rise in my face. "Becky, you do this and you risk everything we own."

"Everything *I* own." She turned on her heel.

I watched her walk away from me. This was not Becky behavior at all. "I am going to rip Kermit's arms out of their sockets," I remarked pleasantly.

"You aren't listening to her," Alan told me. *"It's not Kermit."*

"You too? Great, even my own psychosis is against me."

·   Alan made a sound I interpreted to mean he was cutting me off from the pleasure of his company for a while.

Claude joined me and began babbling about the kind of return you could get from off-shore investments. I gathered that he felt the slander clause was so close to being a done deal he was already starting to resent the tax implications. I tuned him out until Janelle came in and walked over to us, and then my head filled with alarm bells. She scooted a chair up to the table and patted Claude's hand affectionately. He beamed at me like a boy with a new toy and I just shook my head.

"Honey, let's go see a movie in Traverse City tonight," she purred possessively. Claude nodded expansively.

I looked at Janelle and she stared right back, her gaze almost a challenge of some sort. She had been homecoming queen, I suddenly remembered. When I was a boy I stood on the sidewalk in front of the Black Bear and watched her ride by in a convertible. The man she wound up marrying had been wearing a football uniform and was driving the car behind her. He wasn't much of a halfback, I recalled, but he got the girl, and then he dumped her. I shook my head again. A couple of decades hadn't really erased her appeal, but it sure had taken away a lot of her options.

Why did Janelle feel complete only when she had a man in her life? The misery she'd been oozing since her husband walked out on her was gone, and the settled contentment on her face just because she'd hooked an easy fish like Claude made me squirm in my chair.

When Wilma walked in half an hour later I was still sitting there at the table with Claude and his new girlfriend as if we were all having a big adultery party. I dropped my eyes away from Wilma's accusatory stare, cursing Claude for making it appear I had chosen sides against her.

"*She knows,*" Alan whispered in despair.

Becky and I exchanged worried glances.

This was not going to be good.

12

What Everyone Does in a Situation like This

Watching Wilma walk across the floor, dark as an approaching thundercloud, I had the epiphany that Claude had never done anything like this before. Janelle was a new sort of disaster in their lives.

We probably all looked like idiots, sitting there openmouthed as Wilma stood in front of our table, her crazy bejeweled earrings flashing like lightning. I realized I was afraid.

She took three deep breaths. "Well, Claude," she said unevenly, her lips twitching. "Congratulations."

The three of us were silent. Janelle had averted her eyes, while Claude was staring at Wilma in dread.

"You've given me syphilis, Claude," she announced, more loudly.

"What!" he gasped, turning pale. Janelle jerked her head around and stared.

"And gonorrhea, too," she added in a shout. "The doctor said you must be *oozing pus*. That's how you gave it to me."

Claude could think of nothing to say, though he swallowed a couple of times. Janelle pushed herself away from the table and muttered "Excuse me" under her breath. Wilma watched her leave with hot, black eyes. The room was now so silent I could hear people breathing.

"For God's sake, Wilma!" Claude protested.

She whirled on him. "The slander clause, remember, Claude?"

"Yeah, but . . ."

"But what?" Wilma regarded Claude's humiliated expression with complete apathy, as if he were just another person complaining about county government services at her office. "Have a nice evening, honey." Her smile was cold as she pushed her way past him. Her sharp eyes flicked at me and I knew it would take a lot to repair the damage done by my presence at the table with Claude and Janelle.

Alan winked out at the same time Becky shut off the lights. My sister and I exchanged weary glances, as if we'd just survived a family crisis. She gave me a look that meant, "I know we fought, and I know you're still mad, but we're still brother and sister and I love you."

My look said back, "I am always right about everything."

Alan was still asleep when I got home, so after dragging Jake out to do his business, I decided to flip through the stack of mail on the table and then grab an Andrew Gross novel and head to bed. "Unless you maybe want to go hunt some ducks or something, Jake?"

Jake didn't seem to think I was funny.

About a year ago Jimmy Growe purchased something sexy for one of his girlfriends from a mail-order lingerie place and had it delivered to my house. He didn't want anyone at the hotel where he lived to see it arrive. As a rather pleasing result, I sometimes received unsolicited lingerie catalogues, like the one I came across as I sorted through my bills.

I opened it and gazed in something akin to bewilderment. "Do women really let you do that, buy them outfits like this to wear?" I asked. Alan, still slumbering, didn't reply, and I realized with considerable consternation that I'd developed a habit of talking out loud to myself. Jake's grunt indicated he wasn't any more fond of the new behavior than I was.

Once I was in bed with the Gross novel I realized I was far more interested in reading the lingerie catalogue, despite the lack of a plot. One of the models bore a passing resemblance to Katie Lottner.

Hi Katie, here's a present I bought for you.

Thanks, Ruddy! I'll put it on right now!

Be careful with the garter belt!

The same model was on another page wearing little more than an inviting expression and a pair of lace shorts, her arms crossed in front of her bare chest. I pictured Katie spreading her arms to me, her smile, those lips, her eyes, the lace coming off in a whisper of sound . . .

"What are we doing?" Alan asked curiously.

"Nothing!" I shouted. I threw the catalogue across the room.

He was silent for a minute. I surreptitiously yanked at the waistband of my boxers.

"I guess we should talk about this," he said.

"I guess we should *never* talk about this," I responded hotly.

"No, look. I mean, it's perfectly normal," he soothed.

"Do you have any idea how crazy it makes me to have a voice inside my head talking to me as if it is my psychiatrist?" I raged back.

"It's healthy. There's no reason to feel ashamed. Everybody does it," he argued.

"Not with another guy in the room!"

"I think you're really overreacting."

"How am I overreacting? By its very definition, it's a solo act. There's not supposed to be another person there. If there's another person there, it's something else!"

"Ruddy, if it makes you feel better, next time I won't say anything."

"There's not ever going to *be* a next time!" I stormed.

"Sure," Alan agreed skeptically. *"Never again. Ever."*

"Ever!" I affirmed. I reached for my book. "I'm going to read now."

"I'll try to go back to sleep," Alan promised, *"let you get back to . . . what you were doing."*

I closed my eyes and groaned.

Alan was still asleep when I awoke the next morning, but I felt him stir as I was reading the paper.

"God, this is awful," Alan moaned.

"Good morning to you, too."

"The way you are reading is giving me a headache."

I snorted. "That's ridiculous. How can you get a headache? You don't even have a head."

"Ruddy, about last night . . ."

"No talking, Alan," I warned. He sighed in frustration. I continued to read the paper, deliberately moving my eyes more slowly. It took a lot of concentration.

"Are we going back to East Jordan today?" he asked finally.

"Yes, soon as I finish my breakfast and take Jake out to water the lawn," I promised.

"A cold Big Mac and a cup of coffee. Breakfast," Alan pronounced.

"Don't knock it until you've tried it."

"I am trying it," he retorted.

"Okay, but look at it this way: You can eat all of the saturated fats you want, and it can't hurt you, because you're already dead."

"If I have to share this body with you I think I should have some say as to what goes into it," he responded haughtily.

"Let me disabuse you of the notion that you have to share my body," I answered.

After breakfast I stood in my living room and looked at something I hadn't seen in a long time: my carpet, vacuumed and free of any dirty laundry. "Why is she doing this?" I wondered out loud.

"Who?"

"Becky. Why is she cleaning up after me?"

Everywhere I looked, surfaces gleamed with something besides spilled liquid. Crushed bags from the drive-thru had disappeared. I sort of missed them—they'd become a little like pets.

In East Jordan I drove out to Einstein Croft's house to see if he'd decided to wash and wax his truck and leave it sitting for me with the keys in the ignition. At the very end of his driveway I encountered a thick Cyclone fence: He didn't have the money for a truck payment, but somehow he'd found the financial resources to sink some metal posts deep into cement and hang a gate that was far too thick for any wire cutters. I kicked at the fence in frustration and Doris the watch goose wandered over and gave me a warning look.

"First thing we do is locate my wife, Marget, talk to her. Next we need to look into Burby's background, see what we can turn up," Alan said, sounding like he was reading from a checklist. He grew pensive as I headed north up Highway 66, away from East Jordan. *"Ruddy, where are you going? What about the investigation?"*

"There is no investigation, Alan," I responded pleasantly. "Who do you think I am, Jack Reacher? You were killed. This is now a police matter. I'm going to the police."

"Jack who?"

"He's a sort of private eye in Lee Child's books."

"You know, I don't get it," Alan responded peevishly. *"You read nothing but mysteries and thrillers. I'd think you'd be interested in solving my case."*

"Alan, I'm a repo man. My forensic lab is less advanced than the sheriff's."

"I just don't think we know enough to go to the cops yet," he argued.

I set my jaw. "Well, I'm driving and I made my decision—that's where we're going. You don't like it, I'll pull over and let you out."

"Why are you acting like this?"

I wondered briefly if Alan could feel the heat in my face. "Because this is my life, my body, and my prerogative. Not yours."

"Oh. This is about last night, then."

"Alan, just shut up. Now. Period." I was gripping the steering wheel so tightly it was making a creaking sound.

Alan seemed to decide it was best that he not speak.

The sheriff's facility in Charlevoix was larger than many in the area, built to handle the summer crowds that seasonally flooded the town. This time of year, though, it was virtually deserted—the crime rate, like everything else, was waiting to thaw out. The sense of inertia was palpable, the deputy looking up listlessly as I stepped in and wiped my feet. I could feel him sizing me up a little as I approached, gauging my potential for making trouble. Must be an automatic reflex similar to what I experience when a couple of guys wearing motorcycle leathers wander into the Black Bear for drinks.

"Help ya?" he wanted to know. His neck was as thick as his head and his big frame supported a lot of beef. His nameplate read TIMMS. He looked like the kind of guy who would drive his elbow into my side after tackling me, but only when he was sure the ref wasn't watching. His hair was so short it stood up like brush bristles.

"I think I know this guy. His name is Dwight Timms. His dad runs a bait shop. I can't believe he's a cop, he used to be in trouble all the time," Alan murmured.

"Hey there, Dwight. Sheriff in?" I asked casually.

He'd been leaning on the counter for support. Now he straightened, a doubtful look in his eye. I gave him a cheerful grin, like we were buddies, and he was plainly disconcerted. "Um, got an appointment?"

"No, but he wants to see me."

Reluctantly, Deputy Dwight Timms slouched away from his post, taking my driver's license and disappearing for a moment. When he returned he nodded for me to follow him down the hallway to a door marked BARRY STRICKLAND, SHERIFF, CHARLEVOIX COUNTY.

The sheriff was standing, waiting for me, and gave me

a look of complete authority as he shook my hand. I told him my name and accepted a seat at his invitation. He settled down behind his desk and fixed me with a pair of clear blue eyes. He was my size, though at least two decades older, with white hair and a face roughened from repeated exposure to sun and Michigan winters. He was chiseled, fit, and handsome. In his snug uniform he looked like a Hollywood version of what he was—a small-town sheriff.

"How can I help you, Mr. McCann?"

How indeed. This was, I reflected, not the most thought-out action I'd ever taken. I took a breath, then laughed lightly at my embarrassment. Strickland's expression didn't change. I was wondering how I might extricate myself from this whole situation when Alan made a barely audible sound and my irritation punched through my caution. "It's about a missing person case you've got from back about eight years ago. An East Jordan man named Alan Lottner. I was wondering if . . . if you ever found his body."

Strickland's eyes registered something at the word "body" and I tried not to wince. "And what is your interest in this matter, Mr. McCann?"

"I'm a friend of Alan's. At least, I was. Until he disappeared."

Strickland regarded me carefully for an uncomfortable minute, then stood. "Wait here," he ordered. I'll bet not too many people disobeyed Sheriff Strickland when he used that tone.

"I don't think you should have used the word 'body' just then," Alan advised helpfully.

"Alan, I really don't want to be caught talking to myself in a sheriff's station," I warned.

When Strickland returned he carried a manila folder in his hands. Grunting, he lowered himself back in his chair, wet his thumb, and leafed through the papers, taking his time. Finally, he raised his eyes and looked at me. "I'm afraid your name appears nowhere in this file, Mr. McCann."

"I didn't make any statement or anything at the time," I responded lamely.

Strickland closed the file and set it on his desk, then eased back in his chair and put his hands behind his head, staring at me. I tried to remain still under his tight examination. "Case is still open," he told me.

I found myself very unhappy that I had aroused the sheriff's curiosity.

"Do you know something about this man's disappearance you would like to report?" he probed, his instinct taking him right to the heart of the matter.

"Not that I'd like to report, no," I answered evasively. I decided the bravest thing to do was flee. I moved to stand. "I'm sorry to have taken your time," I apologized.

"Just a minute." Strickland tried to give me a friendly smile, then, but the effect under those hard blue eyes was even more intimidating than his glare. "Can I get you something, a cup of coffee, maybe?" .

"No, no thanks."

"Mr. McCann. Ruddick McCann, right? That's what your license says."

"Yes, sir."

"Have you ever been in any trouble with the law, Ruddick?" Strickland asked with forced casualness.

I gulped. Why was he asking *that*? "It's Ruddy," I stalled. "My friends call me Ruddy, I mean."

"Ruddy." Nothing in his expression indicated that he

wanted to be considered one of my friends. "Answer my question, please."

"No. Actually, no," I responded.

We sat there as he processed my lie, the disbelief clear in his expression. The clock ticked on the wall with a loud, intrusive pulse.

Strickland opened his desk drawer, pulled out a tooth-pick, and inserted it into his mouth. A flash of insight told me that the slim stick of wood had come to replace cigarettes for Sheriff Strickland not too long ago. "Why don't you tell me what you came here to tell me, Ruddy," Strickland suggested.

I sighed. In for a penny . . . "Well, I think I know where to find Alan."

Strickland waited.

"I was in the woods today. And . . . I think I know where he is. His body."

"Uh-huh." We sat in the room for a solid minute—I know because I heard sixty ticks from his clock. Then Strickland started asking more questions—what was I doing in the woods, how had I come to know Alan Lottner. Every query dug up another lie, until I felt help-lessly lost in my own deceit. I stood up.

"Look, Sheriff, I came to do you a favor, here. Are you interested or not? I need to get back home."

"Sit back down, son," he commanded. As I did he sighed, reaching for his hat. "All right, you give me a minute to round up a couple of people, and we'll head out to take a look."

The "couple of people" turned out to be three car-loads full. I rode with Timms and Strickland, but in the rear seat, separated from the two lawmen by a steel mesh screen. Timms kept turning to stare at me with a burning intensity, but it was Strickland that I was worried about. I imagined most people who came to his attention were ultimately sorry they had done so.

"*What if I'm not there? My body, I mean,*" Alan fretted as we bounced down the familiar one-lane road toward the burned-down cabin. I had no way to alleviate his concerns, and at that particular moment didn't care about them anyway.

When I directed the sheriff to pull over near the fallen oak tree, everyone jumped out and began messing with equipment. Timms carried a shovel, the coroner a black bag, and another fellow a huge tackle box and two cameras slung over his shoulders. He took pictures of the trail and the woods before Strickland would allow us to proceed to the spot I showed them.

"*Here we go,*" Alan said, his voice trembling with tension.

"Sheriff, mind if I wander over there a minute? Take a leak?" I asked.

Strickland surveyed the woods with his cold eyes and then nodded.

I stepped away from the little group, making fresh tracks in the snow. "Look, we've got a problem," I said urgently. "If they find your body down there, how do I explain how I knew where to find it?"

"*You ever see the movie* Ghost Story? *When they find the body, the ghost ceased to exist. That's the rule.*"

"That's not what happened in the book," I replied.

"*Okay, but the book was fiction,*" Alan answered.

"Like the movie *wasn't*?" I snapped. "Would you listen? I told the sheriff I was walking in the woods and I saw your body, and now they're having to dig for it. The ground was covered with snow! How do I explain that?"

"If that happens, if I disappear forever, promise me you'll stay on the case," Alan begged. *"See that Burby and his accomplice go to prison for murder."*

"So this is all about you," I noted.

"Well yeah, it is," Alan shouted. I winced as his voice echoed around inside my skull. *"They are digging for my body. Any moment and I might cease to exist."*

"Okay. Okay, I get it. Though wouldn't that be best? Suppose this is what it is all about—we find your body and then your spirit can stop wandering the earth, searching for repos in northern Michigan. Would that really be so bad?"

"Yes! I want to find out what happened. I want to see Kathy again. Dammit, Ruddy, I don't want to die!"

"Got something!" Timms shouted. More pictures were taken. The coroner knelt in the dirt, spoke to Strickland, and then Timms dug some more, moving carefully. The photographer opened his\box and removed some tools, including what looked like small paintbrushes.

I crept closer, conscious of Strickland's eyes on me. What Timms had found didn't look human to me, just a bunch of dirt. The coroner kept reaching in and gingerly poking at it. "Sheriff," he called softly.

Strickland gave me a glare to freeze me in place, then squatted next to the coroner, who was pointing at the ground.

I saw what the cops saw—some finger bones protruding from the muddy pool that had filled the black cavity in the earth from when the toppled tree pulled up its root ball. Alan was under water.

"Use the shovel and bail this out," Strickland directed Timms. "Carefully."

I turned away, feeling a little sick, when Timms's efforts revealed a muddy skull. I walked a few yards away.

"I'm still here. I'm still here," Alan babbled. *"If that's it, if they found my body, I'm not going to vanish after all."*

After a time, Timms finished his work and the men huddled around the hole. Strickland straightened, looking right at me with an unreadable expression. He brushed off his pants, coming over to put a hand on my shoulder. "Well now, we got a ways to go before we can identify the body as Alan Lottner, but it is definitely big enough to be a male." Strickland was eyeing me carefully, thinking something over.

"Yeah, shot in the head!" Timms exclaimed as he came up to us. A sharp look from his boss shut him up.

The three of us stood there for a moment, and then Strickland made his decision. "Mr. McCann, there's a lot here I don't understand, but the one thing I'm sure of is that you haven't been truthful with me. You're involved in whatever this is a lot more than you've admitted to. Until I get it all sorted out, I need to keep my eye on you. I'm afraid I am going to have to arrest you on suspicion of murder."

With undisguised joy, Deputy Timms clamped the cuffs down on my wrists, sending a quick bite of pain up my forearms. I ignored Alan's outraged jabbering and concentrated on exercising my right to remain silent as I was led to the sheriff's car and put in the backseat.

How could I have been so stupid?

Timms kept staring at me in his rearview mirror as he steered the car down the highway. "Happened so long ago, probably be no charges if you just tell the truth," he ventured after a few miles, using his expert interrogation skills on me. He twisted around and gave me a friendly, innocent look so phony it looked like it was hurting his face.

"Eyes front, Deputy," Strickland murmured.

The color climbed up Timms's neck at the mild rebuke, and the glare he shot my way in the mirror indicated he felt it was somehow all my fault. I pointedly ignored him.

Strickland was mostly quiet, going over things in his mind. He'd sniffed me out as an ex-con and my story was collapsing under its own weight, but other than the fact that I knew where a body was buried there really wasn't any reason to suspect me of killing anyone. He shifted in his seat to glance at me and he could read my resolve in the tight press of my lips—now he might never find out what happened.

A few more deputies were waiting for us as we pulled up to the jail, looking like an overstaffed valet parking service. Though their behavior in front of their boss was strictly professional, something in their high energy let me know they were pretty excited about all of this. Timms was less restrained, grinning openly at his pals.

The booking sergeant instructed me to hand over my personal belongings, and that's when I broke into a sweat. I did *not* want to go through this again. "Sheriff Strickland?"

He raised an eyebrow.

"In my wallet, there, you'll find a business card for a Ted Petersen. Would you mind calling him for me? I think that will get everything straightened out here."

Strickland broke my request into segments. "Are you giving me permission to search your wallet?"

"Yes, sir, I am."

"Who is Petersen?"

"He's a lawyer now, but he used to be my parole officer."

"Parole officer." Strickland gazed at me. People don't have parole officers unless they were convicted of a crime—I was pretty sure Strickland knew that. "So you want me to call your lawyer for you," he stated finally—not saying he wouldn't, but letting me know this was not something he would normally be inclined to do.

"I just think you should talk to him. It will help clear some things up." I waited for the question I knew was coming.

"Parole officer. What were you in for, McCann?"

I sighed, feeling defeated. When I spoke, it was with a considerable ration of self-loathing. "Murder. I was in prison for murder."

13

Out of Control

My words hung in the air for what seemed a full minute.

Strickland hid his surprise behind those steely eyes. He nodded: I'd traded him enough information for him to make the phone call.

Behind me, I could sense Timms and his buddies glancing at each other, and, of course, Alan was going nuts.

"Murder! You've committed murder? You're a murderer? You murdered somebody?"

I let him go on conjugating the verb *murder* without betraying anything in my expression. Strickland motioned for the sergeant to continue processing my admission, and a few minutes later I was led down a row of completely empty cells and shoved into the one farthest from the door. I looked around and shivered. *Not again.*

"My God, Ruddy, would you please tell me what's going on?" Alan pleaded.

"What's going on," I muttered pleasantly, "is that I have just been arrested for the killing of Alan Lottner of East Jordan."

"What was that about your parole officer? What did you mean that you were in jail for murder?"

"Prison," I corrected. "This is jail. I was in prison. Believe me, big difference."

"But why? What happened?"

I took in a big, unsteady breath. "Alan, I'm sorry, but that is one thing I will never, never talk to you about. All right? I don't ever talk about it. To anyone."

"But—"

"No, Alan. Let it go," I interrupted.

There was a long silence. *"With a record, though,"* he said finally, *"this could be big trouble. I could tell by the way the sheriff was looking at you."*

"Could be big trouble? Do you not see the steel bars in front of me?"

Yet I wasn't worried about Strickland—he'd do his duty. Timms, though, was another matter—it was his spiritual ancestors who used to hang people from trees without a trial. I'd met his kind in the joint, men with weak minds and strong bodies who didn't so much control the prisoners as participate in the mayhem. I didn't ever want to be in a position where Timms had me to himself to play with.

Which is precisely what happened within the hour.

When the door opened at the end of the corridor I stood and peered down to see who it was, already so bored with incarceration I was willing to endure any sort of interruption just to have something to do. I caught sight of Timms and instantly realized he was up to something—he had a sneaky look on his jug-shaped face, like a little boy breaking a rule. Someone came in behind him, smaller, standing in Timms's shadow.

"Oh no," Alan moaned softly.

It was a woman. The proprietary way that Timms steered her down to my cell suggested that this was *his* woman—the deputy was showing off his big murder arrest to his honey.

"What are you up to, Timms?" I asked in a low voice.

When she stepped closer, I literally gasped in shock.

Katie Lottner.

She was even prettier than I remembered. I was drawn to her eyes, which were large and blue as they stared at me. She had the sort of long brown bangs that had to be continually pushed away from those eyes, and she did this now, an automatic motion I found charming.

"Careful, babe," Timms warned. "Don't get too close."

Alan was quietly moaning, almost keening—I guess a father would always recognize his own daughter, even after eight years. I ruefully reflected on my resolve not to tell him I had already met her—I felt like that one was going to backfire on me pretty soon.

"You? You're the one?" Katie asked in a quiet, flat voice. Ignoring Timms's restraining hand on her shoulder, she curled her fingers around the steel bars and leaned her face in close. "You killed my father?"

I was trying to figure out how best to answer this when she spat at me, mostly missing her target. I jumped back, startled.

"*Oh no, Kathy*," Alan groaned.

"You . . . you son of a bitch," she choked.

"Now Katie, move back there. Come on," Timms soothed, pulling at her.

The door at the end of the hall banged open and we all turned. Sheriff Strickland stood on the threshold, backlit so we couldn't see his face. "What's going on here?" he demanded in a voice that sounded like he was speaking through a megaphone. He and two other men marched down the hallway. His eyes darted to me first— secure the prisoner, always—and then rested for a moment on Timms, then on Katie. "Miss Lottner, what are you doing here?" he asked finally, his voice carrying a touch of sadness.

"I made him bring me," Katie explained at once, moving a half step in front of Timms as if to physically protect him.

"Oh, Miss Lottner. Katie." Strickland pursed his lips. "You shouldn't be here, now, you know better."

She crossed her arms defiantly. Strickland shifted his gaze to the deputy.

"Timms."

The man visibly swallowed, and I almost felt sorry for him. He was taller than his boss and probably eighty pounds heavier, but the image that came to mind was of a small dog being whipped by its master.

"You know good and well that you are in violation of procedure. Bringing a civilian down here is not only expressly prohibited, but runs contrary to every single bit of common sense I ever thought you had. Do you have anything to say for yourself, mister?"

Timms numbly shook his head.

"You are on unpaid leave for the next seventy-two hours. Please escort Miss Lottner upstairs. Advise the duty sergeant that you are departing this shift immediately. Understood?"

Timms gave a trembling nod. Katie, biting her lip, made as if to say something, but Strickland held up his hand. "Excuse me, Miss Lottner. Deputy Timms, I have just one more thing to say to you. I've told you more than once that that badge of yours doesn't mean you get to break the rules, it means that you, more than anyone else, have to follow them. I've never in all my years in law enforcement seen anyone do anything as lame-brained as this. I've half a mind to ask the board to re-move you from your position. I can't have a man in my department who won't toe the same line as everybody else. We understand each other?"

When Timms coughed up a reply, it sounded like it had been dragged across cement. "Yes, sir."

"All right. Step to it, son. Katie, please leave with Dep-uty Timms; this is a restricted area." Strickland pointed down the hallway. I found myself intrigued by his selec-tive use of her first name, depending on the circumstance.

The two deputies dared a glance at each other as Timms and Katie fled the lockup. You had to admire the sheriff—his public chewing out had been a deliberate act of atonement, giving me something back for the humili-ation I'd suffered. Our eyes met and I nodded.

Strickland motioned one of the deputies forward. He slid the key card through the slot, punched some num-bers, and the cell door clicked open. "So." Strickland eyed me up and down. "Why didn't you tell us you were in Jackson State Prison when the murder was committed?"

I had planned my answer to that question for the past hour. "You didn't tell me when the murder was com-mitted."

If the light had been better I might have seen a glint of amusement come and go in his eye. "Ah. Well, come up-stairs, Ruddy, and we will process you out of custody. And maybe while that's going on you'll tell me just how it is that you knew Alan Lottner's body was buried out there in the woods, since, as it turns out, you couldn't have put it there."

"Sheriff," I sighed, "you'll never believe me."

I had read too much permission into the friendly banter, because his expression hardened. "You will tell me just how it is you knew the body was buried out there in the woods," he repeated.

Oh, great.

As we turned the corner, Katie Lottner jumped up out of her chair, where she'd been fidgeting, apparently planning an appeal of Deputy Timms's suspension. Her eyes widened when she caught sight of me strolling unshackled next to the sheriff.

"What . . . he . . ."

"Please, Katie, you go on, this is official business," he urged her gently, blocking her view of me with his body in case she wanted to spit some more. She didn't move. Strickland sized up the situation and reached a decision. "Now, I don't know what Dwight told you, but this man here couldn't have done anything to your father. He's not the one, Katie. We're not even sure what happened."

"Couldn't have done anything?"

"He was in prison when your father disappeared, Katie. He just finished off his parole not long ago."

"Prison for *murder*," she protested.

"Yes, well, vehicular homicide." Strickland glared at me but I didn't yield: As far as I was concerned, I killed somebody and that was murder. "But he's served his time, Katie, and we have no right to keep him here."

Her eyes were doubtful as she turned back to me. "Then how, how did he—"

I was tired of being discussed as if I weren't there. "I was walking in the woods," I explained. "And I just . . ." I shrugged.

"You just happened to notice a body submerged in

muddy water and identified it as someone who has been missing for eight years," Alan suggested helpfully.

Katie was looking at me with wide eyes, and I knew she was thinking of what had happened back in my jail cell. "Oh," she whispered. "Oh, I'm so, so . . ."

"Hey, forget about it," I advised uncomfortably. "Happens all the time."

She cocked her head, contemplating the sort of life I must lead if people spat on me all the time. Congressmen? Despite the circumstances, we smiled at each other.

Disapproval flickered across Strickland's face. "Miss Lottner, you need to be going," he told her. His voice was still gentle but it held a definite "move along" tone that probably could have quelled a riot. Katie responded with a nod of surrender.

As soon as she was out the door my pleasure at seeing her evaporated and I realized I'd had all of the jail I could stomach for the day. Strickland was giving me an expectant look that I doubted few people ignored, but he'd said himself there was no reason to keep me here. "Sheriff, I have to leave. I have business in Kalkaska."

He shook his head. "It will have to wait, Mr. Mc-Cann."

"He can't hold you unless he places you under arrest," Alan stated. Legal advice from a dead Realtor.

"I have to go, Sheriff," I repeated, giving him a look both honest and unyielding.

After a moment he grunted, acquiescing. *"Told you!"* Alan hooted triumphantly. The sheriff and I made an appointment for the next day. Strickland raised a farewell hand as I backed my truck out of the parking lot, and I had the strange feeling the guy sort of liked me.

Alan and I were both silent for the first few minutes

as we drove, processing the day's events. Charlevoix had long faded in my rearview mirror when I cleared my throat. "So, Alan. I'm sorry about that. About your daughter, I mean. Must have been sort of a shock."

"Sort of a shock," he repeated. *"The last time I saw my little girl she was sixteen years old. Now she's a grown woman. And you say it was 'sort of a shock.' "*

"What's with the attitude all of a sudden?"

"The attitude? When were you going to tell me you knew my daughter?" he demanded.

"Oh, that."

· *"Yes. That."*

"Yeah, well . . ." I sighed. "I met her a week or so ago."

Alan was completely silent in a way that felt heavy with judgment. I rushed to fill the void. "But I just found out yesterday that her last name was Lottner. You were asleep, and I called her and got her answering machine. It's sort of hard to figure out what to do in a situation like this, you know?"

He was still quiet.

"I mean, either I'm so completely demented that I'm sitting in a padded cell somewhere hallucinating this entire thing, or I just led the police to dig up the body of a murder victim based on *his voice in my head.* I think I'm to be forgiven if I'm making a few mistakes in etiquette, here."

Finally Alan spoke, his voice subdued. *"She was still a child when I saw her last. God, she was so beautiful."*

"She's beautiful now," I interrupted.

"She is, isn't she? Ruddy, seeing her today was the hardest thing I've ever done in my life. But I wouldn't have missed it for the world."

A deer caught my attention and I braked. She stood

by the side of the road, appearing alert and wary, but I knew from experience that her species was prone to sudden leaps across the pavement without wisdom. After I crept past she dashed back into the woods.

"I wonder if that was the right thing to do," Alan reflected.

Somehow I doubted he was talking about slowing down for the deer.

"Before today everything was . . . contained. Now my body has been found, the sheriff's suspicious, we know Burby is one of the killers, Katie's involved . . . it feels like it's getting out of control."

"Out of control? You were shot, remember? When was it ever *in* control?" I flicked on the windshield wipers to clear away the light spray of sleet that had begun to fall. "I think we needed a little disorder, shake things up a little. See what we can make happen."

Alan thought about that, and when he spoke again, his voice sounded troubled. *"I just have a bad feeling that things are going to start happening very quickly now, and we have no idea what they are."*

It gave us both something to worry about on the way back to Kalkaska.

14

And There She Was

Alan was asleep as I parked my truck. I walked into the Black Bear and stopped dead, frowning—in what I would classify as an unauthorized activity, Kermit was setting down a couple of beers for a few people at a table near Bob the Bear. Becky was standing with her back to the room, hunched over something by the cash register.

Kermit's eyes widened when he saw me. "Hi, Ruddy," he called in Becky's direction, like a prairie dog sounding a warning. "I was just improvident, here," he explained to me.

"I'll say," I agreed.

Becky was working the little machine that we used to authorize credit card numbers. "So this is Kermit's get-rich-quick scheme?" I asked in a disapproving tone.

Her lips pursed, a sign of stubbornness from childhood, but she didn't look up at me. Curious despite myself, I stepped around the bar to watch. She was entering credit card numbers and dollar amounts from a computer printout. None of the amounts was more than three hundred dollars. "Shucks," Becky muttered, writing *unauthorized* next to one of the entries. I could see that for the entire page, close to a quarter were winding up unauthorized.

"Why would a psychic send us credit card numbers for somebody over his limit? Wouldn't the psychic know?" I asked innocently.

"Are you going to tell the same joke over and over again?"

"Becky, I have a real, real bad feeling about this."

"You do?" Her eyes were bright with resentment. "That's funny, Ruddy. I've already run ten thousand dollars today. That means we've made more than a thousand dollars for a couple of hours' work. Can you see anything wrong with that?"

"Well, yeah. If you're making more than five hundred an hour entering numbers on a little machine, why doesn't everybody do it?"

"Kermit explained all that."

"What does Kermit get out of this, anyway? Besides demonstrating to all of us that he is a financial wizard."

Becky didn't look at me.

"Becky, you're not paying him, are you?"

"He gets a commission, yes," she shot back.

"How much?" I pressed.

"Third."

"A third?" I repeated incredulously. "That's a hell of a commission. I don't think even drug dealers get that kind of percentage!"

"You get your third, too, Ruddy, so I don't know what you're complaining about," Becky responded bitterly.

I thought about this. Instead of my being paid a salary

as a bouncer, the arrangement that had always worked for us was that when the Black Bear made money, Becky divided the profits between the two of us. But this felt wrong, and after a moment I shook my head. "Keep it," I told her. When her eyes grew blank with an emotion I was afraid might be hate, I gestured at the bar. "Put it into your improvements," I mumbled. "Or, as Kermit would probably say, your improvisations."

A genuine smile lit up her face then, full and open, without her hand reflexively covering it, and I gulped back a sweeping affection that literally choked me. If this made her happy, how bad could it be?

Her smile turned even more radiant as Kermit rounded the bar, and in a motion that caught me in complete surprise, the two of them embraced, their lips coming together for a kiss. I realized I was staring, and spun away so they wouldn't see the shock on my face.

Jimmy wandered in an hour later and we played a little pool. We're not any good at it and I don't think either of us even likes it, but we've probably shot ten thousand games over the years. I felt Alan wake up, but he remained moodily silent.

"Hey, what were you doing last night?" Jimmy asked as he gracefully stroked the cue ball, causing it to kiss off the four to no good effect whatsoever. He mournfully shook his head.

"What do you mean?" I lined up and shot, spreading the balls around but not sinking any.

"I saw you out jogging or something," Jimmy explained. "About four miles down the road. I honked, but you just kept plugging. You trying to lose some weight?"

"What are you saying?" I asked indignantly. "You think I need to lose weight?"

"No, uh . . . I just wondered what you were doing, is all."

"Well, it wasn't me."

Jimmy executed an artful banking shot that managed to miss hitting any balls at all, which isn't easy to do.

"Have you guys never played pool before?" Alan asked wonderingly.

"I do push-ups and lift weights at the club," I stated forcefully, recalling that sometime in January I'd had a pretty good workout.

"Bet you can bench a lot, huh," Jimmy patronized with such wide-eyed sincerity I felt ashamed.

"No, I . . . ah, hell. Forget it."

"You should tell him that we tracked the bounced checks to the bank president's wife, see if he recognizes her name," Alan suggested.

I felt myself bristling at what I felt was unneeded advice. "I've found out a few things about those checks of yours, but I'm not ready to talk about it," I said forcefully to Jimmy.

"Okay."

I know Jimmy pretty well, and gradually I became aware that there was something on his mind. When Jimmy has something he wants to say, he is usually completely silent. "So what's going on?" I prodded, accidentally sinking the eight ball and prematurely ending the game. We put away our cue sticks with relief.

"I guess that check bounced. You know, the one I cashed down at the hotel."

"Yes, but we were expecting that, weren't we, Jimmy?"

"The thing is, I got fired."

"They fired you?" I felt a flash of protective anger.

"For bouncing a check? Didn't you tell them they could take it out of your pay?"

Jimmy was carefully aligning the cue sticks with each other.

"Jimmy?"

"Uh, I sort of had sex with one of the guests again. I mean, she wanted me to, but I guess they thought that I shouldn't have done it since they made an official policy about me. So they told me that the bounced check money was me getting severed."

"*Severance*," Alan and I both said at the same time.

"Yeah, that." He met my eyes. "I'm really sorry, Ruddy. I just kinda couldn't help it."

"*How can you not help having sex with someone?*" Alan demanded. I didn't get it either, but then again, I didn't look like Jimmy Growe.

"Well wait, Jimmy, you live at the hotel," I said suddenly. "Are you kicked out?"

He nodded. "Tomorrow."

"Well hell." I blew out some air. "Okay, you can live upstairs at my place until you find something else. There's nothing in the little kitchen up there but you can use mine."

The look he gave me was full of wonder and gratitude, and just like with Becky I felt my throat tighten. Repo Madness was turning me into a softie. I punched him in the arm to keep things manly. "Tell you what, Jimmy," I said. "I'll even cover your tab tonight, if you answer me a question."

His brow furrowed. "Aw, Ruddy, you know I'm no good at this kind of stuff."

"No." I shook my head. "Just . . . what do you think

of Kermit Kramer? And if you say he's got a great vocabulary, I am going to pick you up and heave you out
into the street."

Clearly, this was exactly what he'd been about to say,
and my abrupt censorship rendered him mute for a moment. His mouth opened and shut a couple of times.
"Well . . ." He cleared his throat, took a thirsty gulp of
beer, and then scrunched his face in concentration.
"Becky likes him," he offered finally. "A lot."

"How can you tell?" I pounced.

Jimmy gave me back a blank stare.

"You have to ask?" Alan inquired.

Alan was right—Jimmy could probably sense a
woman's interest the way Jake knows when I've opened
a can of dog food.

"She laughs a lot when he's around," Jimmy mused,
trying to put it into words that an amateur like me could
understand. "I think . . . he seems to like her a lot, too."

"Bull," I growled, my face suddenly hot. "He's just glad
to have someone run his credit card numbers for him."

"What?"

"Never mind. I'm going to go grab us each another
beer."

"What's your problem?" Alan demanded. *"Did you
expect your sister to become a nun or something?"*

"Go to sleep, Alan."

"Why do you treat people like that?"

"You know, I've just about had it with your lectures.
You can either be a separate person or my conscience,
you can't be both."

When I came back, Claude was just settling in at the
table with a war-weary expression. I gave him the beer
I'd intended for me and sat.

"God, what a mess," he moaned.

"What's the problem?"

"It's Wilma. When I call her and she recognizes my voice, she hangs up without saying anything."

"Well, what did you expect, Claude? You gave her a disease."

"I did not!" he shouted shrilly.

Grinning, I got up to replace my beer. Becky was still running numbers.

Not a bad night. Some fellows limped in around eight, their attitude and muddy attire leading me to believe they had been out playing a little baseball, getting some practice in for the season, which would be starting in a couple of weeks. I knew most of them and wandered over to say hello, but I could see I made them uncomfortable so I didn't linger. I sometimes forgot how the local athletes felt about me.

Janelle didn't arrive at all, which was no surprise to me, but I could see Claude had been expecting her. Every time the door opened he glanced over with a hopeful expression, but he was always disappointed. Eventually he threw some money on the table and walked out.

The door shut behind him and then opened right back up, and there she was: Katie Lottner.

15

No, I Did Not Mean to Do That

Katie spotted me and came right across the floor without hesitation. She held out her hand like we were going to have a business meeting, and I took it with a little disappointment, though I don't know what else I'd been expecting. I reflexively checked to see if Alan was awake, which he was, and so what? I'd done nothing wrong, I reminded myself.

"The sheriff told me where you worked. I wanted to . . . I was going to get you a card. You know, for . . ." She gestured toward my face.

"Oh, you don't have to do that. It was all a misunderstanding."

She poked her finger into her hair and twirled it like a fork full of spaghetti. A reddish highlight flashed in her brown hair as she did so, and I found myself staring at it, enthralled. *"She used to do that same thing with her hair when she was little,"* Alan murmured, jerking me out of my reverie. *"It means she's worried about something."*

"Well . . . I'm sorry," she said.

We looked at each other. I couldn't stop grinning at her, even though I felt foolish. "So," I said finally. "What sort of card do you get for something like that?"

Her mouth curved into a soft smile. "I figured they'd have something suitable."

· "Sorry I spit, I'll try to quit?"

"Oh please," Alan protested, but Katie laughed.

I steered her over to a table and sat down. Becky appeared, her eyebrows raised in unwelcome curiosity. My sister could read me so well. I introduced the two women. So what if I was interested in Katie? No big deal—but I could feel my face flushing, for some reason.

Jimmy came over and I found myself tensing, feeling like I suffered mightily in comparison to my supermodel buddy, but Katie was friendly and nothing more. After Becky brought us both our drinks, Jimmy went back to the bar and I had Katie all to myself, like a date.

With her father there.

"So, you're the bouncer here?"

"More like the business manager," I promoted myself. "My sister owns it, and I run it." I glanced over at the bar to make sure Becky couldn't hear me.

"I'm not going to sit here and listen to you mislead my daughter," Alan warned, as if he could sit anywhere else.

I told her how the Black Bear came to get its name, then cleared my throat. "Actually, I don't spend much time here. My profession is collateral recovery."

Katie thought about that.

"Come on, Ruddy," Alan prodded.

"I'm a repo man," I elaborated. *There, happy now?*

"You're kidding me! Have you ever been shot?"

"Not anywhere vital." Her eyes widened. "No, just joking. I've had a gun pointed at me a few times, but not with intent to use it." I thought about Einstein Croft. "Well, maybe once."

"I could never do that." She shook her head, undoubtedly picturing something far more glamorous than the gritty reality of climbing under a car to attach a tow hook to some deadbeat's bumper.

I told her about how I got into the business—Milt hired me because he figured a large ex-football player could intimidate people into giving up their vehicles. I left out the part about being beaten up by a twenty-pound goose.

"So the theme of this conversation is, all about me, by Ruddy McCann," Alan noted sardonically.

"But what about you?" I asked smoothly.

"Well, what about me?" she replied lightly.

I took a deep breath and broached the subject I'd been dreading. "Well, Deputy Timms, are the two of you . . ."

Against my fervent wishes, she nodded her head. Her finger started twirling her hair. "We're supposed to get married."

"What?" Alan shouted.

"Ah. Well, congratulations, then, that's just great."

Her eyes regarded me with an unreadable expression. "Thanks. It isn't official, though. I mean, he hasn't proposed formally; we've just talked about it."

"Oh."

"Ask her about Marget," Alan directed.

I decided that next time I had Alan alone we were going to have a serious talk about when it was appropriate for him to speak. I asked Katie about her family, and she told me her mother had remarried and still lived in the East Jordan area. "I'm living with her, actually," Katie informed me with an embarrassed blush. "But in a trailer, out back. Like, a travel trailer with a kitchen and all? Just until, you know, Dwight and I figure things out."

"I hope that doesn't happen for a while," I said sincerely. I thought maybe I was pushing too hard, but she just gave me a frank and appraising look.

"Did we ever meet before?" she finally asked softly.

"Well, yeah. I saved you from certain doom in downtown East Jordan by using my superpowers to start your car, don't you remember?"

"No, I mean . . ." She shook her head and her hair shimmered and that's all it took to change everything—the sight of her hair, her curls lightly bouncing on her shoulders. It was like my heart had climbed a wall and then fallen over onto the other side. I barely knew her, but I was in love with Katie Lottner.

"It's just that I have this sense from you, like we were friends before, somehow. It's a feeling."

"Well, did you ever hang out with the Kalkaska High School football team?" I asked.

"No!" she replied, laughing in surprise.

"Top ranks of government? Upper strata of society? Internationally recognized cultural events?"

Alan tsk-tsked in my ear.

"No. Well wait, would the East Jordan fireworks be considered a cultural event?" she asked.

"Was there a truck pull afterward?"

"Sorry."

"Then no."

"She thinks she knows you because she senses me, here inside you," Alan chided.

I decided that wasn't right, because I didn't want it to be. "Maybe in a former life," I suggested, "we were together as repo men."

She laughed again. "Do you believe in that, though? In reincarnation, of former lives becoming mixed up in current ones?" she asked me.

"Oh, I do now," I admitted.

"Me too. I believe it, too," she said. We stared into each other's eyes as if sharing a secret.

After an hour or so she told me she had to go and I offered to drive her home. "Well, thanks, but that would mean leaving my car here," she pointed out.

"Not necessarily. Come on, I'll show you."

I drove Katie Lottner home in the tow truck, dragging her Ford behind us. She kept laughing at the arrangement. "This is the first time I've ever done *this.*"

To show off, I demonstrated how hitting the repo switch dropped all the lights both in and out of the truck, so that we were humming up M66 in eerie darkness for a moment. I flipped the switch back on before Alan had a chance to start panicking.

"This is it," Katie said as I slowed for a long curve, my headlights playing across a nice little place on the steep banks of Lake Patricia. The travel trailer was clearly visible in the backyard, the lights on inside.

When I unhooked her car in her driveway we stood there in the chill air a little awkwardly. I thought about taking her into my arms and kissing her senseless, but instead just stood there grinning when she said, "Well . . . ," and briefly touched her lips to my cheek.

I watched her enter the main house and noticed a woman standing at the window. Corn silk hair, not at all like Katie's, but the same pretty features. She watched me impassively as I slid behind the wheel and threw the truck into reverse.

Marget.

Alan served up one of his frosty silences most of the way back, and I stayed quiet myself, enjoying it.

"Well, aren't you going to say anything?" he finally demanded.

"Nope."

"Do you know how hard it was for me to sit there quietly during all that?"

"No, and neither do you. You talked the whole time."

"She's my daughter!"

"She's a grown woman," I reminded him. "Besides, didn't you hear her? She's engaged to marry about three hundred pounds of deputy sheriff."

He groaned. *"No, that's not what she said. She said they were talking about it. Nothing's been decided yet."*

I decided not to tell Alan how much pleasure it gave me to agree with him.

Something like a warm breeze hit my face while I was out walking Jake, as if spring was taking a test run. He lifted his nose to it and seemed to drink it in, and for once didn't drag me back to the house the moment he'd finished lifting his leg. "That's right, Jakey," I told him. "Summer will come again, I promise."

Jake wagged as if he understood me. I pictured him running through the summer grasses, something he still did, if for much shorter bursts. "Such a good boy," I told him. He wagged again. I stooped down and looked him in the eyes. "Hey," I said softly. "I want you to live a long, long time, okay? I need you. You're my dog."

"I don't get it. Why can't you treat people the way you treat your dog?" Alan asked.

I sighed. "Alan, can you just give it a rest sometimes? I get it, I'm not perfect."

Alan didn't answer.

I plugged in my cell phone to charge it and went through the process of adding some minutes to my account. Who knew, maybe Katie and I would be talking to each other.

The next morning I awoke in an irrepressibly good mood, and then things got even better. Milt had a hot tip for me: A skip was back in the area.

"A skip is a guy the bank can't find," I told Kermit, who was along for the ride at his uncle's request. I felt like whistling—my fee doubled on skips. I'd make five hundred dollars if I located this guy's vehicle, which would erase two-thirds of my debt to Milt.

The customer's driveway was a long, muddy rut pointing up a hill to a shoddy-looking cabin at the top. Parked right next to the cabin, front end facing us, was the truck we were looking for, a green Toyota. Across the road from the mouth of the driveway a steep bank dropped down to a stream, the water dark and deep from runoff. I didn't like that: It meant I'd have to slow way down to make the turn out of that driveway to stay in control, and when I'm stealing a vehicle I like to put my foot into it until I'm out of rifle range.

I looked at my hands and they were not trembling. My heart wasn't beating any faster than normal, and my stomach felt fine. Repo Madness, my ass.

"Slide over," I instructed Kermit. "Drive my truck. Follow me."

I grabbed the keys out of the folder and started climbing the muddy driveway, my eyes on the cabin. I was still forty feet from the truck when I saw the customer sitting at his table drinking coffee. His eyes widened.

"He sees us!" Alan yelled.

"No, he sees me. I think you're still safe," I corrected. I nodded at the guy, raising my hand in greeting. "Okay, fine, just coming to see you," I muttered, smiling hugely, with an "I'm-not-here-to-steal-your-truck" expression on my face. He jumped to his feet.

Great.

I sprinted for the Toyota, which was locked despite the fact that there was no one around for three square miles. *"Hurry! Hurry!"* Alan was shouting unhelpfully. The key went in as the customer's cabin door banged open. I jumped inside, locked the doors, and fired up the engine. He started shouting at me but I had it in drive and tromped on the accelerator.

"What'd he say?" I asked, grinning in triumph.

"I think he said 'no brakes'!" Alan replied.

Frowning, I put my foot on the brake pedal and it went to the floor without resistance. I started pumping it, watching in alarm as the road rushed toward me.

"Look out!" Alan yelled.

The driveway dipped where it met the road and the impact was like crashing into a wall. The truck bounced hard, my teeth clicking together, and then I was across the road in a flash. The windshield cracked as a thin tree tried to stop me. The front end of the truck dove toward the river and then I had a face full of air bag.

"I hate those things," I muttered. My nose felt like it had been hit by a basketball.

"Ruddy, we're sinking, we're sinking!" Alan shouted, his voice shrill. We were, indeed, sinking. The front bumper was pointing down at a severe angle and water was rushing in around my feet. I looked out the window and saw that the stream was up to the side mirrors. I searched

my mind for a sense of déjà vu, but felt nothing. This wasn't anything like the last time I'd been in a vehicle in the water.

Alan had become unintelligible with his panic, but he was still shouting at me. "Alan, shut up," I snapped.

"Ruddy, I can't . . . I'm afraid of drowning. We have to get out!"

"Well, no one wants to *drown,* Alan," I agreed irritably. There was a bump as the front end of the truck gouged the river bottom. We started to slide sideways a little, listing over on the right. I tried to shove open my door, but the rush of water pushed it back shut. "My God, that water's cold!" I gasped.

"Ruddy, please."

I pushed the electric window stud and, against all expectations, the window slid down. As it dropped into the door, more water gushed in, and there was a sure sense of the truck growing heavier. I grasped the top of the window frame and struggled to climb out, my clothes sodden with frigid water.

Three heaves and I was free of the truck. I instantly sank, my winter clothes dragging me down. A lot of thrashing and I got my mouth above the river for a quick, choking breath. I groped for and snagged a tree root, pulling myself over to the bank. The cold water sapped my strength, rendering me almost immobile, and my breath came in shallow gasps as I clambered up the soggy slope.

Kermit stood at the top, his mouth open in wonder. "Hey!" he shouted down at me. "Did you mean to do that?"

16

What the Psychic Said

Within an hour of plunging grill-first into the river we had three state patrol cars hanging around, lights flashing as if there were a bank robbery in progress. No laws had been broken, but the local cops were acting as if they'd never seen anything as exciting as a submerged Japanese pickup truck.

I had changed into the overalls I kept in the truck for when I needed to crawl under cars, slipping on heavy rubber boots to complete the outfit. Still, I was a long way from warm, and shivered as I watched local people driving up to view the action.

The *Charlevoix Courier* showed up to take pictures and I told Kermit to stop trying to get a signal on his cell phone and go represent his uncle's firm, so he ran down to the riverbank and stood there, frowning at the sunken truck in a condemnatory fashion.

"So what was that all about when we hit the river?" I asked Alan. "We weren't going to *drown*, it was no more than five feet deep."

"I've just always had a fear of drowning. In fact . . . well, you'll think this is stupid."

"Everything that has happened to me today has already been stupid, so you might as well go ahead."

"A psychic told me one time that I would die drowning."

"A psychic?" I mulled this over. "Did you pay with a credit card? Because Becky could use some more numbers."

"No, I was a kid. It was at a fair, and this woman supposedly could see our futures. She was a real scary-looking lady, and she told me I should stay away from the water, because someday I would drown. It really frightened me. I've had nightmares ever since, and they are all the same—I'm in a river, and someone is holding me under, and I can't breathe and I know I'm going to drown."

"Okay, except no one was holding me under water. We were in a Toyota pickup truck."

"I'm not saying it's rational, Ruddy. It's just a fear I have."

"And anyway, aren't you forgetting something? The woman was wrong. You didn't die from drowning, you died from getting shot by a funeral director."

"Well, right, except that I'm alive now, through you."

"What? What do you mean? You aren't alive, you're some sort of stowaway. And when this is over, you'll go back to . . . to where you were before you showed up inside my head."

Alan was quiet for a minute. *"Ruddy, what do you mean, when this is over? When what's over?"*

"When the curse is lifted, or whatever. You can't be saying that you think we're going to be hooked together *forever*. Is that what you're saying?"

"I'm not saying anything," Alan soothed.

"Don't talk to me like that!" I shouted. "I'm not crazy!"

I stopped, suddenly conscious of the fact that everyone's attention was riveted on me. When a man is dressed like a duck hunter and standing by himself yelling "I'm not crazy," most people are likely to draw precisely the opposite conclusion. The newspaper shot a picture of Kermit looking gravely concerned at my outburst.

"Alan, that can't be. That just can't be," I fumed more quietly. Alan didn't respond.

Well, what a great way to start the day. I told Kermit to ride with the AAA truck and call his uncle from the Toyota dealership. He could ask the mechanics to work up an estimate on what it would cost to convert the submarine back into a pickup. Meanwhile, it was time for me to have some more conversation with the sheriff of Charlevoix County.

The drive to the jail was one of those sloppy, sliding journeys with ruts of wet snow grabbing at my tires and slush from passing semis hitting my windshield as if thrown from a bucket.

"Do you think maybe you should slow down?" Alan asked anxiously. My answer was to put my foot into it until my back end slid a little, and then I eased off, feeling like I'd made my point even if I wasn't sure what it was.

Sheriff Strickland came out to the lobby to greet me, offering a cup of coffee, which I gratefully accepted. "So now, Ruddy. I've made some calls about you," he advised as we settled into our chairs.

I registered the fact that I was "Ruddy" all of a sudden. "You did," I answered cautiously.

"Uh-huh. I know now the whole story of what happened

to you. Real shame." His voice was kind, his expression indicating his sympathy for my plight.

I gave him a look to let him know I wasn't buying. In Barry Strickland's view the only victim was a seventeen-year-old girl buried in the cemetery in Suttons Bay, and the fact that I'd had an assured NFL career cut short by a visit to Jackson State Prison wasn't worth wasting any tears over.

He read me perfectly and decided we'd had enough warm and fuzzy time together. He stuck a toothpick in his mouth and fixed me with those steely eyes. "So tell me how it was you came to know about the body of Alan Lottner being buried out by the Jordan River."

I coughed. "Sheriff, you're going to think this is really strange."

His expression didn't change.

"I dreamt it."

"I think it's 'dreamed,' " Alan advised.

"Is it dreamed, or dreamt? Anyway, it was a dream."

He watched me take a long, stalling sip of coffee, his face hard. "A dream."

"Yes, sir. I dreamed about the place, and I dreamt that Alan Lottner was buried right there, under that tree. So I just figured . . ." I spread my hands, wishing Alan would say something useful.

"You dreamt he was buried there."

"Yes, sir. Dreamed."

"Alan Lottner."

"Yes, sir."

"When did you have this dream?"

"When? Oh, a couple of weeks ago. The night of the big windstorm? It was a very real dream, more like a vision almost. I just couldn't get it out of my head."

"Can't get me out of your head. Cute." Alan snickered. I wondered how I might inflict pain on my good friend Alan.

Strickland leaned forward and stirred his coffee, carefully watching the black liquid swirl around. When he glanced up I could almost hear the steel jaws of the trap closing over me. "How did you know it was Alan Lottner?"

I took far too long to respond. "What?" I finally answered cleverly.

"In your dream you saw a body buried under a tree, right?"

"Yes, sir."

"How did you know who it was?"

"Well, I . . . um. Well, I told you I was a friend of Alan's long ago."

"The body was so badly decomposed we had to use dental records to identify it," Strickland advised me in clipped tones. "You could have been Lottner's twin brother and you wouldn't have known who it was."

I opened my mouth to provide a reasonable explanation, but nothing came out and I shut it again.

"Let me ask you something, Ruddy."

"Yes, sir."

"You seem to have your life back together. You and your sister own the family business in Kalkaska. I know Milton Kramer, you pick up repos for him, nice little income on the side. Off parole, clean start."

"Sure."

"Why do you want to protect him?"

"I . . . Sorry?"

The sheriff leaned forward and I felt my chair pushing into my back as I unconsciously tried to retreat.

"Whoever you talked to in Jackson who told you where the body was buried. Whoever killed Alan Lottner. You're out now, you're a citizen. Why the hell do you want to put all that on the line for somebody you met in prison?"

Wonderful. I'd had more fun when I was in a sinking Toyota.

Strickland reached into his drawer and pulled something out, tossing it on his desk with a sound like a bouncing coin. It was a golden ring, skittering at me across the desktop so that I automatically caught it.

"Know what that is?"

I looked at it. "Kalkaska class ring."

"From your graduating year. Ever see it before?"

"I had one like it," I admitted faintly.

"Uh-huh. You said 'had.' "

"Lost it."

"Look inside. You see any initials?"

I swallowed. "RJM."

"As in Ruddick Jourden McCann?"

I stared at him, speechless.

"Want to tell me how you 'lost' it?"

"I was canoeing down the Jordan River after graduation with some buddies. There was a lot of horseplay. Fell in the water a bunch of times. When we got to East Jordan I noticed it was missing. Must have fallen off. You know. Cold water."

"We found it in the same hole as Lottner's skeleton."

"Right, I forgot. The ring!" Alan exclaimed. And as soon as he said it, a piece of the dream came back—me reaching for something gold in the water, deciding I needed to get it back to the person who owned it.

"You have been lying to me since you opened your mouth, son," Strickland said.

"No! Well, okay. I have to say, I *did* lose my ring, I don't *know* how I knew it was Alan Lottner. But you have to listen to me, Sheriff. I did have this dream, really, I did!" I closed my eyes briefly, remembering just how extraordinarily clear everything had seemed.

He's dead.

No, I'm not.

When I opened my eyes I saw Strickland regarding me, considering. He could sense some truth leaking into my narrative but wasn't sure what it was.

"I think I've got enough to charge you with accessory after the fact right now as it is, McCann. This is a murder investigation and you'd do well to remember that."

I swallowed.

"I do not know how to say it more plain than this: You do not want me and you to wind up on opposite sides of this thing."

"No, sir, I do not."

I watched him watch me, feeling like I should be holding my breath. Probably it was only the fact that he'd already arrested me once that week that kept him from sending me back to his cells for what my mother always called "a little time out."

He eased back in his chair, shaking his head at me. He gestured at the file on his desk. "I wasn't here then, but about the time Alan Lottner disappeared, there was a fire bombing at a nursing home there in East Jordan. Apparently the ATF was called in, and they took a real interest in Lottner for a while."

"Why?" I asked, shocked.

Strickland shrugged. "Seemed odd, him disappearing and then a month later we've got thirty-two people dead."

"For God's sake, I was murdered. And I wouldn't have the first idea how to set a bomb," Alan protested.

"Oh, but Alan wouldn't do something like that. I mean, come on. What does he know about bombs?"

Strickland gestured toward the file. "Says here it was a pretty simple thing, really. Dynamite, blasting cap, a digital kitchen timer, and lots of gasoline to accelerate the flames. Place went up like a matchstick. Whoever did it padlocked the front and rear doors of the place—he wanted those people to fry. Never caught the guy, never came up with a motive, never uncovered a single witness."

"Well, it wasn't Alan."

"Oh, I don't think it was. Your reaction is interesting, though. So you knew the victim really well."

"Ah, no, not all that well," I said uncomfortably.

Strickland just looked sad. He regarded his watch. "Well, that's about all the horse manure this old man can stand to see a person shovel in a single day without choking on it. I'm going to tell you right now that you've used up your marker with me over that little fiasco in the jail the other day. You do know what I'm saying here, don't you."

It wasn't a question. "Yes, sir."

"You ever had a polygraph exam?"

I shook my head. There'd never been any reason; I'd admitted my previous crime.

"You willing to take one now?"

"Maybe you should ask your attorney about that," Alan suggested worriedly.

I licked dry lips. "Sure."

Strickland grunted. "My polygraph examiner is on vacation in South Carolina. He decides to come back to our winter paradise, I'm going to send a car to collect you for another little chat. That be okay by you?"

"Yes, sir."

"You lie to me again, I'm going to place you under arrest for obstruction and anything else I can think of. Clear?"

I nodded.

Once in my truck, I pounded my steering wheel in frustration. "Dammit, Alan! See what you've gotten me into!"

"Me? I think you're forgetting who the victim is, here."

I started the truck. "And I think you're forgetting that if I'm arrested, you're arrested. If I go to prison, you go to prison," I said agitatedly.

"Well, whose idea was it to say it came to you in a dream? I never told you to say that."

"Well, what was I supposed to do?"

"So are you going to tell him about me?"

"About you what, hanging out in my head like some sort of talking brain virus? No, I do that and he'll be locking me up for my own good."

"So what are you going to say?"

"You know what, Alan? Figuring that out should be your job."

The idea of evading Strickland's questions while wired up to a lie detector gave me cold sweats. I spent the next several days spastically turning my neck anytime I spotted someone out of the corner of my eye, expecting to see one of Strickland's deputies bearing down on me with a pair of handcuffs. At home I'd jump to the window and peer out whenever a car passed, gulping audibly when it was a patrol car. My new tenant, Jimmy, picked up my nervousness and would peer out at traffic even if I forgot to.

Jake, however, was impervious to my mood. He enjoyed having Jimmy around, and would lie next to Jimmy's chair when the TV was on, giving me a pointed look as if to say, "I like this guy; he doesn't drag me on forced marches in the cold."

When Jimmy opened the back door to head up the outside stairs to his room for the night, Jake always followed as far as the threshold, but that staircase looked like it wasn't worth the effort. Jake would sigh, glancing at me in disappointment, before collapsing back on his blanket.

"You have to like me best," I informed him testily. "It's in the Dog Manual."

Another side effect of digging up Alan's corpse: I was back to being Kalkaska's most notorious citizen. I decided to avoid the Black Bear after it became evident that all everyone wanted to talk about was me walking in the woods and seeing a skeleton lying there with a bullet in its head. The inference that Alan had been exposed to the elements made him angry, as if it implied he was somehow lazy. I was just glad the story about the dream hadn't gotten out.

Milt called me at home and asked if maybe we should go writ of replevin on Einstein Croft—sue him, in other words, to get the pickup back. I begged him to give me a few more days. A writ of replevin would mean the sheriff would pick up Einstein's ride, and I'd get paid nothing unless I served the summons for fifty dollars. "Any movement on Jimmy's paper?" Milt asked softly.

Jimmy looked up from the pizza we'd put on the coffee table, sensing we were talking about him.

"You know he lost his job at the hotel, Milt. He hasn't got any money."

"I need to see something pretty quick, Ruddy. That motorcycle has bad piston rings; it's not worth even a grand. Why did he buy the thing—what was he, drunk?"

"No, he was just being Jimmy. I'll get right on it, Milt. Got anything for me?"

"Nope, been pretty quiet. Just Croft."

"Okay, okay." I hung up and Jimmy gave me an anxious look. "You go down to the dealership, ask Claude if the shop is hiring like I told you?"

He nodded. "And the gas station. Nothing."

I knew it was the truth. It was the second week of May. The snowmobilers had quit coming, the summer trade was more than a month off—everyone was just hanging on, waiting for the change of season. The saying up here is that we go from mud to mosquitoes with only a week in between.

"I'm going to head over to the Black Bear in a little bit, help out Becky," he told me.

"She can't afford to pay you anything," I snapped.

Jimmy looked hurt. "Yeah, I know that. Just to help out, I meant."

"Sorry, Jimmy," I muttered.

"We need to go talk to that bank president's wife, find out why she's sending the checks," Alan advised, which irritated me because I'd just been thinking the same thing.

The next morning I was on the Blanchards' doorstep at nine A.M., lifting the brass knocker and letting it clank several times. Jake, who'd joined me for the ride, solemnly watched me from the side window of my pickup. I waved at him and his floppy ears twitched. I loved when they did that. A woman answered, regarding me curiously.

"Mrs. Blanchard?"

She nodded. Mrs. Blanchard looked to be in her late twenties, a pretty woman with light-brown hair. Her cheekbones were high and her legs were thin. I felt like a big dumb repo man standing on her front porch. I glanced over and Jake, bored, had already stopped watching in favor of a nap.

I told her my name and the fact that I worked for Milton Kramer, letting the details of how I made my living flow out one at a time to see what she reacted to, which turned out to be absolutely nothing. She remained cool, leaning on the door a little as if ready to slam it on me.

"She's pretty impressed with you," Alan remarked dryly.

"Bad checks, things like that," I was saying. Still nothing.

"Tell her you've got a voice in your head," Alan snickered. When I was finished here I was going to find a river and drown myself just to punish him.

"Mr. Kramer cashed some checks for a guy named Jimmy Growe."

There! Just for a moment, something passed through her eyes, the faintest hint of darkness. Then a forced blandness took over, her eyebrows arching up questioningly.

"It seems the checks were taken from the bank when you were working there. I just came by to talk to you about that."

"Why? What makes you think that I know anything about it?"

"She looks like she's enjoying herself," Alan observed.

Her grip had relaxed slightly on the door, and though we were both still standing she seemed in no hurry to be rid of me.

"Well, you were issuing starter checks at the bank, weren't you, Mrs. Blanchard? You had access to the packets." I was honor bound not to tell her that Maureen at the bank had recognized her handwriting.

"So?"

"Ma'am, may I ask you what your maiden name was?"

A faint flush spread across her cheeks. "Adams," she answered faintly. "Why?"

"Most people choose variations of their own names when they assume a pseudonym," Alan informed me sardonically. *"Hence Adams becomes Wilenose."*

"I . . . Ma'am, I might as well tell you, I know that you were the one who sent Jimmy Growe the checks. What I don't understand is why you did it."

"And this Mr. Growe attempted to cash these checks?" She responded with a forced casualness.

"Yes."

"Is there a . . . can he go to jail for something like that?"

I stared at her, making her wait for a reply, and her eagerness showed itself just a little before she regained control. "Maybe," I told her, but she had her satisfaction wrapped down tight and didn't share any of it with me.

"Well, I'm sorry I can't help you with any of this, Mr. McCann."

I tilted my head. "You didn't know he'd cash them. You sent them for some other reason."

"There is no point in this conversation. I'm sorry I can't help you." She shut the door firmly, the brass knocker lending solid punctuation to the action.

Jake lifted his head when I got back in the cab of the truck, his soft ears swaying. His look seemed to say "what a dumb way to make a living." I kissed him on the nose.

"I'm sorry that I can't earn enough lying on a blanket with you all day," I told him. To a large degree, I meant it.

Much to Jake's disappointment, Jimmy wasn't home when I trooped in a few hours later, feeling defeated. I opened the refrigerator and scanned the nearly empty insides, reflecting on how much electricity I was using just to keep some mayonnaise cold.

Jimmy had continued Becky's initiative, picking up after the both of us. He'd even vacuumed the carpet. I had to admit I liked having him around. Me, Jake, Jimmy, and Alan—our own little dysfunctional family.

"Mrs. Blanchard clearly sent those checks to Jimmy. Did you see her expression? She was toying with you," Alan observed.

"She was not 'toying' with me," I retorted. "I agree, though—she's the one. I just can't for the life of me figure out why."

I moodily picked through the stack of bills on the kitchen table. It was still all quiet on the repo front, and I had something like four bucks in my wallet. The sense of being in the middle of a famine was even affecting my body; my pants were fitting more loosely, as if I were dropping weight.

"Maybe we should go up to East Jordan and stake out Nathan Burby, see if he makes contact with the shovel guy," Alan suggested.

"Well, that would take gasoline, Alan. I need to preserve gasoline so that when I get a repo assignment I don't have to walk to it. I had Milt apply the money for the sunken Toyota to my outstanding debts to him."

"Well, what are you going to do?"

"I don't know, Alan!" I exploded in frustration. I heaved myself off the couch and put on a jacket. Becky would feed me.

17

You and Me, Kermit

The Black Bear was like an easy chair in my mind: worn, comfortable, familiar. When I opened the door the shock made me blink. Becky had been busy.

She watched me approach her across the floor with apprehension seeping into her eyes, but when I glanced pointedly at the curtains, the new paint, and the hardwood flooring that had replaced the linoleum, she straightened a little, her jaw firming in resolve.

"Hi, Ruddy," she greeted.

"What's all this?" I demanded.

"All what?"

"What are you doing? What's with all the artwork, and the curtains?"

"I told you I wanted to spruce the place up, use a warmer color palette."

"But this looks ridiculous!" I railed. "Can you imagine what Dad would say about windows covered with—with lace?"

"Oh, Ruddy."

"Come on. This is the Black Bear. Next thing I know, you'll want to get rid of Bob."

She glanced over at the stuffed bear, then back at me, her eyes unreadable.

"Becky, no."

She shook her head. "I'm not going to get rid of the bear."

"But can't you see what you're doing? You're changing the, the . . ."

"Ambience," Alan suggested.

"The ambience of the place!"

"Exactly." Her eyes glared at me through her smudged lenses.

"But don't you understand that the beauty of this place is that it never changes? You drive through Kalkaska and there's a McDonald's now, and a Burger King, and just when you think the whole place has lost its charm, there's the good old Black Bear Bar and Grille, thank God. Why, we've got people who've been coming here since we were little kids! What are they going to think when they see you're playing dollhouse?"

"Wow, what an asshole you can be," Alan noted.

Becky fixed me with the sort of unhappy, mournful expression she had mastered through a lifetime of practice. "What do you think, that nothing in life will ever change?"

"Just not the Black Bear," I told her forcefully.

She shook her head slightly, and I found her unwillingness to fight back infuriating. "It's that goddamn Kermit," I stormed, attacking from another direction.

That got her. "What about him?" she murmured.

I gestured at her sweater, which was stylish and feminine. "He's got you all . . ." I groped for words.

"Hot," Alan suggested. *"Sexed up."*

"Jesus!" I snapped at him.

"Ruddy, don't you dare even'think of going near him. If you do . . ." Becky warned.

I leaned forward almost eagerly, bearing down on her. When we were growing up my physical bulk so overwhelmed her frail frame I regularly bullied her just by staring her down, and I was doing it now. "Or you'll what?" I taunted.

She backed away from me. "I'll get an injunction and banish you from the Bear. I'll get the judge to say you can never come in here again." She folded her arms.

I sat down on a bar stool as if sucker-punched. "Oh."

"This has got nothing to do with him, Ruddy, except maybe that he's given us a way to make the money to buy some things."

"Running numbers," I muttered glumly.

"Using our nonswipe account to help another vendor," she agreed.

"Would you really do that? Get a judge to have me banned from a place I've been coming to since I could crawl?"

"Would you really hit my boyfriend?"

"Your boyfriend?" I shouted.

"Hush," Becky warned, glancing at our only customers—a couple of guys sitting in the corner. The flush on her cheeks looked less like embarrassment than sheer pleasure. *Becky McCann has a boyfriend.*

"So what else are you going to do around here? Put in a conveyor belt with sushi on it?" I inquired sullenly, not quite giving up.

Her gaze turned unreadable again. "You'll see," she promised.

Jimmy came out of the men's room at that moment

and stopped dead, looking as if I'd caught him in bed with another guest at the hotel. He was wearing an apron, the pockets stuffed with a notebook and some napkins. "You're a *waitress?*" I demanded.

Jimmy swallowed. "Becky said I shouldn't tell you until we saw how it went, but she gave me a job as a waiter. You know, serving food and drinks."

"I know what a waiter *does,* Jimmy." I tromped off and sat under Bob like a soldier determined to give his life to defend his bear. I moodily drank a Vernors ginger ale, occasionally holding my hand up to cover my mouth so I could talk to Alan.

"I'd say she pretty much handed you your balls in a paper bag," he observed.

"You just don't know. These changes would drive my father crazy."

"A lot of friends of your father still come in here, do they?"

"All the time," I affirmed.

"Any here now?"

I looked around. "No."

"Last time you were here, big bunch of them come in?"

"Well, no."

"Previous week? Two weeks? Even one of them show up?"

"You have a point here, Alan?"

"Just that maybe your sister should be allowed to make the changes she thinks will bring in more business. This sure isn't the kind of place I'd want to hang out in."

"You are welcome to leave any time," I told him frostily. I decided the soda wasn't working for me and switched to beer.

Night settled, and Jimmy left to go on a date. No one

came in. By nine o'clock Becky and I had the place to ourselves. She busied herself installing a rack over the bar, from which she dangled shiny new wineglasses that hung upside down like bats. I guessed we would no longer be serving wine in old jelly jars. When she was finished, we stared at each other from across the room, each feeling the lack of business eloquently supported our respective positions.

Kermit showed up around closing time. "Kermit, over here!" I shouted at him. Becky, who'd been disapprovingly tracking my repeated trips to the keg machine like a school hall monitor, gave me a hard look.

"*Ruddy* . . ." Alan said warningly. What was it with everybody?

Kermit came over and stood a little uneasily in front of me. "Sit," I invited, kicking a chair out from the table. The action was meant to be smooth but instead the chair fell over. Becky stared at me and I shrugged.

Kermit righted the chair and eased down into it.

"You and me, Kermit."

He swallowed.

"Tomorrow, we are going to go cook the literal goose of a certain Mr. Albert Einstein."

Kermit stared at me.

"*Einstein Croft*," Alan hissed.

"I meant Einstein Croft. What did I say, Albert Einstein? That's pretty funny." I noticed I was the only one laughing, and cleared my throat. "Anyway, come pick me up in the tow truck at seven A.M. in the morning. We're going to take the thing from his job. That work for you?"

He nodded. "Sure."

"Okay. Okay, then." I stood, formally shook his hand,

nodded with dignity at my sister, and marched out into the frigid night air.

"Well I hope you're satisfied with yourself," Alan lectured as soon as he had me to himself.

"Satisfied, that's the word I've been looking for. I'm feeling perfectly satisfied, yes."

"You're drunk. I hate it. I can't think straight."

"Oh my God, are you telling me you're drunk, too?" I hooted. This struck me as so funny I had to sit down on my front steps, laughing until tears flowed out of my eyes. "Well, there goes my idea of making you designated driver."

"You disgust me."

"Oh, great! I have a voice in my head and he's disgusted!" I shouted out into the Kalkaska night.

"I was killed, Ruddy. We know who did it. We know where he works. Yet you've done nothing about it."

"Yeah? And what, exactly, am I supposed to do?"

"We need to figure out why he did it. We need to find out who the man with the shovel is. We need to do something, Ruddy, instead of just sitting around all day reading mystery novels."

"Maybe I don't care, did that ever occur to you, Alan? You got killed by two guys in the woods. Well I'm sorry, but that's not my fault. I never asked for this, for you to come into my head and start talking to me. You're a total stranger—why should I give a rip about you?"

"You're an abuser. You abuse your sister and you abuse your own body. You're a murderer."

"Yeah? Well you're *drunk,*" I sneered. I stumbled into my house. The stack of bills on the table enraged me and I swiped them off onto the floor, kicking at them and mostly just hitting air. "Maybe I like it messy!" I yelled.

I picked up a pillow off the couch and threw it across the room, where it landed on a kitchen chair and instantly looked like it belonged there, offering me no satisfaction whatsoever. That was the whole problem.

"I changed my mind!" I bellowed. "I am *not* satisfied!"

Jake eased off his blanket and padded over to me, concerned. He shoved his wet nose at my hand and gazed up at me loyally, ready to take a walk or do anything else that might make me happy. "You are the best dog in the world," I assured him. I held his face in my hands and smiled into those sorrowful brown eyes. "The best dog. My best friend."

I shambled into my bedroom and Jake followed me, a question in his eyes. "No, Jakey. In case I ever manage to get a woman in here I can't have you in the habit of lying in my bed. Want me to sleep on the floor with you? I will. Would you like that?"

His look indicated my offer wasn't good enough.

I didn't remember setting my alarm clock, but it woke me up at six A.M. I felt like I'd been beaten. I eased out of bed and went into the bathroom, looking sadly into the old, red eyes of Ruddy McCann. Life was not supposed to turn out like this.

Jimmy had picked up the scattered bills and placed them back on the table. It looked like he'd polished all the glasses in the cabinets, too. I didn't deserve a friend like him. I found some thousand-year-old beef taquitos in the freezer and heated them in the micro, eating them quickly, before Alan woke up and gave me a nutrition lecture.

I was experiencing the hangover of a lifetime. My head was oddly clear, but the rest of my body hurt as if I'd spent the day working out in a gym and then being beaten by a karate instructor. My stomach was tender with the same soreness I'd feel after the first day of crunches at football practice.

I sighed despondently. I was only a couple of years older than Deputy Timms, but he looked a lot younger, his chubby cheeks lending his face a childlike exuberance, like maybe a child with really ugly parents. When Katie compared the two of us, she probably thought of me as over-the-hill.

The light was blinking on my message machine. As if she sensed I was thinking of her, it was Katie Lottner, asking me to come to a memorial service in East Jordan on Thursday at Burby's funeral home. The county had finished its tests on Alan's body and released it to the family. I listened to the message several times, straining through it to find nuggets of passion or affection, but it sounded like I was just one of several on a list she was working. I was glad Alan wasn't awake to hear about his funeral; I wanted to think about a way to tell him about it.

Kermit picked me up at exactly seven o'clock, handing me a tall cup of coffee as I climbed in. Okay, so maybe he wasn't such a bad guy. When he passed over a new folder from his uncle, I decided his behavior was downright acceptable.

The assignment was an easy one—some nut living in the woods "off the land" and selling the bank's collateral—a Ford Explorer—a part at a time to the junkyard so that he'd have a few bucks to his name. I hauled in what was left of the thing, and because the guy was officially a skip, got five hundred bucks for my efforts. "I guess the bank thinks if you don't have a mailbox or a phone you're a skip," I observed to Kermit.

By the time we were headed up to see Einstein Croft,

it was almost noon. The sun was out, the sky was blue, the temperature was flirting with the fifties. We were about to repo Albert Einstein, and I now owed Milt nothing and had a check coming besides. "I'm back to being satisfied," I told Kermit. He eyed me cautiously.

We swung into the guest parking of Einstein's job, avoiding the guard who protected the employee lot. "Okay, here's the thing. I'm going to get the receptionist to let me use their internal phone system. As soon as she does, I want you to distract her, okay? You're good at that kind of thing—just keep talking to her, don't let her overhear what I'm doing, all right?"

Kermit seemed nervous. "Wait! What should I say?"

"I don't know. Explain the difference between swipe and nonswipe."

We pushed open the glass doors and approached the receptionist in the lobby. She looked like she was barely out of high school—thin and pale, her short hair dyed unnaturally black. Up close I could see the small holes where she inserted her lip and nose rings after work.

I hooked my finger over my shoulder at the tow truck. "I'm supposed to phone the guard when I get here, somebody needs a tow. Can you connect me, somehow?"

She seemed unsure about my request, which was good, because it distracted her and kept her from asking me why I didn't just pull up to the employee entrance and talk to the guard in person. She picked up the phone and stared at the switchboard. After moving her lips and nodding as if she had a dead Realtor of her own to talk to, she brightened.

"Jed? It's Charlene. Hang on, please." She smiled at me triumphantly. The second she handed me the telephone, Kermit pounced on her with a focused ferocity.

"Have you thought about handling call overflows from your station?" I heard him ask.

"Hello?" I said, trying to sound like a factory employee, whatever that meant.

"Security."

"Hi, I need a tow truck, I busted my brake cylinder," I told him. "Can you call one for me?"

"Call it yourself, this ain't road service," he advised gruffly.

"Oh, well, I don't know how to make an outside call on this phone."

"Just dial nine, like every other phone system in the universe."

"Okay, so, when the tow truck pulls up, let it in, okay?"

"It'll make my friggin' day," he responded, hanging up.

So far, so good: a call from inside the factory advising the guard to let in the tow truck. Now we just needed to stall for a few minutes. Kermit showed no sign of winding down, so I pretended to be interested in a bunch of pictures hanging on one wall. They were all businessmen and women, each identified with little golden name tags.

When my eyes drifted across one of the photographs, my jaw dropped.

"Hey, Alan." I stood and stared.

"It's him," Alan breathed.

I reached out and touched the golden nameplate. "Franklin Wexler," I read out loud.

Unmistakably, the man with the shovel.

18

The Man with the Shovel

I strode over to where Kermit was still holding the receptionist hostage with a constant barrage of words. Her nameplate said CHARLENE.

"Hey, Charlene," I interrupted. "Can I ask you a question about that guy over there?"

Charlene's mind surfaced slowly, shaking off Kermit's conversation like a dog getting out of the water. "Who?"

"Franklin Wexler."

"Who?" she repeated.

"Come on, Charlene, snap out of it," Alan urged.

"There's a picture of a guy over there, and this little gold plaque says 'FRANKLIN WEXLER.' I take it he works here?"

Charlene frowned as if she had never noticed the pictures on the wall ten feet in front of her. "Those are board members," she decided.

"Okay, right. I'm interested in Franklin Wexler."

"They're board members," Charlene repeated.

"They're members of the board," Kermit interpreted helpfully.

"Right, I get that, but Franklin Wexler. Is he in?"

"Oh, no. They don't work here."

"They're board members," Kermit said again.

"Okay but what does that *mean?*" I snapped, losing patience. I knew Alan was going to say *"It means they're members of the board"* before he said it.

"They don't come in or nothin'. That's just the people on the board," Charlene elaborated.

"They're on the board but they don't come in?" I asked.

"Right," Kermit answered. I shot him a look.

"That's fairly common," Alan lectured me in a Business 101 tone. *"They're on the board and supposedly have oversight of the corporation, but the CEO actually runs the place. Technically, the CEO works for the board, and sometimes the chairman has a lot of power, but usually the board members don't do much but collect an honorarium."*

"I never seen 'em," Charlene avowed.

"Well, I need to talk to Franklin Wexler," I told her.

I saw the doubt in her eyes—a tow truck driver needs to talk to a board member? "Actually, *he* does," I amended, hooking a thumb at Kermit. "He's my boss. It has to do with his nonswipe account. Kermit, tell her the difference between a swipe and a nonswipe account."

Kermit drew in a breath. "Wait!" Charlene pleaded. "I don't know anything about them. They aren't in the company directory. I don't have any way to get in touch with 'em."

I mulled this over. "Okay, thanks."

"Franklin Wexler," Alan repeated in my ear. *"We*

should be able to track him down; that's an uncommon name."

Yes, Alan, I thought, *but I don't have time for that right now, I need to repo an Einstein.* I slapped Kermit on the arm. "You did good," I told him as we walked back out into the sunshine. "Now here's the plan. I'm going to hunch down in the passenger seat and pull a tarp over myself. You drive around to the side, where the entrance to the employee lot is, and tell the guard you're the tow truck for the guy who called. He's expecting you, so he'll just let you in. You drive far enough into the employee parking lot so he can't see you, then I'll hop out and switch places and we'll go hunting for Einstein's truck."

The plan worked like a dream. The guard waved us in without taking his eyes off his television and within a few minutes I was back behind the wheel of the tow truck, slowly cruising the rows of vehicles.

"What if the guard gets suspicious?" Kermit asked nervously.

"Relax, will you?" I muttered. Then I spotted the pickup I was after. "Uh-oh."

"What? What is it?" Kermit pressed.

"Looks like they're having a picnic. Guess we'll have to call it off," Alan remarked.

Drawn outdoors by the nice weather, a group of burly factory workers sat at a picnic table at the far end of the parking lot, eating lunch together and basking in the sun's rays. Parked directly in front of them, the back bumper not more than twenty-five feet from the picnic table, was Einstein Croft's vehicle. Einstein himself sat as if to keep his eye on the prize, facing his truck.

"That's the truck? Right there, in front of the table?

There are all those guys! They'll see us driving up!" Kermit exclaimed in alarm.

"Right, right. Okay." I thought about it, then turned my wheel sharply and drove down another row of vehicles, headed away from the picnic table.

"We leaving?" Kermit asked, relieved.

I turned the wheel again, then stopped. We were now all the way at the other end of the lot, the rear end of the tow truck facing the front end of Einstein's pickup. "Croft's driver's side window is open. That means the truck is probably unlocked. Manual transmission—I can yank it into neutral." I grinned at Kermit, who paled.

"Ruddy," Alan warned.

"Here's what we're going to do, Kermit. You ever notice the sling that hangs at the bottom of the tow cable?"

I nodded out the rear window, and he followed my gesture. Dangling from the high boom was the thick cable, and at the bottom were two heavy rubber skirts joined along the lower edge with a steel rod—the sling. "Okay. In a normal repo situation, you got three parts: the tow hook, the sling, and the safety chains. You put the sling under the front bumper and raise it—the car you're towing rests on the sling, but isn't attached to it—that's why you need the hook, which you affix to the car frame. And then the safety chains are your fail-safe option. That's a repo term meaning that even if the hook fails, the car won't fall off the sling because of the safety chains."

"This isn't a normal repo situation. The men are right there, twenty feet away!" Alan protested.

"But this is not a normal repo situation," I told Kermit agreeably. I slid out of the cab and yanked on the side lever, lowering the sling. Kermit watched me through the back window, his mouth gaping. When the sling was

all but touching the ground, I came back and got behind
the wheel. "I'm going to back her right up to the front of
Einstein's truck, *fast,* jamming the sling under it," I told
him. "I'll jump out and raise the sling just enough to get
the hook on the frame. You slide over to the driver's seat
and get ready to go. I'll open the door and pop the truck
into neutral. When I've got her hooked just enough to
get out of here . . ." I put the gear shift in reverse, grinning at him. "I jump back in and you floor it. We'll do a
better job of attaching things when we're half a mile up
the road. Simple. Ready?"

"What? No, wait . . ." Kermit protested faintly. I was
already backing up, looking over my shoulder, the transmission whining as I gave it some gas.

"This strikes me as very risky!" Alan announced in
alarm.

I was watching the guys at the picnic table. So far, none
of them had done anything but observe our approach. I
pressed down on the accelerator, ignoring Alan's gasp.

"Wait!" Kermit shouted.

We slammed into Einstein's truck with neck-snapping
force, his vehicle bouncing on the sling. I jumped out and
ran back, grabbing the lever and jamming it forward.
With maddening slowness, the sling began to lift. I realized
I was holding my breath, so I forced a casual expression
onto my face and exhaled, glancing over at the men at
the picnic table as I walked to the driver's side door.
Unlocked. I opened it and leaned in and grabbed the
gearshift, rattling it loosely. Neutral. Parking brake off.

Events were unfolding with such speed that no one
had even moved. Einstein himself had a sandwich halfway to his mouth and was frozen in shock. I nodded at
him. Just another five seconds or so and the front of his

truck would be up high enough to attach the hook and haul it off. This was going to work!

Suddenly the tow truck lurched, pulling away from me. I stared in disbelief. "No, Kermit!" I yelled. "Not yet!"

With a blast of black exhaust, Kermit took off, Einstein's truck trailing behind the tow truck. I gazed after him for a moment, then turned and looked back at Einstein. He and his buddies had come to life and were boiling off of that picnic table. They didn't look like they were in a good mood anymore.

For a moment it was my turn to stand frozen, and then I spun and sprinted after Kermit, who was speeding away. "Kermit! Wait!"

Einstein's truck was bouncing on the sling, threatening to let go, but Kermit kept accelerating. Cursing, I waved my arms at him as I ran after him through the parking lot.

In what I could only classify as more bad news, another lunch shift full of workers was emptying out of the big doors to my right and, spotting their buddies in pursuit of me, decided to take up the chase like a second pack of hounds joining a foxhunt.

Kermit reached the end of the row of cars and turned left, heading for the exit. With nothing to keep it on the sling, Einstein's truck decided it would rather keep going straight and dropped off the tow truck, gliding forward until it bounced up against a curb and stopped.

"*Look out!*" Alan shouted.

In front of me a couple of guys lunged out from between parked cars and blocked my path. I sized them up as if I had a football tucked in my outside arm and jinked left, cutting between them. Three more workers reached for me, their eyes widening in surprise as they realized I was already flashing past them. They fell in behind me and I heard the sound of their footfalls fading rapidly away as if it were game day at regionals.

Only one obstacle lay in my path: the security guard, who had stepped out of his booth and stood in the center of the narrow driveway, a bit hunched over, his arms out to his sides as if getting ready to give me a giant hug.

I suddenly remembered that when he played defensive end for East Jordan High School he was like an open valve; all it took was a little head feint, like *this*, and he was groping at the empty air. I sailed past him untouched.

I turned on the road and saw that Kermit was still driving away as if pursued by the hounds of hell. I ran after him, my legs moving up and down in easy cadence. Maybe it was the sunshine getting to me, but I felt better at that moment than I had felt in a long time. I was almost disappointed when Kermit pulled over; my legs wanted to keep going, run to the gym, lift weights, learn Pilates.

I was barely winded and full of endorphins. Kermit regarded my approach like the accused waiting for the judge to pass sentence. "So Kermit, at what point did you decide to leave me alone at the factory?" I asked, flexing my knees.

"Uh . . . ," he responded as eloquently as he could manage.

"Let me drive. You wait until I get up to fifty-five miles per hour, and then jump out," I told him pleasantly. He nodded, swallowing.

"*That was just crazy. Those men would have caught you before you could have gotten that truck hooked up,*" Alan fretted.

"Kermit, the voice in my head wants me to take you out in the woods and eat your liver," I said. Kermit's eyes bulged.

"For God's sake, Ruddy, he's going to think I'm a lunatic," Alan complained.

I called Milt and told him we had to go writ of replevin on Einstein Croft. "I'll serve the summons, though, Milt," I said. I'd at least get fifty bucks for throwing some papers at Einstein's face.

"And where do we stand with Jimmy?" Milt asked.

"You know, Milt, your focus on collecting money isn't nearly as much fun as lending money," I chided. When he didn't give me so much as a dry chuckle I cleared my throat. "Why don't you hold on to fifty bucks out of what I have coming from picking up the Explorer this morning," I suggested.

"You sure that's a good idea?"

"It's Jimmy, Milt," I said simply.

Between the sunshine and the way the oxygen was coursing through my leg muscles my mood remained nearly euphoric, and I opened the door to the Black Bear for Kermit as if he and I were old friends. Becky gave us a bleak look, waving some papers at us. "Kermit, what are these?"

Becky held three notices in her hand, the type that bank computers issue when you've overoptimized your checking account. Kermit read them, his brow furrowed, while Becky looked over his shoulder at me and shrugged.

"These are customer inquiries. What it is, is the customers are disputatious on the nonswipe charge."

Becky and I looked at him blankly. "English, please," I requested.

"See, the psychics are telling the customers that the

charge will be the Black Bear Bar and Grille, but the card-holders forget sometimes, so when they see the charge, they don't know what it is, and they're like, 'Black Bear in Kalkaska? But I'm in Omaha or some dumb place,' so they dispute it with the credit card company. So the bank sends us this notice."

"Wouldn't the psychics know in advance which customers will forget?" I asked cleverly. Both Becky and Alan groaned.

"They should," Kermit agreed.

"What do we do?" Becky asked him.

"The thing is, you have to protect the integration of the nonswipe account. So we don't even challenge it. We credit the customer back the full amount. Our thirteen percent plus the psychic's eighty-seven percent. Take the eighty-seven percent out of today's receipts from the psychic line. How much did we get today?"

I found myself irritated over the "we," but didn't say anything.

"We received two thousand two hundred," Becky stated. I turned a fond gaze upon her and her ability to manage numbers like that.

"Okay, and these are for a total of six-twenty, so we're fine," Kermit pronounced with such confidence I instantly felt apprehensive. "We get any more of these, handle them the same way."

It was on my mind to advise Kermit that he was to ask, not tell, Becky what to do, but I knew Alan would chide me later for always busting the guy's chops, so I bit my lip.

Becky invited me to step out the back door into the alley, and I followed her, curious. I blinked at a fresh wall of cinder blocks. "What's this?"

Becky looked flushed with excitement. "I've never laid bricks or blocks or anything before. See how level it is?"

Okay, well, if it made my sister happy to build a wall in the alley, what did I care? There was still plenty of room for cars to get around. "It's nice," I offered.

"*It* is *level*," Alan agreed.

She laughed. "Well, it's not for *decoration*. Come here, look." She took my arm and pulled me around the wall. It was actually a three-sided corral, with the trash Dumpster sitting in the middle of it.

I immediately spotted what she had done wrong, and wondered how to tell her about it. "You made a little house for the Dumpster," I said, stalling.

"No, it's . . . the county requires it. I told you we had to build one."

"But Becky . . ." I sighed. "The open part should be facing the back door, not away from it. See? Not only is it more of a trip to walk around with a bag of trash, but when the truck comes, it's one way." I pointed up the alley, gesturing how when the truck approached it would be facing the closed part of the corral.

"It's one way but the truck has to back up to get to the Dumpster."

"Oh." I nodded thoughtfully, hoping to appear to be, well, full of thought. When I glanced at her, she was wearing a neutral expression that somehow looked familiar.

We went back inside. *"Your sister is pretty nice not to point out how stupid you sounded,"* Alan advised.

I went to sit by Bob the Bear and Jimmy came over to take my order, just like it was a real restaurant. "You want to hear the special?" he asked.

"The *what*?" I blurted, laughing. I sensed Becky's eyes

on me like gun turrets and choked it back. "Yeah, sure, what is the special?"

The special was plank whitefish. "Do you eat the plank, or the fish?" I joked. Jimmy shrugged uncomfortably— what the heck was wrong with everyone, how come I was the only person with a sense of humor?

"What is it with everybody?" I muttered to Alan.

"They know you're a little irrational on the subject of the Black Bear. Maybe they're afraid of your reaction," Alan suggested.

"I do not need to be psychoanalyzed by a voice living in my head."

"Who better?" Alan retorted.

The whitefish came and Becky and Kermit watched me eat like parents sending their first child off to kindergarten. I gave them a thumbs-up and they heaved visible sighs of relief.

"You don't need that much salt," Alan observed, so I put a little more on. *"Aren't you going to eat your vegetable?"*

"It's broccoli. Nobody eats broccoli," I informed him.

"You have got to eat vegetables!"

"I did, I ate the fries," I responded indignantly. I realized a woman I didn't know was sitting alone at a table and watching me talk to myself over the top of her *Cosmo* magazine. I gave her a cheery nod and she dove back behind the cover.

Claude came in and sat down with me and ordered a chicken burrito as if we had been serving them for a hundred years. "Hey, Claude, there's this weird thing in the sky, you seen it?"

He gave me a blank look.

"Real bright? Heat coming off of it? Been up there all day, very strange."

"You mean the sun?" he asked.

"Oh, is that what it is? Been so long since it's been out, I didn't recognize it," I chortled.

Claude looked absolutely bewildered. Jimmy slid a plate down in front of Claude and asked him if he wanted pico de gallo. No one seemed to think it was an unusual conversation. "Jimmy, Janelle been in?" Claude asked.

Jimmy's look darkened. "Janelle?" His tone was so sharp I blinked in surprise.

Claude didn't seem to catch it. "Yeah, it's like she's avoiding me or something." He gave us a one-of-the-boys look. "I don't understand her. You know we've never even done it? Closest I got is second base. Women," he snorted. "Can't live with 'em, can't return 'em for a full refund."

Jimmy's face turned red. "What the heck is wrong with you, Claude? You and Wilma have been together my whole life. She loves you, man. You got history together. Are you crazy? Janelle? You know what I would give to have the kind of thing you and Wilma got?" His mouth worked inarticulately for a moment, while Claude just stared at him in astonishment. I don't think any of us had ever seen Jimmy this angry before.

Finally he extended an accusing finger. "You are making the biggest mistake I've ever seen, Claude. You think Janelle isn't going to dump you the second someone closer to her age comes along?"

Claude clearly didn't appreciate the "closer to her age" part. He opened his mouth.

"Aw, heck with it. I'll get you some guacamole with jalapeño garnish," Jimmy stormed, turning on his heel.

Claude and I stared at each other as if unsure of what had just happened.

"Uh-oh, Ruddy, look who just came in," Alan said.

It was disconcerting to think that Alan could keep track of things within my vision that I wasn't focused on. I glanced up to see what he was talking about.

A Charlevoix County sheriff's deputy had stepped inside the Black Bear during Jimmy's lecture. I recognized him as one of the officers who had been out with us the day we dug up Alan's body. He was staring at me, a smirk on his face. When he was sure he had my attention, he crooked his finger. Gulping, I got up from the table, following the deputy outside. A gray band of clouds drifted in front of the sun as I climbed inside his patrol car.

Time for my polygraph.

19

A Funeral for a Friend

Strickland left me sitting in the tiny lobby of the sheriff's department for half an hour in what was probably some psychological, "I'll show you who's boss" type of manipulation. I decided I could *not* be intimidated, though my leg bounced nervously and I gave a start every single time the back door opened. Alan had plenty of one-way advice, to which I felt incapable of responding due to the presence of the desk sergeant sitting four feet from me. *"See if you can find out about this Franklin Wexler,"* he instructed, clearly forgetting who was driving my body. I was not going to bring up *any* names—providing the sheriff with information he didn't already have just seemed to get me in more trouble.

Finally Barry Strickland was standing there, crooking his finger in what apparently was a departmentally approved gesture. He led me to a small, windowless room with a mirror on one wall.

"Well this place could not be more bleak," Alan huffed

as I was seated in a wooden chair. *"Could they not spare a single painting on the wall?"*

I tried to imagine a person actually believing that an interrogation room should be *cheerful.*

I guess I always thought that a polygraph machine was a device that somehow measured brain waves, but what those little jumping needles represented was something much more mundane: pulse, breathing, perspiration, and blood pressure. The examiner who told me to call him Justin looked exactly like Bill Gates. "This doesn't hurt, doesn't do any damage of any kind. I'll ask you a series of establishing questions, and then I have a list of questions here that the sheriff has supplied. He's already shown you these questions, is that correct?" Justin asked in sort of a nerdy drone.

"Yes," I answered, swallowing. One of them, *Do you know who killed Alan Lottner?* was making me sweat already. I didn't want to tell Strickland about Burby and Wexler because I didn't want to tell him about Alan dwelling in my head.

Alan sensed my nervousness. *"Don't worry, I'm here with you,"* he murmured. I didn't have any way to inform him that his being here with me was why I was worried.

"First question then. Is your name Ruddick J. McCann?"

"Yes."

"Okay, good!" Alan praised.

Justin was frowning. "Mr. McCann, are you feeling well today?"

"Yes," I answered formally.

Justin shook his head. "No, that wasn't a control question, I'm just asking. Are you currently taking any medication?" He picked up the form I'd filled out a few minutes ago, confirming my answer as I said it.

"No."

Justin pursed his lips. "Let's try another one. Are you a resident of Kalkaska?"

"Yes."

Justin cocked his head, considering.

"Something's not right," Alan observed.

"Let's try this. I will ask you a question, and I want you to deliberately lie. This is called a 'directed question,' okay?"

"Got it."

"Mr. McCann, are you a resident of East Jordan?"

"Yes."

Justin's eyes widened in surprise. He looked up at me. "And you're not, right?"

"Pardon?"

"You list your address as Kalkaska. You're not from East Jordan."

"No. I mean, yes, I'm from Kalkaska."

Justin nodded. "Excuse me for a moment." He stepped out of the room, closing the door behind him.

"What's going on?" Alan asked.

I glanced at the mirror on the wall. "I'm probably being filmed, here," I stated, sounding like I was announcing it to myself.

Alan got the message. *"Justin's acting like there's a problem with the equipment,"* he said, using the tone of voice that meant he didn't expect me to reply.

A few minutes later Justin was back, unhooking me from his machine. "The sheriff would like to see you now," he told me, appearing unhappy.

I, too, was less than joyous. "The sheriff would like to

see you now" sounded like "Please report to the principal's office." "That's it?" I asked. "The examination is over?"

Justin the Bill Gates impersonator gave me a bland, "sorry your computer crashed" type of look.

I could see as I settled into the chair in front of Strickland's desk a few minutes later that I was not going to be on a first-name basis during this particular interview. Strickland's eyes were cold and he didn't offer me any coffee. His toothpick jabbed out at me from the corner of his mouth. "Grubb says there was a problem with your polygraph," he told me.

Grubb, I deduced, was Justin Grubb the Bill Gates impersonator. Apparently he, too, had lost stock with the sheriff today.

"He didn't really ask me any questions," I responded a bit defensively.

"He said you're too jumpy, you responded to the control questions as if you were lying, but then when he directed you to lie, it was as if you were telling the truth."

"I think I know why that might be," Alan mused thoughtfully.

"Well, I have no idea why that should be. I didn't do it *deliberately,*" I protested.

The sheriff regarded me for a long moment. "You know what I've got on the murder of Alan Lottner?" he finally asked me.

I shook my head.

"You, that's what I've got. You knew where to find him, you knew who he was before we dug him up. Now, I can spend a lot of resources cross-indexing you with every inmate in the state prison system you might have run into who could have put a bullet in the victim's head, but that's four years' worth of convicts. It would be a lot cheaper and easier if you would just come clean and tell me what you know."

Strickland's eyes were hard and unforgiving. I sighed in frustration.

"You shouldn't have told him you dreamed it," Alan coached.

"I read about it in the newspaper," I said.

Strickland frowned. "Read about what in the newspaper?"

"About Alan Lottner. I had this dream that someone was buried in the woods, and I wondered who it might be. So I went to the library in East Jordan and started looking through back issues of the newspaper, and when I saw the story about Alan Lottner, I figured that he was the guy. There aren't that many people who disappear like that, up here."

Strickland considered my statement while I shifted uncomfortably under his stare.

"That doesn't make any sense," Alan noted helpfully.

The sheriff asked me exactly when it was I had been going through the microfiche at the library, and I told him. "Wait here," he said curtly, leaving the office.

"Alan, do you think this is helping?" I demanded as soon as the door was shut.

"I'm just offering constructive criticism," he responded defensively.

"No! *Constructive* means I can *construct* something out of it. All you're doing is sitting there making snide comments. If you've got something brilliant to say, then say it, but otherwise shut up, okay?"

Alan made a miffed sound but I was in no mood to apologize. I wiped sweaty palms on my jeans.

After a few minutes Strickland came back in and sat in his chair, regarding me warily. "The librarian confirms you spent a couple of hours going through the microfiche. Why didn't you tell me this before?"

"Because I didn't think you'd believe me. I mean, I know how weird it must sound, me dreaming about it."

Strickland snorted. He gave me a long stare, like he didn't know quite what to do with me. "We had a psychic one time on a missing child, waste of time. The little girl was taken by her uncle, just like we all figured. Is that what you are, a psychic?"

Everyone in northern Michigan seemed to have psychics on the brain. "No, sir," I answered, dreading the idea that he might somehow know that my sister was running what was, in essence, a psychic hotline. He didn't mention it, though, surprising me with his next question.

"You hear voices in your head sometimes, Ruddy?"

I swallowed. "Well, yeah. How did you—"

"I hear you've been spending some time with Deputy Timms's fiancée," he interrupted.

"They're not engaged!" Alan and I blurted together.

Strickland arched his eyebrows at my reaction. "She told me they were only talking about getting married, sir," I explained more calmly.

The sheriff stood up and stared out his window. A gray fog was rolling through the town, erasing the details of the trees visible from his office. "It's my job to protect the citizens of this county," he told me after a minute.

"Tell him you're a citizen, too," Alan urged.

"Yes sir, but I'm a citizen, too," I said.

Strickland turned back to me. "You're an ex-con," he

corrected icily. "You've got psychiatric issues. And you're running some kind of game here, I just don't know what. Probably taking advantage of Alan's family. I want you to stay away from Katie Lottner."

"No!" I responded without thinking. Probably not too many people said that word to Strickland. His face turned dark.

I jumped agitatedly to my feet. "Look, do you think I wanted this? I didn't ask to dream about Alan Lottner. I didn't even know the guy!"

"You've been saying you did know me," Alan murmured.

"I mean, I've been saying I did know him but I didn't, okay? I just had this dream, this horrible . . ." I squeezed my hands into fists. "I came here to tell you about it. If I hadn't, you never would have found him and we wouldn't be having this conversation."

"You will sit in that chair until I tell you otherwise."

I sat back down. Strickland regarded me for a long moment. "You're a confused man, McCann, and every time I see you, some of that confusion rubs off on me. But on one thing I'm very clear. I will not have you messing with Katie Lottner's head. She's burying her father tomorrow and in her state of mind you probably look like some kind of hero."

"Burying me? You mean they're having a funeral for me tomorrow?" Alan demanded.

"You tell her about Lisa Marie Walker?" Strickland asked.

I swallowed.

"I thought not. She know about the voices?"

I just stared at him.

"Here's where we stand. I'm going to continue my murder investigation. If I find you have been withholding important information from me I am going to see you prosecuted and you will go back to prison. I'm tired of your brand of happy horseshit." Strickland opened his door and stuck his head out into the hallway. "Deputy!" he shouted. He turned back to me. "The deputy will take you back home. We're finished here. I truly hope I don't have to talk to you again, McCann."

My neck was bent as I followed the deputy out to the patrol car and slid inside. The sky was dark and his windshield wipers came on before we'd gone a mile. Alan finally seemed to realize I couldn't very well answer his questions, and before long I felt him slip away into his sleep state. The deputy didn't have much to say, either.

At the Black Bear, two kids were playing at the pool table, clacking the balls together by hand-rolling them. It took me a long time to register the significance: I couldn't remember the last time parents had brought their children with them to the Bear.

Jimmy slid up next to me. "Hey, Ruddy, here."

I looked blankly at the wad of money he was shoving at me. "What is it?"

"I worked out a payment arrangement with Milt, and he said you'd already paid fifty dollars, you know, on that check scam I fell for, so I'm paying you back."

"No, hey, you should hang on to it."

"S'okay. It's from tips." I stared into Jimmy's guileless eyes and then took a full survey of the room. Several tables had people sitting at them, doing something almost unheard of at the Black Bear: *eating*. Jimmy jumped up. "I've got to run. Maybe if it slows down we can play some pool later?"

"If you think we can beat them," I said, pointing to the kids. Jimmy shrugged, grinning.

There weren't any bar fights between the families for me to break up that night, so I went home feeling like events were conspiring to render me useless.

As I pushed open my front door, Jake glanced expectantly behind me to see if Jimmy was coming home, too.

"We talked about this, Jake. You have to love me more. I'm the one who feeds you."

Yeah, his look said, *but you don't let me up on the* bed.

I eased down onto the floor and put my arms around my dog. Alan was still asleep and I felt unusually alone in the world. Jake seemed to sense it, his pink tongue coming out for a reassuring lick. I sighed. Alan asked me why I couldn't treat people the way I treated my dog—but why couldn't anybody treat me like Jake did?

As soon as he woke up the next day, Alan started talking. First he wanted to speculate on why I had flunked the "state your name" portion of the polygraph—his theory, that the two of us were somehow melded together, "my truth" mingling with "his truth," made me peevish.

"I don't want any part of you mingling with any part of me, Alan," I said. Then he wanted to talk about his funeral. We were going to go, weren't we? Would Marget be there, even though she had divorced him? Was it going to be at Burby's? That made sense, but what nerve the man had.

"How come you're not answering me?" Alan asked after a while, sounding frustrated.

"You seem to be doing a good job of holding up both ends of the conversation," I noted.

"Well, maybe that's because you're not saying any-thing."

I didn't say anything. Just call me Mr. Irony.

"What's wrong?" Alan pressed.

"What's wrong? You mean besides having a dead man in my head who won't shut up?"

"What a hurtful thing to say."

"Oh that is so *you*, Alan. 'What a hurtful thing to say.' You talk like you're on British television."

"What is your problem?"

"My problem is that sometimes I just want a little peace and quiet. I would like to spend some time by *my-self*. Is that so hard to understand?"

"Well how are we supposed to accomplish that?"

"I don't know!" I went to my closet and pulled out a suit, brushing impatiently at the dust that had settled on the shoulders. I felt Alan restraining himself from com-menting. "Yes, we're going to your funeral," I said.

Alan fell asleep soon after that, but he was awake and ready to assess my wardrobe as I was getting dressed. He seemed unhappy I hadn't purchased a new tie since the last century and fussed over the lack of shine in my shoes, which just served to make me insecure about my-self. "I don't think it really matters, Alan," I griped. I was standing in the bathroom, willing the razor nick in my chin to stop bleeding. "Maybe you should worry less about me and more about whether it's going to be an open casket."

"Oh, that's funny."

"Sorry, Jake, you can't go," I informed my dog for my amusement. Neither Alan nor Jake reacted.

The sun was so bright it made me squint as I drove to

East Jordan. I swung my truck into Burby's lot, parking in the back because of how many cars had turned out. "You're drawing a pretty good crowd, Alan."

"I didn't think I had that many friends," he responded, sounding a little awed.

I didn't tell him that I thought some of the people were probably there out of curiosity: This town didn't dig up very many murder victims. I squeezed into the main room, standing in the back because all the seats were taken, and let Alan attend his own memorial service.

Marget and Katie both wore black. With her curly hair falling to her shoulders, I thought she looked stunning, but sternly reminded myself that this was her father's funeral and that I should keep all thoughts chaste and appropriate.

A minister stepped forward, led a prayer, and then began speaking about Alan. *"I have no idea who this guy is,"* Alan muttered. We listened: Apparently Alan was a kind man, a wonderful father, a generous person who often volunteered to help decorate the church for holiday services. *"I did that one time,"* Alan complained. I shut my eyes, hard, and he stopped talking.

As the preacher spoke, I gradually became aware that people were glancing at me, cutting their eyes in my direction when I wasn't looking directly at them. It made sense: I was the guy who found the body. I wondered what the local rumors were saying about me. Psychic? Repo madman?

Katie picked up on all the looks and swiveled around in her seat, finding me with her clear blue eyes. I gave a solemn nod, and she raised her fingers in a small, childlike wave. I heard Alan catch his breath. Deputy Timms,

sitting next to her, turned and saw me, the blood roaring
into his face. I stared back impassively.

When the minister finished, he spread his hands and
invited all those gathered to say something about Alan,
and there was a long, awkward silence. I wondered if I
should step forward, since I probably knew him better
than anybody there, but before I could open my mouth
or consider what I could say that wouldn't sound totally
demented, Katie stood up. She turned and brushed the
hair out of her eyes, one hand unconsciously grabbing
her dress at the hip as if to hold herself up.

"My dad . . ." She cleared her throat and looked
around the room. I caught sight of Nathan Burby standing in the corner, looking unctuous, and was nearly felled
by the heat of my anger. "My dad called me Kathy. He
liked to go running, and when he got back we would
walk together. He told me I could be anything in the
world I wanted to be." Her mouth trembled. "I knew he
didn't leave us." Her eyes flashed at her mother, briefly,
before settling back on the people in the room. "He
would never leave. I knew in my heart something really
bad had happened to my dad." Her tears ran down her
cheeks, and when she inhaled it was like a hiccup. "I
didn't want him to be dead, but I knew that's the only
reason he wouldn't be there when I was growing up."
She gave us a crooked smile. "He was the best dad in the
whole world."

Her wet eyes probed the room and when they found
mine I was wiping the tears away. Alan and I sat there,
both crying, and the stares were now frank and openly
curious as they assessed me and my reaction.

Marget stood and hugged her daughter and they both

wept, while people swarmed around, wondering how to help.

I caught sight of Sheriff Strickland watching me from across the room. His expression was, as always, dark and unreadable, but I knew he couldn't be happy to see me there.

After a time the room broke into individual groups and then developed some organization: People would file past a display of photographs, sometimes touching Alan's coffin, before murmuring something to Katie and Marget and then shaking Nathan Burby's hand on the way out the door. I waited until Timms was involved in a conversation across the room before stepping forward. I took my time looking at the pictures.

Alan had always been tall and thin, with very dark eyebrows and curly hair that he'd passed on to his daughter. Sometime in the eighties he allowed too much hair to pile up on his head until he looked like a Chia Pet, but his clothing was always pressed and clean. He had lean, muscular legs and arms. In most of the photographs he was not smiling, though whenever he was caught holding his little girl he was grinning through even, white teeth.

"That one is from her fifth birthday party," he said in wonder. Katie was a little brown-headed girl who always seemed to be wearing muddy dresses and chocolate face paint.

I went and stood in front of the coffin, tentatively setting my hand on it. *"I'm in there,"* he breathed in awe.

Actually, no, I wanted to tell him, you're in *here,* inside me.

I met Marget next. She was a pale, pretty woman,

thin, with a weary expression in her eyes. I told her how sorry I was and she nodded distractedly. It must be difficult to be the official widow of a man you divorced many years ago.

I held out my hand for Katie, but she surprised me by pulling me into a tight hug. "Thank you so, so much for coming. It really means a lot to me. I know my father would have appreciated you being here."

"I'm so sorry for your loss," I told her, which sounded stupid to my ears—the loss had taken place a long time ago. We were here for closure.

Katie steered me slightly to the side. "Most of these people were the same ones who said my dad ran away. Do you think they admit that? No, now they all act like they knew something bad had happened the whole time."

I didn't know what to say to this. I shrugged, cursing my inability to help her. I wanted to slay dragons for this woman, pull her out of a burning building, be her hero, instead of just standing there like a tree trunk.

"You heard? They said he was shot in the head." Katie put her hand to her mouth. "Do you think he suffered?" Her eyes searched mine.

He's dead.

No, I'm not.

"No! I mean, no, he didn't suffer, Katie. I can promise you that. Your father died almost instantly and never felt a thing."

"I never even knew I was shot the second time, I just fell down. It didn't hurt at all," Alan told me.

"Katie?" A woman her mother's age touched Katie's shoulder, and I took my cue and said good-bye.

Nathan Burby held out a hand as I headed for the door. "Very good of you to come," he murmured, acting as if he'd never seen me before.

"What will happen to the memorial now that you have a real body?" I asked curiously.

He frowned, not liking the question. "That hasn't been decided yet."

"You were going to show me where it is."

His eyes turned cold. "You're not a cousin."

"No, I'm not."

"You're the man who found Alan's body. Why did you come here and lie to me?"

"I can't believe the nerve of this man," Alan choked angrily.

"I don't know, Nathan, why did you lie to me?" I asked pleasantly.

He clearly regretted engaging in conversation with me. "Good-bye, thank you for coming."

"Poor Alan, do you think he suffered?"

Burby blinked at me.

"Not from the shot in the head, I'm sure he didn't feel that. But that shovel had to hurt, don't you think?"

The color drained from his face. I leaned forward. "I know what you're thinking, Nathan. I was in prison, right? I'm sure somebody from Strickland's office told you that by now. So I couldn't have been there, hiding behind the trees, watching the whole thing. But if that's the case, how do I know? See, that's what you should be wondering about. How do I know?"

"I don't know what you're talking about," he responded faintly.

I slapped him a little too hard on the shoulder, sensing

the room drop into quiet at the sudden noise. "Sure you do, Nathan." I winked at him. "See you soon, pal."

I walked out into the late afternoon sun.

"My God, Ruddy, that was amazing. You just got right in his face."

"He killed a friend of mine. Pisses me off," I explained. The blood was still pounding through my limbs and I half hoped Burby would follow me outside and try to start something. If he wasn't available, I'd take Timms.

After a bit I'd calmed down and Alan and I decided to check out his memorial, which turned out to be a restful park bench set beneath some trees. Off to the side was a large boulder with a brass plaque bolted into the rock. IN LOVING MEMORY OF ALAN LOTTNER. WE WILL NEVER FORGET YOU. I sat down and let Alan work through his feelings.

"Second day in a row with some sunshine. We'll be covered with mosquitoes before you know it," I remarked after a while.

"Why would a funeral director and a factory board member want to kill me? Why would they deprive me of my family, of my little girl?" Alan asked plaintively.

"It was something you saw that day, I'm convinced of it," I replied, thinking of Wexler's shocked expression when he spotted the car bouncing past. Burby didn't appear so surprised, but his profession probably gave him a lot of practice masking his reactions.

"But what did I see? They were just standing there!"

We thought about that for some time. When we stood up from the bench, the parking lot was only half full, and people were leaving in a steady trickle. Nathan and Marget had stepped outside to talk, Burby probably trying to settle his bill before everyone left. He and

Alan's widow were conferring in low, almost intimate tones.

Then she raised her face, smiling, and the two of them kissed. I heard Alan gasp in shock, and I stood there a moment, my mouth open.

"Alan," I finally said, "I think I know why you were murdered."

20

Why They Died

"*How can this be?*" Alan whispered, stunned.

Burby and Marget went back inside, their arms linked. I turned away from the funeral home so no one would see me talking to myself.

"It's the most basic motive in history, Alan."

"*No, wait—even if you're right, it doesn't make any sense. Why would Wexler want to get involved? It was Wexler who hit me with the shovel, and he . . . I'm pretty sure he shot me, I don't know how I know, but it was him. Why would he do that?*"

"Maybe he owed Burby a favor."

"*Oh come on, Ruddy.*"

I thought about it. "Actually I have no idea," I admitted. "But it's pretty clear to me that this isn't the first time those two have kissed."

"*Thanks.*"

"Well sorry, but you've been gone for eight years, Alan, what did you expect?"

"*It's just not an easy thing to hear.*"

"Sorry."

"It's been sort of a rough day, you know?"

"Yeah, okay," I apologized. "You're right."

"Ruddy?"

I turned. Katie was looking at me curiously.

"Who are you talking to?"

"Oh . . ." I laughed, then trailed off weakly. Her eyes were still red and swollen.

"Can you . . . I'd like to leave. I rode here with Mom and Nathan, but I don't want to be here anymore."

"Sure, yes, of course." We walked to my truck and I held the door open for her. "Where do you want to go?"

I wound up heading north on M66, toward Charlevoix. After a minute or so I flicked on the headlights to keep the highway ahead illuminated. Katie stared out the window.

"We should hold her," Alan said, not thinking very clearly. There was no "we," and while yes, her father should hold her, there was no reason to feel like that would be welcome from me. If anything, Katie seemed hostile and cold.

"That was horrible," she said distantly, squeezing the armrest.

"It must have been very hard," I responded sympathetically.

Her eyes flashed at me. "I'm sorry, but sometimes my mother just makes me sick. When Dad . . . when he was first missing, Nathan would come over with everybody else, all the neighbors and her friends, but then he'd stay long after they all left. One time I saw him pulling out of the driveway *in the morning*." Her lips twisted bitterly. "I think it started before Dad was even gone. Them, I mean. Nathan and Mom."

I breathed deeply, feeling like a piece of the puzzle had slipped into place with an audible click.

"I knew she was probably seeing somebody," Alan grumbled. *"There were a lot of clues."*

"She married him like two weeks after the whole divorce thing was finalized."

Ah. Something our funeral director friend had neglected to mention to us. No wonder he reacted so strongly when I showed up claiming to be a cousin from Wisconsin.

"Tell her it's okay, that sometimes marriages fail and that her mother is no more to blame than I am," Alan instructed.

I would not tell her that. "So he's the owner of the funeral home?"

Katie nodded moodily.

"I was wondering . . . didn't the cemetery used to be somewhere else? I mean, how do you move a cemetery?"

"Oh, right. It sold to a company that manufactures some kind of plastic pipe thing. They dug up each body and moved it to the new spot. I remember Nathan telling my mom he got ten thousand dollars a corpse, like bragging about it." She turned in her seat to look at me. "Do you think I'm being a bitch?"

"What?" I asked, startled.

"Nathan's been very nice to me. He wanted to adopt me but I said no way as long as there was a possibility my dad was still alive. He tries, he really does. Do you think I punish him because he's not my dad? That's what my mother says. She says I've been punishing both of them." Katie stared at me. I considered my response.

"Of course she's not a bitch. Oh, Kathy," Alan moaned.

"I think," I answered slowly, "that you lost your dad at a very critical time. That you were no longer a child and had developed a social life of your own and didn't depend on him for day-to-day decisions." I pictured myself at that age. "You were pretty independent, but then when he was gone you felt abandoned, and as the years went on, you weren't getting along with your mother and you sometimes were angry at your father for leaving, and now you feel really bad because it turns out he was murdered." I thought about what Alan had told me. "He would have done anything to be there for you, but somebody shot him and buried him in the woods."

Her eyes brimmed with tears. "It's been the defining event of my life," she whispered. Inside, Alan was crying again.

I nodded. "Sometimes that happens to us, way before we're ready, a moment that changes everything. Life will be going along, like normal, and then one day without warning you find out that nothing will ever be the same." I stared sightlessly out the windshield, remembering the day it happened to me.

"What about you?" she asked softly, as if reading my thoughts. Her eyes searched mine.

"What do you mean?"

"What happened? Why were you in prison?"

As luck would have it, she couldn't have picked a better time to ask the question—I could *show* her. I slowed, pulled a quick U-turn, and headed back to Ironton, Michigan, population twenty-eight, the place where I ruined at least two lives. The scene of the crime.

There probably wouldn't even be a town called Ironton except that it was there that the long arm of Lake Charlevoix was at its most narrow, a few hundred yards across. The county operated a car ferry that shuttled back and forth across this choke. To reach the ferry when traveling south on M66, cars veered off onto a gentle curve to the left. I did this now, putting on my blinker. A trip of less than the length of a football field and there you were at the water's edge. At night, people sometimes made the mistake of going down the ramp to the ferry, thinking they were still on the highway. During my trial, my attorney handed the judge pictures of the pavement, showing all the dark tire marks from people frantically braking their speed after realizing they'd made the wrong turn. The problem was that while the error I made was mundane, the consequences were anything but.

I drove the short distance to the bottom of the ramp and stopped, my headlights illuminating the thin steel barrier erected to keep people from driving into the channel. The ferry was over on the other side, away from us, just as it had been that night. Katie was watching me intently.

"Her name was Lisa Marie Walker. At the trial, they made a big deal over her age. She was seventeen," I began, looking out at the gray water. "But that night, it never came up. I mean, I was only twenty-one myself, and it wasn't like they made it sound. I wasn't planning to . . . I'd just met the girl, that's all." I shook my head. "Well anyway, it was bad enough. We had too much to drink to be driving around, but she wanted to make a beer run to Charlevoix, the 7-Eleven. So I took her. I came down here, down M66 I mean, on the way home." I sighed. "When I got here, to the ferry road, I must have just drifted down it. You can see how it could happen, the highway sort of bends to the right, but headlights don't bend, they go straight, and for a second it looks like *this* is the highway."

Katie nodded, gazing at the road.

I shrugged. "I honestly don't recall. They said I was going fifty miles an hour." I gave her a sad smile. "By all rights, I should have spun out, but I've always had good reflexes and managed to make the turn. There were some people smoking weed in a van parked right over there, and the witnesses said my brake lights never lit up. They rebuilt the approach after my accident, but back then the barrier was like a drawbridge, a wooden gate that laid flat when the ferry was on this side. It was tilted like a ski jump and I just ran right on into it."

Katie's mouth opened in horror.

"I sailed out into the water a good twenty feet, the people in the van said."

"My God," Alan breathed.

Katie heaved a deep sigh, almost a shudder. She looked out the front windshield into the water, picturing it. Then she turned back to me. "She died."

"Yes," I agreed. "She did die. She was actually in the backseat at that point. I had a blanket back there and she wasn't feeling too good and wanted to lie down. Well, anyway, I don't know if it is good or bad that she didn't see what happened. The water rushing in, the car sinking so fast. I got out, and she didn't. They found her body five days later. It washed ashore in Boyne City."

We were silent for more than a minute, staring out at the lake, and then Katie turned to me. "What happened to you? Were you hurt?"

"Me? Not bad. I was lucky. I was wearing my seat belt." I closed my eyes and remembered waking up in the hospital, my parents looking down at me anxiously. They didn't tell me about Lisa Marie Walker until the next day, and then my first words were, 'Who?' The full impact of it all took a while to sink in, but my dad already understood, and his eyes were dark and unreadable as he looked at me and saw an end to my scholarship, an end to my career, no NFL, no glory, no millions.

Lucky. Except there were an awful lot of days when I wished I had stayed in the car.

"So you were convicted of murder?" I could hear the doubt in her voice. Up here the long, empty roads and equally long and empty winter nights brought a lot of teenagers and their cars together with alcohol, so maybe it did seem an extreme penalty for something that happened all the time. But I'd seen the pictures of Lisa Marie. Her parents were there in the back of the courtroom, and when it was my turn to speak I stood up and told the judge it was my fault and I deserved what was coming to me. My mother cried bitterly when the judge sent me to the penitentiary but my father's small nod at least put things right between the two of us.

"Vehicular homicide, yeah." We sat and watched the ferry chugging back across, carrying a single automobile as its cargo.

"You don't talk about this much," Katie speculated.

"No."

Our eyes met. "Ever? You ever talk about it?" she probed. I shook my head mutely.

She reached out and seized my hand. We watched the car trundle off the ferry and drive past us up into the dark. The ferry captain inquisitively pointed at my truck and I shook my head, so he went inside his tiny cabin, a miniscule television bathing his face in flickering light while he waited for another passenger.

Katie sighed again. "See, I was working in Detroit.

For an insurance company, as a facilities coordinator? But I guess I'm just not the big city type. I hated having to keep my car doors locked all the time and how the same people I worked with would go to the bar on Fridays and the married men would hit on me. I missed my mom. Then we had a merger and they offered me three months' salary to leave, so I did. In the summer I do a couple of jobs on the side—I teach lifesaving at the Y, and I lifeguard at the public beach in the summers, but I'm just a receptionist now." She glanced at me to see if the repo man had known he was keeping such low company.

"Well, I steal cars for a living, though for glamour I'm a bouncer in a bar."

"That wasn't my first time there. The place with the bear, I mean. I've been there a few times with my girlfriends over the years."

"Great, my daughter hangs out in biker bars," Alan observed glumly.

"It's not a biker bar," I responded.

Katie blinked. "I know . . . did you think I was a biker?"

"God, no!" I blurted. I felt my face heat up—I sounded like a complete idiot. "Uh, I don't think so."

"Don't think what?"

"Don't think you've been to the Black Bear. I mean, I think I would have noticed you, someone like you."

Alan made an exasperated sound.

"I remember when I saw you in East Jordan, in the rain . . ." My voice trailed off. I could feel something like poetry steering my thoughts but nothing articulate was coming out of my mouth.

She unconsciously began twirling her hair, sadness creeping into her expression. "Oh, Ruddy, I'm . . ."

I wanted to tell her to *wait,* don't say it, don't slam the door on any possibilities yet, but before I could open my mouth the interior of the pickup came ablaze with light. I squinted behind me, where a spotlight was obliterating everything with white glare. Someone had pulled up and parked behind me without me noticing.

"Step out of the vehicle, please," an electronically magnified voice boomed.

Katie held up her hand to block the spotlight, squinting. "What is it?"

A single blaring note from a police siren made us both jump. "You, the driver. Step out of the vehicle."

"You'd better wait here," I muttered. I wonder if my presence at the Lottner funeral had driven Strickland over the edge, though it didn't sound like his voice.

"We weren't doing anything," Alan observed indignantly as I warily stood up out of the truck.

"Place your hands on the vehicle and spread your feet behind you," I was instructed. I knew the drill; I'd done it before. I assumed the position and heard a jangle as a uniformed cop approached me out of the light. I grunted as he pressed into me, a meaty hand gripping my wrist and twisting my arm around my back.

"Hey, take it easy," I complained, keeping all resistance out of my body.

"Shut it. What are you doing here?"

"Dwight!" Katie was out of the truck and staring at us, her lips pressed together.

"Katie. Get over to my car and get in," Timms ordered in clipped tones.

"Oh, that's going to work real well with her," Alan observed.

Katie set her jaw. "What are you talking about? What are you doing?" she demanded.

"I'm taking you home," he told her. "Your mother called; she said you left without telling anyone where you were going."

"So? I don't have to tell my mother anything. Let him go!" she snapped.

"What do you think you are doing here, asswipe?" Timms breathed at me, pushing my wrist higher.

"What do I think? I think I'm going to break your jaw," I responded thoughtfully.

"Are we in a position to be saying something like that, Ruddy?" Alan asked urgently.

"Dwight. Let. Go," Katie grated through clenched teeth, yanking on his arm. He dropped my wrist and I whirled, squaring off at him. He took a step back, his hand gripping his baton.

"Let's go, killer," he mocked.

"How about you take off your uniform so I don't get your blood all over it," I answered.

"Stop it!" Katie cried. "What are you doing?"

Since neither of us were sure to whom she was speaking, we didn't reply, though both of us lowered our guard, letting the tension go out of our postures. She pointed a finger at the deputy. "Dwight. Give me a minute."

He frowned. "Katie, your whole family has been very worried—"

"I said give me a minute!"

He thought about it, then retreated to his patrol car.

Katie blew out a puff of exasperated air as she watched him settle into the front seat, then turned to me.

"Look, I'm sorry . . . ," I started to say.

She held up a hand. "No, stop, don't say anything."

"It's just, I got a little angry—"

"No, no, it's not that." Her eyes flared at me. "I shouldn't be here, you know? This was stupid."

"But *why*?" I asked, trying to keep the anguish out of my voice. I could hear what was coming as clearly as if she'd already spoken.

"Because, that's why. It would be wrong. It would be." She shook her head. "Don't call or anything anymore, okay?"

This was more than a little unfair—hadn't she called *me*? But I didn't protest.

"I have to go." She turned away from me and got into the passenger seat next to Dwight. He stared at me darkly as he backed the vehicle away.

"And so you just let my daughter drive off with Deputy Dumbbell," Alan announced.

I started my truck and headed home. "Well, what was I supposed to do?" I snapped in irritation. "You heard her."

"Why didn't you tell her the obvious? That moron isn't the right man for her."

"And I am?" I challenged.

Alan let that one sit there for a few minutes. *"Well look, don't be offended, Ruddy, but my daughter has a college education. I think she can do better than . . ."* He trailed off.

"Than a repo man from Kalkaska, Michigan," I finished for him.

"I was going to say bar bouncer."

"You were going to say ex-con."

"Okay, yes, that is what I was going to say."

I stared moodily out at the road. "I don't even remember," I said after a long time. "That's what really gets to me. I don't remember turning down that ferry ramp. We stopped to buy some beer in Charlevoix and when I got back to the car she'd passed out under the blanket—she was just a dark lump in the backseat; I didn't even see her. She never said another word to me. And that's all I remember until I'm in the water, sinking fast. It's like the whole thing is a story, told to me by somebody else. None of it seems real. What happened to you out in the woods, I can remember *that,* as clear as if I'd been there. But not the worst night of my own life. Nothing about that."

Alan was thoughtful as I drove. *"You've been saying you had your dream about me the night there was a big storm. Lots of wind. Might have been the night the big tree blew over."*

I grunted acknowledgment.

"One of the last normal thoughts I had before Wexler and Burby came at me with the shovel was that I was going to return that ring I'd found. But I forgot all about it until the sheriff showed it to you."

"Me too."

"Your ring. Yours."

"I know. But I don't know what it means."

"Yeah," Alan said after about ten minutes. *"I don't know what it means, either."*

Jimmy was still awake when I came in the door, flipping channels with a bored expression on his face. He gave a guilty start. "Oh hey, sorry about my dishes." He gestured at the table. "I know you like it neat, I just didn't get to them."

"That's okay, you do enough around here." I pulled a bottle of beer out of the refrigerator and sat down heavily on the couch. I kicked my shoes off and one of them left a smudge where it thudded against the wall. Jake didn't even twitch at the noise.

"Splatter mud all over the place. Nice," Alan commented.

"I'll splatter whatever I want, whenever I want," I answered loftily. Jimmy eyed me but didn't respond.

We watched Jimmy lazily circle through the channels, and after a while I found myself talking about what had happened with Katie. "It was like she was mad at *me,* when I didn't *do* anything," I finished.

Jimmy thought about it. "Maybe she's mad because she had everything figured out, you know, with the cop, and then you came along and now it don't look so good. Women like to have stuff all set, you know? When someone comes along and it changes their plans, they don't like it."

I pondered this wisdom. "I imagine you've run into that circumstance maybe once or twice along the way."

"Maybe," Jimmy agreed.

I heaved myself off the couch. "Thanks, Jimmy. I appreciate it."

I went to my room and settled into bed with a sigh, but didn't go to sleep right away. I stared at the ceiling, remembering Katie's voice in the cab of my pickup. I could have sat there all night, if Dwight hadn't come along.

"Deputy Dumbbell, huh, Alan?" I asked. He didn't answer, but he didn't feel asleep to me. I sighed, shutting my eyes.

When I awoke I was facedown in a melting snowbank, the ice cutting my cheeks like diamonds.

21

Face-to-Face with a Snake

"Ruddy! Take it easy, you're okay, you're okay," Alan urged.

I realized I had been shouting incoherently. I clawed my way out of the snowbank, which had thawed and frozen so many times it had the consistency of pebbles against my palms. I staggered, wiping my face. I was by the side of a dark, wet road somewhere. I was wearing shorts and a T-shirt and a pair of running shoes. "What the hell is happening?" I yelled wildly.

"Hold on, you're okay. We've been running, that's all. We fell. You're fine, you're fine."

"What do you mean, running?" I responded incredulously. I now saw where I was—about a hundred yards from the car lot where Claude worked, more than a mile from my home. A light fog danced around me in the frigid night air and I realized it was steam rising from my sweaty skin. "How did I get here? What is going on?"

Alan didn't say anything. I hugged myself, though I really wasn't cold. A thick sweatshirt was wrapped around my waist and I slipped it on, drawing the hood over my wet hair.

"Alan?"

"There was a pothole, and we slipped," he explained.

"What does that mean? I don't understand!" I crossed the street and began trotting back toward my house. "It's the middle of the night, Alan."

"Look, there's something I have to tell you that you may not like very much."

That didn't sound good. "Try me."

"A couple of weeks ago, you were asleep, and I was awake—"

"You said you slept," I interrupted.

"Yes, but sometimes I'm awake when you aren't. And I was thirsty. . . ."

"What?" I demanded.

"Would you just let me tell it, please? I would never be so rude as to interrupt you like this," Alan answered in a snippy tone.

"Okay, fine, but how could *you* be thirsty?"

"Do we have an agreement that you will let me tell this my own way?"

"Okay, yes, sure, Alan. I just woke up by the side of the road in the dark like I'd been dumped there by the Mafia, but you take your time explaining, that's fine with me."

"All right, then, I suppose you were thirsty, but you were asleep, so I was the only one feeling it. And I discovered that if I wanted to, I could just get up out of bed and get a drink of water, so I did."

"You have got to be kidding me."

"From then on, whenever you fell asleep, I found I could do things. Move around. Clean the house. Go out for a run."

"You've been using my body when I was asleep?" I yelled, outraged. "Are you out of your mind?"

"What's wrong with that? You're getting exercise in your sleep. We're up to five sets of fifty push-ups, three hundred sit-ups, and a run every night. You know how many people in this country would love to be able to do that without waking up?"

"You cannot be serious. Alan, this is like the invasion of the body snatchers." I thought of my initial fear of the voice in my head, that it would start telling me to do things—instead, the voice was doing things *on its own.* "Where the heck did you think we were going?"

"Just up the road to Leetsville and back."

"Leetsville! That's ten miles away!"

"No it isn't, it's only five. I measured it on the odometer," Alan soothed.

"The odometer?" I shouted. "You've been driving in my sleep? Do you have any idea how dangerous that is?"

"Would you stop shouting? Anyone hearing you will think you've gone crazy."

"I *have* gone crazy! I've got a voice of a dead man in my head who is trying to take over my body! It's like I've become some sort of zombie!"

"It's not like that at all—just the opposite, in fact," Alan argued indignantly. *"Do you know how quickly our times have fallen on a five-mile run? You're already a better runner than I ever was, and I was doing forty miles a week when I was shot. I can't believe how strong and fast you are."*

"You make it sound like I'm some sort of Ferrari you've been cruising around in," I stormed.

"I'm giving you a compliment."

"You're stealing!" I bellowed.

By the time we were back on my street I had calmed down enough to make my statements to Alan clean and clear. "You may not do this again. Understand, Alan? I don't care if I'm fat or thirsty or if my truck needs an oil change, you don't do anything but lie there until I wake up. You read me on this?" I realized I was mimicking Sheriff Strickland—not a bad role model for issuing orders. Maybe I should be calling Alan "Lottner." I paused outside my door. Alan didn't reply. "Alan? I asked if you understand what I am telling you."

Still nothing. "I know you're not sleeping. Answer me."

"I don't see what the problem is," he griped.

"I don't care. My body is my body and you're not to take it on any more joyrides."

I went inside and showered off the sweat and the mud. Jake didn't seem at all surprised that I'd been out running; he just seemed glad I hadn't dragged him along. "You knew and you didn't say anything? Why didn't you bark, wake me up?" Jake just gave me a weary look in return.

Alan slipped away, possibly exhausted from running halfway to Leetsville, but I lay in bed and stared at the ceiling and pondered one disturbing thought: If Alan decided to use my body when I was asleep, how was I going to stop him?

By the time I drifted off, the sky was growing lighter with the dawn. I went to Milt's and picked up an SFU assignment—Spot For Unit. Fifty bucks to drive by the house of the customer's relative and see if a canary yellow Corvette was in the driveway—a car painted that color, up here this time of year, would probably be visible as a glow on the horizon.

Jimmy was waiting tables at the Bear. I ordered an omelet without making any sarcastic remarks about the fact that I could have asparagus in it if I wanted. Alan was still asleep.

Claude and Wilma came in together, sat together, and ate together without slander. Claude had a sheepish look on his face when he glanced in my direction. Wilma's expression was warmer—apparently I was included in the general amnesty. I smiled at them and Wilma patted Claude's hand. Jimmy was right about the two of them.

I sipped coffee and took in the general transformation of the Bear. It wasn't just the new curtains and table-cloths; there was a whole new feel to the place. It smelled like flowers instead of stale beer, and I could hear the new grill sizzling in the kitchen. The pool table was gone, which was a little disappointing because I had just been on the verge of mastering the game, and the floor had been polished. Bob the Bear looked less grumpy.

Things change. I thought about Katie Lottner, pictur-ing her here with me, more comfortable in a place that had a stack of new child booster seats in the corner than one with a couple of guys having a fistfight over which company made the best motor oil.

Alan woke up as I was conducting my SFU assignment, driving past the house on the rural outskirts of Traverse City. The driveway to the place was buried under a foot of rutted, muddy snow—apparently the people living there had decided that snowplows were for wussies. The only way to get a Corvette in there would be to drop it in with a crane. I would tell Milt to close file.

Alan wanted to go to East Jordan and stake out Burby to see if Wexler showed up. "But I don't think that the two of them spend a lot of time hanging out together, reminiscing about the day they shot a Realtor in the woods," I objected. "I think we need to go at it a different way."

Alan and I decided that a company with a board of directors probably was a public company, which meant that it would have a prospectus we could obtain from a stockbroker. Actually, Alan did most of the deciding on this, but it sounded reasonable. We stopped at our town's sole remaining phone booth to look for stockbrokers in the yellow pages, and on a whim I flipped to the residential listings and found an "F Wexler" on Peninsula Drive. *"Think that's him?"* Alan asked.

"Let's go see."

The Old Mission Peninsula is an eighteen-mile stretch of beautiful coastline that sticks out into Grand Traverse Bay as if the Ice Age had decided to carve out a neighborhood just for rich people. Wexler's house had pillars and a large front porch, a view of the water, and what looked like two acres of prime real estate growing disciplined grass and hedges. I knocked on the door, wondering if a butler would answer.

No, not a butler—a killer. He stood there and looked me up and down with his cold green eyes. Shorter than I remembered from the dream, which made sense—Alan wasn't as tall as I. "Yeah?"

"Mr. Wexler?" I asked, for something to say. Alan seemed too shocked to speak.

"Yeah?"

I suppose Wexler was handsome, with short, sandy hair, a square jaw, and a solid body, but I felt like I was face-to-face with a snake.

"I was over in East Jordan, at PlasMerc Manufacturing? Saw your picture on the wall, there."

Annoyance tugged at the corners of his mouth. "And?" he pressed impatiently.

"I was wondering if you're hiring. You know. Night shift, maybe? I'm a friend of Einstein Croft."

Wexler shook his head. "I don't have anything to do with that. They've got a personnel office. You should try there."

"Tell him as a board member, you're hoping he'd have influence," Alan coached.

"Well right, I figured that, but you're on the board; they'd listen to a recommendation from you."

"Look . . . what's your name?"

"Ruddy McCann."

I was testing for some sort of reaction, but he obviously hadn't heard about me from Nathan Burby. "Uh-huh. Well, I don't have anything to do with that place, okay? I sold them the land it's on, and part of it is I get paid as a board member, but I don't got the kind of time to go to the meetings or anything."

"The land? I thought the land was from the old cemetery."

He thought for a second, his eyes unreadable. He probably wanted to tell me to get the hell off his front porch so he could go back to practicing his golf swing or whatever it was people like him did all day, but I knew something about him: He was a killer, with a secret to hide. Though he wasn't sure where I was headed, I was blundering around in the area close to an awful truth, and he'd practiced his lies and would feel compelled to roll them out for me now.

"Yeah, right, the city had to cut a separate deal for that, it was a small piece of the parcel."

"So how does something like that work? Did you and

the cemetery guy get together and approach the factory, or did they contact you?"

"They contacted me, but I never met the owner of the cemetery."

"Wait, never met? Why would he lie about that?" Alan demanded.

"Never?"

"So you get it? I sold them the land, but I don't have anything to do with running the factory. It's some outfit out of Memphis."

"What's the name of the guy who owns that cemetery?"

He blinked his cold green eyes at me. "I told you," he said evenly. "I never met the man. So good luck with the job."

He made to shut the door, but I put out a friendly hand and stopped it. His expression flashed at me, then turned unreadable. I bet his hands were itching to get themselves wrapped around a shovel.

"We got a problem, here?" he growled softly.

"I was just wondering, you live here now, but back then you were in East Jordan?"

"You want to let go of my door?"

"It's a pretty place, don't you think? There's that little river in the valley, there. You ever go for a drive down one of those back roads in the fall, see all the pretty colors? You and Nathan Burby, standing around having a conversation when this big wide Oldsmobile station wagon drives past?"

He stared at me.

"My God, Ruddy," Alan breathed. *"What are you doing?"*

"They never found the car, you know. What do you

suppose happened to it? The cops didn't bother to check the junkyards, because they thought Lottner ran away. Did you hear they found him? Alan Lottner, I mean. Dug up his body."

I could read the look he was giving me now because I'd seen it in his eyes before, right before he hit Alan with the shovel. "You have no idea what you're stepping in," he said softly.

"Oh I do, I do, Frank," I responded. I took a deep sniff. "I know because I can smell it."

I turned and walked down his flagstone path. As I backed my truck out of his brick-lined driveway, I glanced up and saw him still standing there in the doorway.

"What in God's name were you thinking?" Alan wanted to know.

"Did you like that? 'I know because I can smell it.' Get it?"

"Of course I get it," Alan snapped impatiently. *"You as much as told him you know he killed me. Why would you do that?"*

"Because I don't know what's going on and it is starting to really irritate me. Burby was sleeping with your · wife and probably wanted you dead. Wexler claims not to know the guy. You'd think that maybe Burby paid Wexler to kill you, except that Wexler looks like he could buy and sell Burby all day long. Burby made half a million dollars moving bodies for the factory, but that's not what bought Wexler that house. What's the deal between these two guys? You and I know they're linked!"

"But now you've got both Burby and Wexler thinking you saw something that day, or somehow know about the killing. What good does that do us?"

I thought about it. "I don't know," I admitted.

"*Should you have told them?*"

"Well it's a little late to bring that up now, don't you think?"

"*I have tried to bring it up. Why are you so confrontational? Have you ever heard of subtlety?*"

"Alan, I go up to people and take their cars away from them. There usually isn't a lot of room for subtlety."

"*So now what?*"

I shrugged. "I don't know."

We were both silent. Finally I exhaled. "Well, let's go call on Alice Blanchard, as long as we're this close to town. We keep showing up, maybe she'll write us a check just to get rid of us."

Mrs. Blanchard's eyes were even colder than Wexler's had been, once she saw who was standing on her doorstep. "Yes?"

"Mrs. Blanchard? I don't know if you remember—"

"Yes," she interrupted, "of course I remember. I told you I couldn't help you."

"Yes, but that wasn't true, was it? You were lying to me."

"I don't have to talk to you."

"You sent checks drawn on an account that was closed. That's a misdemeanor," I informed her.

A contemptuous smile briefly touched her lips. "Really? Doesn't it have to be in exchange for goods or services?"

"*I think she's right,*" Alan noted.

"Look, there doesn't have to be any trouble, here. I don't have to tell your husband, or anything."

For just a moment I thought this might worry her, but then she appeared to decide she could weather that particular storm. "My husband is at the bank, if you want to talk to him."

"Mrs. Blanchard . . ."

"Please don't come back here again." She shut the door firmly, a vague scent of flowery perfume floating in the air.

"*Well, that went pretty well,*" Alan said.

"I don't get it." I leaned back and looked at the house. While not as grand as Wexler's, it spoke of a solidly upper-middle-class lifestyle. Was Mrs. Blanchard some sort of crazy person? What else made sense?

I raised my hand to knock on the door again, but then dropped it. I had no idea what I would say to her anyway.

"*Let's go,*" Alan said softly.

"Okay."

I turned around on the front porch and found myself face-to-face with the reason Mrs. Blanchard had been sending those checks to Jimmy Growe.

22

The Numbers Stop Adding Up

She was probably eight years old. She was wearing a sweatshirt cut impatiently short at the sleeves and her cheeks were flushed with exertion plus just a hint of sunburn. She had something of her mother's bearing, with an upright neck, but the vivid green eyes, the black hair falling casually onto her forehead, even the shape of her face, were all Jimmy Growe, translated into little girl. She eyed me curiously as she bounded up the stairs, banging the front door open like an assault team. "Mom, some man is here!"

Her mother had been standing just inside the house—I got the feeling she'd been watching me through the peephole. Our eyes met.

"Looks just like Jimmy," Alan informed me unnecessarily.

Alice Blanchard reacted as if she'd heard him, her face losing its defiance, deflating into resignation. She eased the door shut behind her, protecting her child from our conversation, and motioned for me to sit on a wooden chair. She settled into the porch swing.

I tried to piece it together. "You took those checks from the bank so—"

"No!" She cut me off with a fierce stare. "I made some mistakes issuing the accounts and I was embarrassed to tell anyone, so I brought them home. Later I found out there was a log for me to sign, so people found out anyway."

"But then . . ."

"Then his name came into the bank on the last day I was there. Jimmy Growe. He applied for a credit card. When I saw it I just stared, I couldn't believe it. I brought his application home and put it in the same drawer. I don't know what I thought I was going to do, and then I decided I wasn't going to do anything. I went upstairs to throw away the application, and I saw the starter packets. That's when I decided to send him a check for a thousand dollars."

"*I don't get it,*" Alan confessed.

"So you sent him the checks to . . ." I spread my hands. I didn't get it, either.

"Look, Mr. uh . . ."

"McCann," I informed her after an awkward pause. I found myself ridiculously disappointed that such a pretty woman didn't remember who I was.

"Jimmy never paid a dime to help with Vicki. When my family found out I was pregnant, I was completely cut off. Do you understand how hard it is to raise a baby by yourself? The church found me a place to live and gave me a job in the nursery, or I would have had to go on welfare."

"Did Jimmy know about your daughter?"

"No! He dumped me before I knew I was pregnant."

I could feel Alan straining as hard as I was to comprehend how it all fit together.

"So those checks you sent . . ." I tried again.

Her stare was cold. "They're as worthless as he is. And every time he got one, it was a reminder of what he did to me, and the obligations he was avoiding."

"That makes no sense whatsoever," Alan stated, sounding almost awed.

"Mrs. Blanchard, if you'll excuse me for saying it, but don't you think that's a little subtle for Jimmy? I'm not sure he's capable of grasping the whole picture, there."

She stared at nothing. "It's not for Jimmy that I sent them."

"She loved him," Alan blurted suddenly. *"It's not about the girl, it's about him leaving her."*

I stirred. "I guess I understand," I said, though actually I guessed I really didn't. Alan's epiphany wasn't helping, either. I cleared my throat. "But when he cashed them, he got into a real bind."

Her eyebrows arched. "Mister, I really couldn't care less about that."

I chewed on my lip a little, thinking it over. I decided she probably did care, that knowing Jimmy had gotten himself in trouble was a bonus for her in this weird payback scheme.

"Mrs. Blanchard . . ."

She watched me in what I could swear was anticipation.

"Don't you think that Jimmy has a right to know his daughter? He's matured over the past few years."

"No, I do not," she replied smoothly. "We have a family here, now. I married William three years ago. He's talking about adopting Vicki someday. Our lives are on track." She gestured to the house, clearly a big step up from her circumstances of a few years ago. "William wants us to have a child of his own." She absently gazed over my shoulder, pulling on an earlobe.

"Still, for Jimmy, it has all turned out to be very expensive."

I let the statement lie there until she understood where I was heading. When she did her eyes widened slightly, then became milky with contempt. "How much?"

"I'd say thirty-five hundred. We'll get some money out of the motorcycle he bought."

"And for you?"

"Pardon?"

"How much is your personal fee?"

"Oh. No, that's not what this is about. I just need to recover my employer's money, that's all." I didn't see the need to mention that Milt had already paid me $500 for this recovery.

She reached for her purse and wrote a check in quick, angry strokes. "This means I'll never see you again, and you won't tell Jimmy about Vicki."

"Not unless you send Jimmy more checks."

"You have a despicable profession, Mr. McCann." She flung the check at me and left me there on the porch.

"I'm going to guess that was not your typical repo assignment," Alan observed as we drove away from the Blanchard house.

I was quiet. *"What is it?"* Alan demanded.

"Well, you're a father, Alan, did you hear what she said? William is 'thinking' of adopting Vicki. He wants a baby of 'his own.'"

"Yeah," Alan grunted. *"You're right."*

"Sounds like the bank president is a jerk."

"That still doesn't connect the dots for me with her sending the checks," Alan complained. *"What was the point of that?"*

"I thought you said you understood her!"

"No, I said that I get that she bears a grudge against Jimmy because he broke her heart."

I sighed.

"What is it? Why are you acting so moody?"

"Alan, Jimmy is my best friend in the world."

"Ruddy, you cannot tell him about Vicki. That's none of his business."

"None of his business? He's got a daughter! You of all people should understand that!"

"What I understand is that we cannot start messing in other people's lives," he lectured.

"Oh, that's just great, Alan. You come into my head, you start calling me 'we,' when I sleep at night you're driving around in my truck, and you think it's a bad idea to mess with other people's lives? Can you not experience *irony* in there, Alan?"

He adopted a hurt silence.

"Why do I have to be the one to handle all this crap?" I asked the world.

By the time I reached Kalkaska, he was back to psychoanalysis. Apparently being inside my head made him feel he could get inside others'. *"Wexler is the evil one. He hit me with the shovel, and he's the one who shot me."*

That didn't sound right to me. "But where's his motive? Burby had motive."

"I just can't see Burby doing something like that."

"You sound as if you like the guy."

"Ruddy. Come on. He's an accessory to murder. To my murder. Of course I don't like the guy."

"Plus, he's sleeping with your wife," I reminded him.

"Thank you for that. Truly. Thanks ever so much."

I pushed open the door to the Black Bear and halted, looking around. The atmosphere inside the place reminded me of Nathan Burby's funeral home, subdued, even mournful. Kermit and Becky stood next to each other behind the bar, watching me with fearful eyes as I walked up to them. "What is it?" I asked.

Becky held out a handful of bank inquiries. "We got more of these today than we got new business to replace them."

I looked back and forth between Kermit and Becky. *"They had to refund more than they got in new business today. The operation ran at a loss,"* Alan explained to me.

"We lost money running numbers," I translated. They both nodded. I took a step toward Kermit. "How could this happen?"

He retreated, inching behind Becky. "We only got in two thousand, and we had to give back forty-eight hundred," he stammered.

"I don't mean the *math,* Kermit," I snapped. "What's going on here? Did the psychic have a flock of deadbeats or something?"

Kermit shrugged. "We don't really have any way of knowing what happened."

"Did you ask the people who send the numbers?"

"We don't get to talk to them, Ruddy," Becky explained. "They just fax us the computer printouts."

I glared at Kermit. "You call them. Now. We need to figure out what's happening here."

"Stop it!" Becky said shrilly. "Stop pushing everyone around."

"What are you talking about? This is his deal, he should get control of it."

"You're not the boss of this, Ruddy. You're not the boss of me!" Her eyes flared angrily.

"I'm not . . . Becky, I'm your older brother."

"So what?"

"She's really angry," Alan murmured, as if I couldn't tell.

I took a breath. "I just think Mom and Dad would have wanted me to look after you," I said reasonably.

"Look after *me*?" Becky's face flushed. "Why do you think they left the business to me? Because they knew you couldn't run it. You were in prison."

I shook my head sadly.

"The truth is, Ruddy, the shame of what you did, that's what killed them."

There. The ugliest thought I'd ever had, the worst notion ever to occur to me, coming from her lips. I stared at her and saw no pity, nothing but anger, cold and cruel. I whirled on Kermit, my finger like a gun barrel. "This is all because of you!"

"Get out, Ruddy. Just get out!" Becky shrieked at me.

I spun and angrily kicked a chair out of the way. In the truck, I vented on Alan. "Didn't I tell her Kermit's scheme was crazy? Didn't I tell her there was something wrong with running numbers?" I raged.

"Maybe it is just a bad day. All businesses have bad days."

"Come on, Alan. It has turned my own sister against me!"

He was quiet for a minute. *"So your parents died when you were in prison?"*

"Yeah." I felt the heat leaking out of me. I realized I was driving toward East Jordan, but didn't turn around. Maybe I'd move there. "First Dad, then my mom."

"I didn't know that."

"Well—there you have it."

"Sounds like you and Becky have some things to work out about it."

I didn't reply.

"I'm just suggesting that the two of you need to talk," Alan elaborated after a pause. *"Okay? Why aren't you saying anything?"*

"I really can't talk right now, Alan," I whispered hoarsely. I gripped the steering wheel and stared straight ahead.

For want of anything better to do, I drove to the East Jordan Library and camped out in front of the microfiche machine. We found another story about Alan in the "Still Missing" category, though vague reference was made to police seeking to question him in relation to the fatal firebombing at the nursing home. Alan was incensed. I combed backward, seeking stories about the PlasMerc factory, but most of the ink from that time was devoted to the aftermath of the nursing home fire, the worst disaster in the county's history. I glanced through the profiles of the victims, most of them elderly people, and stopped dead at one name: Liddy Wexler.

"My oh my," I breathed.

Liddy Wexler had been survived by her only son, Franklin. Her family was best remembered for a huge ranch they owned in the 1940s, much of which had been parceled off, but of which 240 acres still remained in the family.

Another piece of the puzzle.

"I don't see what this has to do with me," Alan complained from his position in the center of the universe.

"It's interesting, don't you think? If Liddy Wexler hadn't been in the fire, her son wouldn't have owned the ranch, and wouldn't have made the money from the sale to the factory."

"And that ties him to Nathan Burby how?"

"I don't know."

"And motivates him to murder me why?"

"Look," I said agitatedly, "it's a clue. You're killed. A month later, a nursing home is firebombed, and one of the people who dies there just happens to be the mother of your murderer. There's a chunk of land involved in her estate, and it winds up six months later being sold to a company that sticks a big factory on the site."

"Are you saying Wexler blew up the nursing home?"

I rubbed my head with my hands. "I don't know."

"I wish you'd warn me before you'd bring your hands up in front of your face like that. It startled me," he noted.

I slapped my hand against my forehead.

"Hey!" he protested.

"I'll touch my face any damn way I want," I informed him. I realized that several people in the library, startled by the sound of the slap, were staring at me as I ranted to myself. I smiled and pointed at the microfiche machine as if its presence explained why I'd just hit myself in the face. When they looked away, I stood up.

"What now?" Alan wanted to know. He sounded

disappointed we weren't going to waste any more time trying to find stories about him in the newspaper. I delayed responding until I had closed the library doors on all the quiet eyes that had been tracking me as I left.

"The only person who has given us any information we can use is Katie," I reasoned. "So probably the best thing to do is to just go ask her if she can think of any connection between Wexler and Burby." I felt pleased with myself—a perfectly acceptable excuse to call on Miss Lottner.

Alan was silent while I started my truck and backed it out of the library parking lot. *Ruddy, I don't know how to say this . . ."*

"But based on past experience I'm going to guess you'll say it anyway," I observed.

"It's just that Katie didn't exactly seem, well, receptive to you last time you saw her."

"Alan, if I went through life only talking to people who were glad to see me, I wouldn't be much of a repo man, now would I?"

I pulled out my cell phone from the glove compartment and dialed Katie's number. A woman answered on the second ring. "Hello, may I speak to Katie, please?" I requested formally.

"May I tell her who's calling?" came the cautious reply.

"Yes, it's Ruddy McCann. From . . ." I trailed off. Nothing I could use to complete the sentence seemed very promising. The repo agency? A bar in Kalkaska? Prison?

"Oh hi, Ruddy. It's me. I thought that was you."

"Katie! Hi!" I chuckled, feeling my brain cells dribble out my ears until I was completely drained of anything else to say. I sat there, snorting witlessly.

"Use your words, Ruddy," Alan encouraged.

"I thought you were your mother. I mean, answering the phone." There, two complete sentences.

"No, she and Nathan went out of town. They said it has all been a little much."

"I'll bet it has," Alan muttered.

"Ah. Well, look. I'm sorry, about, you know, the last time I saw you."

"Why are you sorry?" I thought I could hear the hostility returning to her voice, and cursed myself for reminding her.

"Well, you just seemed . . . I just thought it sort of ended badly."

"And you are apologizing to me?" she said in disbelief. "Dwight threw you up against the car and practically broke your arm, and you say you're the one who is sorry?"

I frowned. "Well, he didn't throw me, I leaned there myself. I wasn't fighting back, or anything."

There was a long pause, and then, to my surprise, she burst out laughing. "That is such a guy thing to say."

"I guess it is."

"I'm the one who should be sorry. And I wasn't mad at you. Dwight and I . . ." She sighed. "I told him . . . well, let me just say that the two of us don't belong together. Never did, really."

"Yes!" Alan cheered. *"See? What did I tell you?"*

"I'm so sorry about your engagement breaking up; that must be hard," I said properly, giving myself points for sensitivity.

"Oh, I bet you are," she replied sarcastically.

My heart decided it was time to turn up the volume on its pounding a little bit, and for another long silence, that's all the noise we made between the three of us. What did that mean? That she knew of my interest? And approved?

"So are you calling from the bar? It seems awfully quiet," she finally asked.

"No, actually, I was just in East Jordan, and I thought I should call you."

"You're here?"

I looked around. "Yeah. Down the street from the library, actually."

"Oh." She thought about it for a bit. "Come on over, then."

23

Katie, Me . . . and Her Dad

I imagined her in her travel trailer but she was standing in the house doorway, framed in yellow backlight, so graceful and feminine my mouth went dry as I pulled up in my truck. Her eyes seemed lit with a mischievous humor, and they never left mine as I stepped inside. "So you split your time between a bar in Kalkaska and the East Jordan Library?" she asked lightly.

I felt myself blushing. "Oh, well . . . I was looking up things from when your dad disappeared."

As soon as I said it the light went out of her eyes and I wanted to shout *Wait, come back!* at her.

"I sold this house once. They've remodeled the kitchen since then," Alan noted, sounding like a Realtor.

"What sort of things were you looking for?" Katie asked, her voice a bit flat.

I shrugged, oh so not wanting to talk about this. "Did you remodel your kitchen?"

"What?" She looked around, bewildered.

"It looks modern, like maybe you had it worked on," I explained lamely.

"The countertops and cupboards," Alan supplied helpfully, as if I cared about any of this. I wanted to slap my forehead again.

Katie offered me a beer and I eagerly accepted, but she seemed stiff as she got one for each of us. I sat on her couch and she settled into a chair, curling her legs underneath her body as she regarded me warily.

"Why would you be doing that, looking into my dad?"

"Ask her about other stories; there must have been some more coverage that we didn't find," Alan instructed. I could feel myself hating him.

I took a breath. "I just want to understand him, that's all. Ever since the dream, I can't get him out of my head."

Alan had already heard that particular joke and didn't laugh. Katie was watching me steadily.

"There were a couple of stories about the nursing home fire."

"Oh, *that,*" Katie said in disgust. "Right, my dad disappears and then a month later there's a fire, so he's a suspect?"

"Did you know any of the people who were killed?"

"No, I don't think so." She looked sightlessly into the distance. "I remember I was pretty angry. Everyone forgot all about my father; all they wanted to talk about was the bomb and how all these people were killed." She seemed to catch herself. "I mean yes, it was horrible that people died and everything. I get that. But my dad was still missing, and no one cared anymore. The only person to even mention it was this guy from the ATF or whatever it is called. Oh, and Nathan, of course."

I went very still. "Nathan Burby?"

"*Oh, I'll bet* he *mentioned it,*" Alan fumed.

"Right, he was always asking how I was doing." She flipped a wrist as if getting something off her hands. "I'm past that, though. What's done is done."

"Then he sold the land," I prompted.

"What?" Her eyes regained their focus.

"For the factory, I mean."

"Oh, no." Katie shook her head. "That was a huge shock."

"I guess I don't understand."

"The city didn't tell him. They didn't have to; it was in the lease. The city council was working with the company that bought it, but Nathan didn't find out about it until the deal was already set. I mean, he wasn't exactly unhappy about it, because he got paid ten thousand dollars for every coffin he had to move, and he's got a lot more room at the new property, but still, he had no idea." She gave a sigh. "Why?"

"Oh. Nothing. I just, you know, was curious."

Katie glanced at her watch, and I felt my heart sink. "*It's getting pretty late,*" Alan remarked.

"I had a repo up here the other day," I blurted, grabbing at something to say just to stay there. She smiled encouragingly so I told her about trying to pick up Einstein Croft, starting with the first try, the encounter with Doris the Attack Goose, and my efforts since then. When I told her about Kermit dropping the pickup off the tow truck, she threw back her head and laughed with delight.

"Now I just have to hand him the court summons, and my work is done," I finished.

"How are you going to do that? It seems like he's hiding from you."

"I haven't figured that out. It's not worth it to me to sit in front of his house all day and night, waiting for him to make a run to the grocery store." Maybe I would make Alan do it while I was asleep.

"Then the sheriff's department goes and gets it? How do you feel about *that*?" she inquired, her eyes twinkling. She laughed again as she saw the implication of her question register on me.

"Well yeah, but those guys are armed. I mean, they can just see Einstein driving by and pull him over."

"I was kidding."

"They drive police cars. It's not a real repo," I argued.

"I know." She shook her head, grinning. "Want another beer?"

She jumped up before I could reply and went into the kitchen. I watched the rear end of her jeans as she walked away from me.

"Hey!" Alan shouted.

I jerked my eyes away.

"We shouldn't be drinking and driving," he admonished.

Katie was still smiling when she came back from the kitchen. "Let's go look at the lake," she suggested, handing me a brown bottle of beer.

"Sure, okay," I agreed, pretty much willing to do anything she wanted. I followed her out the back door. The lights were off in her trailer, but the moon glinted off the silver sides and the yellow grass glowed white as I treaded beside her, my breath making foggy swirls.

"We're not going in the trailer," Alan informed me tightly. The trailer, I recalled, was where Katie usually slept.

He was right; that's not where we were going. Just past the trailer the backyard, which had been bulldozed flat by the homebuilders, dropped away sharply, a steep hill that became steeper the closer it got to the lake. We stood at the lip of the hill, regarding Patricia Lake—a still, black body of water, a hundred acres or so, glimmering below us.

"We built the steps," Katie informed me.

"Steps?"

She pointed and I squinted. Where the hill became too steep to walk down, a long flight of stairs took over, leading all the way to a sliver of beach. "The people who lived here before us never went down to the lake, if you can believe it. I mean, trying to get down there would be like falling off a cliff. So Mom hired these guys to put in the steps."

We were talking about this, I realized, just to have something to talk about. "They did a nice job," I noted lamely.

"They look too steep to me," Alan complained. *"They should have put in a landing."*

If he were there next to me instead of in my head I would grab Alan and fling him down the hill.

I saw that Katie was getting aggressive with her beer, tilting the bottle up for long swallows. Something was going on with her, but I was both figuratively and literally in the dark. I snuck glances at her in the night, tilting my own bottle up and ignoring Alan's puritanical sighs.

"Okay," she announced. "I'm cold."

The lake-viewing portion of the evening was over. We retreated from the lip of the hill and trooped back into the house. Katie grabbed the empties and I heard them hit the recycling box as she grabbed two more from the kitchen.

"More beer?" Alan observed sourly.

When Katie returned she sat down on the couch next to me, hard, bouncing me a little like it was a game. We clinked bottle necks in a gesture that was both silly and fun.

"It's probably time for us to go," Alan observed frostily.

He repeated variations on this declaration for the next ninety minutes, while I took the tiniest possible sips of that beer, dragging out the experience as long as I could. Being with Katie felt free and easy and natural, so of course I had to screw it up. "I'm glad you're not going to marry Dwight after all."

Her expression sobered. She gazed at me, no longer smiling.

"I mean . . ." God, what did I mean?

"He's not a bad guy," she said.

"Oh, no! Of course not. I didn't mean that. He's a great guy."

She pushed the hair out of her eyes. "I'm not some sort of prize for you two to compete for, you know."

"I agree with her," Alan said primly.

"What? No, of course not."

Katie shoved herself off the couch and it took all my strength to keep from reaching for her and pulling her back down next to me.

"Neither one of you is the . . ." She stopped herself, but her eyes were angry.

The man my father was, I knew she had been about to

say. I felt the truth of it deflate me. How could anyone compete with the memory of the man she had been searching for since she was a little girl?

"My dad died when I was in prison," I said haltingly. I didn't know where I was going with this because I'd never allowed myself to say anything more than that, but now I tried. "He used to be so proud of me, it felt like my life and his life were the same thing, you know? He would throw the football to me until it got so dark I couldn't see it. When I heard about him dying, I realized I couldn't picture the world without him in it. I was glad I was inside—in prison, I mean—because it meant I didn't have to go places where he should be but wasn't anymore."

Katie's expression was unreadable.

"And now my sister . . ." I had to pause for control before I got the rest of it out. "She told me she thinks it was the shame that killed them. I don't believe that, but I do think, without me playing football, it gave them a little less to live for." I gave her a crooked smile. "I know what it is like to have your whole life figured out." I remembered being read my Miranda rights while I was still in the hospital, feeling like my life had become like a derailed train. "I mean, you were on track to marry Dwight, right? I think sometimes we get angry when we realize our plans aren't going to work out." The wisdom of Jimmy Growe. "But then in the end, it turns out to be better. This'll be better."

One moment she was staring at me with hot, weeping eyes, and the next she was on the couch, her warm mouth on mine. My arms went around her as naturally as anything in the world.

"Ruddy," Alan gasped.

I broke from the kiss. Katie blinked, looking a little puzzled. "I think maybe you've had too much to drink?" I said weakly, unable to believe what I was doing.

"Oh no, don't worry about that," she assured me. She came back into my arms, searching for me with her mouth.

"Uh . . ." I backed away, retreating into the couch. She stood up, smiling.

"Come on."

"Uh, where . . . where we going?"

She slid her eyes sideways. "When Mom's out of town I sleep in the guest room down the hall."

"What do you think you're doing, Ruddy?" Alan demanded furiously.

What I was doing? I wasn't doing anything—wasn't he paying attention?

Katie held out a hand and I followed, completely unable to prevent myself from taking any other action.

"I certainly hope you don't think you're going to seduce my daughter," Alan stormed.

I blew out a shuddering breath. "Katie . . ."

Her reply was a sly smile. She began twisting the buttons on the front of her sweater, the material falling away from a silky camisole underneath. Before it was the guest room it must have been Katie's bedroom, and it was still a little girl's room, with a canopy bed and stuffed animals on the pillows, all of whom jumped to their deaths to make way for the grown-ups. In contrast to the rest of the house, everything here was neat and orderly, which made it seem all the more wanton when Katie unbuckled her pants and dropped them to the floor, standing before me in all lace, the most desirable woman I'd ever seen.

"Leave. Now. Get out of this room," Alan ordered, a note of desperation in his commands.

I simply could not imagine a worse situation. Katie lit a candle and then coiled on the bed, still smiling, and I moved toward her.

"Could we . . ."

"Yes?" she replied, reaching for me.

"This is going to sound really weird."

That stopped her: "Really weird" is not the most comforting phrase to hear from someone right before you have sex with him the first time. "Yes?" she prompted again, more cautiously.

"Could we just lie here? Would that be okay?"

She was so quiet I could hear the sputter of the flame gaining purchase on the candlewick.

"Are you . . ." She gestured to my crotch, and I was a little hurt she couldn't see the obvious answer to *that* question.

"No, of course not," I assured her. "I'm fine there. Better than fine, I mean. Hugely better."

She laughed.

"I would just like to hold you; would that be okay?"

"You mean you really don't want to?"

"Oh," I nearly sobbed, "oh, I want to, but I just think it would be better. Trust me, okay?"

With a puzzled look she slid over and I climbed in, lying on my back. She put her head on my chest. "Like this?" she asked, her voice vibrating my heart.

I touched her hair, wrapped my arms around her, and sighed. "Yes, just like this."

We didn't talk after that. I lay in bed and stared at the ceiling, watching the gentle circle of light from the candle dance above me.

When I awoke the birds outside the window were starting to chatter about the possibility of sunrise. I was sitting in a soft stuffed chair by the bed, with no memory of having pulled away from Katie's embrace. She was huddled in her sleep, her face turned toward me, and I stared at it for several minutes before I stood and went down the hall into the bathroom.

I flipped on the light and looked in the mirror. "What's up, Alan?" I asked softly.

"I wanted to look at her. She's so beautiful."

"Yeah, she really is." I poured myself some tap water in a small paper cup. "Look, Alan, about last night, I'm really sorry."

"Don't be. After you went to sleep, I got to lie there and hold my daughter against my chest, just like I used to do when she was a very little girl. It was the most wonderful night of my life."

I nodded slowly. "Yeah, me too."

"I was a lot of things in my life, and if you had asked me then I would have told you the things I thought defined me: Realtor, businessman. But that would have been wrong. Nothing was more important than being a father. Those men, Wexler and Burby, of all the things they took from me, that was the worst."

"She's wonderful, and it's because of you, Alan. You were there for the most important years of her life. And you're still there now, I can see it in her."

"Let me ask you something, Ruddy."

I put my eyes on my reflection, sort of dreading the question, but Alan surprised me. *"Why didn't you play ball after you got out? If you were really that good, you served your time, why not make a couple million dollars while you still could?"*

"A couple million? Yeah, well, that would be just great, wouldn't it?"

"Wouldn't it?"

"Picture what that would be like for her parents, Alan. One day they turn on their TV and there I am being interviewed by ESPN, having the time of my life. And their daughter was buried when she was seventeen years old, never even got to have her life. I'm making millions and Lisa Marie Walker lost everything. Can you imagine how they'd feel?"

For a long time Alan didn't reply, and when he did, his voice was a quiet whisper in my ear. *"I thought it might be something like that. You're a good man, Ruddy."*

"You're telling me it would be okay for your daughter to date a repo man from Kalkaska, Michigan."

"Something like that."

"Great. Got any ideas how that's going to work? I'm not even comfortable talking about it with you. Can you imagine how it's going to go with you *watching*?"

There was a soft rap on the door. "Ruddy?"

Katie's hair was tousled from sleep. She had pulled on a thick robe and looked so cute in it I just had to grab her, though my hug was as G-rated as I could manage.

"Good morning!" She laughed. She looked over my shoulder into the tiny bathroom. "You always talk to yourself?"

"Yeah, it's called Repo Madness."

"Okay, good for you. It's pretty early, are we really getting up?"

"Sure, why not."

"Well . . ." She drew a finger down the length of my jaw, and I nearly shivered. "Wouldn't you rather come back to bed?"

"Yes, I really would."

"Well then, why don't you?"

I looked into her smiling eyes. "Because there's something I have to do, and I'm afraid if I don't go do it right now, I'll lose my courage, and then I won't do it at all."

24

Too Subtle for Me

Jimmy was awake when I walked in my front door. He was eating a donut and frowning at some cartoons on the television. Jake was sitting next to him, giving the donut significant glances. "Cartoons suck now," Jimmy declared.

"What?"

"It's like all fake, or something."

"Jimmy, I don't understand what you are trying to tell me. Fake cartoons?"

"He's right; the animation's awful," Alan agreed. *"Remember* Jonny Quest?"

"This conversation is making me nauseated," I said.

"Oh, sorry, would it help if I changed the channel?" Jimmy asked innocently.

"That was a great cartoon," Alan insisted.

"Jimmy!" I yelled over Alan's babbling. Jimmy jumped in surprise. I held out a hand. "Sorry. Jimmy, there's something I need to talk to you about."

"Sure, Ruddy."

I sat down heavily and regarded my friend Jimmy. He sensed that this was going to be an intimate conversation, so he reacted as I would, turning to the TV and flipping channels. I watched him do that for about five minutes before clearing my throat. "Hey, turn it off a sec, would you?"

He switched off the TV and held out the remote in submission. I took it from him and set it aside. "Jimmy, there's no easy way to tell you this."

"Ruddy, what are you doing?" Alan asked in alarm.

Jimmy's eyes were trusting as he nodded for me to continue. "Remember I was asking if you knew Alice Blanchard? And you said you didn't."

Jimmy looked thoughtful. "Right."

"Well, you do know her, Jimmy."

"Oh. Okay." Jimmy shrugged.

"Maybe we should just leave it at that," Alan suggested desperately.

"The thing of it is, Jimmy," I said sternly, "a friend of mine once told me there is nothing more important than being a father, and that no one in the world has the right to separate someone from his child, you know what I mean?"

Jimmy's look was completely blank. "Sure, yeah."

"Jimmy, you've got a daughter. She lives in Traverse City. I've met her. She's maybe seven or eight years old."

Alan gave a sigh of resignation.

Jimmy blinked at me for what seemed like half a minute, then sat bolt upright as his synapses, straining, finally connected with each other. *"What?"*

"Yeah."

Jimmy stood up, whirled around, then sat down.

"Well, I can see that this is even more upsetting than the decline of animation," Alan observed.

"Are you sure? I mean, how do you know?"

"The mother told me. Alice Blanchard? She's the mother."

"I don't even know an Alice Blanchard," Jimmy protested.

"Well that's her married name, Jimmy. I don't know what it was before she got married."

"Adams, her name was Adams," Alan prompted.

"That's it. Alice Adams."

"I don't know an Alice Adams!" Jimmy wailed.

"Look," I said impatiently, "cut it out. I'm telling you, it's your daughter."

Jimmy sat there, his face slack, while I avoided the temptation to snap my fingers in front of his eyes.

"What's her name?" he finally asked. "My daughter."

"Um . . ."

"Vicki," Alan whispered.

"Vicki."

He nodded, as if confirming that the name made sense. "What should I do?"

"Shower."

He focused on me. "Huh?"

"Go take a shower. You don't want to meet your daughter looking like that, do you?"

When Jimmy left the room, I turned the television on to see if I could find any good cartoons, but Alan wanted to talk.

"You know how angry Alice Blanchard is going to be over this?"

"I guess I do, yeah."

"It doesn't seem like you to meddle like this."

I felt the blood rush to my face. "Is that what I'm doing, Alan? Meddling? This morning you told me the worst thing that Burby and Wexler did was rob you of time with your daughter, and now you want me to do that to my best friend?"

Alan couldn't think of anything to say to that.

Jimmy came out of the shower looking as if he'd managed to wash all the color out of his cheeks. He trudged numbly after me outside, sliding into the truck and staring sightlessly through the windshield. Though it was a relatively mild day for that part of the country, he was dressed for an Arctic expedition, a parka pulled over a bulky sweater.

As I backed up, I had to brake a moment to let another vehicle go past, a gleaming SUV the color of midnight. The man behind the wheel gave me a quick glance and then looked away, but not before Alan and I both recognized him.

"That was Franklin Wexler," Alan said tensely. *"What's he doing here?"*

I decided to find out. Jimmy's head snapped back as I put my foot into it, closing rapidly on the black SUV as it slowed for the town. The light ahead turned yellow and Wexler stopped. I eased up behind him, staring at his rearview mirror, but he didn't raise his eyes. I tapped the horn, but Wexler remained resolutely focused on the road ahead.

Jimmy stirred. "Do you know that guy?"

"Yeah. We're good friends." I took my foot off the brake and crept forward. My front bumper kissed the back of the SUV, rocking it a little, but still no reaction from Wexler.

"What are you doing?" Alan asked, though I thought it was pretty obvious.

Still nestled up against the SUV, I tromped on the accelerator and my engine surged. Wexler's vehicle, held fast by its own brakes, bounced up and down as my truck valiantly struggled to push it forward. With a low chugging sound, my motor died.

Finally, I had him. Wexler stared at me in his mirror, and I gazed back calmly, raising my eyebrows a little. *Wanna play, big fella?*

The light turned green and with a shriek his vehicle leaped ahead. I started my truck and took up pursuit, but Wexler drove without restraint, and I couldn't bring myself to match his speed as we sailed past the Black Bear. The SUV was probably doing ninety as it rocketed out of sight. I followed at a sedate pace, chuckling.

Jimmy was wrestling with his demons and didn't even ask me what that had been all about—I wondered if he'd even noticed. Halfway to Traverse City I pulled over and listened sympathetically as he vomited by the side of the road. "You going to be okay?" I asked, concerned.

His look indicated he honestly didn't know. "Maybe we should get a toy or something," he muttered when we were in town. I drove him to a Target and he spent an hour pondering his choice, eventually settling on a small stuffed rabbit with innocent, unaccusing eyes. He gripped the thing as if it was giving him strength as we cruised toward where the Blanchards lived.

"Will she be home?" Jimmy wondered.

"It's Saturday."

"Oh, yeah."

"If she's anything like her biological father, she'll be watching cartoons," Alan predicted.

Jimmy's hands were shaking as he pulled open the door to the truck and followed me up to the Blanchards' porch. I dropped the large brass knocker a few times, giving him a wink as the vibrations from within the house indicated someone's approach.

When Alice Blanchard opened the door her anger at seeing the repo man turned to shock when she glanced at the person standing next to me. She raised a hand to her mouth.

"Oh, *Alice*," Jimmy said in recognition.

As she had done before, Alice stepped out and pulled the door quickly shut behind her. She darted a look left and right around her yard, then glared at me with hot eyes.

"What do you think you are doing?"

"You can't ask me to stand between a father and his child," I lectured, feeling significantly less self-righteous than I had when I'd argued with Alan.

"*His* child?" she hissed.

"*This was not the best idea,*" Alan stated.

She raised her hand as if to strike me, then whirled on Jimmy. "What are you doing here?"

"Uh . . ." He half lifted the stuffed rabbit, then shrugged.

There was a sudden flurry of sound from the side of the house and little Vicki burst into view at a dead run—I got the feeling this was her standard method of getting from place to place. She stopped when she saw us, recognizing me, then switching her curious gaze to Jimmy, who had drawn in a sharp breath. When Vicki's eyes found her mother's, she sensed something, and looked back and forth between these two men, trying to figure out what was going on.

We stood there in the morning air for what seemed

like a long time, though it might have been only an instant. I saw Jimmy try a trembling smile, for the first time in his life unsure of himself around a female.

"Vicki," Mrs. Blanchard said. Her voice sounded distant. "Remember when I told you that your father had to go away, and he would never be back?"

Vicki blinked, processing this. Suddenly her eyes grew wide. She flung a panicked look at me, but before I could even shake my head she was staring at Jimmy, and I knew she had seen the rabbit.

"Hi," Jimmy choked.

She was past us like an explosion, up the steps and to the door, which she threw open with such force that the recoil brought it back to a close. The three of us gazed after her, and then Mrs. Blanchard sighed.

"Okay?" She turned to me. "Okay now?"

"Maybe, I could like send money . . ." Jimmy stammered.

"No! I don't need your money," she snapped.

Jimmy turned pleading eyes to me, but I shrugged, helpless to assist him. He tried again. "Well for college, like a college fund? I'd like to do something."

"Now? Now you'd like to do something?" Mrs. Blanchard repeated contemptuously.

"Alice, I *didn't know,*" Jimmy begged.

"You said that you weren't ready for a relationship," she said, her voice bitter as she mocked Jimmy's words. "'Maybe things have gotten too serious too fast,' you told me. And when I asked you if there was someone else, you said 'just once.' Just *once.*"

Jimmy swallowed. "Yeah, I'm . . ." He shook his head in self-loathing. "I'm sorry. . . ."

"Oh, for God's sake, don't say you're sorry," Mrs. Blanchard said furiously. "Don't say anything, Jimmy."

He hung his head.

"I got over you a long time ago. Please don't insult me by pretending any of it matters now."

We stood there for a bit, and there was the sense of waiting to see if there would be any more punishment. Finally she drew in a deep breath, looking toward the closed door. "It was a mistake for you to come here. Vicki doesn't need you."

"Okay," Jimmy agreed.

We turned to leave, sort of slouching down the porch steps like whipped dogs. Jimmy was biting his lip, staring sightlessly ahead of us as we walked along the cement path toward my truck.

"Wait!" came a call from behind.

We turned. Vicki was running down the sidewalk after us. She stopped, her face almost identical to Jimmy's as it gazed up at us with an open innocence. "Want to see my pictures?"

They weren't drawings, but photographs, each carefully mounted behind plastic in the small album in her hands. They sat down together on the curb and went through each one, Vicki chattering easily with her biological father, already miraculously okay with the situation. Jimmy hugged his knees, clinging to them for support, and kept staring at his daughter in disbelief.

I strolled away to give them some privacy, stopping to examine a swing set in the corner of the yard. From that vantage point, I could slide a sideways glance over to the front porch and see Alice Blanchard's face as she watched Vicki and Jimmy sitting at the curb. There was none of the hostility I'd expected—if anything, her gaze seemed to contain a small measure of satisfaction.

"That's why she did it. Not for revenge or anything

complicated. She wanted Jimmy to find her. She couldn't call him, her husband would never forgive that. But this way, he tracked her *down,*" Alan proclaimed. "*Mr. Bank President might provide a house, but he refuses to truly accept Vicki as his own.*"

"And every child needs a father," I murmured.

"*That's right. She did it for her daughter.*"

"Still a little subtle for me," I confessed. I thought about what it must have taken for Alice Blanchard to decide that even though he had torn a hole in her heart, Jimmy was safe, even essential, for her daughter. He might be useless when it came to resisting the easy seductions of life, but no one who knew him could deny that he was anything but a gentle, caring person.

Alice's eyes were completely unreadable as they settled on mine when we got into my truck. Vicki jumped up and down, waving, and Jimmy grinned and waved back, but Alice was going to have to deal with her husband over this, and that was going to take some strength. I wanted to raise my hand in some sort of a salute, but dismissed anything but a nod as being inappropriate. In all likelihood, Mrs. Blanchard still thought of me as despicable.

Alan fell asleep, and Jimmy was deep in his thoughts, so I had an uninterrupted opportunity to think about Katie Lottner for an hour—a very pleasant way to pass the time.

We went straight to the Bear so that Jimmy could be on time for the lunch shift. We walked in and Becky came across the floor and put her arms around me.

"Oh, Ruddy." She sighed. "It's a sex line."

25

Those Psychic People Are Crazy

Financially choking on the bounces from the bank, Becky had finally figured out how to call the person who had been sending us the credit card numbers—not the contact number we'd been given, but the line the customers called. For a buck ninety-nine a minute, a breathy, sultry voice on the other end promised to discuss anything the caller wanted in the way of "hot, hot, hot sexy talk."

"The operative word being hot," Alan suggested, but I was not amused.

"What happens after that?" I asked.

"They want a credit card number."

"Well, what about the contact number?"

"They called Kermit back once and told him they would send us more credit card numbers to process, but they haven't responded to our messages since then."

"Would that work, send us more numbers?"

"Well, maybe, but Ruddy, *most* of the numbers are bouncing! We didn't know the cardholders were disputing the charges because it takes a full billing cycle for us to get the notice. We'd have to run a huge amount of business through our account to get out of this hole, and Kermit says the bank would shut us down before then. Ruddy, I . . . I was just going to put in new Caesarstone counters." She turned and surveyed the Black Bear, no doubt seeing all of her planned improvements going away.

I called the number Becky gave me, impatiently tapping my foot as the recording moaned and whispered its way through the sales pitch. Finally a human voice' picked up.

"Credit card number?" the woman asked, sounding less sexy than bored.

"You the person I'm going to be talking to?" I demanded.

"No, I just take the credit card. One of our models will be handling your call," she responded.

"Sounds like she's said that a few million times before," Alan noted.

"Then you are the person I need to talk to. We're getting all these bank inquiries. The business you're sending us is crap, it all bounces."

There was a long silence. "Who is this?" she finally asked.

"We're the people who have been running your numbers."

"Running numbers?" she repeated.

"Processing your credit card numbers. Swipe, nonswipe." I put my hand over the phone. "Where's Kermit?" I hissed at Becky. She gestured toward the kitchen and I jerked my head at her to go get him. "Hello? You there?" I asked into the phone.

"I'm here," the woman responded reluctantly.

"Well, we have to do something about this. No one

told us you were a sex line; we thought you were a psychic. Your transactions are bouncing all over the place."

"I don't talk to you."

"What?"

"I don't talk to you. You got problems, you take it up with Mr. Drake."

"Mr. Drake? Who's Mr. Drake?"

"He's the business manager."

"Well, put him on."

"Oh, Drake's not *here,*" she told me scornfully. "I'll have to take a message."

"I don't think you understand me."

"We finished, here?"

"Finished? You tell Mr. Drake that we're not running any more numbers for you. You got a lot of transactions today? Well, you might as well tear them up, because I'm not putting a single one through the bank. What I am going to do is call my lawyer and the state district attorney and we're going to get to the bottom of this!"

"Can't do that."

"What?"

"You can't do that," she repeated more distinctly. "We have a contract."

"You have this number?" I looked over at Becky, who nodded. "You have this number. You tell Drake what I said. I'm going to wait ten minutes, then I'm calling the D.A."

I hung up the phone. "Tell Kermit to get out here."

"He's making chili," my sister replied. She stuck her chin out.

"Becky, this whole thing is his doing!"

"He didn't know! He thought it was a psychic line."

"Well, he should have known—it's his business, for

heaven's sake. Kermit!" I bellowed. "Get the hell out here!"

Kermit peeked around the corner, wiping his hands on an apron. The phone rang and I snatched it up.

"Black Bear, Ruddy McCann speaking," I said, just as my parents had taught me. I found myself wishing I'd come up with a tougher greeting, like, "Yeah?" or something.

"You wanted to talk to me?" Drake had done a much better job preparing himself to sound threatening.

"This Drake?"

"Yeah, and the first thing is, you don't ever talk to my girls like that, got it? Some kinda problem, you deal with me. Otherwise, we have a little conversation."

"That made no sense whatsoever," Alan complained. *"We* are *having a conversation."*

"Here's what I understand, Drake. We were supposed to be running numbers for a psychic line, and instead you've got us doing sex talk."

"So what? Lot more money than psychics. Those people are crazy."

"So they don't pay their bills, that's so what. We have . . ." I looked at Becky and she mouthed "ten thousand," which caused my eyes to bulge. "We have ten thousand dollars' worth of bounces we have to refund."

"Yeah," Drake grunted. "Happens. Somebody steals a credit card number, first thing they wanna do is call a sex line. Customer sees the charge and denies it but by then it's too late for us. Bane of my freakin' existence."

"Your existence? We're the one getting the bounces!"

"Well come on, McCann. Did you really think you were going to get to keep all that money, just for entering numbers in a little machine? This is a tough racket."

I decided I didn't care about his business problems. "The point is, we're shutting this down, and you need to send us ten thousand dollars."

Drake laughed heavily. "That's not going to happen. I've been through this before, friend, and let me tell you, the only way out is to grow through it. I'll get you some more volume to process. I can get some Internet stuff, too."

"Are you stupid? We can't grow our way out of this, it's a disaster!"

Drake was silent for a long time. "I'm going to ignore that little remark, friend, because we've got a business relationship."

"Not anymore. We don't want you to send us anything but the money to get out of this."

"Don't even think that. I've got an operation to run here and you're my source for credit card processing. That's the deal. Period."

"No, the deal is, send us ten thousand dollars or we call the D.A. Period."

"Oh, don't even start with that. A deal is a deal. We've got a contract. You want me to come up there and enforce this contract?"

"Sure."

"I have to tell you, friend, you do not want to see me in that little pissant town of yours."

"Why, are you as ugly as you sound?"

He breathed into the phone. "Well maybe I *will* be paying you a visit."

"Good idea. Bring your checkbook."

"What I'm gonna bring is a world of pain."

"Looking forward to it." I hung up. "Kermit!"

"What did they say, Ruddy?" Becky asked anxiously.

"He said he's going to come up here in the pain-mobile. Kermit!"

Kermit came out, looking fearful. Becky put a hand on my arm as if to keep me from hitting him. "Do you know how much this place means to me and my sister?" I seethed. "This is going to ruin us. Ten thousand dollars!"

"Are they going to send us the money?" Becky asked.

I stared at them, their eyes hopeful and frightened, like children. The anger left me and I shook my head wearily. "People like this don't pay what they owe other people, Becky."

"How can you be sure?"

"Because I make my living off people like this." I ran my hands through my hair. "Becky, I need to talk to you a minute." I pulled her over so that we were standing under the protective arms of Bob the Bear.

"What are we going to do, Ruddy?" I had never seen Becky so frightened. I put an arm on her shoulder.

"It's going to be okay, Becky. I'll talk to Milton. He'll give me the money and take a note on the house."

She nodded. "I'll pay it back, Ruddy, I swear—"

"I know, of course you will," I interrupted. "I'm not worried about that. There's just one condition."

She searched my eyes. "Ruddy, *no*."

I nodded. "I want Kermit out of here. He's been nothing but trouble for us, can't you see? This whole thing has been a disaster. He's just using us for the credit card account. He wants his *third*."

"No, he loves me," Becky whispered in a tiny voice.

"Becky, you don't have to settle for someone like Kermit!"

She made her calculation, standing there, and then

straightened, pulling back from my arms. "No, Ruddy. If that's the condition, then no deal."

She turned from me and strode away, heading back into the kitchen to be with Kermit. I watched her go with my mouth open.

"She sort of called your bluff there, didn't she?" Alan's dry voice asked.

I walked out into the street so that Alan and I could talk. "I wasn't bluffing."

"Oh, really. So you're just going to let the Black Bear go out of business, then?"

I didn't answer because I didn't know what I was going to do.

Monday morning I was awake before dawn, agitatedly pulling on clothes and scooping up the court papers for Einstein Croft. Jake, afraid I'd drag him out for a walk at that unholy hour, wouldn't even look at me as I headed out the door. Time to earn my fifty bucks.

Alan came awake on the highway. *"We're headed to East Jordan,"* he noted.

"Yeah."

"Shouldn't we go up to Traverse City and find Wexler?"

"I think Wexler is doing a pretty good job of finding us. Besides, what do you want to do, just sit and watch him all day?"

"See what he's up to," Alan agreed.

"Well, that sounds like a complete waste of time to me. Besides—and this may be difficult for you to comprehend—but occasionally I involve myself with things that have nothing to do with you."

"Ah, the good mood you were in all weekend continues to make its presence felt," Alan observed.

He had no idea. I wanted to punch somebody. I

wanted to punch *him*. I felt as if my skin itched, as if I was sitting on the bench while my team lost the game.

The gray overcast sky became gradually lighter, which is how dawn presents itself in a northern Michigan spring. I turned off my headlights and automatically twitched my fingers toward the repo switch, but I didn't flip it—there was no point. I stopped twenty yards away from Einstein Croft's new gate, chewing on my lip.

"So now what, we wait for him to come out and go to work?" Alan inquired.

"That's the idea."

"And what, follow him? How do you get him to pull over so you can serve him the papers?"

"I don't know."

"They probably aren't going to let you back on the PlasMerc lot."

"Probably not."

"So how is this going to work?"

A light popped on in Einstein's house. He was awake.

"You can't very well serve him from a moving truck," Alan argued. *"He's moving from behind the fence at his house to the fence at the factory."*

I put my truck into gear. "Good point." I punched the accelerator.

"What are we doing?" Alan shouted.

"Improving my mood!"

I hit the fence full force with the front bumper of my truck and it popped right off the hinges. I charged up the steep driveway, rocking to a stop behind Einstein's truck.

I got out, tasting blood in my mouth. I must have kissed the steering wheel.

"Are you out of your mind?" Alan asked.

I walked up the steps toward Einstein's front door,

which flew open. He charged out in his bathrobe, holding his rifle out in front of him. His face was full of fury and he pointed the gun at me and I lunged forward and grabbed the thing, twisting it up and to the side, pulling it from his grasp. I spun and threw the rifle over by where Doris lived. Einstein, his expression black, swung his fist at my face. I ducked the punch, then stepped in and slugged him in the chest. He sat down.

"Good morning, Mr. Croft." I took the court summons and stuffed it in the pocket of his bathrobe. "You've been served."

He was still sitting there as I backed my pickup down the steep driveway, over the broken gate, and out into the street.

"Can you do that?" Alan demanded.

"Did it."

"Destroy property? Hit him?"

"Did you happen to notice the rifle he was pointing at my head, Alan?"

"I think maybe you're upset about what is happening at the Black Bear and decided to take out your anger on Einstein Croft."

"And I think I'm sick to death of your psychotherapy."

Milt wasn't particularly pleased to hear that the fence had become defective during my service of Einstein Croft. "I'll call the sheriff, see if the customer filed a complaint," he told me. "Also, I see in the paper this morning that the cosigner died a couple days ago."

"Einstein's father?"

"Yeah. I don't know what this means for the account, I'll call the bank today and ask. Maybe if there's an estate, they'll just sue that and won't bother with writ of replevin."

"So you punch the guy out a couple of days after his father died," Alan translated for me after we left Milt's office.

"Well I didn't know that at the time," I replied peevishly. "Otherwise I would have let him shoot me."

My afternoon consisted of tailing a guy from his house to the hardware store and driving off in his pickup when he went inside. I wrote up the recovery and called Milt with a certain listlessness—it seemed like somehow the joy had gone out of stealing cars.

I perked up when it occurred to me I was near enough to East Jordan to see Katie. I called her at work and asked her out to dinner, and when she came to the door in a pair of jeans and a dark red sweater I realized that Alan was asleep and grabbed her for a kiss I'd been storing up for forty-eight hours.

"Whoa!" she said with a laugh. "I take it you're glad to see me!"

During dinner in Charlevoix, at the Grey Gables where the whitefish was much better than the Black Bear's, I decided nothing I had ever accomplished in my life was as important as making Katie Lottner smile. I felt better than if I'd crashed into a thousand fences. We lingered over coffee and dessert until the hostess turned up the lights so the cleaning crew could close up.

"Where to?" I asked as I slid behind the wheel of my truck.

Katie was giving me a mischievous grin. "Nathan and my mom are still out of town," she informed me.

And Alan was still asleep.

"Good," I said, starting the truck. She slid over next

to me like a high school date and I prayed my thumping heart wouldn't wake up her father.

As I hit the East Jordan city limits a patrol car swung out from behind me and then its flashing lights went on. I groaned aloud.

"Were you speeding?" Katie asked.

"Well . . . yeah," I admitted. She laughed because she knew exactly why I had been in such a hurry.

I was ready for a confrontation with Deputy Timms, if necessary, but the officer was someone I'd never seen before. He didn't pull out his ticket book. "Mr. McCann?"

"Yes, sir?"

"Sheriff Strickland would like to speak to you. Would you step over to my patrol unit, please?"

The deputy used a cell phone to call the sheriff, which disappointed me—I'd sort of expected that he would use the radio. He handed the phone to me and I awkwardly held it to my ear.

"I've been looking for you all evening, where have you been?" Strickland asked without preamble.

"Charlevoix, sir. We went out to dinner."

"We. Who's we?"

"Katie Lottner, sir," I told him, though I really didn't want to.

There was a long pause. "Put her on a minute," he instructed.

Just great. "He wants to talk to you," I told her, holding out the phone.

"To me?" Katie took the phone. "Sheriff?" She listened, nodding. "Yes, sir. All evening. Starting at I'd say seven. Yes, sir. The entire time. Okay."

She handed the phone back, eyes puzzled.

I'd used the time she'd been talking to Strickland to

formulate a speech about how I could date anyone I wanted—a *fast* speech, due to her mother being out of town and Alan still asleep—but the sheriff surprised me.

"I need you to come to your house, Mr. McCann," he said. It didn't sound like a request.

"Um, can't we do this tomorrow, Sheriff?" I asked, trying to keep the pleading out of my voice.

" 'Fraid not, son."

"But why?"

"Ruddy, there's been a homicide in your living room. Occurred around nine o'clock this evening. I'm looking at a male, late twenties, shot in the head. I need you to come down here, help us identify him and figure out what happened."

I gripped the phone, sucking in a deep breath.

Jimmy.

26

Free and Clear

The deputy gave Katie a ride back home and I drove through the black night toward Kalkaska, my chest feeling as if I held my breath the whole way. "Alan! Alan!" I kept shouting, trying to wake him up. I had never felt so alone in my life. I reached for my own cell phone, wanting to call my sister, anybody, but I couldn't get a signal and in a fit of irrational rage I chucked the thing out my window. I can't be the only person in the world who has ever done that.

My house was a circus of police tape and patrol cars. Strickland met me at the end of my sidewalk.

"Is it Jimmy?" I blurted.

He shook his head. "I don't know who it is."

I started to move forward, but he stopped me with a firm hand. "I'm going to take you into your house. You are to touch nothing, understand me, Ruddy? We walk in on the plastic. You look at the victim. We come back out. Got it?"

I nodded.

"You up to this, son?" he asked more softly.

I swallowed. "Yeah." But I wasn't, not if someone had killed Jimmy.

I followed Strickland into my house. I numbly registered broken glass on the carpet before I saw the sprawled body, his face turned away from me, the back of his head a bloody mess.

"Come over here." Strickland gripped my arm and moved me carefully to where I could see the face. "Know who this is?"

He was a large man, muscular, a tattoo of some kind reaching blue tendrils from inside his shirt to the base of his neck. I shook my head.

"No. I've never seen him before." My relief was so overwhelming I felt tears collecting in my eyes. I hastily raised a trembling hand and wiped them away. If I lost Jimmy I didn't know what I would do.

Strickland frowned at me in concern. "You okay?"

"Yeah, I just . . . I thought it might be Jimmy Growe. He's staying with me in the upstairs unit." I let out a breath.

"I should talk to him, too, then. Know how I can get in touch with him?"

"No, not at the moment." I was seized with another alarming thought. "What about my dog? Did you see my dog? He was in the house."

"Hold." Strickland snapped a radio off his belt and held it to his face. "Strickland here. Anyone have eyes on a dog?"

The silence gave me my answer even before someone came back and told the sheriff no sir, didn't see any dog.

"Jake?" I shouted. Strickland grunted in feeble protest as I stepped off the plastic and went to my bedroom. The door was open and there, lying completely still, was my dog, sprawled motionless on the bed where he was never allowed.

I almost didn't want to look at him. In the dim light from the hall, his eyes were open and he didn't seem to be breathing. Why would Drake kill my dog? What kind of bastard kills a man's *dog*?

"Oh, Jake," I said softly. Strickland's shadow filled the doorway behind me. "Jake, Jakey" I whispered. I put my hand on him. He was still warm.

His eyes looked at me.

"Jake? Jake!"

He feebly wagged his tail. I put my face to his neck, laughing into his fur. Probably he figured that with Drake breaking in and gunshots going off and the cops overrunning the place, all rules were out the window and he could sleep on the bed as long as he was quiet. "You crazy mutt. What kind of watchdog are you? There must be twenty people here."

Jake's look indicated I wasn't paying him enough to be a watchdog.

"Come on, Jake," I ordered. With a world-weary sigh, Jake eased off the bed and followed me into the living room.

Strickland escorted me back outside. "Your back window is broken and the back door was open. From the position of the body, it looks like he was standing there, looking out your front window at something, maybe a car in the street. We pulled a slug out of your paneling; that's where it wound up after exiting." Strickland was eyeing me carefully, seeing how I processed what he was telling me. I nodded, but my thoughts were on Jimmy. He was probably out doing something with some female.

"Pretty big fellow," Strickland observed.

"Yeah."

"The light on behind him, someone standing out here with a deer rifle would probably think it was you." We looked at each other. "Anybody got reason to want to put a bullet in you, Ruddy?"

I evaded the question, jamming my hands in my pockets and turning back to my house. "I think you'll find out that guy's name is Drake. I don't know his first name. He's from Detroit. You look around, you'll probably come across his car parked nearby."

Strickland nodded. "I've got someone doing that right now. Who is this Drake person to you?"

I told him only that a business deal had gone south and that a man who claimed I owed him money had said he was going to come up to Kalkaska and talk about it.

"So he broke into your house?"

"He kind of implied it was going to be that sort of talk."

Strickland didn't like any of it—I had a feeling I would soon be back to "Mr. McCann." I felt Alan come awake, making a startled noise when he saw to whom I was talking.

"You got anything else to say?" the sheriff asked.

"No, sir. This guy Drake threatened me and obviously came up here to have it out. He broke into my house and someone shot him from the street. But it wasn't me, I was out with Katie Lottner." There, now Alan knew everything.

"And that's it."

"Well . . ." I took a breath. "When you do ballistics on that rifle slug, you might compare it to what you took out of Alan Lottner's body, see if they came from the same gun."

"Ruddy!" Alan exclaimed, shocked.

Strickland stared at me. "What in God's name are you implying?"

"It's just a hunch, sir."

"A hunch."

"Yessir."

Strickland leaned over and spat his toothpick out onto the grass. "Like your dream. Same thing."

"Yessir."

He mournfully shook his head. "Move along, McCann. My office will let you know when you can get back into your house. Probably tomorrow."

Jimmy and I spent the next two nights on cots in the back room of the Black Bear, Jake happily sleeping on the floor between us.

When we were kids, Becky and I thought sleeping in the bar was a special treat, and would stay up half the night telling spooky stories to each other. I was never scared, though, because I felt sure that Bob the Bear would protect us. Now, though, I was being hunted by Franklin Wexler—it was up to me to provide protection for everybody else.

Two nights twisting and thrashing on a rickety steel-springed cot with a thin, almost prison-issue mattress should have played havoc with my back, but I felt remarkably pain-free each morning.

"Yoga," Alan said simply when I remarked on it.

"Yoga," I repeated. "Alan, we talked about this."

"What do you expect me to do when you're asleep?"

"I expect you to lie there."

"So stretching and exercising so you don't wind up paralyzed from a night on that hideous contraption you call a cot is against the rules?"

"Doing *anything* is against the rules. What if Jimmy saw me doing yoga?"

"What if he did?"

"People like me don't do *yoga*," I snapped.

I was back to being the most exciting attraction in town. Everyone wanted to ask me who Drake was, why he broke into my house, and why he got shot. "I can't talk about it while there's a police investigation going on," I said glumly. This was like trying to calm a crowd by setting fire to it: My lack of comment galvanized every gossip in town.

"They're saying Kermit shot him, to protect me," Becky told me on Friday.

"Maybe he did," I speculated. Kermit was standing there, trying to figure out if he should look proud over this. Alan was asleep.

"What was the damage today?" I asked. With every mail delivery, more bounces arrived, and we had no new business to replace it.

"Just eight hundred," Becky responded faintly.

"I'm going to go over and talk to Milt in a little while. I'll borrow what, fifteen thousand?"

Becky's eyes were sorrowful as she nodded.

Kermit cleared his throat. "I looked into new business, but we're not likely to find someone to let us decimate the funds like that."

My patience broke with an audible snap—I'd had it with Kermit's wonderful vocabulary. "Decimate. To destroy," I said to him, my voice shaking with anger.

Kermit looked a little surprised at the heat in my response. "No, I mean, to keep a tenth of the business."

"You said decimate. It means to destroy, like blow up," I shouted.

Kermit glanced at Becky. "Ruddy . . ." she began.

"No! No, Becky." I pointed at her. "I've had it with Mr. Vocabulary. Let's get a dictionary. We're going to settle this whole thing once and for all. Right here. Right now."

"What whole thing?" she asked timidly.

"No!" I yelled. I marched into the back room and grabbed a dictionary, flipping agitatedly through the D's. "Decimate!" I cried. I stopped, moving my lips a little.

One of the meanings of the word "decimate" is "remove one-tenth of."

I slapped the dictionary shut. "Okay! Fine! You win, Kermit! Happy now?" I stomped out the door.

Alan came awake as I was trudging down the muddy sidewalk. *"What are you so angry about?"* he asked.

"What makes you think I'm angry?" I challenged.

"I can tell by the way you're walking. And your fists are clenched."

"Let me ask you this, Alan. What does the word 'decimate' mean to you?"

"Decimate?"

"Just answer the question."

He thought about it. *"I guess it means to destroy something."*

"Aha!"

"Also to remove every tenth man from a group, or withhold ten percent of something," he reasoned.

"Well, why do you keep dropping off to sleep all the time? What kind of person are you? You're never around when I need you!" I stormed.

"Sorry?"

"Alan, this is one of those times when you should just stop talking," I fumed.

Milt was in his office when I got there. "That fence you hit, Einstein's place?" he greeted.

"That I allegedly hit," I responded. Alan snorted.

Milt waved his hand. "Doesn't matter. Turns out Croft put the thing in without a permit, and get this—it wasn't even on his property, it was too close to the road. You want to, you can sue *him*."

Milt handed over a couple of assignments—the death grip of winter was finally relaxing its hold on business a little bit, and we were heading for a far happier time— repo season.

With business picking up it felt like a good time to tell him I needed to borrow some money, at least fifteen thousand dollars, maybe more, and that I had a free- and-clear house he could attach as collateral.

"For the Bear?" he asked when I explained what the money was for. "I guess I don't understand, I was in there last night. A lot more business than I've ever seen on a weeknight. My nephew says they're going to have to hire someone to help cook."

"It's not that. I just got us into a bad business deal, Milt, and this is the only way out of it."

Milt said he'd get going on the paperwork, and Alan was silent when I got into the tow truck. "Okay, Alan, what is it?" I demanded testily.

"*Why didn't you explain about Kermit's numbers- running business?*" Alan asked. "*Seems like it would have been a perfect opportunity to let him know what's going on with his nephew.*"

"I don't like that sly tone in your voice, Alan."

"You can't help it, you like the guy."

"Who, Kermit? I loathe the guy. But I love my sister. So . . ." I shrugged.

"So you decided not to tell Milt because it would have gotten Kermit in trouble with his uncle," Alan finished for me. *"Ruddy McCann, repo man with a heart of gold."*

"Yeah, well, don't let it get out," I grunted.

I spent the afternoon hauling a Chevy Malibu out of the middle of a cow pasture. According to the file, the customer decided he was too inebriated to drive on the roads one night and attempted to make it home from the bar by traveling directly overland. He made it through some barbed-wire fences without a problem, but became bogged down in the mud and concluded he shouldn't have to pay for such a defective automobile. He called the bank and told them where to find it. The bank's collection department was headquartered in Los Angeles and apparently the folks there thought that *cow pasture* was roughly the same as *shark tank,* so instead of calling a tow truck they elected to contract out to a repo man the task of recovering their collateral from amid the dangerous animals.

In truth, the biggest danger from cows is their curiosity. As I shoveled and cursed and squirmed around in the mud trying to hook the car frame solidly enough to winch it out, they stood around and watched, their flat expressions communicating a complete lack of comprehension. When I finally managed to get underneath the car I looked over and three of them had their heads lowered so they could watch what I was doing. They didn't seem particularly awed at this feat by a superior species.

"What if one of them is a bull?" Alan asked nervously.

"You see any horns, Alan? Only thing we have to worry about is one of them stepping on us while trying to get a better view."

We had a busy Friday night, busy enough that I could let Becky serve Janelle bourbon without making it appear I was avoiding her. Janelle, though, kept turning her eyes toward me, so finally I steeled myself and went over to her table.

"Hey, Janelle."

"You've made some amazing changes in here. I love the new floor," she greeted. "Engineered wood. Nice."

"Becky did all the work," I replied.

She looked good—hell, she looked very good, everything pulled together, a black sweater and black skirt clinging tightly but tastefully to her curves. She sat back in her chair and gazed at me for a long moment, while I stood there getting more and more uncomfortable. Alan, of course, was asleep.

"I'm going to visit my sister in Kansas City for a month," she said softly. "Might look for a job while I'm there. Get out of this place."

"Wow, really? That's great."

"I leave tomorrow. I have a bunch of food in the fridge. Rather than me throw it out, why don't you come over after the Bear closes and pick it up? It won't last for as long as I'll be gone."

Her eyes were watching me steadily.

"Oh, well, that's really nice, Janelle. The thing is . . ." I cleared my throat. "I'm sort of seeing somebody."

I couldn't tell if she thought I was lying—it certainly *felt* like I was lying.

"I'm just offering you the food from my fridge, Ruddy," she replied, her voice faintly mocking.

"I can't."

She looked away from me. "Suit yourself."

I watched her walk out that night, in heels no other woman ever tried to wear in the Black Bear, and not for the first time felt slightly regretful over my decisions surrounding Janelle. But you can't have everything, and with Katie I was trying to direct all my efforts into having *something*.

The next day was Saturday and Katie and I had planned a picnic on Lake Michigan. Since I was going to be in East Jordan I decided to take care of a little errand and drove over to Einstein Croft's place. I pulled a thin envelope out of my folder and walked up the steep driveway, which had been completely cleared of any fence. Doris was picking at the ground and pointedly ignored me as I mounted the stone steps and knocked on Einstein's door.

Einstein looked and smelled like the inside of his house, stale booze coming off his breath. He smiled a little when he saw me, and for an uneasy moment I wondered if he had a pistol stuffed in his belt.

"*I don't like this,*" Alan muttered. "*He looks too happy to see us.*"

"Mr. Croft?"

He stepped outside. "C'mere a second."

"Sorry?"

He pushed past me and clumped down the steps. "Got something I want to show you."

"*I wouldn't go with him,*" Alan stated nervously.

"I'm just here to give you something," I said.

"And I've got something for *you*," Einstein replied. He kept walking.

Curious, I followed.

"*Ruddy . . . ,*" Alan pressed anxiously.

Einstein strode toward the back of his property line, not looking back. Glancing over, I noticed the rifle was still lying in the mud where I'd thrown it. My father would have killed me for treating a weapon like that.

"Here ya go, Repo Man. She's all yours." Einstein grinned at me and gestured expansively to what was left of his truck. He'd burned it in the center of a patch of concrete that looked like it had once been the floor of a garage. The tires had melted off the rims, the interior had turned to ash, and everything made of aluminum or plastic had run off onto the ground.

"*That's insurance fraud,*" stated Alan the amateur lawyer.

"You can't file an insurance claim on a fire you set yourself, Mr. Croft. That would be fraud," I advised him.

He threw back his head and laughed. "In-surance! I don't got any in-surance. I'm telling ya you can have it. Sorry it got a little burnt." He laughed at my expression, loving the moment.

Sighing, I handed him the envelope. He took it from me suspiciously. "What's this?"

"It's a free-and-clear title, Mr. Croft."

He blinked at me in noncomprehension.

"The cosigner had a life insurance policy on the loan. Your dad. When he died, it paid off in full. The truck's all yours, free and clear."

Einstein stared at me.

"Have a nice day, Mr. Croft."

I resisted the temptation to glance back, but I sensed

that Einstein Croft was still standing there, frozen in place, as I came out of the trees and walked down his driveway. "Nice meeting you, Doris," I called to the goose, who raised her head and watched me go with a disapproving expression.

I was just driving past the PlasMerc factory when a patrol car lit up its emergency lights behind me. "Every time I go to East Jordan," I muttered, pulling over.

It turned out to be the same deputy with the same message as the night Drake was killed: The sheriff wanted to talk to me.

"Can you follow me to his office, please, sir?" the deputy requested.

"To the . . . to the jail?" I repeated.

"Just to the sheriff's office, sir."

"Couldn't we do this on the cell phone?"

Apparently not. *"What do you suppose Strickland wants?"* Alan wanted to know as we followed the deputy.

"Well, let's see, Alan. He's had two murder victims turn up this year, both having something to do with me. I'm surprised he hasn't decided to make me a permanent guest of the county by now."

Strickland was standing at his window when the deputy led me in, and lowered himself into his chair with a weary sigh. He pulled out a file. "All right, then. Tell me why you thought the ballistics from the rifle that killed Drake would match the one from Lottner."

"Did they?" I blurted.

Strickland gave me a stony glare. "Tell me why you thought the ballistics from the rifle that killed Drake would match the one from Lottner."

"Because Franklin Wexler and Nathan Burby killed Alan Lottner, and I think they blew up the nursing home, and I think they shot Drake in my living room, believing it was me."

There was a long silence, during which Strickland just stared at me.

"*Oh, Ruddy,*" Alan said sadly.

27

A Meeting with Sheriff Strickland

Strickland was quiet for so long I was afraid he was thinking of just pulling his weapon and shooting me. Finally he cleared his throat and spoke very quietly. "Why do you think these two men committed those crimes?"

"Because that's what I dreamed. I mean, I didn't dream about the nursing home or about Drake, but in my dream, that's who killed Alan."

"Why would they do something like that?"

I shook my head. "I don't know. Maybe Marget Lottner was seeing Nathan Burby and he decided to get rid of the competition."

"So Mrs. Lottner is involved, too," Strickland speculated neutrally.

"No!" Alan shouted.

I cocked my head, considering. "Well, maybe, but I don't think so."

"Ruddy, you know that's not right," Alan lectured me.

"I mean, I *don't* know that's not right, but it could be," I said, trying to keep the irritation out of my voice.

Strickland was pondering something. "I've read the file on the nursing home explosion probably one hundred times. Did you know a woman named Elizabeth Wexler was killed in the bombing?"

"Liddy Wexler, yes I did."

"Everyone with a relative at the home was looked at. Franklin Wexler was in Las Vegas that night. I remember that because in the file there's a picture of him shaking hands with Wayne Newton."

I shook my head in frustration. "Well, okay, look. I can't explain it. But, Sheriff, what if when we die, there's a . . . a remnant of us, something of us that stays around sometimes after we're gone. Something no one can explain or prove, but that can get a message to the living."

"You're saying what, that Alan Lottner is communicating with you from beyond the grave?"

"Please don't tell him, Ruddy," Alan begged.

"No, just that I think the dream came from him. Sheriff, if you search Burby's and Wexler's houses, I know you'll find the rifle that killed Alan and Drake."

He shook his head. "No, I won't."

"How can you say that?" I asked in frustration.

"Because it wasn't the same gun. You were wrong about that."

"Oh."

"I don't have probable cause to search anything except *your* home—there was a dead body in the living room, last time I was there."

"Yes, because Burby and Wexler thought it was me."

"Nathan Burby is out of town, according to Deputy Timms," Strickland observed.

"Oh, yeah. Right, I knew that. So it must have been Wexler."

He sighed.

"If you pull in Wexler for questioning . . ."

Strickland raised his cold eyes to mine.

"*Oh-oh,*" Alan murmured. "*He looks angry.*"

But when Strickland spoke again, it was without heat. "When I was a cop in Muskegon, twenty years ago, one of my first calls was on a woman, shot to death in her bedroom. We were out canvassing the area, checking garages and backyards to see if maybe the perp was hiding in the area. I rang the doorbell of a neighbor and when the guy opened the door, I knew he was the one. I don't know how I knew it, I just had it, that feeling in my gut, that I was looking at the guy who shot the victim.

"I was just a beat cop then, but when I told the homicide detective about the feeling I had, he followed up on it, and they nailed the guy on forensics."

Strickland stood up and stared out his window, his hands in his pockets. Then he shook his head. "I am not going to pull in anyone for questioning based on a dream, McCann. You say you have a, a remnant of some kind, but that doesn't do me any good. I can't take it to the D.A. and I certainly can't as a police officer act on it. A man was killed in your living room the other night and you're an ex-con—those are things I can act on."

"*He's going to arrest you!*" Alan squeaked.

I swallowed. Absurdly, the only thought I had was that if I were taken into custody I would miss my date with Katie to see the sunset.

Strickland wasn't arresting me, he was dismissing me. "My gut's been telling me all along that you're clean on this, that you didn't kill Alan Lottner. I think you made a mistake you're going to have to live with the rest of your life, but you're not the same kind of criminal that lived next door to the murder victim in Muskegon. And I understand that there are some things we can't explain, like how I knew I was looking at the perpetrator twenty years ago when he opened the door. But what was true then is true now—it takes police work to solve a crime." He turned away from the window, giving me a sober appraisal. "It's best you go home now, Ruddy."

I left the station feeling as if I'd just somehow been found not guilty—but only by reasonable doubt.

Katie and I watched the sun expand into a huge orange ball and drop into Lake Michigan with our arms around each other, and then decided nothing would be more fun for her than to watch me help Becky tend bar.

We drove to Kalkaska, but as we drew close to the Black Bear, traffic—and there never really is such a thing in Kalkaska that time of year—was at a standstill. The congestion seemed at its worst right in front of the bar.

"Why all the cars?" Katie asked curiously.

I looked at her. "I don't know. Something's going on."

We parked at my house and made our way back to the Bear on foot. The place was packed to the walls; I had to shove my way in.

"I had no idea this place was so popular!" Katie shouted to me over the crowd noise.

I shook my head. "It isn't!"

We fought our way to the bar and found out why there was such a mob: Becky was pouring everyone free champagne. "Ruddy!" she shrieked when she saw me, giving me a huge hug and a kiss.

I reminded Becky that she had already met Katie, and Becky gave her an ebullient hug, too. "I take it that we're drinking what we're not giving away?" I asked.

Becky tugged on me and I nodded at Katie to give me a minute. In the back room, things were more quiet.

"This is the best day of my life, Ruddy," Becky told me. "You know what we got in the mail today?"

"The new Home Depot catalogue?"

"No!" Becky shook her head wildly. She was, I decided, drunk, a state in which I'd never seen her before. "The money."

"The money?" I repeated stupidly.

"The sex line sent us the money back. Everything we sent to them, they sent back. We can cover everything and have some left over!"

"You're kidding."

"They must have interpreted the death of their business manager as a sign of the way you work," Alan speculated. *"They decided to send you the money before you came down to collect it in person."*

"Kermit says that twenty percent of the charges are ultimately good, so we'll wind up making a profit!" Becky proclaimed.

"That's great, Becky. It means the Bear is no longer an endangered species?"

"Yes!"

"Okay. But free champagne for the entire town? Isn't that a little excessive?"

"Oh, Ruddy, it gets even better." She held up her fist and I looked at it.

"The ring," Alan suggested. I stared at the diamond on her finger, and then up into her radiantly happy eyes.

"I'm engaged, Ruddy! I'm going to be married!"

I opened my mouth.

"Don't say it," Alan warned. *"Don't say anything except 'congratulations,' Ruddy. Please."*

"Congratulations, Becky," I grated.

She threw her arms around me and hugged me fiercely. "Oh, Ruddy, I've never been so happy."

"Okay, good. Good, Becky," I told her, patting her back. "But enough with the free booze, okay? Go tell everyone that we're back to being a pay-as-you-drink enterprise."

She nodded joyously and all but skipped out of the room.

"You see anything coincidental about the fact that we get this money and all of a sudden Kermit wants to marry my sister?" I demanded.

"Easy, Ruddy."

"Isn't he supposed to ask my permission so I can say no?"

"Who are you, the Godfather? Why should he ask you—seems to me asking Becky would be sufficient."

"I'm not going to talk to you if you're going to be like this."

"I thought you were going to give Kermit a break because he makes your sister happy."

"Yeah, but that doesn't mean I want to be related to him!"

Trying to spend time with my date proved to be impossible: even with the free alcohol spigot shut off we were crammed with people, and I worked the bar without pause, darn near pouring myself into carpal tunnel syndrome. Katie ran into some girlfriends who ultimately gave her a ride home, laughing off my apology with a quick kiss on the cheek.

"Call me?" she asked, though we both knew the answer. As long as I had permission, yes, I would call her every day.

After last call I went into bouncer mode, forcing people to leave. Jimmy sat in a chair, his black hair matted with sweat, and my sister and Kermit were cooing to each other in the corner. What looked like a thousand empty beer bottles littered the place, and I knew the floor would have to be scrubbed and waxed.

"Good thing tomorrow is Sunday, give us some time to clean up," I observed. When football season ended the Bear was closed Sundays until Memorial Day—a policy we might have to rethink now that people were eating our food.

I walked home with Jimmy, the cold air refreshing on my face. "Look, Ruddy," Jimmy said uncomfortably. "I kinda said that I would see Vicki tomorrow."

"You mean," I replied, stopping and staring at him in disbelief, "that you'd rather spend time with your daughter than help clean up the bar?"

He frowned. "Well . . . yeah."

I slapped him on the shoulder. "Don't worry about it." I was just glad he was alive.

The bar looked even worse when I limped in after noon the next day, especially compared to the sunshine and warmth outside—we were having one of those exceptional days that fooled you into thinking this part of the country was paradise. Jake trotted in on my heels and sniffed disdainfully at all the spilled beer. I rubbed his ears and he groaned a little.

Becky was tiredly picking up trash and empties. "Up late celebrating?" I asked her.

She blew the hair off her face and gave me a lazy, satisfied smile. "A little."

I was so overwhelmed with unexpected emotion at that moment that I felt my eyes tear. I turned away so she wouldn't see. My sister Becky was going to be married. She was happy. God, how I'd wanted her to be happy for so long and now here she was, smiling without covering her mouth.

"You should tell her," Alan murmured. *"Life's too short and precious to keep things like this hidden. Tell her what you're feeling."*

I cleared my throat and turned back. "Becky."

She looked up from the collection of glasses she was stacking.

"I love you," I choked. My mouth trembled a little, and I nodded, overcome.

"I love you, too, Ruddy," she said simply. She went back to her work.

We labored side by side, cleaning up the Bear on a Sunday morning the way we used to when we were younger. Okay, so maybe we had tablecloths and soup du jour and windows you could actually see through, but it was still the Black Bear, still home.

An hour later I ran to the store for some cleaning supplies and when I returned Becky had a message for me. "Sheriff Strickland called for you," she said. "He wants you to meet him out where you found the Realtor's body at one o'clock."

"Did he say why?" I asked.

She shook her head. "Just that you need to be there."

I looked at my watch. "Okay then. I'd better leave. You don't have to do all of this, though; I'll get to it when I get back."

"That's okay."

"Where's Kermit?" I asked with forced neutrality.

"He'll be back. Milt sent him to Traverse City to pick someone up at the airport."

I took Jake with me as I walked home to get my pickup. The cops had cleaned up and left. My dog seemed disappointed to leave the bar: he wanted to sleep between Jimmy and me. I looked at him sadly regarding the blanket on the floor, and it was as if I could feel the stiffness in his old joints. Life was *too* short. "Hey, come here a minute, Jake."

He followed me into my bedroom. I patted the bed. "Up."

He regarded me in astonishment.

"Up, Jake."

He launched himself onto the bed, his tail wagging. "Good boy," I told him as he circled three times and lay down with a contented sigh. The new rules were instantly approved and accepted. When I scratched his ears, his eyes closed and he moaned with pleasure. "You go ahead and sleep here. I'll be home soon, Jakey."

I drove north and soon was winding my way through the Jordan Valley. The trees were all feathered with green, the grass looked new and tender: In a few weeks it would be summer, unless it snowed.

I sensed Alan's uneasiness as we turned down the now-familiar dirt track that led to the scene of his murder. Though we were just crawling out of winter instead of rushing toward it, the day felt much the same as it had when Alan had been killed, with sun streaming through the gaps in the branches and lighting up the ground with dancing sparkles. We cruised past the felled oak tree with the huge hole, the ground next to it still black from everyone tramping around in the mud.

"I expected to see him here," I said, frowning. It was ten after one; it didn't seem like Strickland to be late.

"Maybe he's up where the cabin used to be, next to the river."

I drove on, pulling right up to the old foundation. When I shut off the truck, the woods were completely silent. There was no sign of the sheriff.

I walked down to the water's edge. The stream was swollen with meltwater, more than four feet deep here in what was usually a shallow rapid. Where the waters sluiced their way past some fallen trees they laughed out a loud, wet gurgle, a pleasant and welcoming sound that lifted some of the dread away from this place. My eyes found the spot where Alan had picked up my ring. I could remember it vividly now, feel the icy water as he plunged his hand in.

"There's still something we're missing," Alan muttered. *"Some connection we're not getting, some reason I was killed."*

"Alan, what if it wasn't complicated at all? What if it's just that Nathan Burby wanted you out of the way so he could marry Marget?"

"But it was Wexler with the shovel. Why would he kill me? You heard Katie, they didn't even know each other," Alan argued.

"But they did, remember? The way they were talking, they weren't strangers."

I watched the waters flow past. The property was still for sale, and I pictured myself sitting on a dock in this very spot, dropping a fly on the water to seduce a couple of trout to join me for dinner. And that's when it hit me. They weren't strangers, but they claimed not to know each other, even to this day. There was only one person who could put the two of them together.

Alan Lottner.

"Alan. Who called you that day? Who said they wanted to see the property?"

"I told you, I don't remember."

"But think about it. Could it have been Nathan Burby?"

While Alan pondered this, I heard a noise behind us and turned. Nathan Burby and Franklin Wexler were coming down the hill toward us.

They both had rifles.

28

Fear of Drowning

"Afternoon, fellas," I called, forcing a casualness I didn't feel. Inside, Alan's anxiety was nearly boiling over. I didn't blame him: Last time he'd encountered these two out in the woods, it had not turned out well.

Wexler and Burby approached silently, looking intent.

"Glad you're here. Sheriff Strickland will be along in a minute, and I think he's going to have some questions for you."

The two of them exchanged a look, and the slight smile on Burby's face made my heart sink. "Oh, Nathan, did you pretend to be someone else again? Like you did the day you killed Alan Lottner, and you pretended to be interested in real estate so that he'd come out here and see the two of you together?" I turned to Wexler, who was now only ten feet away, his rifle leveled at me. "Did you know about that, Frank? Or did you think that when Alan showed up it was all some sort of accident?"

Wexler's expression flickered and I nodded at him. "That's right, Frank . . . ."

"Ruddy!" Alan shouted.

Burby's rifle butt slammed me in the back of the head with such force I lost track of where I was. Stars drifted across my vision and my palms hurt from where they'd hit the ground.

Then I was up, driving forward, reaching for Burby. I got under his arms before he could do anything with the rifle and then I was fighting my fight, just as Alan had once told me to do. Burby gasped and crumpled as I punched him in the stomach and the chest and then I went down, felled by Wexler's gunstock.

He'd hit me at the base of my neck and I wouldn't be getting up anytime soon. My head rang and my limbs felt useless. I lay gasping in the mud, stomach churning, barely able to breathe.

"I'm not dead," I slurred.

They grabbed me under the arms and I tried to move my worthless legs, get some power underneath me, but all I could do was flail limply. I strained to see what they were doing, but I couldn't bring my eyes into focus.

And then I hit the water.

"Oh no!" Alan cried. *"Not the water!"*

The cold shock put some strength back into my body but there were two of them and they were pressing down where Wexler had hit me and the pain was paralyzing. I heaved, everything forgotten but the need for air. I put all my strength into it and burst from the surface and whooped in a single breath before they got a better grip and slammed me back down. My right arm was bent behind me but my left was free and I groped around, trying to find balls, eyes, something, but the angle was wrong.

"*Ruddy*," Alan shouted in anguish. *"We're drowning, we're drowning!"*

I wanted to say something to him, but he couldn't hear my thoughts.

My legs grew heavy and my arms stopped obeying instructions to move. Alan went quiet and a blackness leaked into my vision that was far darker than the swirling, muddy waters. *Becky,* I thought. *Katie. Jimmy. Jake.* Good-bye.

"Hey, Ruddy, it's okay," Alan said. The pressure in my chest was building and I knew I was through. I tried one last kick, but had nothing to give.

"Ruddy, this is it, this is my dream," he soothed. *"I know what to do now. You just need to sleep, okay? I've been through this before. Let me do it. I promise, it's okay. Let go now, Ruddy. Give me control of your body. Go to sleep."*

With a frustrated yell I lost my grip on my lungs and sucked the river inside.

"Good-bye, Ruddy," Alan murmured. *"Good-bye."*

29

No Time Left on the Clock

I came awake in darkness and in the middle of a gasping, choking spasm. Water flowed from my mouth and nose and for a panicked moment I couldn't breathe. Coughing, I flailed my hands, coming into contact with a rough blanket that I shoved off my face, gratefully sucking in air past the sodden feeling in my chest. A cramp seized me and I brought up river water from my stomach.

I was in the back of a truck, the steel bed vibrating as the tires hummed down the pavement. Once I stopped throwing up, the shivers started: I was colder than I'd ever been; it felt as if my very bones were frozen. My head ached and I was so weak that for several minutes I lay there expecting to die.

Alan was gone. There was a different quality to his silence, deeper than the odd absence I'd felt when he was asleep. He had died back there in the river, somehow stepping in and taking my death for me. Drowning, just as he'd always feared. I was truly alone, now. Quaking, I clutched my legs and bit back the pain of loss.

After a time I gained control—Alan's voice came to me, almost as if he were still inside. *"You've got to get out of here."* I cautiously looked over the edge of the tarp through the back window into the cab. In the dwindling light I could plainly see Burby and Wexler, two rifles hanging on the rack behind them.

I didn't know where we were or where we were going, but I'd had enough and just wanted to escape. We were moving too fast for me to do anything, though, but ride helplessly down the highway.

They must have a plan for me. At some point, they would come back to check under the tarp and I would be easy prey, unable to defend myself.

Opportunity presented itself a few minutes later. With a screech of brakes that slammed me forward in the truck bed, Wexler stopped, hitting the horn. "Idiot!" he shouted at the vehicle that had sagged onto the highway in front of him, nearly causing a collision as it pulled out of a driveway.

We were rolling again in a second. I had no time. Gulping, I seized the side of the truck and vaulted over, landing heavily in the muddy ditch next to the highway. I held my breath, watching Wexler's brake lights, but nothing happened.

I took my bearings and realized Wexler's truck was headed toward Kalkaska. I was standing only a couple of miles outside of city limits. I ran in that direction, my legs rubbery and useless. Every inhalation seemed to bubble in my chest, and the first mile I coughed more than I breathed, bringing up lungfuls of phlegmy water. Gradually, though, I straightened myself out. My feet were completely numb, hard to keep on track, but after a while a thousand needles stabbed them, and my shivering stopped. My breath sent out billowing clouds of fog.

Thanks to Alan's midnight exercise program, I was a runner now.

There was no traffic, not particularly unusual for a Sunday night—and I wasn't sure what I would do if I saw a vehicle anyway. I was drenched from head to foot, my shirt torn, my shoes missing. Who would pick me up looking like this?

My thought was to get to the Bear, get some warm clothes, and call Strickland. I encountered some traffic once I hit the Kalkaska town limits, but by that time I decided I would get there faster on foot than if I had to try to explain to someone what had happened.

The Bear's front door was locked. Impatiently I dug into my wet pockets and pulled out my keys, my hands trembling as I opened the door. "Becky?" I called.

No one here. I flipped on the lights, noting irrelevantly that the place had been completely cleaned up. A clean towel sat on one of the tables and I picked it up, wiping my face. The cloth came away wet and streaked with mud.

A sound alerted me and I glanced up, startled. Becky stood behind the bar, very still and quiet. "Becky!" I gasped. I took two steps toward her and then stopped. "What's wrong?"

She didn't say anything.

"Becky?"

Franklin Wexler stepped out of the back room, his rifle held steadily on my sister's head. "You sure are tough to kill, boy," he told me.

"Pull that gun down from my sister's head or I'll take it from you and bust you up with it," I said pleasantly.

"First you come on back here and sit down," Wexler

directed. For emphasis, he leaned forward, nearly touching his gun to Becky's head.

"Ruddy, I'm so sorry," Becky murmured.

"You did nothing wrong, Becky."

"I let them in. They said they were your friends."

Wexler grunted. "Enough with the chitchat. Come on."

He kept the rifle on Becky as we walked to the back. As I saw that, the rage left me, left me because the fear doused it like a scream drowning out a whisper. *Becky*.

"She doesn't know anything, Frank. I didn't tell her *anything*. You can let her go, okay?"

Wexler's face was devoid of emotion and humanity. He was going to murder my sister because he'd already decided to. He wasn't going to put any more thought into it than that.

Nathan Burby was waiting for me in the back. He had me sit in a chair while he wrapped duct tape around me, securing me tightly. Next was Becky, whom he sat down across from me. Terror showed on her face and I didn't know what I could say to fix it.

Once we were both stuck to our seats, Burby went to work on something he'd put on the table. His back was to me and I made note of a pistol shoved into his waistband, though I didn't know how I could get my hands on it easily. Wexler dipped his rifle, but kept it handy—having failed to drown me, he was probably less confident that he could keep me taped to a chair than he would have been otherwise.

I stared, realizing what Burby was doing. It was just as Strickland had described: a simple device, just dynamite, a plastic gallon jug of gasoline, and a digital timer.

I had to stall for time. "You set the bomb in the nursing home, didn't you, Nathan? No one would look at you, what motive would you have? Frank here couldn't do it, because his mom was inside. While you were killing old people, Frank was off having his picture taken with Wayne Newton."

Becky stared at me.

"Alan thought you weren't the kind of person who could kill, but you're the worst kind of monster, Nathan. You're a mass murderer."

Neither of them said anything.

"What's wrong, don't either of you assholes *read*?" I taunted. "Now's the time for you to brag about how smart you are, how you managed to pull everything off. You know you want to. It's at the end of every book."

"Shut up," Burby ordered. Wexler, predictably, said nothing at all.

"That's why you had to kill Alan, Nathan. You weren't supposed to know each other. What happened, Frank, your mom didn't want to sell the ranch? So you told Nathan here all about it, and he agreed to help out. After all, he was making ten grand a body to move his cemetery. The firebomb just added some last-minute sales. But Alan shows up while you were still in the planning stage and that meant someone could connect the two of you. So you hit him with a shovel and shot him in the back." I wanted to spit.

"You 'bout done there, Nathan?" Wexler asked.

"Almost," Burby responded.

"Must have seemed like a real coincidence later when your partner married the victim's wife, huh, Frank? He played you for a fool, inviting Alan down there to look at the property. He act all surprised? No idea how Alan happened to be there? Because he made the call. He set you up, Frank."

Burby straightened. "All done."

"Are you listening? Your buddy Nathan can burn up a bunch of old ladies but he doesn't have the guts to kill somebody face-to-face. He wanted Alan Lottner dead, so he arranged for you to do it for him. He sold you out and he'll do it again, Frank."

Burby bit his lip. "I said to shut up."

"I told Strickland that you two killed Alan Lottner. I told him that Frank hit him with the shovel and then you chased him down in the truck and shot him in the leg and then the back of the head. He knows, boys."

Burby's eyes were glassy and he shot a glance at Wexler, who regarded me without blinking and then picked up the duct tape.

"What was supposed to happen today? I disappear, and there's a bombing, so they blame me, like they blamed Alan last time? You two are about the most stupid killers I ever heard of."

Wexler patiently wrapped tape around Becky's mouth. Her eyes grew frantic with fear as she inhaled through her nose. When he came for me his expression was the same as when he swung the shovel: implacable.

"This isn't going to work. It makes no sense!" I shouted in frustration. Then the tape was over my mouth. A minute later, and they were gone.

The red digits on the timer were counting down from five minutes, and I spent the first one of those fruitlessly trying to burst the tape by spreading my arms apart with all my strength. My feet were lashed together to the chair legs, so I couldn't even get to an upright position. I kicked downward, trying to toss the chair backward against the wall.

Becky was watching my furious efforts with wide eyes.

I wanted to sob: she was trusting me to fix it, somehow, but I couldn't.

At two and a half minutes I'd managed to bounce over to an old wine rack and was attempting to catch the tape on the rack's edge. Suddenly there was a bang as the back door of the Bear opened. Becky and I exchanged wild glances.

"Hello?"

Kermit.

I rocked my chair, throwing everything I could into making noise. The digits ticked backward on the timer, and then finally Kermit stood on the threshold, peering into the dim room. "What are you doing?" he asked, puzzled.

We both yelled through our masks and he came inside, jerking in surprise when he saw our bonds. He strode across the room and reached down, pulling at the tape on my mouth, easing it off.

"Sorry." He winced. "You okay? Sorry."

Finally there was enough off of my lips for me to talk. "Rip this off! Hurry!"

He hesitated for just a second, then yanked the tape.

"That's a bomb! There on the table!"

He turned and looked numbly at the kitchen timer, which read 1:30. Ninety seconds.

"Get Becky loose! Get her out of here!" I shouted.

Kermit darted to Becky and began scrabbling at the tape, pulling at it with his fingernails. He ripped the tape off her mouth.

"Oh, Kermit!" she wailed.

He made as if to pick her up, chair and all, then realized he wouldn't be able to get very far that way.

"Get a knife! Kermit, get a knife!" I told him.

He nodded and turned to a drawer, yanking it out with such force the contents spilled to the floor. We had forty seconds. He picked up a small kitchen knife and started sawing away at the tape, his hands shaking. The tape started to part, but slowly, too slowly. Thirty seconds.

Kermit stopped, his shoulders going still.

"Kermit! Hurry!" I bellowed.

He and Becky were staring at each other. He reached a hand up and touched her on the cheek.

"Kermit, no!" she sobbed.

Kermit dropped the knife and ran to the table. He gathered Burby's device in his hands, cradling it like a football, and turned to leave, leaving the jug of gasoline behind.

"*Kermit!*" Becky screamed in anguish.

I thought of Becky's new Dumpster corral. If he threw the bomb in there the cinder-block walls might protect him from the blast. "The Dumpster!" I shouted.

He stopped on the threshold for just a moment, giving me an unreadable look, and then he was gone.

Becky was wailing and straining at the tape, working her one arm completely free, as the back door to the Bear slammed shut.

"Becky," I said.

She raised her eyes to mine, and then the world disintegrated.

The shock of the explosion was like nothing I'd ever felt. The concussion seemed to last for an impossible length of time, punching the air from my lungs, ripping the light from the room. My limbs went limp and useless, my brain fuzzy.

Kermit hadn't managed to throw the bomb into the Dumpster.

Gradually I came to realize that I was cocooned in a false silence, that pieces of ceiling and wall were dropping all around me, though I could hear nothing but a high, clear whine.

The chair I had been sitting on and the tape that had held me to it were both in tatters. My first thought was for the gasoline, but the plastic hadn't ruptured and the jug lay on its side, not leaking. Coughing and choking, I crawled across the floor, feeling my way toward my sister. I saw now that the back wall of the Black Bear was gone, and that the light streaming in was from the bulb in the alleyway, which had somehow emerged unscathed.

"Becky!" I shouted, my own voice silent to my ears.

I found her lying on her back, her glasses gone. When I bent over her, she focused on me, so I knew she could see me. The floor beneath her was slick and dark with what I realized must be her blood.

"Becky, I was wrong about Kermit!" I yelled, still unable to hear myself. "Do you understand me? I was wrong about Kermit!"

Becky raised her hand and grabbed my arm. She was nodding. She said something, but I couldn't hear what it was.

"I was wrong about Kermit!" I said again.

Becky smiled at me, squeezing my arm, and then slowly closed her eyes.

30

Have You ID'd the Body in the Alley?

I'd been concussed a few times in my football career and my body knew the symptoms—an odd dislocation, like watching a movie with frames missing, as the brain sputters and misfires and loses track of time. A sense that the ground is moving when your blurry vision can see very well that it's not. I stared at my hands on the wooden floor, my ears ringing, and willed the world to stop spinning.

I knew I'd been unconscious for a bit but had no sense of how much time might have passed. When a hand grabbed my shoulder I glanced at it lethargically, not really caring if it was threat or assistance.

I was pulled onto my back and found myself staring with confusion into the eyes of my seventh-grade science teacher, Mr. Barnett. Oh yeah, he was one of the Kalkaska volunteer firefighters.

"You hear me okay?" he asked. "Ruddy?"

"Yes." I turned my head and was shocked to see three men loading my sister onto a stretcher—when had they arrived? I blinked, trying to clear my vision, fear piercing my apathy. I looked back to Mr. Barnett. "How is Becky?"

He reached up and stroked his mustache, which I recalled from class meant he didn't like the question. "A piece of wood impaled her in the back, we're going to leave it in place until we get her to Munson Medical. Got the bleeding under control, though."

I put my hand out and grabbed Mr. Barnett's with it. "Is she going to *live*?"

"Live?" The question alarmed him. "Well yeah, of course she'll *live*. I mean, she's as banged up as you are, but nothing fatal."

"She has blood coming out of her ears."

"*You've* got blood coming out of your ears. The left one, anyway."

I snapped my finger by my left ear and heard almost nothing.

Barnett took a breath and surveyed the room. More men were trouping into the Black Bear, some of them in full firefighting regalia. They seemed disappointed there was nothing burning. "Gas line explosion, maybe?" Barnett guessed.

I closed my eyes as if it would help block out the image of Kermit hunched over Burby's homemade bomb. When I opened them, I knew they betrayed the sick feeling in my stomach. "Tell your men they need to look in back. There was a man in the alley."

Mr. Barnett stared at me, then looked wordlessly at the hole where the wall used to be. We were both thinking the same thing: The alley was blast central. He raised a radio to his lips, then lowered it. The firefighters were

right there. "Hey, guys. Check out back, there was someone back there when this happened."

They exchanged glances and three men bolted out the
back, crunching through the debris.

With Becky out of danger, a new thought jolted my
mind. *Katie.* I rolled onto my hands and knees, a wave
of nausea rolling with me. How much time did I have to
get to her before Wexler did?

"Whoa, hang on," Mr. Barnett warned. "We called a
backup from Traverse City; it should be here soon."

"Backup?"

"Ambulance."

"I'm okay."

"No, you're *not.*"

I stood up, taking a deep breath. "I said I'm okay." I
looked toward the back wall, seeing nothing but a giant
hole and that one miraculous lightbulb. Kermit, I knew,
was not going to be okay.

I headed toward the front door, Mr. Barnett discover-
ing along the way what a lot of defensive linemen knew,
which is that if I wanted to go somewhere it was pretty
difficult to stop me. His hand was still clutching my arm
as I stepped out onto the sidewalk.

Sheriff Strickland was hustling in our direction, his
cruiser out in the street, its lights pulsing. Somehow enough
time had passed for the cops to bottle up the main drag
for several blocks in either direction. Strickland's was
the only car in the road. The sheriff drew up in surprise
when he saw me come staggering out of the Black Bear.

"Ruddy. You're up," he noted, as if he'd heard I'd been
taking a nap. He stuck out a hand and I shook it, both
of us taking a moment to exchange odd grins.

"We're waiting for the ambulance from Traverse City. Maybe another twenty minutes," Barnett told him.

Strickland eyed me. "Time enough to talk, then," he decided.

I considered it, and it was tempting: tell Strickland, head out to Katie's house with sirens screaming, bust Wexler and Burby if they were there or go find them if they weren't. Then I thought about Becky screaming Kermit's name, and how complicated my story was, and about a jury sitting through it all, basing the whole case on the testimony of a discredited repo man with a murder on his record and a voice in his head. And it added up to a different conclusion.

I needed to take care of Wexler and Burby myself. Tonight.

"Ruddy!" We all turned to see who had shouted, and Jimmy came running up to us, his face pale. He piled into me, grabbing me and holding me tight. Then he released me, looking apologetic. "Oh, hey, sorry."

"It's okay, Jimmy. It's good to see you, too, actually."

"There are police cars all over the place. You can't even get here." Jimmy glanced at Strickland accusingly.

"I know, son," Strickland said. "It's a crime scene."

His statement brought us all out of reunion mode and back to the matter at hand. I knew how it would go. If I convinced Strickland I was well enough not to need an ambulance, I'd be stuck here answering questions. A ride into Traverse City in an ambulance would be just as bad, carrying me in the opposite direction from where I needed to be. I had to shake loose of the cops and the fire department and make my way to Katie.

Strickland was watching me and I knew too much

speculation was showing on my face. "We need to discuss a few things," he told me.

A firefighter walked up to our little group then, looking official and powerful in his rubber boots and thick fireproof clothing even though it was just Larry from the appliance store.

"Hey, I'm supposed to tell you that the ambulance from Traverse City got diverted. There was a rollover accident on 131, so it's going there instead. Triage." Larry was speaking to no one in particular, not sure to whom he was supposed to address this information.

"Jimmy can take me," I blurted, inspired.

Jimmy nodded, eager to help.

"You should go in an ambulance," Barnett objected. "We can get one from Charlevoix, be here in less than an hour."

"Why? When I lie down it just makes me want to throw up," I argued.

"I have bucket seats, they don't even recline much," Jimmy supplied helpfully.

"I shouldn't wait an hour to get to the hospital, right?" I appealed to Strickland, turning my head so he could see the blood in my ear. "And I get to pick who drives me."

"Okay," Strickland pronounced decisively. "You can ride with Jimmy."

I nodded, trying not to look either devious or triumphant.

"Hey, Sheriff," the radio at his side squawked. He raised it to his lips.

"Go for Strickland."

"We've got a guy in the back alley."

Strickland was watching me as he pressed the button

on his radio. "Copy that. Secure the area, I'm coming back."

"It's Kermit Kramer," I said, my throat growing inexplicably tight. I took a deep breath, blinking. "He was back there."

"He do this? The bomb?"

"No. Of course not. He died to save us."

Strickland raised the radio. "The ten-seven in the alley, he have any ID on him?"

"Come again, Sheriff?"

His irritation showed in the tiniest flicker in his eyelid. "I asked, have you ID'd the body in the alley. Check for a wallet."

"Oh, he ain't dead. He's in the Dumpster and he's afraid to come out."

What? Despite all I'd been through I felt like leaping in the air. Kermit hadn't thrown the bomb in the Dumpster; he'd climbed the thick block walls and thrown *himself* in there.

"Just what the hell happened here, Ruddy?" Strickland asked softly, eyeing me with suspicion.

I shook my head, forcing myself to look damaged and beaten. "I need to go to the hospital," I mumbled.

Strickland wasn't happy with my response, but with a last look at me he left to talk to Kermit.

"Let's go, Jimmy."

"Copy that," Jimmy replied. I had to hide a grin. We headed toward his car. "You cold? Jesus, Ruddy. What happened? What exploded? Is Becky okay?"

I stopped. "This is where I say good-bye. You keep going and drive on out of here—I don't want Strickland coming out and seeing your car still parked up there; I want his men saying you left."

"Wait, what do you mean?"

"There's no *time,* Jimmy. Do it, okay?"

His gaze was confused and even wounded, but a lifetime of seeing me as his big brother led him to do exactly what I asked.

My pickup was, as far as I knew, still out in the woods. Despite the fact that I felt that I'd done enough running for the night, I dashed into the darkness. I stuck to the shadows and within a few minutes I was slipping inside the fence at Milt's repo lot. I scooped the keys off the tow truck's left rear tire and cranked up the engine, which leaped to life as if it understood that I was in a hurry.

The back streets of Kalkaska were clogged with traffic picking its way through unfamiliar territory, so I flipped on my warning lights and the drivers dutifully pulled over and let me charge past.

I kept my brights on and hoped I wouldn't see the red eyes of deer charging across the road, because I wasn't going to be able to stop for them. My speedometer quivered at eighty and I threw myself recklessly into turns that threatened to flip me.

I wasn't at all sure that Wexler and Burby would actually do something to harm Katie. She didn't know anything that could get them into trouble with the law, and as far as they knew, Ruddy McCann was at that moment being scooped into body bags by the Kalkaska volunteer fire department. I just wanted to know that she was safe. Then I would figure out what to do with the two killers. No, not do with. Do *to.* I was going to do something to them that would make it impossible for them to ever hurt anyone I cared about, ever again.

My optimism stuck with me up until the point where

I steered my truck into the long curve in the road where Katie lived with her mom and saw, so, so clearly, Frank Wexler peering out of the window of Katie's travel trailer in the backyard, a rifle cradled in his arms.

I had the sense there were others in the travel trailer, whose lights were ablaze, but I kept my foot on the accelerator and blasted past, thankful that the inside of my cab was repo-dark. I kept going until I was out of sound and sight, then cranked my truck around and stopped facing the way I'd come, my heart pounding.

What are you doing there, Wexler?

But I knew what he was doing there. "He's going to tie up all the loose ends tonight," I said out loud to Alan, who, of course, was no longer there to hear me. Katie, her mother Marget, and probably Nathan Burby. Bang, bang, bang.

I flipped my repo switch and my electronics went dark. I stealthily headed back down the hill toward the house with only the moon to guide me. I killed the motor when I was about twenty yards away and wrestled the power steering around so that I rolled into the driveway. I was coasting silently at about fifteen miles an hour over the back lawn as I approached the travel trailer, and caught a full view of Katie standing up against the sink, talking, looking relaxed, not at all as frightened as she should be. Wexler was out of sight, but Nathan Burby stood next to his wife, his shiny head in stark contrast to his wife's wispy white-blond hair. No one noticed a tow truck ghosting by in the night.

I nearly ran out of momentum before the front wheels hit the lip of the steep hill down to the lake and pulled me forward. I kept my foot lightly on the brake, working harder because the power brakes were out, thinking, not for the first time in my life, that I was glad Milt put the brake lights on the repo switch.

I stopped just a few yards shy of where the pitch in the yard got serious and plunged steeply toward the black water of Patricia Lake. I eased out of the driver's seat and looked up the hill to the travel trailer. My plan, such as it was, was to go into the trailer, get the rifle from Wexler, and kill him with it.

Out of habit I glanced at my watch as I started climbing. It was just past midnight.

Prime time for the repo man.

31

The Midnight Plan of the Repo Man

After I had trudged halfway up the hill I thought of something and reversed course, dashing back to the tow truck, the steep declivity turning my gait into ridiculous, Superman-sized leaps. The problem with walking into the trailer and grabbing the rifle was that Wexler might not like it. He'd already tried to kill me twice and I doubted there was much I could say to dissuade him from taking another shot at it. I needed an edge, something to turn the tables my way.

I slipped on gloves and released the brake on the winch, so that I could stand behind the truck and pull the tow hook off the spool with no resistance. Working frantically, I yanked steel cable off in big loops, trying to estimate how much I'd need. A lot, I'd need a lot. It pooled at my feet, gleaming like dozens of coiled snakes. Finally I figured it had to be good enough, and as quietly as I could I flipped the lever. The electric motor obliged by humming and slowly winding the tow cable back onto the spool.

I grabbed the tow hook and scrambled back up the

hill, working my legs against the gravity, dragging the heavy cable behind me.

The travel trailer's thick, heavy tow tongue rested on a stack of cinder blocks in a reasonably stable arrangement. Without the blocks, the whole trailer would tilt forward like the deck of a sinking ship. If it happened suddenly, it might give me time to lunge across the inside of that trailer and get my hands on the rifle. The winch would pull the trailer off the blocks and it would drop hard.

As I affixed the tow hook to the trailer hitch tongue I despaired to see far too much slack in the cable. I had way overestimated how much I would need. My diversion would be awfully late in coming.

I'd have to think of something to say to keep Wexler from shooting me until the cable snapped taut and the trailer was yanked off the blocks.

I could hear them quite clearly through the open window. "We just need to know what you said," Burby was saying in his unctuous voice, funeral-director nice.

"Honey, like to Dwight, did you tell him anything about what's going on?" came a female voice. That would be Marget, Nathan's wife.

Wait, why was *she* asking that question?

"Think, Katie," Marget urged.

"Anything McCann might have said," Wexler interjected impatiently.

When I opened the door, everyone turned and gaped at me. I suppose I must have made for quite a sight—oil-smudged face, dried blood trailing down my neck, plus, of course, the fact that two of the people in the trailer assumed I had been blown into pieces by Nathan's bomb.

Nathan himself looked more shocked than anyone,

ready to crumple into a dead faint. His pistol was still tucked in his rear waistband, though, so he was far from being a neutral threat. He was closest to me, on my right, standing in an odd little space created by folding the dining table up against the wall. Marget was sitting on the bench seat just inches from him, while Wexler leaned against the sink to the left and Katie stood at the far end. It was all pretty close quarters. The rifle was leaning butt-down against the sink counter next to Wexler, as if people came over with weapons all the time and said, "Oh, let me just set my deer rifle here in the kitchen while we have a friendly chat."

"You were in on it, weren't you, Mrs. Burby," I said to Marget.

Katie looked as if she had been getting ready to rush to me but my flat, hard tone halted her in her tracks. Confusion flickered in her gaze—but not in Marget's. I didn't know the woman at all but the cold glare in her blue eyes let me know I was right on target.

"Was it your idea?" I asked her. "I mean, Nathan calls Alan, asks to meet him out by the Jordan River, the same place where Nathan suggested he and Frank have their little meeting? You thought that one up, didn't you? A divorce is expensive and takes a long time. Murder is more messy, but with all the bodies you three were planning to stack up, what's one more?"

Ah, that one got to Wexler, who had shifted his gaze from me to the married couple, calculating.

How much longer before the cable yanked us off the blocks?

"Mom?" Katie asked.

Burby licked his lips nervously, looking in obvious

panic at his wife, who was staring intently back. I knew what Marget was thinking, so I said it.

"You probably don't have more than a few seconds to use that pistol in your belt, Nathan," I advised quietly.

Everyone froze. Katie's eyes were huge.

"You want to die? Shoot Frank, Nathan," I shouted. "Shoot!"

Burby took a breath and his arm twitched and Wexler reached down and swung his rifle up and pointed it at Burby in one motion. We all heard the click as the safety went off.

There were ten feet between me and Wexler. I wouldn't have a chance. My diversion was too late.

"Hey, Frank," Burby whined.

Wexler fired, the percussion lashing my ears, and Burby's head flew back and he went down with a crash. Katie and Marget both screamed. Wexler's face hadn't changed expression. He turned the smoking eye of the rifle toward me, and that's when a shudder went through the trailer, unsteadying all of us.

Now.

I leaped forward just as the trailer tongue dropped off the blocks. The shock of it was everything I could have hoped for, completely disorienting everyone. The rifle dipped and fired again and then I was there, falling on Wexler, using my weight to bring him to the ground. He thrashed beneath me while a hot pain spread through my left shoulder. I'd been hit.

"Katie, run! Get out of here!" I shouted. My right hand was on the lethal end of the rifle, pushing it away from me, but my left arm was flopping uselessly, blood leaking from my shoulder. I tucked my chin to my chest and put my head to Wexler's chin and tried to keep him pinned, sucking in my breath when he got his right hand free and punched me right where the bullet had gone in.

I was aware of Katie screaming and Marget dragging her up the pitched floor to the door, and then the abrupt change in sound when they plunged outside. *"Ruddy!"* she cried.

Now it was just Wexler and me, and I knew I wasn't going to win. I could keep the rifle pointed away from me but that's all I could manage, and Wexler hit me again in the shoulder and I pulled in air to stay conscious. The floor seemed to be dropping away beneath me.

The pain was so dizzying it took me a moment to realize the floor *was* dropping, that the trailer was in motion. The cable had done its job and then continued to do its job, dragging us relentlessly toward the spool. Once it had pulled the trailer off the flats the steep hill took over and we were bouncing and careening and picking up speed, outrunning the cable as we headed toward the lake.

The cupboard doors flew open and plates and glasses tumbled out and the body of Nathan Burby somersaulted over to where Wexler and I were still clutching the rifle and then in one awful, seasick motion the trailer hit the stairs down to the lake and flipped.

The sum total of the strength in a travel trailer comes from the heavy steel frame underneath it all. The walls and ceiling are relatively flimsy, designed to withstand nothing more than highway-speed wind. Once we rolled over, the walls collapsed, the ceiling came down, and I lost track of Wexler and rifle and of everything else. I saw the night sky and was hit by flying debris as I ducked my head.

With a final, momentum-ending impact we were up-side down in the lake. Water rushed to fill the space where the trailer had once been, cold, *cold* water that extinguished all sound. I barely had time to take a breath and then I was under, a searing pain in my leg.

Bubbles streamed all around me. I blinked, trying to get my bearings. Debris was everywhere. Oddly, the ceiling lights, which were directly beneath me, hadn't shorted out, and I could see what was causing all the pain in my leg: the heavy trailer frame, which had been overhead when we hit the water, had crashed down and was jammed against my shin, holding me helplessly in place.

Wexler was worse off—the frame was across his chest, and he was wriggling like a pinned bug. He'd already realized what I was just now figuring out: We were being held underwater by the sheer weight of the steel frame. If we didn't get out, we'd drown.

There was a tremor in the frame as he heaved, trying to push it off of him. The flash of pain as the steel bar bit down harder on my leg was nothing compared to my alarm when I saw the entire assembly slide a few inches. If he managed it, he'd escape and be free to go after Katie.

If I worked with him, we might both get out from underneath the crushing weight that was threatening to end our lives. Instead, I leaned as far forward on the bar as I could, pressing down, squeezing that trailer frame closer to the remnant of the ceiling, tightening it like a vise. When he realized what I was doing he jerked his head around and stared at me, his expression full of disbelief. I gazed back, giving him nothing in return.

Wexler's moves were getting more frantic, his eyes

bulging. He must not have had a chance to draw in a last breath.

I knew what he was going through, how his lungs were hurting, how desperate he must be feeling. I'd felt the same way, just a few hours before, when he'd held my head underwater. And now I was doing it to him.

How ironic.

There was a blast of air from his mouth and I stopped pressing, because it didn't matter anymore. I turned away from his eyes, feeling the swelling ache in my own chest. The pain in my shoulder had receded, either from the cold water or because my brain was shifting its focus to the urgent need for air.

What I heard then was bubbles, a relentless stream of them, as if there were an aquarium bubbler going somewhere. I looked around frantically. Right next to me was the upside-down oven, and it was from the back of this that a trail of bubbles danced merrily in the flickering yellow ceiling lights.

What if . . . ?

I reached for the inverted oven, opening it up from the bottom like my garage door. The whole unit was tilted forward, and up in the back was a solid wedge of air. Right there.

I pulled myself into the oven, using the door for leverage, straining with all my might. I ignored the pain in my shin as I rotated my ankle enough to let me thrust my head inside. A little closer, a little closer, and then my face broke the surface and I brought in air, pure delicious air, one gasp and then another.

My whole body was being held by my right arm and I couldn't sustain it. I drank in one more lungful and then relaxed, falling back. Okay.

With my body no longer screaming at me for air I could take stock of my position. I was, I realized, in no more than six feet of water. If I could stand up, I'd be fine. If I could roll my ankle the other way so that the beam pinned me at the crease between ankle and foot, maybe I could raise my head to the surface of the water, call out for help. Breathe. Live.

I went back to the oven for more air and made a horrifying discovery: The air had mostly bubbled away in the half minute or so that I'd been gone. It was all I could do to get my lips to the surface, and I sucked and blew and sucked and blew, pulling in as much air as I could, trying to build oxygen in my blood.

When I withdrew my head I went for Plan B. The trailer frame, though, had other ideas, and it took precious seconds of yanking and kicking and twisting, biting my numb lips against the pain, before I finally got that beam down closer to my foot, my toes pointed toward the sky. I could now rise, and I did, aiming for the surface, my face up and eager.

I didn't make it. I was maybe five inches short but it might as well have been five miles. My foot was pinned and I couldn't get it out, and the water wasn't shallow enough for me to stick my head above the surface.

This was it.

There was no Alan to take over for me this time, no way to do anything but find out what happened when the air left my lungs and the cold waters came for me.

Even though I'd been through pretty much the same experience just a few hours ago, I still ultimately couldn't accept it, couldn't really believe this was happening. I had so much to live for now, it just didn't seem to be possible that I was losing everything. Not *now*.

⌐I heard a splash, a big one. I turned and saw Katie swimming toward me. She ducked her head under and took my face in her hands.

I misunderstood, thinking she was trying to give me one last, farewell kiss, and my heart swelled when her lips met mine. But then I felt the blast of air as she blew forcefully into my mouth.

Right, she taught lifesaving at the Y.

It didn't work, because I wasn't ready for it, but I nodded vigorously at her and she nodded back. *Okay. I get it.*

Katie raised her head, visibly expanding her lungs, and this time when she came for me I deliberately blew out, and we carefully sealed our lips against each other before I felt bubbles against my face and inhaled.

I didn't get much, just a fraction of what I required. Sensing my growing need, she went back up and came down quickly and did it again. This time I adjusted and got nearly an entire lungful.

She went up, grabbed air, came back down. Every third or fourth breath I would exhale as she returned, and the oxygen debt in my blood was slowly repaid. I didn't feel so urgent, now, and when she came back again and again I tenderly touched her face. I would always love Katie Lottner.

The cold, though, was sapping my strength, making it harder and harder to focus, and I realized it must be doing the same thing to Katie. We couldn't keep this up forever; we might not even be able to do it for five more minutes. Tremors were wracking my body. I tried to tell her this with my eyes. I even pointed, jabbing my finger.

Go for help, I mouthed.

She shook her head at me.

Come on, Katie!

Then she jerked her head at me, staring. I nodded, and she nodded. She went back up, came down for one last lifesaving breath, and then, in a swirl of bubbles, she swam for shore.

The ceiling lights winked out as she left, the trailer's circuitry finally getting the message that it was underwater and should have shorted out by now. I floated in the black water and willed myself calm, forced my pulse to slow. I needed to conserve energy, save oxygen.

If she ran up the hill it would take her what, twenty, thirty seconds? She could dash into the house, dial 9-1-1. Another thirty seconds, say, to connect, scream at the operator to send the fire department, drop the phone, and race back. They'd have her address on caller ID. I'd need to hold my breath a minute and a half—could I do that?

My pulse was pounding dully in my skull, and the pressure was already building in my lungs. How much time had passed? No more than twenty seconds.

I wasn't going to make it. In my artificially relaxed state, I understood this without panic. I thought about Katie—would she forgive herself for leaving me here? I'd asked her to, but that would be little comfort when they managed to wrestle my cold body out from under the trailer frame.

There was a sudden red flash. What was that? Then the flash went away, but a white light flooded the waters. I could even hear a truck. Milt's truck. Katie had flipped off the repo switch and started the tow truck.

I figured out what she was doing at the same moment I saw the red flash again—brake lights. She had turned the truck around and was now pointing up the hill.

If she drove up the hill she would take up all the slack in the cable and tow the frame right off me. It would work, as long as she didn't drive too fast and snap the cable when it drew taut. *Don't panic, Katie honey, nice and slow,* I urged her in my mind.

Then there was a pain in my shin so hot and searing it felt as if my foot had been torn off. But the frame, and much of the debris still bolted to it, was on the move. I ducked under and ignored the agony as I gripped that steel beam with both hands, the water like a rushing river as I was drawn with the frame toward shore. I thought my leg would break and then I was free, whooping in air in just a few inches of water, while the frame trundled upside down toward the hill. I heard the door slam and looked up as Katie ran down to me in the faint red glare of the running lights.

"Ruddy?" she was screaming. "Ruddy?"

I felt weak, nearly unable to move, but I flopped on my back and breathed. She fell on me, sobbing, frantically kissing my face. I kissed back with lips so numb they felt like they belonged to someone else.

"Ruddy, my God, my God," she said. "Don't die, don't die, please don't die."

He's dead.

"No, I'm not," I said. "I'm not dead."

"What? What?" She wildly shook her head, pulling her wet hair away from her face.

"I'm not dead, Katie. You saved me. I love you."

"I love you, too. Ruddy, I was so scared."

"You did everything right, Katie. Everything."

This was her. The woman I could trust, the woman I could hold, the woman I could love forever. I looked into those amazing eyes and I wasn't *falling* further in love, I was rising up to it, being lifted.

She helped me stand up. My foot felt utterly destroyed, my leg below the knee bleeding and in terrific pain. My shoulder wound felt safe to come out and play, too, and gave me a jolt as we staggered toward the truck.

"I think I'll let you drive," I told her.

This actually made her laugh. I took a deep breath. I had a lot to tell her, and wasn't sure how much of it she needed to know, or already knew. But her mom had participated in killing her father, and Marget and Burby and Wexler were mass murderers. That was what I was going to tell Strickland, anyway, so that much she needed to hear from me.

"Okay," I said. "Let's take a ride."

Epilogue

I was afraid.

Well, okay, not afraid, but nervous, somehow.

Alan's body was interred underneath the heavy stone with the memorial plaque, and I'd come down a few times before to chat, sitting on the stone bench. His voice might be gone from my head but I still felt his presence, and the urge to talk out loud to him was so strong I'd succumbed to it without thinking a few times before I'd caught people regarding me warily. Now I limited my discussions to this place, to this bench. People did that, right? Came to talk to their dead friends? Normal people?

"So Alan, hey," I greeted.

I sniffed in the clean air, not expecting an answer or anything, but just giving a normal pause to the conversation. It was early June and Michigan was acting as if it had taken an oath to be Hawaii. The sky was impossibly blue, the leaves had burst out of hiding and were lifting their faces to the sun. Birds were singing, bugs were buzzing, and people were delinquent on their car loans. A perfect day.

"So the reason I'm here is to ask you something. It's been more than a year since that day at the river, the day you saved me. A lot's happened. My sister . . ." I trailed off. I hadn't realized I was going to talk about Becky. "She's a different person now. You'd hardly know her. The married life, it really agrees with her.

"We've rebuilt the Bear, and Jimmy's sort of managing the place. Not the books, Becky still does that, but you know how people love him. He greets everyone; it's fun."

I sighed. I was avoiding it.

"Then there's Katie. Mostly, she's doing really well. She and her mom aren't talking, but that's no surprise. The D.A. declined to prosecute, says there wasn't any evidence, but Katie knows what happened, what Marget did to you, and she's not letting it go. I don't know how you would feel about that.

"Anyway, about Katie. She's the best thing that's ever happened to me, Alan. Every moment I'm with her, I'm happy. And I'm good for her, too, Alan. I really am, which is why, okay, I want to ask her to marry me. So that's why I'm here. I'm just letting you know. Man to man. Your daughter, if she says yes, will be married to a repo man. Like that."

I let it sink in. I had a foolish grin on my face—this was the first time I'd said it aloud. "I'll be a good husband to your daughter, Alan," I finally added. "The married life, it'll agree with me, too."

I stood, feeling oddly relieved. "Okay then," I said. I looked over to where Jake was sniffing at a headstone.

"Jake, respect the dead," I warned him. He glanced back at me and did exactly that, lifting his leg and giving a deferential sprinkle. "Great," I muttered.

I turned back to the large rock. "You were right. Life's too short, you have to say what's on your mind. I really miss you, Alan. You were the best friend I ever had. I hope I get to see you again, someday. Good-bye, Alan."

I walked away, clapping my hands so Jake would join me for the ride back home.

Acknowledgments, Apologies, and Afterthoughts

Ruddy McCann is based on a real person: me. Well, okay, I didn't play football for Michigan State or have my football career cut short by a prison sentence or play football in high school or play football. I'm under six feet tall instead of over, and I couldn't be a bouncer in anything tougher than a donut shop. But I was, for several years, a repo man in northern Michigan. I was born in Petoskey, and have spent at least some pòrtion of every year of my life in the East Jordan / Charlevoix area. When I was repossessing cars, I lived in Traverse City and had a lot of customers in Kalkaska. So if you're looking at the book jacket photo and thinking the author looks suspiciously like someone you saw driving away in your pickup truck a couple decades ago: yes, that was me. I feel pretty awkward about the whole thing and I'm hoping we can put it behind us.

Ruddy McCann and I will both be back in the sequel, *Repo Madness,* as will the cast of characters from the Black Bear and, of course, Jake the dog.

Being so familiar with my subject and the local geography can be a curse, because I assume I know all the answers to everything, when in fact my memory can't even accurately describe yesterday's lunch. I apologize for any errors I've made in the telling of this story, whether they be related to distance, topography, or history. For example, there is a Patricia Lake and it does appear to be pretty steeply banked, but I couldn't find a way to get down to it and therefore described it entirely from my imagination. I've never been in the Charlevoix County Sheriff's station, which is probably a good thing, and I most likely made a mash of the procedures for arresting someone who reports a dead body found in the woods.

None of the characters except Ruddy are based on real human beings. Well, Jake's personality is a lot like my dog Tucker's—Tucker hates to go for a walk. What kind of dog hates to go for a walk? All he ever wants to do is sit at home and read e-mail.

I've made a lot of fun of northern Michigan, especially the weather, but the truth is I love the area—it's in my bones. In fact, there is currently no Black Bear Bar and Grille in Kalkaska, but I think it would be a great idea to open one! Make it exactly as described in the novel! My wife doesn't care how many exclamation points I slap on this concept; she lives in Los Angeles and is not moving to any place where she would have to use a snow-thrower.

But speaking of my wife: Cathryn, your ideas and edits, as always, dramatically improved this novel through every draft. Thank you so much for your contributions, so vital to my work, and thank you for marrying me because I don't know what I would do if I couldn't wake up every morning and see your face.

Submitting a manuscript to a publisher and then getting editorial notes is a bit like dressing a child for school and then having the teacher call to complain that you sent your first grader to class wearing a tennis shoe on one foot and a moon boot on the other. Since this actually happened to me, I can attest to how painful it is. Thank you, Kristin Sevick, for your tact, and for your great ideas and thoughts.

I feel lucky to be with Tom Doherty, an imprint of Forge, a division of Macmillan. I think I got that right. Thank you, Linda, Tom, Karen, Kathleen, and everyone else for adopting me and publishing my novels and making them a priority and a success.

Thanks Scott Miller of Trident Media for living in New York so I don't have to, and for helping reinvent me as a novelist instead of a humor writer.

Thanks to my three Steves for being my Hollywood Triple Threat: Younger, Fisher, and Iwanyk. Iwanykly, Iwanyk is Younger than Fisher. Deb, thanks for working Deuble time.

Thank you Gavin Palone for being a sword and a shield. I'm proud to be working with you.

Thank you Tracey Nyberg and Rodney Ferrell for the great Christmas present!

Thank you Monica Perkins for organizing and caffeinating my office. Now that you're here I have time to write!

Because my writing didn't cover the bills for so much of my life, I developed the habit of always having a day job. Currently that job is producing independent movies, and by the time you are reading this I hope at least one of them—*Muffin Top: A Love Story*—is in theaters and available via VOD. Elliott Crowe has taken on the majority of the work that I was supposed to do. Thank you, Elliott, for literally saving the movie. And thanks to the people who contributed to our Kickstarter campaign so that we could take our finished film on the road! There were a thousand people, but I want to specifically thank Katherine Fugate, Liz Cameron, Linda Slater, Jay Kogen, Joyce Kemph, Roger and Vivien and Burke and Kellie, Laura and Dick Flanigan, Barbara and Robin Foster, Sudy Hurst, Niki McDowell, Tim Gillin, Ginger Truitt, Geoffrey Jennings, Tracy Beckerman, David Tausik, Ellen GoldsmithVein, Gigi Levangie Grazer, Monsie Cameron, Jennifer Altabef, Nitanee Paris Lawson, Jeff Jacobson, Pamela Norris, Kati Johnston, Iris Dart, Lissa Collins-Gudim, Alex Gudim, Melissa Berryman, and Diane Edwards.

Thanks to Connection House Inc. for its research into some key aspects of car repossessions that I had forgotten. All I could remember was sweating and panting and fibrillating.

Thanks Fly HC and Hillary Carlip for building and beautifying my websites: wbrucecameron.com and adogspurpose.com.

There are some writers I can always turn to for support, encouragement, and psychological counseling. Thank you Claire LaZebnik and Samantha Dunn—you both are better at this than I am.

Thank you Carolina for listening to me even when I'm spouting nonsense. Thank you Annie for letting me hang out with the popular kids. Thank you Pam Norris for letting me visit Casa de Squillo il Telefono.

Thank you Jody and Andy Sherwood, and Diane and Tom Runstrom, for all you did for my family the fall of 2013.

Thanks to my award-winning teacher sister Amy Cameron for writing the study guides for *A Dog's Purpose*, *A Dog's Journey*, and *Emory's Gift*. All three books are being successfully taught in the classroom. If you, dear reader, know an educator who would be interested in our grant program, please have him or her visit our website to read the study guide and download a grant application!

Thanks Julie Cameron MD for continuing to promote my books to all of your patients. Let's talk soon!

Chase, you are a master. Chelsea, thanks for G-Bru. Georgia, thank you for Tucker. Eloise, you are a joy— remember, just say "No." You're good at it. Gordon, I know there's some Cameron DNA in there somewhere— probably you'll wind up getting your father's looks and my running ability.

My mom sells, on average, 1.45 of my books for every 1.0 people she meets. Thanks, Mom, for being my biggest supporter and best salesperson.

I would never know anything about Michigan if my grandfather hadn't bought a stone cottage on Lake Charlevoix about eighty years ago. When the cottage passed into my father's hands, my parents drove their family from their home in Kansas City to the place on the lake every single summer, so that I could experience the same childhood my father had enjoyed as he was growing up. After college I moved to Michigan because I couldn't imagine living anywhere else. My father died October 5th, 2013, right where he wanted to be: in that stone cottage that had been in his family his whole life. Thank you, Cameron Family, for the gift of all those cottage memories. Thank you, Dad, for working so hard so that your children could enjoy such a marvelous home. I miss you and think of you every day.

—W. Bruce Cameron
Monday, March 10, 2014, Marina del Rey, CA

— Read on for a preview of —

REPO
MADNESS

W. BRUCE CAMERON

*Available in August 2016
from Tom Doherty Associates*

A FORGE BOOK

1

Nothing like You in the Literature

I flipped the light under the little sign that said JOHNSTON and then took my seat, pensively glancing at my watch. I was close to fifteen minutes late.

The small anteroom had a coffee table layered with magazines for every possible sort of person who might be seeking psychotherapy: fishermen, people who cared about fashionable clothing, people who wanted their houses to look like someone else's house, women who were pregnant or wanting to be pregnant or had recently been pregnant. I picked up one whose cover had a snowmobile straddled by a woman in a bikini. The girl and the machine were both impressively muscular. Maybe where she lived, that's how everyone dressed for snowmobiling.

I've never actually owned a snowmobile, but I've stolen a few.

The door popped open, and I blinked in surprise at the guy standing there—fit, wiry, fifties; short, sparse hair receding from a freckled forehead; green eyes. My regular psychiatrist was a trim and frankly attractive woman who I felt was really helping me because she laughed at my jokes. "Mr. McCann?" he asked.

I stood and tossed aside my magazine. "Where's Sheryl?" I asked.

He bent and arranged the snowmobile magazine so that its edges lined up with the magazine for people who dress their dogs in sweaters. I'm not an edges-lined-up kind of guy and didn't feel bad about my apparent negligence.

"You call your doctor by her first name?" he asked mildly. "Why are you late, Mr. McCann?"

"I had to repo a Mazda from a guy who got fired from his job for threatening his boss with a baseball bat."

"Oh?" He raised his eyebrows in interest.

I shrugged. "The guy still had the bat."

"Come on in. Dr. Johnston was in a skiing mishap. She's all right, but she won't be able to work for a few months, so I am helping out. My name is Dr. Schaumburg. Robert Schaumburg."

I followed him into Sheryl's office. There was a couch, of course, but I always sat in a chair across from her, and I settled into my habitual place uneasily. After eighteen months of dealing with one psychiatrist, I was feeling awkward starting up with another.

"I've been reviewing her notes, to which I am allowed access under the terms of your probation." He settled into a soft chair, tapping a thick green folder. My file, I gathered.

"Okay, so should we wait for her to recover, probably?" I suggested helpfully.

Dr. Schaumburg regarded me blandly. "We have no

idea how long that might be, unfortunately," he responded finally. "Shall I call you Ruddick? Ruddy?"

"Ruddy. No one calls me Ruddick except those phone calls at election time."

"Ruddy, then. Are you still taking your meds, Ruddy?"

My discomfort increased. "Well, yeah, of course. Why do you ask?"

"People on your mix of medications usually exhibit small changes in facial muscle tone and general body movements. I'm pretty good at spotting those, and you don't seem to have any."

"Guess I'm just lucky that way."

"Under the terms of your probation, you are required to be on your medication. I'm sure Dr. Johnston advised you of this."

I used my facial muscle tone to give myself a frown. "Did you talk to her? Because this whole probation thing is BS."

Dr. Schaumburg settled back slightly. "Tell me about that."

I shrugged. "Not a lot to tell. A bomb went off. A couple of people got killed. I wasn't to blame for any of it, but I was in the middle of everything and the D.A. felt like I had to be charged with *something*, even though I did nothing wrong."

"Because you're an ex-con."

"Because I went to prison, yeah. So we worked out this sham arrangement where I would get probation for obstruction of justice, because instead of taking matters into my own hands, I should have called the cops and let innocent people get killed while we all waited for them to respond, I guess. Sheryl agrees it's ridiculous.

I didn't *obstruct*. I *solved*. Things could have been a lot worse, let me tell you."

Schaumburg reflected on this. He looked at his notes. "You were in prison for . . ."

I blew out some air. "Murder."

"Because you were drunk and crashed your car and a woman died."

"I was not drunk," I corrected. "I tested well below the limit. And many people accidentally took that turn down to the ferry before they reengineered it."

He regarded me blandly. "But you *were* drinking."

"Yes." I bit off anything else I might add.

"You don't seem to have any remorse."

I wanted to stand up. That's what guys my size do when we're getting pissed off: We stand up. A lot of times that ends the conversation. But something told me that was not a good idea here, so I jammed my hands into my pockets. "No remorse? I think about that accident every day of my life. Didn't I plead guilty? Didn't I stand up in front of a judge and say I deserved to go to prison? Don't you think I would give anything to have it all back, to have her back? That I would have traded places with her if I could?"

"Lisa Maria Walker."

"Yes. That was her name."

"Your girlfriend."

"No." I looked away. "We had just met."

Schaumburg nodded as if I had just confirmed something. "Before that, you were something of a local hero," he observed. "Football star, NFL career all but assured. And now you are a repo man and a bouncer in a bar."

"You say that like it's a step down or something."

"You're getting agitated."

"Well, who wouldn't? It was the worst thing that's ever happened to me."

"I would expect someone on your dosage to be more calm. A deadening of response is typical."

Okay, now I wanted to stand up and also punch him in the face. He was needling me, picking at a deep wound to test me. "I *am* calm. Bob."

A tiny smile played on his lips, but it wasn't amusement. "All right, then. Has Dr. Johnston ever discussed with you something called dissociative personality disorder?"

"Mostly we discuss sports."

"Let's talk about the voices in your head."

I sighed. We sat there, silently regarding each other for a full minute before I nodded wearily. "One voice, actually."

"Under what sort of circumstances do you hear the voice? Is there something that triggers it?"

"I don't hear it anymore," I replied dully.

"The meds are working, then." He was giving me a look full of irony, and I didn't reply. "But you also told Dr. Johnston that there were times when the voice would take over your body."

"No, not 'take over.' Look, I had a voice in my head that said his name was Alan Lottner. That's all."

Schaumburg pulled out a pen and clicked it, positioning it to write something. I waited patiently. "Alan Lottner," he repeated. "Who was once a real person? Now deceased."

"He died, yes."

"And it turns out you are engaged to his daughter?" His green eyes flicked up to meet mine, glinting slyly.

Jesus, had Sheryl written down every single one of my

personal secrets for this schmuck to read? "Yes, but that was just a coincidence."

"A coincidence."

"Meaning, I didn't know Katie when Alan showed up. Okay, I had met her, but I didn't know who she was. In relation to him, I mean."

"You met a woman you were attracted to and then started hearing her father in your head," he summarized.

I was developing a real dislike for this guy.

"It's not typical for someone who harbors the delusion of a voice in his head to tie it to a real person," he informed me. "Historical figures, maybe, but I've never heard of it being the father of a fiancée. Does she know?"

"Who, Katie? That I had her father talking in my head for a while? No, I guess none of the bridal magazines in your lobby suggested I should bring it up. He's gone now, anyway. Alan, I mean."

"Which makes you sad."

"What? *No!* Where do you get that? Did Sheryl say that?"

"Your reaction is interesting. Your . . . vehemence. Why do you deny it with such force? Would there be shame if you missed the voice?"

"Shame? No, of course not."

"Then what is the matter with admitting you might, at times, regret you no longer hear the voice?"

"What is the *matter*?" I repeated incredulously. "If I went around saying I used to hear a voice and I want him back? People would think I was crazy."

"Well . . ." Schaumburg gave a lazy shrug. "People. Perhaps. But in here, I think it is important to probe these areas."

"Okay, sure. Let's *probe*."

"What do you want to tell me about how you feel about the voice? Today, I mean."

"I want to tell you that the voice is gone," I replied firmly.

He looked amused. "All right, then."

I glanced longingly at the door. The clock said I had to endure just a few more minutes of this.

"Tell me about when Alan would control your body," Schaumburg prodded after neither of us had spoken for an awkward while.

"That only happened a couple of times. I would be asleep, and he would sort of take my body out for a spin. He never did anything bad with it. Like, he would fold the laundry, stuff like that."

Another long silence. I regretted bringing up the laundry—it made me sound pretty crazy somehow, even though doing my shirts was Alan's idea.

"I'm not able to find anything like your case in the literature," Schaumburg told me. "Schizoaffective disorder, which is how Dr. Johnston has classified your condition, is entirely separate from dissociative personality disorder, though people commonly make the mistake of believing schizophrenia means having a so-called split personality. In other words, patients never describe their alter ego as a voice; they just morph from one personality to another, spontaneously and, sometimes, conveniently."

"I see we're out of time and I'm sorry I was late," I replied sincerely. "It took longer to get that bat out of his hands than it should have."

"Did you hit him with it?"

"What? *No*. That's not how it's done. You think I would last long in this profession if I went around braining people with a baseball bat?"

"What if Alan were running your body: Would *he* hit someone with a bat?"

"Alan?" I laughed. "No. A badminton racquet, maybe. Or he'd write them an angry note." I stopped chuckling at Schaumburg's expression.

"You really miss him, don't you?"

I wasn't buying the sympathy. This guy was playing me, and I needed to pay more attention before I talked myself into trouble. "He's gone," I responded unequivocally.

"There have been cases where people miss the voices; they crave their delusions. You've perhaps seen the movie *A Beautiful Mind*? It's even hypothesized that some patients could so yearn for the return of their imaginary companions that they re-create the voice. Bring them back, in other words."

"Sounds like something we should talk about next time," I noted amiably, standing up.

"Why don't you sit down? I have some time before my next appointment."

It didn't sound like a suggestion. I sat, flexing and unflexing my fists on my knees.

"What is your pharmacist going to tell me when I call him to find out the last time you filled your prescription?" Schaumburg asked.

"Tom? That I was just in there last week," I replied with all the truthfulness my soul could muster. I had, in fact, been in there just four days ago, getting some medication for Katie.

"All right, Ruddy. I'm your doctor and interested in what is best for you. But if I call your pharmacist and find that, as I suspect, you have not been getting your medications, I'm going to report your lack of cooperation to the court. And you do know what that means, don't you?"

I licked my lips. "It means I would go back to jail," I finally rasped. I believed this bastard would do it, too—put me behind bars just for not taking some stupid pills.

"I'm glad we understand each other," Schaumburg said.

I thought about giving him the stare I had successfully used to close down bar fights and get people to hand over their unpaid-for cars, but I knew it wouldn't work here. Schaumburg had all the power. In the end, I just stared at him helplessly.

I did not know what I was going to do.

TOR

Award-winning authors
Compelling stories

Please join us at the website
below for more information
about this author and other great
Tor selections, and to sign up for
our monthly newsletter!

Printed in the USA
CPSIA information can be obtained
at www.ICGtesting.com
LVHW010218160724
785623LV00033B/491